AF245013

COLLODION

GREG MORGAN

Copyright © 2020 Greg Morgan

All rights reserved. No part of this publication may be reproduced,
stored in a retrieval system, or transmitted in any form or by any means —
by electronic, mechanical, photocopying, recording, or otherwise — without
prior written permission from the author or publisher.

ISBN: 978-1-7349657-2-8 (Paperback)

www.greg-morgan.com

This is a work of fiction. Yep, that means it ain't true and didn't really
happen. More specifically, it is historical fiction, which also means the story
that ain't true occurred in a historical period of time that did happen. Most
of what's written here are the products of the author's imagination and/or
used in a fictitious manner. Then again, several of the characters were, in fact,
true historical figures of the nineteenth century, but the roles they play in this
narrative are entirely fictional, and so is their dialogue. Yep, I made it up,
all in my imagination. Any resemblance to actual living persons is purely
coincidental, and since this narrative took place in the mid-nineteenth
century, if you think I'm writing about you, you're crazy, oops,
I'm sorry, I mean peculiar.

For the rainbow
of those on the spectrum of autism
who see the world from a different angle.

CHAPTER I

June 1862
Henrico County, Virginia

The two men, one dead, one alive, sat alone and across from each other in the great room so cavernous it would've echoed if they had spoken. Instead, the thunder of distant cannon fire and the tinkling of crystal from the swaying chandelier filled the space. Dust and bits of ceiling plaster floated about the air as the two men coldly regarded each other through the legs of a tall tripod. The dead man's icy grin sent a shiver down Osborn's spine. An embalmer had sewn the lips into the smile with a well-concealed thread knot. It made the dead man look like he might be jealous of Osborn for breathing. The embalmer had also opened the dead man's blue eyes. They stared at him, but Osborn could not return the favor as he found eye contact with anyone difficult, even a dead man. Removing his oval-shaped blue steel spectacles, he blew the dust off them.

Osborn jumped when the door flew open. "Are you all right?" asked his seventeen-year-old nephew, Ray.

"I am fine, I am fine," replied Osborn, flapping his hands up and down from the fright.

"I'm sorry, Uncle. Did I frighten you?"

"Just a bit, just a bit. I'm fine." Osborn shook off the surprise and walked behind the dead man slumping in his richly upholstered Fauteuil armchair.

Ray asked, "Are you ready yet? The cannons are getting closer."

"No, not yet, not yet." Taking the dead man by the armpits, Osborn sat him up and readjusted him. Bits of ceiling plaster had fallen into the man's grey hair. Osborn bent down and blew.

"What are you doing?" Ray asked in a loud whisper.

"There was dust in his hair, dust in his hair, yes," replied Osborn as his fingers fastidiously flicked off the large white specks from the hair. "Is the glass plate ready?"

"I was working on it. I just wanted to see if you were…well, you know how you get, and that was a loud one."

"Bring me the plate, bring me the plate, Ray."

"Fine, I'm doing it. Can I let the family in? They are all out here." "No, no, no. I must work alone, must work alone."

"Fine, I'll be right back," Ray replied before closing the door.

Osborn flicked off the last speck and adjusted the iron stand, embracing the skull. Reaching down, he tightened the cleverly hidden fourteen-gauge wire affixing the wrists to the wooden chair arms. Walking around to the front, Osborn stepped back, tilting his head side to side like an artist critiquing his painting. The man's family had dressed the sixty-eight-year-old Union army general in his finest uniform to prepare him for his first and last photographic portrait.

"There, now, you look better," he said before ducking under the black camera shroud. Osborn peered through the viewing glass, displaying a blurry, upside-down image due to the lens's refraction. As he pulled apart the camera bellows, the general slowly came into focus.

The room shook from another volley of cannon fire, and the door flew open. Ray hurried in with a cough and waved away the plaster dust from his face. He carried a thin wood box containing the glass plate negative in his hand. Ten family members of the dead man followed him, all filing in behind the camera.

"We have to get out of here. I have the glass plate here."

"Yes, yes. Put it in. I am prepared, yes," Osborn said from under the shroud.

Ray blew the dust off the camera before sliding the box in. "All set."

Osborn emerged from the shroud and wrapped his thin fingers around the brass lens cap. "Please hold still," he told the dead man as he pulled the lens cap off for ten seconds, ensuring the gentleman's likeness for posterity. He replaced it softly with a twist. "Thank you for your patience."

As Osborn and Ray removed the various posing accessories from the general, the family members whisked him away to the funeral procession waiting outside. A tall man walked over to them. "Mr. Roche, your fee," he said with money in hand.

Osborn raised his hands as if being robbed. "No, no! Give it to Ray, give it to Ray."

Ray leaped over a footstool, jumping in front of his uncle. "I'll take it. Thank you." The man studied Osborn's face oddly before handing the money to Ray and walking off. Osborn shuddered and dropped to the floor from the sound of another explosion. A cloud of dust fell from the ceiling, covering them both. Osborn rose and shook it out of his brown hair with gray at the temples, disclosing his age of forty.

"You all right?" asked Ray.

"Fine, fine," Osborn said with disgust growing on his face as he tasted plaster dust on his tongue.

"Eww, eww, eww." Osborn tried to wipe it off with his dusty hand. "What?"

"The dust, it's…yuck."

Ray also shook the dust from his head and said, "We can pack up the wagon and head back a bit away from the noise if it's bothering you."

"No, no. If I am prepared for it, I'll be fine, fine. We need to be first on the field after the ruckus, the ruckus, yes."

They loaded the equipment into their fanciful red wagon with O. Roche Photography, Portraits of All Kinds painted in yellow on both sides.

Osborn climbed up on the wagon's bench and took the reins of their mammoth jackstock mule, Hoady. "The general was prepared by an embalmer," said Osborn as he slapped the reins to move Hoady along.

"One of those doctors that make a body last longer?" "Yes."

"I seen the sign back at the camp. Big ol' tent on the south side. It said embalming."

"Yes, I had read the President authorized it to send the unfortunate home. Replacing blood with chemicals, they do. Blood with chemicals."

"Not a job I would want." Ray picked up Moby Dick from the bench next to him. The latest novel from author Herman Melville. "The smile was quite good, quite good."

"I suppose. So, we were at chapter seven, if I'm not mistaken," said Ray. "The Whiteness of the Whale."

"Yes, yes, we were," replied Osborn with a smile.

The wagon pulled up on a Union forward observing post atop a grassy knoll, half a mile from the battle raging in the distance. The staff members of Brigadier Major General John Sedgwick stood some twenty yards off. Osborn climbed down, turning to them for some sign. Their arms pointed here and there, and their mouths anxiously twitched and flapped, providing no clue.

"Can you hear me?" Ray shouted.

Osborn turned to him with a blank expression. "You say something?" he asked, pulling the tobacco-filled plugs from his ears. Though he invented them for his nose, they served double duty, dulling the loud noises that would disturb him.

"Oh, did, when did you...? Did you have those in the whole time? Did you hear the last chapter?"

"I did not. The cannon fire was too much, too much," Osborn replied as he put the nose plugs back into his ears.

"Could've told me," said Ray, wiping the salty rivers of sweat under his red hair with his shirt sleeve.

General Sedgwick sat twenty feet from them atop his brown stallion, field glasses to his eyes. Osborn had met him a few times in the past. "Quite a fine uniform he has. So clean, so clean," said Osborn, smoothing his shirt and straightening his bowtie.

"What's that?" asked Ray.

"The general. His uniform. I like it."

"Osborn!" called a sharply dressed man walking toward them with a gold pocket watch and a red tie. Ray waved at Osborn for his attention, pointed to his ears, then pointed to the man approaching them.

Osborn turned and recognized him. "Mathew," he replied as he again pulled the nose plugs from his ears. Mathew had an impressively waxed mustache and light brown hair slicked back with pomade. Osborn thought it looked a bit like melted chocolate ice cream.

He stuck out his hand to Osborn with a grin. "Good to see you on the field, Osborn. How have you been?"

Ray jumped from the wagon bench. "Uh, I'm sorry, sir, my uncle doesn't shake hands."

Osborn sharply turned his head away. "He knows. He's only doing that to make me angry." Osborn twisted his wiry goatee.

Mathew pulled his hand back. "Naw, it's a little joke between us, son, that's all."

"How is that a joke?" asked Osborn, pushing up the spectacles on his nose. "You know I do not like to touch. I do not like it."

"Come on, now, Osborn. I didn't mean it like that. So, how have you been?"

"I have been well," said Osborn, snubbing him as if searching for friends at a party.

Ray flashed his eyes at his uncle and turned to Mathew, saying, "And… how…are you…?" with a glance back to his uncle and a confirming nod at the end.

Mathew stuck out his hand for Ray and said, "Very well, thank you. You are his nephew?"

Ray's face brightened as he replied, "Ray," and he shook Mathew's hand.

"Ray, nice to meet you, Ray."

"Very excited to meet you, Mr. Brady. I've heard so much about you."

"Thank you, young sir." Mathew turned back to Osborn. "So, Osborn, I saw your book for sale while I was in New York. Excellent work. Is it selling well?"

"It is, thank you," replied Osborn with disdain.

"Yes, I saw it while I was there for the exhibition of my daguerreotypes from Shiloh. I called it 'The Forgotten Dead,'" he said, wiping a hand across the sky. "I plan to turn it into a book as you did."

Osborn's eyebrows jumped. "Humph."

"I also saw your daguerreotype of Willy Lincoln—"

"God rest his soul," they all said.

"Portrait. Portrait of Willy Lincoln, yes."

Mathew glanced at the wagon's painted signage and pointed to it with his hat. "Ah, yes, I see you prefer the term."

"Yes, yes, I prefer the term portrait to 'daguerreotype,' yes."

"What about 'photograph,' Osborn? Everyone seems to be using that term now."

"Portraits are of people; photographs are of things. I do not take photographs of people. I make portraits of them, portraits of them, yes."

"It's the same thing," said Ray as he rolled his eyes, having heard this from his uncle a thousand times.

"Portrait is a more beautiful word, beautiful word, yes," added Osborn.

Mathew pointed again to their wagon, half again larger than a typical wagon and decorated with gilded wood carvings on red sides that sloped outward toward the eaves of the arched roof. "Still with the Romani vardo, I see. What'd we call it? Big Red?"

"Yes, yes. Big Red, you called it. Big Red."

"It'll be quite a field today. Got to get out there quick. My carts are fast and light." He pointed to a line of six portable hand-pulled darkroom carts in the distance. All the size of four stacked hay bales with two eight-foot poles jutting out in front for the photographer to pull and maneuver. Inside, they contained all the chemicals needed to develop a print. He had painted "Mathew Brady & Co. Daguerreotypes" across each side.

"It won't be how fast you get there. No, the better photograph will win, not the fastest. It's never the fastest," said Osborn.

"Yes, but the carts are far more nimble in rough terrain," said Brady, putting his hands on his hips and eyeballing Osborn from head to toe. "We have one like it in the wagon. We used it at Shiloh," said Ray. "You should pull it out and use it now."

"Our dark cart is used only for special, special circumstances. The Romani vardo allows me to have all the tools at my disposal, at my disposal, yes," added Osborn, continuing to look around as if Brady weren't there.

"And we can sleep in there. It's real comfortable," added Ray. "The Romani vardo can float across any water. I sealed all the joints with tar, with tar, yes. Not a speck of light comes in if we don't want it to." The light was his most significant ally to take a photograph and his biggest foe to develop it.

Brady rocked back and forth on his heels. "Anyhow, I also employed three runners to take our daguerreotypes to my publisher right away." Brady cleared his throat and raised his chin. "You should have come to work for me. I'd have your 'portraits,' as you call them, out in a jiffy."

"You always use that word, jiffy, jiffy. What is that word jiffy?" "Mr. Roche, good to see you again, sir," called General Sedgwick as he approached atop his horse, his staff following close behind.

Osborn tipped his hat. "And you, General."

The general turned to Mathew and said, "Mr. Brady."

"General," replied Mathew.

The general turned back to Osborn with a grin. "I understand you are now a captain, sir. Congratulations are in order."

"Captain?" asked Mathew.

"Yes, appointed by General McClellan himself. It's an honorary rank, but that still deserves respect." The general turned back to Osborn. "Are you still his personal photographer?"

"He prefers me, but I needed to seek other endeavors and photograph the grit of war, the grit of war, yes. The general appreciates my contribution, contribution to the historical record of the rebellion."

General Sedgwick nodded his approval. "Very good. I suppose that is needed."

"Photography is my contribution..." continued Osborn as Ray looked to the heavens and covered his face with his hands. "...It's the way I fight a battle for us all." The general's brows furrowed; interest piqued. "I fight time. Time is the enemy to all men, an ally to none. My portraits and photographs are the only weapons to fight it, to fight it as they capture a moment of it like capturing one soldier from time's endless army, time's endless army."

The general clapped his hands with pleasure. "Bravo, sir!" he said, a great smile upon his face. "Well played! I would like to see some of your captured soldiers later in the day." The general raised his field glasses to the battlefield. "Let's move to see our right flank," the general yelled to his staff. He turned back to Osborn. "Good day to you, Captain. I wish you luck in your endeavors with time!"

With a surprised expression, Brady said, "Well, Captain—" "Will you be photographing today?" interrupted Osborn. "Well, no, I am only here to supervise my employees and—"

Osborn walked away mid-sentence. Hands on his hips, Brady rocked on his heels. He turned to Ray's confused face and shrugged. "Go on, boy. Go get him," he said disappointedly.

Ray ran off and caught up to his uncle. "What happened back there? Everything we've worked on for years. After he asks you how you are, you ask him how he is. And you didn't introduce me. How many times have I explained that one to you? I had to introduce myself. The worst part was you walked off without saying a word! That was very rude, Uncle."

"I remembered all that. I just didn't want to do it. I don't like him, don't like him."

"Mathew Brady is the most respected photographer in the world." "He is not a photographer."

"He is a photographer. He has just escalated his business and now employs other photographers."

"Which he takes credit for. That's unfair. It's cheating."

"Yes, but it was still rude, and I can see he likes you. He admires you enough to want to hire you."

"I work for myself. It's my art."

"I know, I'm saying if you want friends like you say so often, you have to play by—"

"Different rules, different rules. Yes, I remember. I will work on that, but not with him, not with him, no. The best kind of friend to have is one you respect."

CHAPTER 2

The bright red wagon bumped and jostled over the scarred landscape of the battlefield. Once a vast field of bright green grass, it was now a scene of desolation. In the distance, women and children walked among the fallen, rolling bodies over in desperate hopes it wasn't someone they knew. Soldiers and stretcher-bearers searched for the wounded. A little boy's voice called out, "Over here! Over here!" like he'd found an Easter egg on Easter morning.

"It looks like a big farm," said Osborn. "How's that?"

"A big farm of freshly tilled soil. See, the stretcher-bearers are the farmhands, yes, farmhands collecting vegetables from the ground, putting their carrots and lettuce heads in their baskets, in their baskets, yes."

Ray scoffed. "Morbid, Uncle."

"See, that soldier dragging that man by the armpits? He's a farmer pulling his, pulling his hand till through the soil, see?"

"Yeah, I can see that."

The buzzing of flies overwhelmed the singing birds. Osborn swatted one away and sniffed. "Ooh!" he said with a disgusted expression. Osborn reached into his coat pocket for his nose plugs. He checked one pocket, then the next. Panic rose on his face.

Ray pointed to his ears. "They're in your ears."

"Oh!" said Osborn before he moved them from his ears to his nose. Stinking, bloated bodies dotted the landscape. In a few hours, they would solidify into statues of various positions. Their legs would often stiffen at odd angles, even pushing their lower halves up and away from the earth. Some would have arms raised as if to ask God a question with fingers as twisted as the roots of a cherry tree. Ahead a group of wild hogs roamed like underworld creatures rummaging for their dead and rotting flesh as the sun beat down on body parts strewn about; leg here, daisies there, hand here, dandelions there.

Ray cracked the reins a moment before they hit a big rut. Both bounced up from the bench. "A jackstock mule can only go so fast, Ray," said Osborn. "Maybe I should be back there and make sure everything stays tight."

"I put everything away secure," said Ray as the wagon's right wheel hit a rut and cracked apart. The wagon lurched forward, crashing down and to the right. Hoady slammed to a stop, rearing with a hee-haw as Osborn and Ray flew forward off the wagon to the dirt on either side of Hoady. Picking himself up, Ray ran to Osborn. "Are you all right?"

Osborn rose with his hands paddling the air in front of him. "Oh, we won't get our photograph, our photograph. Mathew, Mathew, Mathew. I'm not happy. I'm not happy!"

"You need to calm yourself, Uncle. It's a broken wheel. We'll fix it." Ray dusted himself off and walked over to the broken wheel. "Do we have spare wheel parts?"

"We might have some spokes under the bed floor. I'll have to remove everything, remove everything to get to them." Osborn stamped his foot. "It won't be easy. We'll be here all day, all day. We're gonna miss our chance. Mathew is going to get it. He's going to get it."

Osborn stomped over to the wagon, fists at his sides, and peered in the rear door. With one wheel gone, it lay on a forty-five-degree angle. The contents of every cabinet had fallen to the floor. Osborn climbed in, picking up various bottles and equipment and tossing anything broken out the doorway. From the corner of his eye, he spotted one of Brady's dark carts passing him. Brady himself walked beside it. He waved at Osborn as he passed. "And a good day to you, Osborn," he said, laughing. Osborn came outside and sat, dejected.

"We can do that. I'll put together the dark cart," said Ray, walking to the other side of the wagon and pulling it out. A few moments later, Ray returned, sat next to Osborn, and said, "Its wheel is broken too." Osborn shut his eyes and pulled handfuls of grass from the ground. The wind blew his hair in the sweltering afternoon. Ray said, "Suppose I should get started on the Romani's wheel."

Osborn opened his eyes and stood. "I'll get the spokes from the wagon, from the wagon, I'll get them." Two steps toward the wagon, Osborn stopped. The cicadas stopped singing, and the sounds of battle thundered from the east. He squinted into the sweltering heat as it played with the landscape. "Wagons. They're coming back." Ray turned—the wagons raced in their direction. One passed and then another. Osborn raised his hand to one of the closer ones, yelling to them, "Where ya off to?"

"Lines changed!" the man yelled. "Better get on outta here! Rebs are flanking!"

Ray walked up to Osborn. "Flanking?"

Osborn stiffened. The entire contents of the wagon lay about them like a photographer's yard sale. He jumped into action, putting things back.

"Uncle, don't do that. Maybe we should take Hoady and mosey on outta here. Leave the wagon," said Ray, spitting out the words.

Another wagon came by. "Leave it and head out! It's gonna be a battlefield!" yelled the driver.

Osborn turned to Ray, his eyes moving across his face and down to the ground. Sucking in a breath, he returned with feigned calmness. "Take Hoady and follow them, follow them to wherever they're..."

Ray's arms flew out like a pair of wings. "What?! You mean, let's take Hoady! I ain't leaving you. We gotta get on outta here!"

"Please don't yell, Ray, and I won't leave all my equipment."

"Are you soft?!" yelled Ray, spinning around, hands and face to the sky.

"Don't call me names!" Osborn shut his eyes and scrunched his face. His hands paddling the air.

Ray rushed back to Osborn, softer. "I'm sorry, I'm sorry, all right?" Osborn's face slowly relaxed. "But we need to pull foot and to get to walking," added Ray in the sweetest tone he could muster.

Osborn's eyes narrowed on a Rebel soldier casually walking by. Ray followed his uncle's line of sight. The Rebel waved. "Photographer, eh? I got me one of them back in Georgia," he said as he walked off. "Have a pleasant day, now."

Ray turned back to Osborn, stone-faced. "Uncle, this is serious now, let's get on outta here…" Osborn's eyes narrowed again. Ray spun back around. Grey uniforms poured out from the east woods. They stood frozen as hundreds of Rebels swarmed around them and passed them like a stone in a stream.

The rebels smiled, waved, or said hello as they passed. Some shouted, "Take a portrait of me," "Get a photo of the Yanks running," and "Don't I look pretty," as they made silly faces. Ground troops, cavalry troops, and horse-drawn cannons continued passing them until it came down to a trickle and all the grey uniforms disappeared into the west woods across the battlefield.

"Well, that wasn't so bad, not so bad at all," said Osborn.

A plume of brown erupted from the soil like a fifty-foot geyser two-hundred yards from them—the ensuing boom knocking them down like an unexpected sucker punch. Osborn rose to his feet in shock, put his hands out, fingers splayed, and flapped the air. "No, no, Uncle, this is no time for a conniption fit."

Ray grabbed Osborn by the shoulders. Osborn screamed, jumping back. "Oh, oh, oh, no, no! I'm sorry, Uncle! Lie in the rut as low as you can!" They jumped in the rut as Rebels came running back from where they entered with Yankee cavalry chasing, firing, and killing. "If we run, we're dead. The wagon and this road rut are the safest places to be!" Rebel forces from the east woods flew out to reinforce, catching them in the middle.

Osborn's eyes slowly opened, and his mouth relaxed. The voice in his head grew louder than the battle around him. "It's the best photograph! Not the fastest!" he yelled before jumping to a stand. He turned to Ray with a determined expression Ray had never seen before. "Get me a plate! Get me a plate! Get me a plate!" screamed Osborn above the booming sounds of battle.

Running to Hoady, Osborn slapped him on the rear to scare him off before picking up his equipment. Ducking, jerking, and slamming his eyes closed with every explosion, he fought the need to close his eyes and disappear. He ran past Ray, still lying in the rut, and screamed, "I said, get me a plate!"

Ray jumped up and ran after him. "What?! Are you mad! You're gonna get killed!" he screamed, red-faced.

"I said, get me a plate! And never call me mad again!"

Ray shook his head at him before turning and saying, "Who are you?!" as he ran for a plate. Osborn grabbed the stereoview; a camera with two lenses producing three-dimensional photo cards. The wagon door flew open, and Ray came running out with the first plate as Rebel cavalry thundered by him, swords out, sending him flying back against the wagon's side, eyes bulging with fear. He stumbled back over to Osborn, handing him the plate.

"Get two ready at a time and bring them to me!" screamed Osborn.

Ray ran off again, saying, "This is crazy! This is crazy! This is crazy!" to himself on the way back to the wagon. Osborn shot him a sneer for use of the offensive word before focusing on two soldiers, ten feet away, stabbing each other with bayonets. Ray returned and slid another glass plate into the camera.

Osborn said, "Please hold still," a split second before a cannonball blew through the dark cart and exploded beyond, splattering them with dirt and mud.

They stared at each other in amazement until Ray said, "It's all right. I didn't put anything in it."

"Good, then get me some more plates!" Ray ran off as Osborn ducked under the shroud to focus on Union cavalry prepared to charge.

Rifle balls hit the wagon as Ray brought out another readied plate and took one from Osborn to develop. "Keep your head down!" yelled Osborn as a rifle ball zipped by clipping wood from a tripod leg. The unexposed plate lay next to it. "Hey, bring me two! I said two!" yelled Osborn as he slid in another plate.

"I can only do one at a time! Remember, I'm also developing!" screamed Ray as Osborn aimed the camera and pulled the lens cap on a line of Union infantry, dropping to their knees to fire on the retreating Rebels. Ray ran to the back of the wagon with the exposed plate. A Rebel loaded his rifle in front of the wagon's open door, using the wagon for cover. "Excuse me," said Ray as politely as he could yell.

"Sho nuff," he replied, aiming his rifle and firing.

Ray went in, shutting the door behind him. He readied a plate while developing an exposed one. Finishing those, Ray flung open the door. Two more Rebels had come to use the wagon for cover. Rifle balls hit the wagon, sending splintered wood flying everywhere as he ran to Osborn, again swapping plates. Running back to the wagon, Ray skidded to a stop. Three more Rebels had joined in by the wagon, firing and using it for cover. One stood blocking the door. Ray tapped him on the shoulder. "Excuse me."

The Rebel turned to Ray with wide, bloodshot eyes as he put the stock of his rifle in the dirt. He casually studied Ray from head to toe as he ripped off a gunpowder bag with his teeth, poured it in the barrel, dropped in a ball, and mashed it in with his ramrod. He gave a polite nod before moving from the door, turning, aiming, and shooting. Ray went in, shutting the door behind him. Bullet holes had punched tiny rays of light into the wagon. He grabbed a rag, ripped it up, and plugged them as two new ones appeared, sending wood splinters and Ray to the slanted floor of the dark wagon. Jumping back up, he plugged those before concentrating on his work. Ray continued bringing, taking, and developing plates. When Osborn handed Ray his fifth exposed plate, he said, "Thank the Lord for this bright day. I hope they're not too blurry!"

A rifle ball whizzed by close to Ray's ear. "They look great from what I can see!" yelled Ray. "But there's no more glass plates. Should I reuse them?"

"No! Bring me tintypes, and I'll get the portrait camera!"

A few yards away, Union General Howard took a bullet and flew off his horse. Osborn focused on him with the last glass plate as he sat up, holding his bleeding shoulder. Osborn removed the lens cap and said, "Please hold still," to himself.

Ray flew out again with five prepared tintypes, avoiding two dead Rebels. He stopped to pull out the last bottle of collodion. He raised it to the sunlight—half full, until a bullet flew through it, splashing his shirt and face. He dropped to the ground and ran in a hunch to Osborn.

"That's it! No more collodion!" said Ray, ducking low into the rutted soil. Osborn moved, focused, and shot, moved, focused, and shot with the single-lens camera, dropping each one into Ray's lap until all five tintypes had their image.

"What are you doing?! Bring me more!"

"I told you there's no more collodion! Now lay in that rut till I get back," said Ray, running to the wagon to develop the last five. The war still raging around him, Osborn sucked in a deep breath and laid in the rut. He turned to the direction Hoady ran off, thanking God that he was nowhere in sight.

Ray returned and lay in the rut with him. "That's it?!" asked Osborn. A two-inch splinter of wood stuck in Osborn's cheek.

"Yes," said Ray, spotting it. "Everything developed?!"

"Yes, and hanging in the wagon to dry. Let's hope a cannonball doesn't get it," said Ray.

After twenty minutes, the battle's rage had cooled to an occasional rifle shot, finally stopping a minute later. The cicadas resumed as blue uniforms trickled out of the west woods with larger numbers following the retreating Rebel force. Most walking like a day at the fair.

As the Rebels had earlier, Union troops now called out to them, "I need a portrait!" "Can you make me look like a colonel?" "How much?"

Ray turned to his uncle's face: filthy, blackened from gunpowder, browned from dirt, and still with a two-inch splinter impaled in his cheek.

"You don't feel that?" asked Ray, pointing to it. "Feel what?"

A smile grew on Ray's lips. "Yeah, yeah. Feel what? Exactly. Do you even know what you just did for the last few hours?"

"Photographs, photographs. I do so hope they are in focus, in focus, yes."

Ray rubbed his dirty face. "Yep, they're in focus, all right. But the photographs weren't the only things in focus; you were." Osborn turned to Ray with a blank expression. "What? You don't remember what you did? You charged hell with a bucket of ice water! I've never even heard of bravery like that from anyone, let alone you. I was the one panicking. You had more guts than you can hang on a fence." Osborn cocked his head, confused. "Oh, yeah, uh, guts have something to do with fear and bravery, like when you're scared, you feel it in your stomach…well, never mind. I just mean, you were so brave. Braver than brave."

"I was quite upset that Mathew, Mathew was going to win the day with his photographs. He is not a photographer. He is a cheater."

Ray shook his head. "Mathew? That... I mean, they were shooting at us—both sides! Explosions, rifle shots...? It's like you didn't hear any of it. You just kept asking for another plate. You screamed at me for calling you mad! I still can't wrap my mind around it."

"It was only that I did what needed to get done, did what I needed. I only hope they are better than Mathew's."

"Have you seen what's hanging in that wagon?! It's amazing! No one will have what we have. No one will ever get what we got. Not Mathew, not anybody. These photographs will make a book that will sell all over the world," said Ray.

"I'd like to see them, but I also want to sit here now. I am so tired." "You should see yourself. You're filthier than I've ever seen you," said Ray, his eyes again locking on the considerable splinter.

"You're not so pretty yourself, not so pretty," replied Osborn.

Ray's face brightened. "That's a joke. You just said a joke."

"I did. I did say a joke. I learned it from you."

Ray brought his hand up to the splinter. "Hey, hold on a minute." Osborn's eyes followed his line of sight. "Don't touch me."

"I won't," said Ray as he took the splinter between thumb and forefinger and pulled it out.

"Ouch!" Blood trickled from the wound.

"Put your sleeve on that," Ray said, pointing to the wound and standing. "I'll get started on that wheel." In the distance, Hoady slowly walked back to them. "There's Hoady. Where did he run to?"

Osborn put his sleeve on it, then off, grimacing at the bloodstain.

"I slapped him on the ass, and he ran off."

"Hmm. Guess he's the smart one."

CHAPTER 3

A blackened, bloated arm stuck out of the soil ahead as they headed back to the Union lines with their wheel repaired. It's five fingers stuck straight up as if waving hello. A few feet from it, a living arm was. "Water, can you spare a bit of water?" the Rebel attached to it asked.

Osborn pulled the reins on Hoady and pulled the brake. "Water is the second most spoken word we hear on the battlefield," said Osborn.

Ray jumped down with a canteen, kicking dirt at the bloated arm as he walked by.

"Oh, yeah, what's the first?" asked the Rebel.

"Help," replied Ray as he handed the canteen to him.

Osborn pointed. "There's a hog over there, Ray. It's over there." Ray picked a stone and threw it, hitting the hog. It squealed and ran off.

"Should 'a just shot it," said the Rebel with a raspy voice. The clean-shaven, gap-toothed Rebel, no more than seventeen, lay on his back, his head propped up on a dirt mound. His hand pressed against a dark bloodstain on his leg as he slugged down the water. Ray tried to take it back as he took a breath, but the Rebel refused to let it go.

"Ya don't want me dying parched, do ya?" asked the Rebel as he winced in pain, took another slug, and handed it back to Ray.

"You aren't gonna die," said Ray.

"Ain't no stretcher-bearers 'round here, and they can't see me down in this ditch."

"We'll find one for you. We'll take you back if we don't."

"You with the Yankees?" "Yep."

"I'll wait."

Osborn climbed off the bench and walked closer to the soldier, pointing to his bleeding leg. "I'm sure that hurts." "A bit. That's a fancy wagon ya—"

Osborn's eyes sparkled as he turned to his precious wagon. "It's a Romani vardo caravan. A Romani vardo, yes. I bought it from the son of a dead British Romani Traveller who said in his will that he wished to be, to be cremated in it but, at the last minute, his son refused, as he needed the money for funeral expenses."

The Rebel appeared half surprised and half confused. "That's quite a tale there."

Osborn continued, describing it with his hands as if he were in the wagon, "Inside, since you can't see it with the condition you're in, it is decorated with bright red walls with gold leaf carvings, yes, gold leaf. In the corner, over here, we have a cast iron cooking stove we use for heat as well, yep, we use it for heat. Over here, we have a bed against one side with a chest of drawers beneath. Across from it here, we have a desk—"

"Uncle, stop! He doesn't want to know."

The Rebel shook his head and said, "Whew! I bet your tongue is plumb tuckered out from that one. You one of those daguerreotype people?"

"Yes, but I prefer the term photographer," replied Osborn. "Louis Daguerre was the Frenchman who invented this photographic process..."

Ray walked in front of Osborn, facing him. "Uncle, he doesn't care." Osborn quieted and walked off.

"You can do one of those of me if ya desire to."

Osborn stopped, turning back to Ray with a gleam in his eye. "We gotta get the photographs we have back," said Ray.

"We don't have any collodion anyway," said Osborn.

"I found another bottle when I was putting everything back," Ray admitted.

Osborn returned with a disappointed face. "Ray, I could have used that during the battle!"

"I didn't have it then, Uncle."

Osborn exhaled and turned back to the hand. It stuck out of the ground behind the Rebel and would make an exciting background.

"You don't mind?" Osborn asked the Rebel. "I could use the company."

Osborn nodded to Ray, and they both headed to the wagon. Osborn stepped up and into the wagon, unbuckled the tripod, and handed it to Ray standing outside. Ray set it up as his uncle pulled the camera from a compartment and handed it down to him. Ray attached the camera to the tripod as Osborn shut himself in the wagon and draped the door, eliminating sunlight from the cracks. Putting on a pair of rubber gloves, Osborn took a thin sheet of tin from a cupboard. The brown glass bottle of collodion sat on the desk. He pulled out the cork with his mouth while holding the bottle in one hand and the tin sheet in the other. Slowly, he poured the gooey, syrupy substance onto it, tilting it in all directions to cover the entire surface, then sticking the corner back into the bottle to collect the excess. He stuck the collodion coated tin into a wooden box filled with silver nitrate and quickly closed the lid. As he waited three minutes for it to soak, he fitted a red window into the clear glass above the desk. It illuminated the wagon with red light, a color from the spectrum insensitive to the silver nitrate.

His hands did the rest by memory, removing the tin sheet from the silver bath and placing it face down into a wood frame with glass in front. In front of the glass was a thin wood panel called a "dark board" that would block light. They could slide the dark board out once the glass plate was inside the camera. Precise and delicate, Osborn rarely lost a drop of chemical or broke a frame.

Osborn left the wagon and brought over the readied box to the camera. "That's also quite a fancy daguerreotype you have there," said the Rebel, motioning his head toward it. Osborn made it himself from pinewood and stained and varnished it to a smooth finish.

"Thank you," replied Osborn, heading quickly off like a man with a great secret. Ray turned to the Rebel, picked up the canteen, and returned it to him.

"Thank ya, kindly. Much obliged."

"It's my pleasure," replied Ray as his uncle dragged a dead Rebel officer over, placing him a few feet from the Rebel.

"You work for him?" asked the Rebel. "Yep. He's my uncle."

"Is he a bit touched in the head?"

"He's just peculiar, they say." Ray called out to Osborn, "Need some help?"

"I'm fine. Give the boy some water," Osborn said, not noticing the Rebel already had it. The Rebel smiled and raised the canteen to Ray in a silent toast.

The Rebel turned to the body Osborn placed near him. "That's my captain. I got shot trying to save that ole' boy. He was most likely dead before I got to him. When I saw he'd gone coon, I tried to skedaddle on outta there, but they was all now shooting at me like I was General Lee himself. I pulled foot on outta there fast as a coon hound. And zigzagging like a Virginia fence, I was. They couldn't get me until one lucky boy did. Dang, it all. Just my…" the Rebel trailed off as Osborn gathered a gruesome collection of body parts; a leg from the knee down still with a sock, another leg with a twelve-inch black boot, and lastly, an arm and hand without a pinky finger. Osborn ran over and tossed the assemblage around as if he had collected logs for a campfire. Manipulating a scene like this would produce ostentatious but hugely sellable photos.

The Rebel's expression lay somewhere between disgust and fear as Osborn callously handled the body parts.

"Ain't there any stretcher-bearers about?" asked the Rebel, cringing from his leg wound.

"Saw some a bit back. I'll let ya know," replied Ray as Osborn dove under the black camera shroud. Osborn slid the back of the camera away from the front, and the Rebel slowly came into focus. He replaced the lens cap, and Ray slid in the box with the tin plate and slid out the dark board in front of it. "It's ready, Uncle."

"Have you been photographed, photographed before?" asked Osborn.

"Yessum. I have."

"Just remember not to move, all right?" added Ray.

"Yes, sir," said the Rebel as he grimaced from the pain. "Would it be fine if I could have a copy for my pa? Show him how I got shot and alls?"

"Of course," replied Osborn as his hand gripped the lens cap. "Please hold still. Please hold still." The lens cap came off for eight seconds, enough time for the amount of light that day. Ray placed the dark board into the camera, pulled the wood box out, and handed it to his uncle. "I wish you well, sir, wish you well," Osborn said to the Rebel before he went inside his wagon.

"Thank you kindly, sir. I'm obliged to ya," replied the Rebel as Ray folded up the tripod and carried it and the camera toward the back of the wagon. Ray stepped up and in, shutting the door behind them. Together, the pair developed the photograph within six minutes. Ray dried the tin by holding it over the flame of an oil lamp.

They came out, and Osborn's eyes went to the dead Rebel captain. Osborn turned to Ray with a question in his eyes. "Go ahead, go ahead and pack up, yes, pack up," said Ray as he took the camera and tripod and disappeared behind the wagon. Osborn walked over to the young captain and stood over him. Ray removed the framed red glass from the small window above the desk and opened it. Osborn stared down at the captain, specifically at his pockets, like a drunkard to liquor.

"Whatcha thinking on there?" asked the Rebel.

"The stories, the stories this man can tell," replied Osborn. He turned and found Ray watching him from the window.

Ray said, "You might as well," and Osborn dropped to his knees beside the captain. His hands dove in, rummaging through the pockets and sending them on a treasure hunt of discovery.

"Hey, hey, hey, there! Ya ain't stealing his stuff. He's got kin. Now—"

From the window, Ray said, "He isn't. He'll put it all back."

"I put it all back, yes. Nicer than how I found it, than how I found it." Osborn pulled out a small, double locket from the topcoat pocket.

"Then what in the tarnation are you doing?" asked the Rebel.

Ray came out from the wagon. "You don't want to know. He just does it, is all."

Osborn opened the locket, revealing the captain's mother on one side and his father on the opposite. "It's just something I do, yes." He closed it and placed it back.

"Is he looking for guns?" "No, he isn't."

"No, I'm not," repeated Osborn as he rolled the dead captain to his side and went into his seat pocket, pulling out a letter, Osborn's crown jewel. He laid the body back and read it. "Father and Mother, I hope this letter finds you all well. I am doing smartly and having a fine time with the boys of my platoon. They are a good lot and do right by me most of the time. We are good fighters and have proved our own in more than a few scraps with the Yankees—"

"You don't have to read us the whole letter, Uncle."

Osborn quickly scanned the rest and said, "Da, da, da, da, send my love to Beth Ann and Daisy. Love to you all. Your devoted son, Warren." Osborn turned to Ray. "His name was Warren."

"I heard."

Osborn folded the letter back into the envelope, replaced it, and gently returned the body to its original position.

"I just knew him as Captain McCullan," said the Rebel.

"Ray cried when I told him why I do this, why I search the pockets. Yes, he cried."

The Rebel turned to Ray. "You cried?"

Ray took in an exasperated breath. "You'd get a tear from a glass eye with the story he told."

"A tear from a glass eye is not possible, not possible," said Osborn as he pulled out coins and put them back. "Ray's lip quivered, I saw it, and he turned away after I told him why I wanted to search the pockets, but I knew, yes, I knew he was crying."

"Uncle, please. Can you please not tell everyone this? It's humiliating."

"I saw Ray's arm wipe away the tears he was trying to hide. I said, 'Please don't cry, Ray. Don't cry. It's not a sad thing. It's a happy thing. It makes me happy. Remember, Ray?"

"I remember. From behind, you looked like a vampire taking his blood meal, though."

"But I wasn't. Vampires are not real creatures." Osborn pulled off a boot looking inside—nothing.

"Well, now ya might as well tell me. I, I just have to know."

"It was Corporal John Haggarty, a Union corporal. He had died from a stomach wound, but he wrote out a letter, yes, a letter, as he lay dying. So sad, so sad. I had a strange desire, strange desire, yes. I wanted to find the story behind the corporal. So, I read the letter and searched his pockets for more secrets. Corporal John Haggarty is now one of my old friends—"

The Rebel shook his head. "What?"

"Yes, you see, I piece together their lives. They are a mystery to be discovered, a mystery. What they did before the war, who their loved ones are. Did they have a sweetheart or not." He pulled out paper money from the Captain and an unspent bullet which he rolled between his fingers. "What they have in their pockets, what they wear, if their shoes are clean or muddy..." he said, finding a gold tooth. "...if they brushed their teeth...," Osborn reached in the captain's wide-open mouth, his finger finding a fresh gap. "...their hair. All those are clues, all clues, yes. I learn, I learn, I learn about them with what I find, and then I imagine how their life was when they were alive," he said, glancing at Ray, then to the Rebel, his eyes smiling. "Then, the best part is, I make up a story, make up a story, yes, about them with me. Like I've known them all their lives, or I lived down the street or went to school with them. They become my friend. It gives me a friend, you see," said Osborn with a smile. "As a boy, I never had any friends, no friends for me, no. I was always picked on and considered peculiar, although they would say meaner words, meaner words like fool, muttonhead, or stupe. It hurt me, it hurt me, so I avoided many children my age. Except for my mother, I don't like to remember my childhood. Making up stories works for me. It gives me a childhood worth remembering. It gives me friends and enjoyable things I did with them as a boy or even a young man. I turn the stories into pleasant memories with old friends, old friends, you see?" Osborn fixed the captain's uniform and wiped the blood off his face.

"That's... Uh, yeah, I don't know what to say," said the Rebel. "You didn't cry," said Osborn.

"He doesn't know you as I know you," said Ray.

"I told him it's not a sad thing. It's a happy thing. It makes me happy." Osborn crossed the captain's arms across his chest, straightened his legs, and stood up.

Spotting something in the distance, Ray waved his arms and shouted, "Hey, hey!" Osborn slammed his eyes shut and froze. "Oh, sorry, Uncle. I just saw some stretcher-bearers."

Osborn opened his eyes. "Yes, just a shock, just a shock." "You gotta handful, there," the Rebel told Ray.

"He's worth it," said Ray, walking to the wagon's bench. Osborn followed.

"The stretcher-bearers are coming," said Osborn, climbing up. "Thank ya. Nice meeting ya, both."

Osborn slapped the reins on Hoady. The wheels of the wagon creaked, groaned, and bumped along the rough dirt terrain. Osborn glanced over to Ray. "Don't know if I told you, but Captain Warren McCullan and I went to school together. He was a good sort and fell for this Esther gal. She was a pretty one. He had two sisters, Beth Ann and Daisy. Daisy was a bit younger, but she was sweet on me, but most fellas thought Beth Ann was real pretty. His mother and father were good people." Having heard Osborn's tales countless times, Ray switched his nose plugs to his ears and closed his eyes.

CHAPTER 4

The branches of a forty-foot dogwood tree took root in the sky as its roots did in the soil. Osborn lay underneath it, his eyes following the trunk up into its limbs, covered with creamy white blossoms. One fell gently to his face like a landing butterfly. Startled, he knocked it off like a mosquito.

"Done with your plate?" asked Ray. They had finished lunch inside their portrait tent, a canvas room with four sides, a door, and no roof. This gave them the working space and privacy of a studio, with all his backdrops and mirrors that used the sun as a light source.

"Yes," said Osborn, rising and walking out of the tent. Hundreds of division tents assembled down the hill, fifty feet away. Their campsite was far enough away for fresher air but close enough for the men to stop by for their portraits. It confused Osborn why no officers had chosen this shady site, or maybe he'd been lucky enough to find it first.

Ray swept out the blossoms from the tent as Osborn returned to work on his new but unfinished invention: a device that would allow the photographer to photograph himself alone. Osborn could easily pull off the lens cap. The trick was how to replace it. Osborn came up with an idea. He fashioned a small wood box, open on two sides, and installed it in front of the lens. He cut a slot into the box and slid a thin piece of wood into it with a long dowel attached. Osborn sanded it down to smoothly slide it up to allow the exposure and quickly drop it down to stop it.

"I'm gonna lie down for a bit in the wagon," said Ray.

"All right, I'll call, yes, call you if someone comes in." Osborn ran his fingers down the length of the dowel to the end, which lay in the portrait chair. He raised the thin wood piece with the dowel in his hand and dropped it down like a miniature guillotine. "Click." Off with his head. "Click." Off with another. "Click." And another. Osborn made a different face for each miniature death.

"Excuse the intrusion, sir." A large sergeant with bushy brown muttonchop sideburns came in. Osborn jumped from the chair, trying to hide his embarrassment by walking to the other side of the room. "Might you be able to portratise my brother for my family? He's passed on now, and they sent word that they'd like something to remember him by," said the sergeant in a deep voice. "He was shot last week in the attack at White Oak Swamp."

"A week? Was he on ice all this time? All this time? He can't be looking fresh enough for a portrait. Can't be, can't be," said Osborn with his back to the sergeant.

"Oh, yes, he is, and no ice. The embalmer fixed him up. Even fixed up his face to make him look real alive again. Remarkable."

"Oh, yes, yes, the embalmer."

"Yessum. The division just got us a full-time embalmer person." "Well, yes, it'd be our pleasure. Can you bring him by, or would you like us to come to you?"

The sergeant grinned. "I'll bring him by in the shake of a rattler's tail," said the sergeant before heading out the door and passing Ray coming in.

"Why would he want to shake a rattler's tail?" Osborn asked Ray. "It's a figure of speech, meaning he'll be back in a short time."

An hour later, the sergeant busted through the tent flap carrying his sheet-covered brother by the arms. A man with a mottled complexion, wearing a bloody smock with rubber gloves to his elbows, held the feet.

"Where should we put him?" asked the sergeant.

"Please put him in this chair," said Ray, pointing to the armchair where Osborn sat. Osborn hopped up, narrowly missing the heavy body dropping into it. He pulled off the sheet. "Phenomenal," Osborn uttered to himself.

The body slowly fell forward, and the sergeant stopped it with his hand. "Whoa!" said the sergeant.

"Ray, get out the posing stands, the posing stands, yes."

The bloody smock man grinned, revealing two missing teeth. "You're the photographer, Mr. Roche?" he asked. "Wrote the book and all?"

"No, I didn't write a book. I made a book of photographs. Book of photographs," said Osborn, his attention fixed on the cadaver. "Are you the embalmer? Phenomenal work on this man."

"I am, but my brother Henry did this one. I'm Ben."

"Did you do the work on General Wool?" asked Osborn.

"Uh, yeah, the old guy from Ashland? Yeah, that was us."

"Tell him it's amazing work."

"Isn't it?" replied the sergeant with a pleased grin as if it wasn't his dead brother they referred to. "It's my uniform he's wearing. His was shot up a bit. The poor bastard."

Osborn took note of the pressed uniform and the clean-shaven face with makeup that gave life to it. They called it "setting the features," and Osborn also did this for his clients. The embalmer of this man had paid as careful attention to his work as he would have.

The sergeant asked, "Can you do something about his eyes? Make him look like he's awake?"

Ben stepped up. "Oh, I didn't know you'd want that. I could've done that for ya."

"I can do it. Certainly, I can either paint on eyes on top of his eyelids now or on the portrait. Both end up being lifelike," replied Osborn, his attention fixed on the body. Ray brought in the stands and set them near the body.

"Paint the portrait, so I don't have to wash his eyelids."

"Of course." Walking behind the man, Osborn clamped the pole onto the dead man's skull behind the ears, steadying it. Placing the dead man's arms on the armrest, he positioned the man's fingers to wrap around the carved mahogany and moved his legs to a relaxed position as if coming home from a stroll, slightly angled, one over the other. Osborn stood back, critiquing his work, but went up to him again, tilting the dead man's head a bit.

"As if in thought," said Osborn to himself.

"Yep, like he just got done reading a fine book," said the sergeant. "He loved them books."

"Is the glass plate ready? Is it ready?" asked Osborn.

Ray's eyes snapped open. "Oh! Sorry, Uncle. It'll be right quick!" Ray ran off to the wagon. Three minutes later, he returned and loaded the glass plate into the camera. He stepped back, allowing his uncle to approve the scene through the lens.

Osborn stepped aside, hand on the lens. "Please hold still." Osborn pulled the lens cap and replaced it at a precise moment.

"I can do the developing," said Ray as he slid out the box containing the glass plate.

"No. I would like to do this one," replied Osborn.

Ben appeared confused. "Were you saying hold still to him or us?"

He pointed his thumb at the corpse.

"Hmm?" said Osborn absently.

Ben shook his head. "Nothin'. Can I take him back now?"

"Yes. We have him now for all eternity. All eternity," said Osborn, walking out.

Alone in the wagon, sunlight from the red glass window illuminated the room. The photograph soaked in its final rinse bath. Osborn took it and hung it to dry, clipping it to a string with a clothespin. He stood back regarding the photograph of the week-old dead man that appeared so much alive. The fact that he was dead would remain a secret to all except for the family, himself, and the embalmer. He said to himself, "You showed me your work. I will show you mine."

CHAPTER 5

Osborn clutched the photograph in his hand, his grip tightening as he and Ray marched toward the embalming tent. The twelve-by-twelve canvas structure loomed ahead, its two large poles stretching towards the sky like the pillars of a circus big top. Above the entrance, a three-by-six-foot wood sign announced, "Embalming." The tent sat a mere hundred feet outside the Union encampment, a distance that felt both too close and too far. As they approached, the faint odor of chemicals wafted through the air, a sickly sweet scent barely masked death's stench.

Ben sat in a chair outside, reading a newspaper and smoking a pipe as if he had just gotten home from work. As they reached the door, Ben stuck out his leg, blocking the entrance. His brown hair covered head slowly tilted up to them. He carefully set down the newspaper and took his pipe from his mouth, all with an arrogant flair.

Osborn coughed and waved away the pipe smoke from his face while saying, "Oh, my. Oh, no, no—"

"Why, it's the photographer. What can I do for ya?"

"May I meet the man associated with the corpse you brought over?"

"A bit occupied at the moment." "How long shall I wait? How long?"

"I'm finished! It's fine!" came from inside the tent.

"He ain't lookin' for you," yelled Ben from the side of his mouth. "If it's the photographer, he's looking for me. I did that man." "Henry won't be happy!"

"Let him in, Ben!"

Ben shook his head and dropped his leg. Osborn raised his eyebrows and entered. Ray tried to follow, but Ben's leg went back up. "Not the boy. Trust me, that place ain't for him."

Osborn shrugged, and Ray backed away.

As Osborn stepped into the embalming tent, the cavernous interior defied his expectations, dwarfing the unassuming exterior. The sight transported him back to a distant memory, to a time when his mother's gentle hand guided him through a traveling church revival at the tender age of eight. The congregation stood with arms raised high, their faces awash in the radiant love of the Lord, a sight that both captivated and unsettled the young Osborn. His mother, the sole person he ever permitted to touch him, clasped his hand tightly as she navigated the outer aisle, her eyes scanning for an open pew amidst the sea of worshipers. With a polite request, she secured two seats at the end, the man beside them obliging with a nod and a shuffle. The backs of the worshipers obscured Osborn's view of the stage, their arms raised and bodies swaying in a hypnotic rhythm. He turned to face those behind him, their eyes closed, hands up, and lips moving in an unintelligible chorus of whispers and mutterings. Some shook and convulsed like birds that had flown into windows, their movements erratic and unsettling. Fear gripped Osborn's heart, and he closed his eyes, desperate to escape the rising panic that threatened to consume him. But then, a gentle squeeze from his mother's hand drew his gaze to hers, and he found himself lost in the mesmerizing flicker of her unique green irises. A condition she had since birth; her eyes twitched back and forth rapidly, never resting for a moment, like leaves dancing in the wind. As he stared into their depths, Osborn's breathing slowed, and his jaw relaxed, the calm washing over him like a soothing balm.

Today, he stood in the embalmer's tent that held a different congregation. These worshippers all lay on gurneys covered with sheets instead of sitting in pews. The embalmer stood at the far side of the room with his back to Osborn. Possibly in his late teens or early twenties, the embalmer dressed like a street urchin, wearing beige pants held up by suspenders over a white cotton shirt. He had a smock over it, tied in the back. As he worked, he swayed his hips back and forth like he needed to pee. He pulled a sheet over a milky white soldier's body with tubes gruesomely entering and exiting his neck.

The embalmer reached back and untied the smock before turning to face Osborn with it covered in blood. The embalmer pulled the smock over his head and walked towards Osborn, his hands held low, fingers dancing in a constant, invisible piano performance. An unusual trait, thought Osborn as he reached for his goatee, twisting it.

As the distance between them closed, Osborn's jaw dropped, his eyes widening in astonishment at the sight of the embalmer's light brownish-gold eyes. They flickered as his mother's did. The embalmer's lips curled into a curious, half-grin. "Can I help you?" the embalmer asked with a giggle. The question hung in the air momentarily, the embalmer's eyes studying Osborn's face intently. "Are you all right, sir?"

Osborn struggled to find his voice. "My Lord in Heaven. Your eyes, your eyes, they flutter to and fro like... butterfly wings," he said as he stepped closer, unabashedly staring into them.

The embalmer's smile grew wider as he let Osborn examine him. "I don't know how to respond. I've never been told. I mean, most people call them odd. Or worse."

"It's the most amazing thing. My mother had eyes just as yours are. They moved just as yours do, just as yours do. Like a little girl waving to her father as he returns home from a long trip."

The smile faded from the embalmer as tears filled his eyes. "That is the most beautiful thing I have ever heard. No one has ever said that to me," he said as he swallowed the tears down a throat with no Adam's apple.

Osborn's awe suddenly vanished, and his head jerked back in surprise. He stepped back, examining the embalmer up and down. The voice, the wider hips, the soft features..., "You're a woman, a woman."

Her sleeve wiped her face as she stepped back. "Most don't notice. You're..., you're not gonna tell anyone, are ya? I do my job here, and I do it well."

"Oh, you most certainly do, and that is why I'm here. And I will tell no one."

Her shoulders eased. "My name is Lou Cattell."

"I am Osborn Roche. I am a photographer," he said as if it was a secondary conversation to another he was having in his head. Osborn walked around her, surveying her like a display mannequin in a clothing shop. Her small mouth and thin lips rested upon a round face. She had cut her brown hair short and wore spectacles, oval-shaped blue steel, the same as he wore.

"Osborn Roche? Yes, we have your book," she said, pointing to the corner of the room.

His fascination blocked her words from his ears. "You do that with your fingers. Move them like that, like the tentacles of a sea anemone." Lou laughed. "Or like you are playing the piano. Yes, a piano. May I ask why?"

"I don't know why. I've always done it. It calms me."

"Yes, yes. Interesting. I am calmed by someone reading to me. Do you play the piano? The Piano?"

"I do not." She took a deep breath as he circled her in strange amazement. She pushed her spectacles up on her nose as her eyes behind them grew curious.

"With my photography, I discover the souls of people and photograph them. Questions and jokes help me reveal them. I get them to drop their guard and show me their true selves. But yours is there, revealed so easily. There it is in your smile, like a child, when she pets a dog for the first time, and in the crinkle in the corners of your eyes. A bit more when you bite your bottom lip like you are..." She stopped biting it, and a smile crept on her face. "...doing right now." His head tilted down and to the side, as he watched her under his brow like a shy boy. "Every feature on your face is divulging and expressive. An unusual trait. Do people tell you that? Tell you that a lot?"

Her nose wrinkled, adding to the unceasing smile on her lips as she shook her head in tiny, fast motions. "I've never been told that," she giggled.

"Yes, Magnificent."

Osborn stood staring into her eyes. She giggled again. "Are you flirting with me, Mr. Roche?"

Osborn stiffened, his expression falling. "Uh, I don't... I don't know what I..." His eyes dropped to the floor, away from her.

Lou's smile fell like a duck from a scattergun. "Oh, no, it's perfectly fine," she pleaded. "Please, come sit down."

Osborn's eyes stayed on the floor, and he backed up toward the door. "I've never. I... don't... I don't know where I am."

"Mr. Roche? No, please. I didn't mean to say anything. I, I've never been flirted with—"

"I wasn't flirting!"

"No, no, I meant I've never been flirted with, so I don't know what it's like."

He shook his head. "I shouldn't have said those things. What came over me I do... don't... I... Forgive me, will you? Forgive me."

"There's nothing to forgive," said Lou as she closed the gap between them.

His head buzzed, his stomach queasy. He wanted to turn and run, but his legs wouldn't move. He needed his nephew. He needed Ray now.

"Please, Mr. Roche, please sit."

Osborn slammed his eyes shut and raised his elbows to his sides, hands up in front. Lou's brows went up as fast as his elbows as she watched him in a surprising panic of her own. His face grew red and scrunched up, his body tensed, his fingers spread wide and flapping up and down.

"I need Ray! I need Ray!" he demanded.

Ray came flying into the tent with Ben on his heels. With a quick glance at Lou, Ray stepped in front of his uncle.

"Uncle! Uncle! I'm right here. It's all right. Nothing's happening. No bad things here," he said in a rushed but calming tone. "Let's go this way and follow me out the door. Follow my voice. We'll have tea at the wagon. I'll get it ready for us. Yes, some warm tea."

"Yes, yes. Warm tea. Warm tea," repeated Osborn, calming. A smile returned to his face.

"What the hell is happening?" asked Ben. Lou stood frozen, mouth open in shock.

Ray walked backward toward the flap, with Osborn following his voice like a blind man. Ben stepped aside to let them out.

"Thank you," said Osborn as calmly as if he had just paid for groceries.

Lou stood expressionless as Ben's eyes narrowed with curiosity, staring in the direction they exited.

Reaching the wagon, Ray pulled over the footstool for Osborn to sit. "What set you off in there?" Ray asked.

Osborn sat. "Nothing."

Ray's tense shoulders dropped as he squinted and shook his head. He drew a breath as he sat on a footstool, wiping his face with both hands. "Still want me to make tea?"

"Wonderful."

Ray rose and brought the teapot to the fire, now smoldering. "We are out of firewood."

"Don't fuss. We'll make tea at our regular time. I'm feeling much better. Thank you. Thank you, Ray."

Ray put down the pot and sat on the other stool. "Was his embalming disgusting?"

"No, no, it wasn't that. She thought I was flirting with her."

Ray's brow raised. "Her? That was a girl?"

Osborn stopped, mouth ajar. "I, I wasn't supposed to….She told me not to say."

"I won't say anything. I'm just surprised. A woman, eh?"

Osborn stood, wiped off his undirtied coat with his hands, and paced in front of the wagon. "And an incredibly beautiful one."

Ray's head snapped up. "Beautiful?! You think she's beautiful? Did we see the same filly? She dressed like a buck! And those eyes? They moved all back and forth like. Quivered-like."

"My mother's eyes did that. Did that, yes. Your grandmother. Did I ever tell you that? I thought she was… beautiful. Just beautiful."

"Your mother or this filly?"

Shocked, Osborn stood and said, "Both, of course."

Ray gave in, waving his hands. "I'm sorry, I didn't understand. Maybe you should sit down. You're still all wound up," said Ray gesturing to the stool.

"That's nice that you think she's beautiful. I ain't never heard that from you before."

"I'm not all wound up! I know beauty when I see it."

"Beautiful, eh? I suppose ya can't beat that with a stick."

Osborn's head jerked. "Why would you beat that with a stick?"

"No, it's 'can't beat that with a stick,' and you've heard me say that before. Remember I told you?"

"Ah, yes, the euphemism, I remember. Referring to be acceptable or something."

"Yes, that's the one," said Ray. "Such a strange way of putting it."

"It is, but it makes language enjoyable." "It makes it confusing."

"But back to this gal——"

"She thought I was flirting."

Ray jumped up with a laugh. "Flirting?! Were you?"

"No! I do not flirt. I do not think I know how."

"You said she was beautiful."

"I said her eyes were beautiful."

Ray laughed again. "That's flirting."

CHAPTER 6

The crisp morning air carried a welcoming chill, thin enough to allow sounds from distant sections of the regiment to reach Osborn and Ray's ears. The echoes of clinking spoons against tin plates and the gentle swish of coffee being poured into cups mingled with raspy morning voices uttering their first waking words a jangle from a distant banjo, laughter, and chirping birds created a lovely contrast to the previous day's sounds of battle.

Osborn and Ray sat outside their tent on three-legged footstools, eating their typical breakfast, bread with the bacon fat drippings from last night's dinner of bacon with potatoes.

"You seem quiet this morning," said Ray.

"I was thinking of trying something different today. With the portraits, with the portraits, I mean. Bring me the plate or the tin before they begin their story and sit there quietly as they tell it."

"What if their story is long? The plate will dry."

Osborn brought his forefinger to his lips and tapped it against them. "Hmm. Yes, but it is a chance we need to take. We need to take, Ray."

"If it dries, I'll have to make a new one."

"When you come in the middle, it interrupts their concentration, and at the end, they lose that gleam in their eye."

"All right. I can prepare them while you loosen them up with the jokes I taught you."

Osborn's eyes brightened with excitement. "Yes, yes! I need them to forget about the camera, forget about the camera, and their armor will fall."

"All right, we'll try that."

Osborn took his forefinger from his lips to the sky and said, "It's those moments when the armor falls off, and you see their true souls. That's when the lens cap comes off."

"I know, I know, Uncle. You've said—"

"There are many photographers that take photographs now, but for a portrait to be like a Rembrandt or a DaVinci, you need to see more than skin and smiles. You need to see their soul." Osborn took another bite.

"You've told me this ten times at least," replied Ray, paying more attention to the camp's activities.

"Eight at the most, but I tell you this to teach you, Ray. That's what the great painters of yesterday did."

"I know they did because you told me ten times."

"It was not ten, not ten. More like seven. It is important to remember the soul is what makes us who we are. Not the skin and muscles. To capture the soul of a person, you need to see what others can't. Scrape off that armor the person wears and wants you to see, wants you to see, Ray. Enough that a loved one can say, 'Yes, that is him! I see him there.' We are doing God's work in revealing it to them."

"I know, Uncle, and that is why I am teaching you how to tell a joke."

"Yes, yes. They have worked quite well, quite well."

Ray put down his plate and turned to Osborn. "Besides that, yesterday, you spoke about your mother. You've never mentioned her before."

Osborn snapped his head toward Ray. "Haven't I? She was your grandmother. Did you ever meet her?"

"No," said Ray.

"Your father never...?"

"Not that I remember. Maybe when I was very little. I don't remember much before the time I met you," said Ray.

"Your grandmother was beautiful, so beautiful. I wanted flickering irises like hers. She was the only person who could touch me. The only person I let touch me."

"Oh, I didn't think anyone could touch you."

"She could, she could hold my hand, brush my hair, help me get dressed. She wanted to kiss me, but I didn't like kisses. No, sir. No kisses," said Osborn, wiping imagined saliva from his cheek.

Ray laughed as four soldiers approached, all formally dressed and carrying their rifles and gear, ready for their portraits. "Good morning," said Osborn, scraping up bacon fat with his slice of bread.

"Morning, sir, remember me?" asked Private McDonnell, a sixteen-year-old soldier.

"I see a lot of soldiers, but you, I remember. You, I remember."

"Me and the boys want to get a group portrait."

"I wanna get one by my lone self as well, if possible," a thin Corporal Douglas chimed in.

"For you, corporal, anything's possible in this man's army, this man's army," said Osborn. "Just like last time, we can give you four tintypes, which are normally five cents each, but I'll make 'em four cents because there's four of you, or I can do albumen paper…"

"We all ain't got much money. Let's do tintype, what ya did for me last time," said McDonnell.

Ray ran to the wagon to prepare the tin sheets. A one-of-a-kind positive print, each tintype would be prepared separately and quickly exposed as the tin needed to remain moist.

"Very good. Give my nephew a minute to prepare the first tin. Come into the tent, and we'll be all ready for you in just a minute, just a minute." The soldiers walked past Osborn into the tent.

Osborn finished his breakfast, putting his plate and fork on the ground beside his footstool. As he stood, he wiped his lips with his fingers and put them one by one into his mouth to suck off the remains of the breakfast. Walking into the tent, he said, "You boys figure out how you want to pose." The boys practiced different poses, fixed their uniforms, and smoothed their hair in front of the long mirror.

"Now you boys have to stand over there. Put your backs to that wall and set up how you like." Osborn went under the shroud to adjust focus. He pointed to the giant soldier on the end, Private MacPherson. "You there, hold your rifle a bit higher and scoot in closer to that lad. Where you boys from?"

Private MacPherson spoke up. "We're all from Fond du Lac, Wisconsin."

"We're with the 14th Wisconsin," said McDonnell as he took a proud stance and put his chin up.

"Michigan, eh? Yes, yes, I like Michigan," said Osborn.

"No," he said, "Wisconsin. We's Wisconsin men," insisted McDonnell.

"I know he did. I'm just saying I like Michigan. I like Michigan," replied Osborn. The four men had a two-second moment of confusion before bursting into laughter. Ray walked in with the first prepared tin and put it into the camera.

"You are one funny fella!" said McDonnell as the laughing settled down.

Osborn replaced the lens cap before Ray pulled the dark board. Osborn leaned closer to Ray and said, "I used the joke where you say a different state than the one they mention, they mention. It worked."

"Told you."

"But I still don't understand the humor behind it. No, still don't." Osborn turned back to the soldiers. Now, I'd like to ask you a question. Can each of you tell me in just a few sentences what the saddest moment you've encountered on the battlefield was? The saddest moment." Confused at first, the men looked at each other in thought before one stepped up with his story.

As the last man finished telling his story, Osborn asked, "Now, tell me about the greatest moment you enjoyed with your grandparents?" Each soldier told his story and listened to their comrades'. After the last one finished, Osborn softly said, "Boys, please hold still." He removed the lens cap and counted in his mind to ten for the right amount of exposure needed in the morning light. With the lens cap on, Ray immediately replaced the tin plate with another until he exposed all four.

"How'd we look?" asked McDonnell.

"Like a bunch of damned fools," said Ray as he walked out of the tent to develop them.

Osborn flinched at the men's outburst of laughter. "That's good because if I didn't, my daddy wouldn't recognize me!" said Private MacPherson.

Osborn took a seat on a supply trunk. The men laughed at each other's banter, flipping their heads back and forth amongst each other. Their laughing and yelling annoyed his senses, but these boys had a friendship he had never experienced with a living person other than Ray, and Ray was family. These longtime friends knew each other's deepest secrets from long ago and laughed about them now. Friends who protected each other when young and now shared in each other's accomplishments, marriages, and children. He wouldn't ask for three friends like this, but one special lifelong friend wasn't asking for much.

CHAPTER 7

With a fountain pen, Osborn added a dot to the right side of his favorite bowtie. The left side already had one—a stain from one of the chemicals he worked with. This morning, Osborn dressed in the tidiest clothes he could find. Ray sat on the footstool, whittling a stick as he came from the wagon.

"I'm going to the privy. Be back in a bit, back in a bit," Osborn quickly said as he headed toward the privy, but that wasn't his destination.

"Yup," replied Ray, focused on his whittling.

Wood planks were laid over the muddied pathway between the two regiments. Osborn walked carefully on one as if crossing a drawbridge to her castle ahead. Without the mottled-face man guarding the gates, Osborn advanced in with no announcement. As he entered, the smell of the dead and chemicals drifted about the air. Instinctively, Osborn's hand reached for his nose plugs, seeking to block out the overwhelming stench. But then, he spotted her, her back turned to him as she worked. Osborn froze, his heart pounding in his chest, the desire to turn and run growing with each passing second.

As if sensing his presence, she turned, her eyes widening in surprise. She seemed taken aback momentarily, caught off guard by his unexpected arrival, until a smile spread across her face. "Oh! Hello, I'm pleased you came back."

Osborn's lips seemed glued shut. He didn't know how to respond, even if he could utter a coherent sentence. Her cheeks rose with her smile. "Can I help you?"

"I would. I would like to apologize for..."

"There's nothing to apologize for, Mr. Roche."

"But there is. I was…"

"You were kind and sweet, is what you were. No one has ever told me such kindnesses before. You are a very charming man."

Osborn's shoulders eased as his eyes rose to meet hers. Lou removed her bloody smock, setting it aside before walking to a small table. "Would you like some tea? It's oat straw tea." Osborn awkwardly nodded yes.

She took two cups and a kettle from atop a heating oil lamp. She walked to a bamboo mat on the dirt floor in black knee-high boots, sat on it, and crossed her legs. She poured the tea into one cup, then the other with delicate motions, her fingers moving about, playing the role of the sea anemone between every item she touched. With her head, she gestured for him to sit. Her short hair and boyish clothes suited her. Now that he knew, he found seeing her as anything other than a woman impossible. Walking over, he sat in front of her and crossed his legs as she did, something he hadn't done since he was a boy.

"I saw the man yesterday. The dead man your worker brought over," said Osborn.

"He's my uncle."

"Oh, I'm sorry. I'm so sorry."

"No, not the dead man. The worker is my uncle. His name is Ben." Osborn's cup sat on the mat before him, a short twelve inches away. She picked it up and handed it to him.

"Oh, yes. He told me his name. He said his brother worked on that corpse." Osborn took the cup from her with both hands, careful not to touch her fingers, and brought it to his lips.

"He always says that in case they find out about me being a woman. I stay hidden for the most part. Were you pleased with my presentation of the body?"

The tea ran down his throat, warm and pleasing. "I was. He looked alive. You are an artist." Her slight smile played hide and seek behind the cup, revealing itself after every sip. "I like to watch your fingers move. I can see why it is calming. I can see that, yes."

"Thank you," she said.

"Why are you doing this? This embalming."

Lou wrinkled her nose. "I am good at it. You said I'm an artist. Are there not women in art? Caterina van Hemessen, Mary Beale, Marie-Denise Villers?" she said, revealing her education.

"But you work with the dead. Doesn't it upset you? Upset you?" Her eyelashes fluttered. "You do as well. I have seen your photographic book, 'Portrait of Shiloh.' Those photographs are full of dead soldiers. Did it upset you when you photographed them?"

Osborn shook his head. "Working with the dead makes me appreciate life more."

"Me too."

"Does your family approve? Approve of this?" he asked as she carefully put down her cup.

"My father taught me. My father is Henry Cattell. We provided our services for President Lincoln's son, Willy, last February—"

"I made a photographic portrait of Willy just a few months prior."

"Really?"

"Yes, requested by the President himself."

"He requested us for the embalming. All of us work for Brown and Alexander, a surgery and embalming company. My father has now made the firm well known because of Willy. My father taught me the process, but I am the one who turned the craft into art." Her finger delicately circled the rim of the cup.

She leaned in. "Would you like to see how embalming is done?" Her lips curled into an inviting smile. Her eyes, like his mother's, emanated kindness and patience.

Rising, she reached out for his hands. He pulled back. "I'm sorry, I do not like to touch."

"That's all right. Follow me."

Osborn rose and followed her to a covered body on a gurney. She turned to the gurney and removed the sheet, revealing a man's pale, blue-lipped face.

"He was a Union captain. Took a ball through the chest," she said, her voice steady and clinical as she pointed to a small hole in the man's chest. With a fluid motion, she pulled the sheet off further, exposing the naked body, save for a modesty cloth draped over his groin. Caught off guard by the sudden reveal, Osborn turned away momentarily, embarrassed, but curiosity brought him back.

Her hands moved with the delicacy of a concert pianist as she worked, each motion precise and purposeful. Taking a rag, she washed the body in calm, circular patterns, her touch gentle as she massaged the rigor mortis stiffness out of the muscles. Osborn glanced over to her, curiosity in his eyes, marveling at how the naked man's body didn't seem to faze her in the slightest.

With a deft hand, she took up a scalpel and made a small incision at the soldier's collarbone. The pale captain, his lips slightly parted, seemed to grant her silent permission, a final act of surrender to the inevitable. Like a skilled surgeon, she put down the scalpel and took up a rubber tube, inserting it into the opened artery, followed by a second tube into the nearby vein. The tubes led to a foot pump that she rhythmically tapped like a caller at a square dance.

An arsenic-based fluid flowed into the body through one tube while the other tube carried away the blood. As she tapped, her hands continued to massage the captain, evenly distributing the liquid into him.

"Please inform me if this disturbs you," she said.

Osborn remained silent, too fascinated to respond. The process was both mesmerizing and unsettling, a dance between the living and the dead. The prodding, poking, aspirating, and cleaning would have been a revolting procedure to anyone else, but, similar to himself, Osborn took note of the respect she showed the dead. He witnessed the preciseness, the gentle actions, and the perfection in how she treated her art. She stopped pumping and removed the tubes from the body. Taking a small glass bottle from the tray next to her, she popped off the cork with her mouth and poured a small amount into the incisions.

"Now, I use collodion to seal the incisions," she said as her thumb and forefinger held the incision closed until it dried.

Osborn's eyes opened. "Collodion? We use the same chemical in photography. We pour it onto the tintype, and the silver nitrate sticks to it."

"The doctors here also use it to seal wounds in the field hospitals," she said. "And now I wash up so that I can set the features."

"I set the features as well for my postmortem work." He followed her to a half-full water basin. Standing centimeters away, the scent of her hair came to his nose. Rarely liking any scents, her hair drew him nearer, replacing some of the smell of death in the room. His nose moved closer to the back of her neck, and he sniffed twice.

Her hands swept across and over each other in the basin as she poured water on them, washing with a brown washcloth. A twinge of jealousy poked him like a needle as the cloth slid across her porcelain skin from fingertip to elbow. Again, she sunk the cloth into the water. It swirled about in the basin like a water moccasin in a river, clinging to her fingers, wrapping around them as it sucked in moisture. The snake hypnotized the charmer as it brushed over her small hands and up and down her forearms. She pulled it out and wrung it gently. The water gushed out, then dropped as tears into the bowl as she released.

She set the cloth next to the basin and turned to him. "I think we are very much alike, Osborn. In so many ways. Am I right?" Her eyes gazed into his. The warm, moist air from her lungs caressed his neck.

"Oh, excuse me," interrupted a man entering from the rear tent flap. Osborn's head snapped up to him, and Lou turned around.

"Father," said Lou.

With a mind of its own, Osborn's hand jumped for the damp brown cloth, stealing it into his pocket behind her back. He hoped her father didn't see. Henry Cattell, a bald gentleman with a grey horseshoe mustache down to his jowls, walked up to them. "Father, I'd like you to meet Mr. Osborn Roche, the photographer."

Henry Cattell smiled and outstretched his hand. "Nice to meet—"

"He doesn't shake hands," said Lou.

"That's probably good with all the chemicals I have on my hands. I am a great admirer of your work, Mr. Roche. We have your photographic book, and I saw your photograph of Willy; God rest his soul—"

"God rest his soul, his soul, yes," interrupted Osborn.

Henry curiously studied Osborn before continuing, "Yes, well, the President showed us."

"Thank you, Mr. Cattell," replied Osborn. "Your daughter told me you have the book. Told me you have it. And I am also fascinated by your profession."

Henry turned to Lou with raised eyebrows, and she said, "He knows I'm a girl. He saw I was a girl right away."

"Oh, yes. I saw it right away. Right away. But it was her eyes that attracted me. Attracted me."

Henry raised his brows higher, and Lou stammered, "Oh, he means, I mean.... Well, he said that because his mother had my condition. My eyes... I mean. He didn't mean they are beautiful like that. They are like his mother's."

"No, I meant they are beautiful. Oh, yes, beautiful. And like my mother's, yes. But I was not flirting. Not flirting, no, sir."

"Yes, he was absolutely not flirting. Just observing," she said as Henry shifted uncomfortably.

Her hand reached out behind her to Osborn, attempting to signal him to be quiet as he said, "Just observing, just observing." As she touched his arm, he jumped back with an, "Ah!"

She whipped around to him and said, "Oh, I'm sorry, I forgot."

Osborn took a step toward them with an awkward grin. "Quite all right, quite all right," he said as if nothing had happened. "Oh, all right then," said Osborn uncomfortably, not knowing where to look with his anxiety growing. "Suppose I should get back to work. Nice to meet you both." Osborn turned and walked out. His gait turned into a run after leaving the tent, and as he ran, he smiled and pulled out her brown cloth from his pocket, grinning like a successful thief.

She could be the one. She could be the friend he had always longed for. There was something about her. Something peculiar. Something peculiar like him.

CHAPTER 8

"Can't I get a portrait done?" asked a ten-year-old drummer boy as he came from around the wagon. He dressed in full regalia with three sergeant's stripes on both sleeves, gold epaulets on the shoulders, a gold aiguillette rope draped off his shoulder, and shiny, polished boots. His mother must have embellished the uniform.

Osborn and Ray sat on their stools, leaning against the wagon. A supply box sat between them with their morning breakfast of baked beans and salt pork. "Come back in an hour, young man," said Ray as he took another bite.

"I'll take care of this one," said Osborn. "What will it be, a tintype?"

"Yes, sir. I'd like to get two of the same, please. One for my momma, one for my aunt."

"Good, goo. Tintypes are less money. I can do two tintypes, same pose. Go on in there and set yourself how you want to be."

"You have a rifle I can borrow? I would like to look like everyone else."

"Ain't got one, son, but with that fancy drum, I'll make you look like the best of 'em," said Osborn, turning to the wagon. "I'll be right in with you."

"Thank ya kindly, sir," replied the young drummer, turning to Ray to whisper, "You got a gun or a rifle?"

"Sorry, I don't," said Ray as he took another bite. The drummer lowered his head and turned to the portrait tent.

Osborn came from the wagon carrying the tin plate box. "Follow me."

"There ain't no roof in here," said the boy as he walked in. "That's because we need the sun's light for this to work. Go ahead and stand over there, in front of that tarp," he said as he slid the glass plate in. "I can put the flag behind you if you like. Put the flag behind you."

"That'd be nice. My momma would like that." Osborn went to a box next to the boy, pulled out the flag, and draped it behind him.

"Uncle!" said Ray, walking in with a big smile. "You have a visitor."

Osborn turned to Lou, walking in. "Good morning. I just came to see how the master photographer does his work. Would you mind?"

Osborn's hand reached for his beard, twisting it nervously. "Well, it'd be my... certainly, of course. Of course," he stammered.

"Where can I sit?" She walked to a barrel next to the camera. "Can I sit right here? I'll just listen," she said, turning to the drummer boy. "Hello. Here to get your photograph done by Mr. Roche?"

"Portrait," corrected Osborn.

"Yes, I am," said the boy.

Lou faced Osborn and asked, "Pardon?"

"You said photograph, and well, photographs are what you take of nature and things and—"

"Portraits are what you take of people," finished Ray, rolling his eyes. "It's the same thing."

"No, it's not. No, it's not, Ray."

"I can see that. All right, I'll be quiet now and just listen," she said with a finger to her lips.

Osborn turned to the boy and asked, "Can you show me how you'd like to pose?"

"How about this? The boy faced them with closed fists at his waist and his chin up.

"Very good," she said.

"Are you gonna use your drum?" asked Osborn. "No, sir. I'd like a rifle."

"We do not have a rifle. We do not have one."

"They don't give us rifles. I think they should."

"They would shoot at you, shoot at you if you had a rifle. You don't want to get shot. I would not want to get shot," said Osborn.

"Suppose," said the boy.

"They don't shoot at you if you are a drummer boy?" asked Lou.

"No. Drummers are off-limits on both sides," replied the boy.

"I think you'd look right fine with the drum," said Lou.

"Well, since there's two, I'll do one with and one without?" he said, retrieving the large drum and strapping it on.

"Sounds reasonable. All right now, remember that pose, but for now, take in a very deep breath and think of something pleasant. When I say, please hold still, take that pose again. Take that pose again, understand?"

"Yes, sir."

"So, let me ask you a few questions before we get started. Are you enjoying your time with the army? Your time here?"

"Yes, sir."

"Please provide me more detail. How are you? What is fun? Who do you stay with?"

"All us drummers stay together. There are six of us. Fun? I guess. We play lots of games, card games. The other fellas taught me."

"You been in battle yet? What was that like? What was it like?"

"It was scary. It's scary every time. But the Rebs don't shoot at me since I'm a drummer, like I said. But I seen a lot of dead men I know and met. That's scary."

"Your momma proud of you for doing what you're doing?"

Lou turned to Osborn with a curious expression. The boy smiled and thrust his chest out. "She's worried but very proud, I believe," he said with a gleam in his eye.

"She let you join up at your age? At your age?"

"I followed my Pa here. The Lord took him early in the war at Cheat Mountain," he said, as Osborn slid the dark board out of the tin plate box. "But I wanted to stay on, figuring I was doing my part 'cause he couldn't."

"Your ma want you home?"

"Yep, I got letters from my ma, but I wanted to see the country, the plains, the west, so I stayed."

"That's the reason you stayed, just to see more country, just to see more country?"

"Yessum. Ya see, back where I lived, it was all green. Most folks think that's pretty and all. It's nature. But when you grow up with it it's all that's there, always. Everywhere you go, green. Green, green, green. Green in the trees, green in the meadows, green in the garden," he said, his face brightening, tilting up. "And coming to the army, I saw gold—the golden fields of the prairie, the gold saber handles and aiguillettes, and epaulets. But now, Pa is gone, and I've seen so much death, mud, tents, and destruction. Gold turned to brown. Brown everywhere. I've missed home and my ma being gone for so long. I look up to the trees when we're marching or whenever. I look up to 'em, ya see, and ya know what? I'm seeing green again. And it's special green like pine leaf green or the green of crick moss, ya know. When I march now, I see that green in every leaf waving at me. And in that green is my momma. In the other leaf, there's my pa, in another one; momma's fresh-baked cherry pie, in another; pa's whittled…"

As soft as a grandfather would say goodnight to his sleeping granddaughter, Osborn whispered, "Please hold still."

"Oh my, oh, my," said Lou as she entered the wagon, her mouth wide open. "Your wagon is beautiful. I mean, it's beautiful from the outside, but inside… it's a delight."

Osborn perked up and told her the same story he told the Rebel, beginning with, "It's a Romani vardo caravan…" He showed her around and said, "It's quite comfortable. I sleep here, and Ray sleeps here below me on the floor. We bring out that mattress over there."

"I see. But that over there was supposed to be bunk beds?"

"Yes, but we needed it for storage."

"Yes, and this stove? You can cook in here?"

"Yes, yes. And it warms the room."

"Delightful. And these lamps and the colors and the shades. It's fit for a king."

"I'm happy you like it. Go ahead and shut the door," said Osborn as he fitted the framed red glass into the window. Lou shut it, and Osborn unloaded each tin plate from its box in the wagon's red light while sneaking a glance at her. "The red light will not affect the silver nitrate of the photograph, but I have become familiar with working in total darkness," he said as his fingers laid them gently into the developer bath, moving the fluid back and forth over it. He didn't want to touch her, but the desire to stand closer formed within him like the boy's image developing in the bath. "You can see the image of the boy coming through? Now, I take it and rinse it with water in this bath."

"Your questions to the boy, why do you ask them?"

"That's how I get what I want. Just what I want. I wait for that perfect instant—the point where the boy wouldn't be the drummer anymore. You see how he wanted to hold a rifle? He's trying to be someone he isn't, someone he isn't, no. He'd be that boy who he used to be—his truest self. The one who ate supper, ate supper with his parents, played with his friends, listened to his grandfather's stories, his authentic self. The boy that didn't have anything to prove. Nothing to prove."

She carefully studied Osborn before she said, "Yes, I see."

"And now it's safe to let light in if you want. Next, I'll move them to this bath and put in the fixer chemical, which prevents the image from changing. I rinse it again in the water bath with fresh water. Then I move it over the lamp to heat it and dry it." Sunlight came through the red glass window and reflected off the various baths, creating wavy shadows on the walls. "And lastly, I pour varnish on it and heat it again to seal it on there."

They came out of the wagon to the boy waiting outside. Osborn handed the two tintypes to him. "Wood frame, you said, right? Wood for both?"

"I did, and yes," said the boy as he examined the photograph, producing a smile broader than his face. "My, oh my! Thank you kindly, sir. It's just perfect."

"You're welcome," said Osborn as the boy walked off.

Lou turned to Osborn, arms behind her back, a smile on her thin lips. "That was beautiful. Your fingers were so precise they reminded me of little ballerinas on a stage of water, knowing each subtle dance step."

Osborn cocked his head to the side and smiled. "I like that, very poetic. Do you read John Keats?"

"Oh, yes! And Lord Byron," she replied.

Ray walked up to them. "Can I make you both some tea inside the tent? My uncle forgets his manners sometimes."

Osborn raised his eyebrows. "I'm so sorry. I do forget my manners sometimes."

"I would love that," she said.

Walking into the tent, her arms raised to the open ceiling. "A beautiful dogwood. I love their white blossoms. We had dogwood like this in my front yard where I grew up."

"Where was that?" asked Osborn as they sat on the footstools.

"Johnstown, Pennsylvania."

"Yes, yes. Our home is in Pittsburgh. I have worked in Johnstown. Yep, worked there with an undertaker. Mr. Parker? Do you know the Parkers?"

She nodded. "I do."

Ray came out with the tea and placed it on the table before them. "My name is Ray, Ma'am," he said, leaning to her, one arm behind his back. "My uncle fails to introduce me."

She smiled. "Nice to meet you, Ray. It looks like you take good care of your uncle."

"Nope, he takes care of me, Ma'am."

"Ray, Lou is from Johnstown."

"Oh, not too far away from us. We're up there quite a lot. Or used to be, before the war."

"Yes, he told me," said Lou.

"Now, I'll be off. You two rapscallions have a delightful time," said Ray, turning to leave.

"Why would you call us rapscallions?" asked Osborn, crossing his arms.

Ray looked surprised. "I've called you that before. I told you it's a term of endearment."

"But you called my guest that."

Ray turned to her and said, "I'm sorry. Did you know I was—" "I knew. It's fine."

"See? Now, you both have a delightful time," said Ray, shaking his head as he walked out.

"He's a nice boy, Osborn, your nephew."

"Yes. My brother and his wife passed on years back. I've been taking care of Ray since he was eight. I am like a father to him, I am told." Osborn twisted his beard.

"I see that. And he is a pleasant young man. Not too many pleasant young men these days."

"He was not pleasant at eight. Not pleasant. He was not nice to me at all."

"Apparently, he grew into a pleasant young man."

"At around thirteen, if I recall. Yes, thirteen, I have a good memory.

He became interested in my photography, and I showed him."

"Before Ray, where did you live?" asked Lou.

"Philadelphia is where I grew up. My brother moved away after university. I stayed. I never went to university."

"Did you want to?"

"Our parents didn't think…Well, my mother didn't think I was ready to leave our house. But my father insisted, and eventually, I moved out and got my own flat. I lived by myself above a tea shop in Philadelphia. I did everything for myself: shopping, cleaning, laundry, and such."

"I've never lived apart from my father."

"Where is your mother?"

"She passed away when I was twelve," replied Lou.

"My mother had done it all for me before I moved out. Just moving out on my own almost killed me. I was frozen with my anxieties most days. Then I got the letter, got a letter from my brother that forced me to change again. It was just another change after getting used to the first change. Move to a new city and meet a nephew I never knew I had, never knew. I had already made a life change and didn't want to go."

Osborn shifted in his seat. "Speaking of parents, I do hope your father liked me. I was awkward that day, and I, well, you should know that I am not very good with people. I have no friends. No friends."

She laughed through her nose. "Aren't you forthcoming?"

"Yes, they call me strange or worse."

"That's funny because I've been called the same. I used to get picked on because of my strange eyes and the way I dressed."

"I did too," said Osborn. "I mean, well, not the way I dressed. But I was picked on too, for all sorts of reasons or no reason at all."

"Yeah, it wasn't easy. I also had no friends, and when I tried to make friends, they just made fun of me."

"Me, me as well, yes."

"We seem to be very similar people in ways."

"Yes, we both wear men's clothes."

Lou laughed. "Yes, we do," she said, putting down her cup again and studying him. "You twist your beard a lot. I move my fingers, or as you say, play the piano." She giggled again.

"Or act like a sea anemone," said Osborn with a grin.

"That time you panicked, you went like this," she said, demonstrating his hand flapping up and down with her eyes closed.

He laughed. "I did?"

"Yes, but I have those times too, just like you. I like to rock back and forth. It calms me. Do loud noises bother you? Because they bother me considerably."

"Why, yes, they do. They do indeed, but I have gotten a bit better with them over time, over time, yes. Waiting for a battle to end, you must. If I know the loud noise is coming, I am prepared or, I should say, more prepared."

"What about smells? Are you bothered by them? Certain smells bother me considerably, considerably, yes."

"Yes!" she said, laughing. "We both are in the wrong businesses, it would seem, with all the sudden, loud sounds of battle and the bad smells afterward."

"Ray tells me I am like a balloonist with the fear of heights. Do you see the metaphor?"

"I do. To be in a balloon, you must enjoy flying high," she said. "Yes, yes. But I must be here. I do it all for my photography."

"Me too, for my embalming."

Osborn reached into his shirt pocket. "Oh, wait, I have something for you," he said, pulling out his nose plugs. "These are my inventions. They are nose plugs with tobacco inside and wrapped in linen. Ray and I use them all the time on the battlefield or during a postmortem." He displayed them to her in his open palm. "Tobacco is something that doesn't give me a headache, except for the smoke from it. Ray adds perfume to his. I do not. Once, I put his in my nose by accident—it gave me a headache for two days."

She giggled. "Oh, perfumes are the worst. Strangely, I got used to the smell of death. I do not like it, and in the past, I could not be around it, but I can tolerate it now."

"Not me. That is why I use those."

Her hand darted in, swiftly taking the nose plugs from his palm and barely touching him. He recoiled from the slight glance. "Ah!" he said as he yanked back his hand.

"Oh, sorry," she said before smelling the nose plugs and sticking them up her nose. With a giggle, she asked, "How do I look?"

With worried eyes, he said, "Well, those…were… mine…" She quickly removed them. "I have some new ones for you over there," he added as he pointed to the far side of the room.

"You mentioned you were not very good with people. I am very much that way, too, but strangely, not with you. Does it seem that way to you as well? Are you comfortable with me?"

"Yes, yes. I do not believe I have ever had a conversation like this with anyone except Ray."

Her moving fingers stopped as they brought the cup to her mouth. She took a sip, reminding him to do the same. "My father says what we have is a condition—"

"What's the condition? What's the condition?"

"Some doctor in Harrisburg says it's an illness of my mind, a problem with the passions or drives in the mind, I was told."

Osborn looked up from his tea. "Drives?"

"Well, yes, that's what they tell me. I don't know. I don't feel I have a condition. I like being different. But it'd be nice if other folks liked me for being different."

"Yes, yes, I agree, but I wouldn't say you're different. If others choose to label me, I prefer the word peculiar. It is how I describe myself. I'd say you were peculiar. Peculiar like me."

CHAPTER 9

"There's word we might be moving out soon," said Ray as they ate supper in front of their campfire. Osborn put down his plate. A hound dog popped up from under the wagon and licked the gravy.

"I heard," said Osborn as he petted its fearless head.

Ray eyed him curiously. "What's wrong?"

Osborn's eyes skimmed across Ray's face as he shrugged his shoulders. "I like, I like this place."

Ray tilted his head to the side. "Is it that gal? Is she moving out with this division?"

"I am not certain. I have not asked."

"I'll bet they'll move out with this division. The army tells them where to go. You sweet on that gal?"

"No, I am not sweet on her. Not sweet on her at all, Ray. You know that."

"I do not know that, Uncle."

"Well, I am not. I might like her to be my friend."

"Maybe we could follow along with them."

"You wouldn't, you wouldn't mind?"

"We would get more customers going with a different outfit, but there's still a few portraits to be had. You should try to be friends with her."

"I have never been successful at making friends."

"That was when you were young, Uncle. Youngins can be cruel. I was cruel to you when I was young."

"Your parents had just passed."

"I was cruel for long after they passed, and you know it."

"You are not that way any longer, Ray, and you have apologized."

"Yes, but—"

"And I accepted your apology, Ray. I accepted it."

"I know, but what I'm trying to say is, you can make friends. When we met Mr. Brady last week, I'm sure he would want to be your friend. I could tell."

"I do not like him."

"Well… And I'm sure she would want to be your friend too. You should try, at least."

"She could be a good friend. I do not have any friends, Ray."

Under his breath, Ray said, "Not live ones; that's for sure."

Osborn and Ray sipped their morning coffee while sitting with other soldiers on a long stone wall. Ray fed an apple to Hoady while they all watched a sergeant try to break a young black stallion with little success. Other soldiers gathered behind them at the wall, shouting and laughing as they urged the cowboy sergeant on. The young stallion whipped its tail and shook its head angrily. Dirt kicked into the air. It bucked hard and high, flinging off the cowboy to the crowd's applause. The young cowboy rose, dusted himself off as he turned back to the horse with disdain.

"Good morning," came from a voice behind him. Osborn and Ray turned. Lou walked up to them with her father, Henry. Osborn immediately stopped fingering the cloth in his pocket like a boy caught stealing candy.

"Hello, Lou. Mr. Cattell," said Osborn.

"Good morning, gentlemen," she said with a bright smile. "My father would like to invite you both to breakfast this morning. Would you like to come?"

Ray frowned. "We already—"

"Cooked up some bacon," interrupted Osborn. "We'll bring it by. We'll bring it by."

Osborn's heart skipped a beat as he and Ray stepped closer to Lou's tent. A square table sat in front of it, set with plates and utensils. Lou came out, bringing a skillet of eggs and grits. She turned to them as they approached. "I thought you said you had bacon," said Lou, placing the food in the middle.

Ray glanced at his uncle with a knowing smirk. "Someone must have stolen it," he replied.

"Oh, well, no harm. Please, take a seat," she invited, gesturing to the empty chairs.

Henry came out of the tent, pulling up his suspenders. "Mr. Roche, good to see you," he said, nodding in Osborn's direction.

Lou passed the skillet around. "Have you heard? These boys are moving out in the morning, following Lee east close to Sharpsburg."

Ray nodded, reaching for the skillet. "We heard. We already started packing up," he confirmed, scooping a generous portion onto his plate.

Osborn turned to Lou, "What, what were you planning to do, to do?"

"We will be following them," interrupted Henry. "This division seems to have great need for our services."

"We were thinking of following it, too," said Ray.

"Delightful, how about we caravan together?" asked Henry.

Osborn's eyes darted to Lou's smile, surrounded by blushed cheeks. "That'd be fine," said Ray.

Henry turned to Osborn and said, "So, Mr. Roche, this photography science... it really has become an educational art."

Osborn's eyes darted about at the thought. "I believe so. It is a manner of...It is a manner of visual communication," said Osborn.

"Visual communication. Interesting. How so?" asked Henry. "Like my book, it presents the viewer with not only the history of what happened but ideas, yes, ideas. Someday, they will be putting photographs in newspapers with a story describing the scene or giving additional information about the scene, about the scene, yes."

"Photographs in newspapers, yes, wonderful idea," said Henry, sitting back in his chair. Lou and Ray's heads turned back and forth between the men. "You seem an intelligent man, Mr. Roche. And an artist as well, it seems. Those two don't always go hand in hand."

"A very talented artist," said Lou, her eyes lighting up at Osborn.

"Speaking of that, Mr. Roche, it seems I have a business proposition for you. Louise and I were invited to provide our services to a young lady who passed away due to unfortunate circumstances, and they are in need of a postmortem photographer. Would you be interested?"

"Most certainly so."

"Where is the home?" asked Ray.

"In Powhatan. Same direction as the army is heading. Two hours out."

"How much does it pay?" asked Ray.

"We'll take it," said Osborn. Ray turned to his uncle and chuckled. "They stated that it is a rather large home, and they will have beds and would like to invite us to meals, of course."

"Do they have a bath?" asked Osborn. "I love baths."

Henry laughed. "Not sure about that one. But I'm sure if they have one, it wouldn't be a concern."

"Does she need her features set?" asked Osborn.

Henry looked puzzled. "Uh, yes, but that is what we do."

"Of course. Of course. May we watch your techniques? Postmortem is my specialty."

"Tell him your motto, Uncle," said Ray.

Osborn put both hands in the air in front of him, spreading them wide as if unfolding a large invisible sign in the air. 'Gone from the world, but alive again in our hearts.'"

"Very good. It'd be our pleasure to show you our techniques. And I'd be interested in your opinion, Mr. Roche."

Osborn spotted a book on a trunk behind Henry. "Did you read that one? Persuasion was Jane Austen's last completed novel."

"Yes, it's mine," said Lou. "Austen is my favorite author."

"Do you read much, Mr. Roche?" asked Henry.

"Everything he can get his hands on," said Ray.

"I do enjoy reading," said Osborn. "And being read to."

"So, what have you gotten your hands on of late?" asked Henry.

"I just finished Moby Dick by Melville. I am in need of a new one."

"He is like a ravenous lion with books. You need to throw in whatever scraps you find when you run out of meat," added Ray.

Lou turned to Osborn with a beaming smile. "You are? I'm a ravenous lion. I am."

Osborn couldn't stop himself from staring. Her smile, the way she cocked her head, her giggle, and those beautiful eyes. He drifted off into them, attracted to them like a bee to flowers.

"He also just read Dickens. A new one called Great Expectations," said Ray.

Henry glanced back and forth from Osborn to Lou. Curiosity rose on his face before he reached over and took Jane Austen's Persuasion from the trunk behind him.

"I read it too," added Ray.

Lou said, "I didn't like Estella. She wanted to break Pip's heart."

Henry dropped the book flat onto the table from two feet in the air. Osborn and Lou jumped from their seats, panic on their faces. Ray's face jerked to Henry in confusion.

"Oh, please forgive me," said Henry.

Lou yelled, "Father! What—"

"An accident, my dear. Just an accident," said Henry.

Osborn, flapping his hands, said, "I believe I must go, I must go."

"I'm sorry, Mr. Roche," said Henry.

"We'd better go," said Ray. "You all right, Uncle? Let's get on home."

"Home? No. I want to go to the wagon, to the wagon."

"That's what I meant."

As Ray and Osborn walked off, Lou asked her father, "Father, did you do that on purpose?"

"Of course not, my dear."

Osborn stopped and turned around. "Uh, yes, I believe you may be wrong about Estella, yes." Lou and Henry turned to him. "It wasn't her fault. It was her adopted mother, adopted mother, Miss Havisham."

"Oh?" asked Henry.

"Yes, Miss Havisham. She used Estella to break Pip's heart. It was her mother. Her mother broke Pip's heart, yes."

CHAPTER 10

The camp buzzed with frenzied activity, soldiers scurrying about like ants from a kicked anthill as they packed up their belongings and prepared to march out. Amidst the controlled chaos, Osborn and Ray sat on their wagon bench, watching the organized commotion unfold. The steady stream of soldiers marched past, their footsteps creating a rhythmic beat against the dirt. A familiar wagon pulled up behind theirs, the horses' hooves clopping to a halt. Osborn's heart leaped as Lou and Henry jumped down from the wagon. Ben remained on the driver's bench, his hands on the reins.

"Sirs! How are you this fine morning?" asked Henry. Lou's eyes met Osborn's, and a smile bloomed.

"We are well. Very well, sir," said Osborn.

"Mr. Roche, why don't you ride with my brother, Ben, and get acquainted?"

Osborn stepped down and turned to Henry. "No, I would not like that, no."

"No?" asked Henry.

"No, I would not like that. I will ride in the wagon."

Lou beamed excitedly. "I will ride with you. Is that all right, Father? It is so beautiful inside their wagon."

"Uh, I suppose," replied Henry. Osborn swallowed hard as his hand showed her the way to the back of their wagon.

The wagons took off down the road, fitting in between two platoons of marching soldiers. Osborn had the back door open, with the hinged staircase up in the doorway. Ben drove the other wagon behind them, staring in. Lou sat a mere two feet from him on the bed. Goosebumps rose on his neck from sitting close to her. He shivered.

"Are you all right?" she asked.

"Certainly," said Osborn as he reached into his pocket for the cloth. Finding it, he slowly exhaled. The wagon bumped and jostled them on the bed. His head jerked to his arm when hers bumped it.

"What?" she asked.

"You bumped my arm."

"Oh, sorry," she said, turning to the window.

"I don't like to be touched."

"I remember." Each of her fingers tapped its thumb like a mama bird's beak feeding its four chicks.

"I, I, I well—"

"Hey, when you set the features for one of your postmortem clients, do you do makeup as well?"

"Yes, I do. I'm very good."

"I'm sure you are. Do you do makeup for both men and women?"

"It makes no difference to me. I am very adept at the dead and reviving their color, and bringing back sunken features. I also suture up smiles, puff the cheeks with cotton, and I'm excellent at drawing beautiful eyes on eyelids, or I can do it after, on the portrait itself."

"Our professions seem to cross paths quite a bit, just like the collodion we use," she said.

"Yes, they do."

Hearing voices from the front of the wagon, Osborn raised a brow and turned to Lou, placing his index finger over his lips. It was Henry's voice. "Yesterday, when I accidentally dropped the book. I noticed that your uncle reacted in the same way my daughter does to loud noises. Is that a typical reaction?"

"Wouldn't it be for anyone? It woke me up," replied Ray.

"Please, indulge me, but I must ask you…Well, there is something I have previously investigated." Osborn stood and walked closer to the wagon's wall, tilting his head toward it.

"Investigated?" said Ray.

"May we speak frankly, young man? I believe your uncle might have the same medical condition my daughter has."

"Medical condition? And what condition is that?"

"How is he with people? Blurt out strange things that have nothing to do with the conversation?" Osborn shook his head.

"I wouldn't say so," said Ray. "What's this about?"

"When Louise was young, I saw something wasn't developing correctly with her. She wasn't like the other children. Several doctors diagnosed her as an idiot, but that wasn't possible. Her intelligence was just too great to be simply idiotic. I sent her to a specialist, a man named Doctor Samuel Howe, who diagnosed her with a defect of the mind. He called it 'idiot savant syndrome.'"

Lou smirked with a confirming nod to Osborn.

Ray scoffed. "My uncle doesn't have a defect of the mind, I'm telling ya."

"I'll try to be as delicate as I can, but let me explain. Passions or drives in the mind help satisfy human needs and are consequently necessary attributes to a human being. We all have them. Each drive develops on its own as we grow into adulthood due to stimuli. These drives help satisfy human needs like eating and drinking, and the need for companionship, the need to have children. A lack of morals can lead to drive disharmony, or one drive may develop at the expense of others and lead to insanity."

Ray disagreed, "Drive disharmony? Lack of morals? Uncle has read the Bible five times. There's not an evil thought in his head."

Osborn nodded.

Henry added, "Please forgive me for upsetting you, son. But even you can see Louise and Mr. Roche are similar?"

Osborn nodded again to Lou. She grinned.

Henry continued, "I believe your uncle has idiot savant syndrome, the same condition Louise has."

"Hogwash," said Ray.

"But I'm sure you've lived with his strange behaviors."

"They aren't so strange. He's getting better over the years with people. Not as awkward anymore. Besides, he's a well-admired photographer."

Lou rose from the bed and faced Osborn against the wagon's wall.

"Very true, young man, I didn't mean anything—"

Ray interrupted, "He's the farthest thing from an idiot savant, as you call it, as anyone could be. He's the smartest man I've ever met. He's far smarter than any professor I've ever had, and he's had an answer for every question I've ever asked him. Toss a mathematical question his way, and it only takes him a few minutes to figure it out. Wanna talk about history? He knows everything, including the day it happened, the number of troops, who were there, and what was happening in other parts of the world at that time. There is no one smarter. If he's got this condition you speak about, the world would be a better place if more people had it."

"My boy, you are correct. Forgive an old man his indulgences. Your uncle is indeed a very well-known and admired photographer. He needs no help in that department. And my Louise is the same except it is with embalming. She is the most talented embalmer I know, and she is a woman. I would say she has more talent than even myself."

Lou slapped her hands over her mouth as she danced on her tiptoes.

"I was only informing you of what I discovered. But there was one last fascinating thing I saw last night that I must beg you to indulge me. Something highly unusual. Did you notice they both didn't glance about when they looked at each other?"

"What do you mean?"

"I watched them. Like I said, Louise doesn't like to look people in the eyes. Not even me, and I see neither does your uncle."

"Yeah, that's true."

"Well, I saw that, apparently, they can with each other."

Both listening with eyes to the floor, Osborn and Lou's gaze rose to meet each other's.

"Maybe that means this condition you speak about is going away."

"I don't believe so. It worries me. Louise has never held any interest in men before."

A sudden blush rose on Lou's cheeks.

"Why would that worry you if they like each other?" asked Ray with irritation in his voice. "They both need friends."

"Because, my young man, two people with mental deficiencies should not procreate. That would lead to a malformed child, and that is absolutely out of the question."

Lou's expression fell, and she walked back to the bed, chin to her chest.

"I've had just about enough of this conversation, Mr. Cattell."

Osborn sat on the bed with her, leaning close to her ear. "Don't you listen to that, Lou. You know that's not true, not true," he whispered.

"He thinks he knows everything."

"He did say you were more talented than him. He did say that, yes."

"But what he said about you? You are wonderful the way you are, a charming man who is a renowned photographer."

"Yes, yes. Oh, and thank you. Oh, and you are charming as well. Can charming be used for women?" she asked.

"Hmm, delightful or enchanting, maybe?" Osborn suggested.

Lou added. "Captivating."

Osbirn grinned and said, "Beguiling."

They both snickered. Lou lifted her legs up from the edge of the bed and clicked her heels together. "But we both know we are different from others."

Osborn nodded. "Different? Yes."

Lou jumped back with unexpected excitement, leaning her back against the wall of the bed. "You know what I think? I think most people don't notice the incredible amount of information that enters their minds. Their minds can strain out the unnecessary, unimportant, and unpleasant things, like using cheesecloth to strain seeds from juice. They see just what they need to see and hear just what they need to hear. Our minds don't have that strainer most people have. Everything comes into our heads: all we see and all there is to see. All we hear and all there is to hear, you know? You and I are sensitive, and with that sensitivity sometimes comes pain and anxiety. There are times when we need to shut it all down," she said, her smile rising. "But on the other hand, it could be that sensitivity lets us be artists in our way. You create beautiful photographs, and I bring the dead to life as an embalmer."

Osborn flashed a smile. "Yes, I suppose you are correct."

"But one thing he said was right. Our eyes connect. They stop on each other like magnets. That's astonishing! You can look into my eyes, and I can look into yours," she said, beaming.

"Yes, just a bit after meeting, I felt comfortable with you. So comfortable, I spoke too much. Ray says I do that. Or maybe it was your beautiful eyes that fascinated me so that I wasn't uncomfortable. I noticed that with me but never knew you even had that issue."

"I never knew you did either. I surprised myself by not having to look away. I agree; it felt comfortable."

"Yes, comfortable. Comfortable like coming home."

CHAPTER 11

"A daguerreotype man?" asked Mrs. Harriet Turner as she raised the argand oil lamp and squinted at their faces in the dark parlor of her two-story home. Already a widow at forty-five, Mrs. Turner now suffered the loss of her only child, Tabitha. Next to her stood Frank Griswold, her fifty-eight-year-old brother.

"I thought I'd give you the gift of having Tabitha's visage on your mantle or in your bedroom so you can revisit your beautiful memories of her," said Frank, the lamplight gleaming off the sweat on his face.

"Frank, that is so kind of you," said Mrs. Turner.

"This is Mr. Roche, the daguerreotype man, and this is Henry Cattell, the embalmer I spoke about," said Frank.

"Oh, Mr. Cattell, nice to meet you," said Mrs. Turner. Her black mourning dress and bonnet gave the impression of a floating disembodied face in the dark room.

"Nice to meet you, Ma'am," said Henry.

Harriet brought up her lamp around them, searching. "I was told you would bring your daughter?"

"Yes, Ma'am, I'm Lou, Louise, Ma'am."

Mrs. Turner showed surprise. "Oh, dear. In this dim light, I thought you were a boy. Gracious me."

Lou looked down at her shirt and pants. "Yes, Ma'am. Many do."

"Well, it's nice to meet you, Louise, Mr. Roche, and Mr. Cattell," said Mrs. Turner. "Frank, maybe we could light up some more candles and lamps. I wasn't expecting any guests this eve."

"Certainly, Harriet, certainly, in just a short spell. Mr. Roche here has a published photo book, he does. Of the war."

"But do you do other types of daguerreotypes, Mr. Roche?" she asked.

"Yes, Ma'am. I do. I specialize in postmortem portraits. I always say, 'Gone from the world, but alive again in our hearts.'"

"Oh, that just pleases me to no—"

"Is there a bath here?" interrupted Osborn.

"Well, yes—"

"I do so enjoy baths."

"Uh, certainly. Frank will—"

"Of course, Harriet."

Mrs. Turner turned back to Lou. "And you, Miss Louise, it's a blessing you have come. My dear Tabitha is still in the dress she passed in, and I just couldn't bear to remove it. I could not even bear walking into her bedroom. No, I could not bear it."

Lou took Mrs. Turner's hands in her own. "I can do that for you this evening, Ma'am. Make Miss Tabitha comfortable for her eternal rest."

"When did your unfortunate circumstance occur?" asked Henry.

"Four days ago. Saddest day of my life."

"I'm certain it was. Well, I can make Miss Tabitha look like she did five days ago," replied Henry.

"Oh, that is just wonderful."

"Do you have her burial dress?" asked Lou.

"It is up in her room with her. Oh, my manners. Would you like to sit? Would you like some tea? I can whip some up right quick."

"Please, no, Mrs. Turner. My father and Mr. Roche will be needing to rest and get started on prettying Miss Tabitha up in the morning. As for me, I would like to get started this evening and have her pretty as a picture for the men tomorrow morning. We have been advised of your ground setting early tomorrow. Is that correct?"

"Yes, it is," Mrs. Turner said, her head dropping. Frank placed his hand on her back.

"Harriet, get some rest. I'll show them to their quarters."

"Of course. Goodnight to you all. And Frank? Thank you so much. It's wonderful of you, as usual."

"No, Harriet. The pleasure is all mine. And I'll be able to view the portrait as well, so the gift is ours to each other."

Griswold's face flickered in the warm glow of the oil lamp, shadows dancing across his weathered features as he addressed the trio standing before him in the hallway. "All right now, I'll leave you to it," he said, his voice echoing through the darkness that enveloped them like the depths of a cave. The presence of the deceased in the adjacent bedroom hung heavy in the air. "You can light some candles in the hallway if you'd like," Griswold continued, gesturing towards the unlit wicks lining the walls. "Just put 'em out before you retire. I hope you find everything comfortable." He pointed towards the rooms. "There are enough blankets in your room to make a comfortable spot, and Mr. Roche, your room is right over there. It has a soft bed with all the fixings." Griswold's gaze settled on Osborn. "You sure you don't want your boy out there to stay in with ya? There's plenty of room."

"He'll be fine. He'll be fine. The bed in the wagon is quite comfortable. Quite comfortable."

Griswold nodded before turning to Henry. "And yours, Mr. Cattell, is down the other end on the right. I'm in that room right over yonder. I'll say goodnight to ya." Griswold's footsteps receded down the hallway as he retired to his own quarters.

Henry turned to Lou. "Good night to you, dear," he whispered, placing a gentle kiss on her cheek. He then nodded to Osborn. "And to you, Mr. Roche."

"And to you," replied Osborn.

As Henry and Osborn parted ways, their footsteps carrying them in opposite directions, the hallway seemed to stretch into an infinite abyss. Henry reached his room first, the click of his door closing behind him. As Osborn's hand hovered over his doorknob, a whisper cut through the darkness. "Psst!

Psst!" Lou's voice, as delicate as a moth's wing, beckoned to him. She raised a finger to her lips and motioned for him to come closer.

"Come in here with me. You can help," she urged. With a furtive glance down each end of the hallway, Osborn tip-toed towards Miss Tabitha Turner's room, his heart pounding. As he crossed the threshold, he paused to recheck the hallway before gently closing the door behind him.

In the center of the room, Osborn and Lou stood frozen, their faces contorting. Flowers and potpourri battled against the unmistakable stench of death and the musty odor of wet dogs, creating a wave of overwhelming scents that assaulted their senses. In a synchronized movement, their hands delved into their pockets, emerging with nose plugs that they hastily shoved up their nostrils. A shared sigh of relief escaped their lips as the plugs settled into place.

"It's the flowers and perfumes," said Lou.

"It's everything."

Miss Tabitha lay on her bed in the corner. Osborn walked around the room, lighting the candles as Lou went to her body. "She's soaking wet," she said as she ran her fingers across Miss Tabitha's wet, yellow dress clinging to her body.

"How did she pass?" asked Osborn. "My father didn't tell me."

Osborn walked over and rubbed her dress between his thumb and forefinger. "It hasn't rained. Maybe she drowned?"

"Could be," she said as Osborn walked over to the fireplace. "Except for the sunken features, and a little skin blistering, she's in decent shape. But who knows what's under these wet clothes?" The darkness and the late hour made them speak in low, late-night voices, a hair above a whisper. "I'll need your help in removing them."

"But she's a woman," said Osborn as he attempted to light a log in the fireplace.

"She's dead."

"She could be watching us from above right now, right now. I don't believe she would like it."

"Wouldn't bother me any, but that's just me. I've always been that way. My mother would catch me naked all the time. Running through the house and even outside. I preferred the air on my skin to the scratchy clothes when I was little. I got in a lot of trouble."

Osborn blew into the kindling, catching a log on fire. He turned to her and said, "I prefer softer clothes too."

Lou untied the wet bows on Miss Tabitha's dress. "You've never seen a woman's body before?"

Osborn turned away, embarrassed. "I've never been married." Lou grinned. "Do you ever desire to be married, Osborn?"

"I do not like to touch or be touched. I would not provide what a wife would desire most—children. I wouldn't make a good husband."

"Hmm, yeah, that might be a problem. Well, anyway, we'll have to move her body about to get her out of these things. Then we get her into that white dress next to you. Avert your eyes if you need." The dress provided by her mother lay at the foot of the bed. "Help me flip her over?" Rolling her to her side, Osborn held her as Lou unbuttoned the back of her dress. "She has minimal bloat, considering it's been four days. This will be a simple job for my father."

Lou finished unbuttoning. Spotting a pocket in the wet dress, Osborn instinctively reached for it but stopped himself. "Oh, please, do you mind?" he asked.

"What?"

"Can you let me...?"

"Let you what?"

"I just want to see if she has anything in her pockets. I'll put it back. It's something I..."

"Oh, all right. Yes, of course. Would you like me to help?"

"No, no, thank you. I prefer to do it myself. I always return it to where I find it."

"Always?"

"Yes, always."

Standing at her feet, he bent over and delicately pulled up the laced trim of her sock with thumb and forefinger, leaning further over to peek in from an inverted position. "I mean, you do this a lot?" asked Lou. Nothing in her left sock; he repeated it with her right.

"Yes, but only since the war started. The war provides you with a considerable amount of recent passings." His fingers gracefully searched through the folds of her yellow silk dress, finding one pocket on the right, sticking his hand in with a smile that immediately faded. Osborn didn't know where to go in her dress without touching something he shouldn't. He moved from her feet to her side, next to Lou.

He tenderly took up Miss Tabitha's pagoda sleeve-covered arm in both hands, sliding down from the armpit to the wrist. Finding nothing, he moved to the next arm—nothing.

He swiftly moved to her feet again. "Would you be so kind? Well, I mean to say, I have never done this to, uh, with a woman. Do women keep stuff in other places or hidden pockets?"

"I don't know. I don't wear dresses."

"Could you see if there is anything in her petticoats or…?"

She took a deep breath. "Surely." Osborn turned his back, giving Lou a one-sided smile. "Are you bashful, Osborn?" she teased as she continued to search.

"I, well, yes, a bit. I never, I mean, I've only searched men's pockets. Check that upper area."

"The corset? Nothing in her dress. Here's the locket from her neck." Osborn reached back for it without turning his head, and she put it into his open palm. He opened it to the initials TT.

Lou propped Miss Tabitha up and pulled down the top of her dress to her waist, revealing her corset. "That's it, nothing else."

"Quite unsuccessful. I typically find quite a bit on a soldier." Osborn took his lamp and walked about the room, stopping at a dresser. An unaddressed envelope sat upon it. He picked it up and turned it over; it had never been sealed. Osborn's eyes lit up, and a smile came to his face. "This is what I always hope for." He pulled out the letter, unfolded it gently, and turned to Lou gleefully.

She giggled. "Read that later. We need to finish this."

"Yes, yes," he said absently. He spread out and flattened the letter on top of the dresser.

Tabby,

We have been fighting one battle after another but doing quite well. The boys of the fighting 33rd are a proud sort, and we take care of each other. We were just in a skirmish at Cedar Mountain over in Culpeper County. Have you been there? But we gave those Yanks a wallop. It's been four days now of quiet and no marching. My boots are almost bare! I've been reading. . .

"Osborn, I need your help," she insisted. He set the letter back on the dresser. Lou stripped down the wet clothes, the limbs flopping about. "Can you find me a towel?"

"Yes, yes." Osborn took his lamp and headed out the bedroom door. A minute later, he returned with a bedsheet and set it on the foot of the bed. "It's all I could find." Lou removed the remainder of Miss Tabitha's clothing. His attention focused on the letter on the dresser, begging to be read. With an accidental glimpse of Miss Tabitha's nakedness, he gasped, and his eyes slammed shut.

"It doesn't count, Osborn. It's a corpse now, not a woman." Lou shook her head at his bashfulness and covered the body with the sheet.

"Still has the shape of a woman, the shape, yes."

With the sheet on top, Lou massaged the body as she dried it. Avoiding a second sighting, Osborn turned to pink and white wallpaper covering the walls, with shelves that held dolls, rocking horses, and porcelain figurines sitting in neat rows.

Lou rolled Miss Tabitha to her side, rubbing down the sides of her buttocks, flipping her back, and rubbing her limbs, thighs, and breasts vigorously.

"We just need to get her dressed. The portrait won't see what's underneath," his whisper insisted.

"Massaging her will make her body easier to work with and slow the bloat." She lifted the sheet again and pointed to Miss Tabitha's backside. "See how the blood accumulated on her backside? It pools where it drains to." Covering her again, Lou continued to massage. "Massage recirculates that and brings up the sunken features like the cheeks and eyes. Can you hand me those clothes?" She pointed to the chair behind him. "I'll need your help putting these on." She threw off the sheet, exposing her pale blue body. Osborn's eyes went wide, and he turned away. Lou took the bloomers, sticking each leg into them. "Here, hold her feet up."

"I don't like touching people."

"She's dead, Osborn. You've touched the dead before. I know you do postmortem photographs."

"But she's a woman," he pleaded.

"She's not. She's a corpse. Now, hold her feet up."

Osborn turned around and took the feet, one in each hand, but kept his gaze anywhere but down. Lou went to her side, hiked up the bloomers to the waist, and tied them. She grinned at his innocence. "I will need your help here. I'll sit her up, and you put the dress over her head."

"Well, what if I sit her up and you do that?"

"It really doesn't matter," she said. Osborn walked to her head, reaching under her arms to sit her up. His fingers poked the sides of her breasts, and he immediately let go. Her body flopped back to the bed. "What?"

"You sit her up. I'll put her dress on."

Lou grinned and shook her head. She lifted Miss Tabitha's arms to the sky as Osborn slipped the dress over her head. He pulled each arm through the sleeves, avoiding the sight of the breasts at all costs. Instead, he gawked at the letter on the dresser as a dog does to the supper table.

"I'll finish dressing her from here."

Osborn spun on his heels to the letter.

I've been reading your letters. From what you describe of your dress, you'll be something to see in it. I'm certain from your list we will have the whole town at our wedding because my mother is also making a list! It'll be quite a boodle...

"There now. Beautiful," Lou said, smoothing the wrinkles from Miss Tabitha's burial dress and placing her hands neatly on her chest. The log in the fireplace popped and crackled as he read the letter. She walked over to the rug in front of the fire and sat. "Why did you want to do that so badly?" Osborn turned to her, setting the letter down on the dresser. "So, why do you do that? Can you tell me?"

Osborn walked over and sat with her on the rug. As he unfolded the story, his smile grew while her eyes filled with tears.

Osborn stopped. "I didn't mean to upset you. I'm sorry. The same thing happened to Ray when I told him. I saw his arm wipe away the tears he was trying to hide. I don't understand. I won't tell this story again. I think it's a happy story. It makes me happy, makes me happy."

Her hand wiped the tears from under her spectacles. "I'm sure it does," she said with a sniffle.

"Ray says, you'd get a tear from a glass eye with that story. At first, I thought that's not possible, but as the tear duct is separate from the eye, I suppose it could be."

"I reckon he was making a joke."

"Yes, he told me later. Ray explains his jokes and euphemisms to me after he tells them. I see others laugh, but I don't see the humor most of the time."

"Me too. That happens to me a lot. I have learned to laugh when others laugh. I've learned to watch for smiles or frowns or any clue on people's faces to know how to react to things."

"I've learned that as well, but it was mostly Ray. He helped me and still helps me be less odd with people, say hello and thank you, and ask them questions like, 'Would you like to come in?' or 'Would you like some tea?' or 'How have you been?' It doesn't come to me to do these small kindnesses. Others connect to you better when you do these things. In my portrait work, I started asking the questions to be polite and to be more like them and less peculiar but also, I was hoping they might ask me questions in response, and maybe I could make new friends. Unfortunately, it turned out that they never did."

"Making friends has always been hard. When I was young, my sister had to explain to me that who I thought were my friends were actually laughing at me. I didn't understand."

"That happened to me too, me too. Yes, asking my questions didn't find me friends, but the consequences of asking them were that I saw the portraits revealed more, what I call soul. That something about you that can't be seen; it has to be felt. I saw that in you, and you saw that in me without questions, without the questions, yes. We don't have those masks."

"It's like we wear who we are on the outside. That's why we are so sensitive."

"As you said before, we feel everything with no cheesecloth strainer, no strainer. And in my portraits, I remove their masks, and they become a little more like you and me; who they are shows on the outside in the portrait."

Lou sat in front of him, her eyes smiling as much as her lips. The firelight played on them as her flickering irises wandered across his face.

"I have no friends either, Osborn. I'll be your friend. We can be best friends. We can laugh with each other, not at each other." She stood, took the blankets in the corner, and made a bed by the fire.

"I have been hoping you'd say that," he said, rising and moving to the door. "Well, I should be getting on to bed. I'll be up early to prepare for the portrait."

"Ah, you're leaving?" She pouted with an exaggerated frown.

He stopped and turned to her. "It's late."

"Hey, Osborn. Since we're best friends, ever had a sleepover?"

"No. What is it?"

"We just sleep in the same room, talk, play cards, tell jokes."

"I'm not good with jokes. Oh, and I don't have a deck of cards, but I don't know any card games anyway. I do play chess. I'm quite good."

"Well, we can talk then."

"Talk more? I also play checkers even though it's a silly game. Silly game."

"Yes, talk. Tell each other our deepest secrets," she said with a gleam in her eye as if revealing an evil plan.

"How do we sleep over?"

"Well, next to each other."

"I don't like to be touched."

"I know that." She rolled her eyes. "You could even sleep over on that side if you want."

"No touching?

"No. Stop it. We're friends."

He smiled. "No, we're best friends."

CHAPTER 12

The candles had all gone out, and the fire smoldered as morning light came through the window. Osborn awoke under a blanket two feet from Lou.

Osborn sat up, the fog of sleep still clinging to his mind as he rubbed his face. "Is there a chamber pot in here?" he asked. "I need to perform my necessaries, my necessaries."

Lou stifled a yawn as she stretched. "There's indoor plumbing. It's down the hall. You go first."

A knock on the door shattered the morning. "Good morning. May I come in?" Henry's voice, muffled by the wooden door, sent a jolt of panic through Lou's veins. Her eyes widened in shock, darting towards the door as if it might burst open at any moment, revealing their compromising situation.

Osborn clutched at his groin, his fingers digging into the fabric of his trousers as if he could somehow hold back the impending flood. He danced about, his movements a frantic ballet of desperation as he looked to Lou for guidance.

Lou's mind raced, her thoughts scrambling for a plausible excuse. "I'm dressing, Father," she called out, her voice wavering.

"All right, let me know when you are finished."

Osborn's eyes darted around the room, desperately seeking an escape. Lou pointed to a spot behind the door. Osborn rushed over and pressed his back against the wall, his hands still firmly gripping his groin, a futile attempt to stave off the inevitable.

"Uh, yep, come in?" she said as a question. The door swung open, its wooden frame pinning Osborn behind it, concealing him from Henry's view as he strode into the room.

Henry's gaze fell upon Miss Tabitha. "Oh, you did a fine job dressing her. She looks nice."

Ben came in next, walking backward as he pulled in the embalming equipment cart. His head jerked towards Osborn, his eyes widening as he spotted the man hiding behind the door. With a subtle shake of his head and a finger pressed to his lips, Ben silently implored Osborn to remain still.

Henry, oblivious to the silent exchange, turned around, his brow furrowed in confusion. "Oh, Mr. Roche. Where did...? Were you... in here?"

"No. He followed me in," said Ben with a wink to Osborn. Henry's eyes narrowed.

"But I didn't see... well, all right."

Lou chimed in with a cheerful greeting. "Good morning, Mr. Roche."

"Good morning, yes, morning. I have to go to the privy," said Osborn, running out and down the hallway. By the time he returned, Henry and Lou had the tubes inserted into the artery and vein.

"Just in time to make a dead person look alive," said Ben with another wink.

"Yes, yes. I would like that," Osborn said, his words a veil of feigned interest as he struggled to regain his composure. His eyes, drawn like a magnet to the mysterious letter on the dresser, kept darting back to its tantalizing presence.

Ben leaned casually against the far wall, his gaze fixed on Osborn.

Ray entered the room as Henry and Lou finished the process. Ben asked Ray, "Hey, what's your name again?"

"Ray."

"Can you help me take the body down?"

"Of course." Ray turned to his uncle. "Everything's waiting for you, Uncle. We have a nice spot."

"Very good, Ray. I'll be right down."

"All right, then. They have coffee and biscuits down below. Shall we?" asked Henry.

"You all go on ahead. I need just a moment."

Henry stuck his thumbs in his suspenders. "For the artist to prepare for his art. Very good."

Lou raised her brows at Osborn as they left, leaving him alone in the room. Osborn went straight for the letter.

. . .It'll be quite a boodle. My heart is sorely missing you, and I'm praying for the day I return to you. I would cross lots to be with you right now.

The letter stopped and started again in different printing.

Dear Miss Tabitha,

I am writing you this note below what your betrothed, Jeremy Guss, wrote but never got the chance to mail to you. I am so deeply saddened and full of pain to tell you of the loss of your beloved and betrothed. Jeremy and I were close and fought in scraps side by side most of the time. He was taken at the battle of Manassas, as were thirty-three others of our fighting 33rd. Please take with you good thoughts that he is now with the Lord. As well, please forgive me for taking much time to inform you of his passing in this letter. I have held it closely, knowing I would have to write to you eventually, but could not bring myself to do it until now.

All my prayers are with you now in your time of sorrow,
Private Robert MacGruder, 33rd Virginia Infantry

Folding the letter, he put it back into its envelope. His image stood staring back at him in the mirror. His head dropped to a second envelope. It must have been lying under the first one. "Mother" was printed on it. He slid his finger under the seal and pulled out the note.

Forgive me, Mother, for I cannot go on. A broken heart is the reason for my passing. You will soon hear that Jeremy is with the Lord. Killed in battle. I aim to follow him and join him in the hinterlands beyond the clouds. Please forgive me. I mean no pain to you, but only to stop my own.

"Uncle, they are waiting for you," said Ray as he entered the door. Osborn folded the note and placed it back where he found it before going downstairs with Ray.

"Now, don't you look like some pumpkins!" said Lou to Mrs. Turner, in her finest dress, her hair up in a perfect bun.

"Aren't you sweet. It's the first time out of that old mourning dress since it happened," said Mrs. Turner.

Osborn swiveled to Lou and asked, "She looks like some pumpkins?"

"It means very pretty," replied Lou.

"Yes, it does," said Mrs. Turner. "And I have the prettiest bonnet to go with it, just you see."

"I'm certain it will be lovely," said Lou. "Now, you'll be standing up next to her?"

"I will," she said with pride. "I've always wanted a portrait of us together but had never taken the time when I should've."

Miss Tabitha sat in a seat in front of the parlor room by the fireplace. Osborn walked over with Ray to make the final adjustments. "You did a fine job, Ray. Is the camera ready?"

"Of course," said Ray before raising an eyebrow at his uncle and leaning in. "Are you feeling all right, Uncle?"

"It's been a peculiar morning." Osborn turned. "Mrs. Turner? You may come over and sit next to your daughter."

Mrs. Turner approached. "Ah, there's my baby," she said, holding back tears.

Griswold approached, handing her a handkerchief. "Harriet, you all right?"

"Thank you, Franklin."

"Now, your baby is sitting by the side of the Lord. Basking in his glory," said Lou.

"I know, I know."

Lou said, "And today she'll be surrounded by people all remembering her and—" Mrs. Turner burst into more tears and left the room. Griswold followed, only to return a short time later.

"Is she all right?" asked Lou. "Bless her heart."

"She's upset because Tabitha won't be surrounded by loved ones. None of the family is coming."

"None?"

"None, but it's not their fault. We have boys in the war relatives too infirmed and sickly or old. Some live too far away. I tried my best."

"We'll be there. All of us. There's five of us and two of you," said Lou.

Ray approached. "Lou, we gotta be getting on."

"No. We're gonna be here for that woman," she said. The determination on her face allowed no argument.

"Yes, yes. We're gonna be here for that woman," added Osborn as he thought, *This is what best friends do for each other.*

Mrs. Turner held the portrait in her hands, her eyes filled with wonder. "My, oh, my, this is a beautiful portrait, Mr. Roche. Just beautiful," she said, her voice trembling.

Osborn's eyes gleamed with pride as he replied, "You needed a portrait that you can view the rest of your years and feel her spirit's right there with you." Harriet smiled back at him.

As the pallbearers, Ray, Ben, Henry, and Griswold, carried Miss Tabitha's coffin outside into the warm, sunny day, Osborn and Lou followed behind, making their way through the knee-high grass towards the oak tree that stood two hundred yards in Mrs. Turner's back acreage.

Osborn leaned closer to Lou, his voice a conspiratorial whisper. "She was betrothed to a Reb soldier."

"She was? Ah, that's sad."

Osborn yanked up some tall grass, his fingers fidgeting with the blades as he spoke. "Miss Tabitha's death was not accidental."

Lou glanced at him. "The letter?"

"Suicide note."

"You found one?"

"Yes."

Lou's voice dropped to a hushed tone, urgency lacing her words. "That's one treasure you shouldn't put back, Osborn. You gotta get that and destroy it."

Osborn's mind raced, the gravity of the situation sinking in. With a curt nod, he turned and ran back to the house, his feet carrying him swiftly across the grass.

By the time Osborn returned, slightly out of breath, the group had already gathered at the gravesite. He took his place next to Lou, the simple pine box resting beside the freshly dug grave under the oak tree. The gravedigger, an old, thin black man, stood nearby, his hands resting on top of the shovel handle, his chin perched atop them.

As the preacher began the ceremony, Osborn's eyes fixated on the gravedigger, yet his mind wandered, his lips moving silently as he crafted the story of Miss Tabitha in his thoughts.

When the ceremony concluded, Osborn lingered, waiting for the others to make their way back to the house. Once alone, he approached the grave, the pine box now resting at the bottom, adorned with the flowers tossed by the mourners.

The gravedigger eyed Osborn.

"Would you mind if I slid this letter, slid this letter in with her before you cover?"

"Why would I be minding?" said the gravedigger.

Osborn bounced on his knees at the edge of the grave, hesitating for a moment before making the final leap.

Lou walked over and peered into the grave. "You're gonna hurt yourself. Take my hand and climb in." Osborn made a half move for it before stopping and shaking his head.

"Just toss it on in there," said the gravedigger. "I'll make sure she gets it."

Osborn tossed it in and said, "Guess I coulda done that from the beginning."

Osborn and Lou made their way back to the house, the rhythmic sound of the gravedigger's shovel piercing the earth behind them. Osborn suddenly stopped, a chill running up his spine. "I love that sound," he said, his voice filled with a strange reverence.

Lou turned to him, her eyes sparkling with understanding. "I was thinking the same thing. The stabbing of the spade into fresh dirt."

"Ooh, yes," Osborn replied, closing his eyes to fully immerse himself in the sound. Lou's giggle filled the air.

Lou stopped on a dime, turning sharply on her heels to him, her face beaming. "Hey! I would like to try something, and I'm hoping you want to try it."

"I will certainly try to try it."

"You know the strangeness of how we can look each other in the eyes but have trouble with everyone else? Let's continue to walk, and I want to see if I could hold your hand." She beamed at him as Osborn's smile faded. "You could stand it with your mother, right? Just try it. If it's awful, we'll let go."

"But Lou, what is that? Sweethearts hold hands."

"Friends do too! Are we not best friends? Now let's go and try it," she said as she turned, walking next to him again. "Now, my left hand is gonna..." Osborn took a deep breath, his eyes fluttering shut as he walked blindly through the tall grass. Suddenly, he felt the gentle slide of her hand into his, and with a reflexive movement, he grasped it tightly. As if emerging from a dream, he opened his eyes to the sight of their joined hands. His amazed face turned to her beaming smile.

"We're doing it, we're doing it!" she said like a giddy child learning to ride a bike.

Osborn struggled to find the words. "This could never... I've never..." Lou swayed their arms, her giggles filling the air. "And I can't feel your fingers moving."

She shook her head. "Not while they're holding your hand," she said as if he was silly for saying it.

Suddenly, Henry's voice rang out from the porch of the house, shattering the moment. "Louise! It is time to leave." Their hands dropped to their sides, the spell broken.

Osborn made his way to the back of his wagon, settling himself on the bed as he watched Lou through the open door. Henry's words cut through the air once more. "Lou! You're riding with us in our wagon."

Lou hesitated, reluctantly turning back to her wagon. Turning back to him, she called out and asked, "You created the story about Miss Tabitha?" He nodded, a smile playing at the corners of his mouth. "Did you give it a happy ending?"

Osborn's smile widened, his eyes sparkling. "She's married now. She's married."

CHAPTER 13

The smell of sweat and fear hung in the air as their wagons pulled into the Union Army headquarters sitting on the east side of Antietam Creek. Couriers on horseback flew by carrying messages to the front. Ray and Osborn climbed down from their wagon as the cannons unleashed their deadly burden. Osborn immediately sat in the dirt and stuck the nose plugs into his ears.

"You all right?" asked Ray. Osborn nodded as Henry and Ben pulled their wagon next to theirs. Ben jumped down, went around to their wagon door, and opened it to Lou, hands over her ears, shaking with fear inside. With each distant explosion, Lou shuddered.

"Ray, if you are not too occupied, would you be so kind as to help Louise set up her tent away from the foray? We were thinking back at the hospital. Ben and I need to be closer to the front. Louise cannot tolerate this," yelled Henry above the cannon fire.

"Not a problem," said Ray. "He doesn't like it either, and we won't be busy until after the battle." Ray walked around back to help Ben load Lou's tent and equipment into their wagon.

Henry helped Lou out and walked her over. Osborn still sat on the ground as Henry came out. "Mr. Roche," said Henry, standing above him, an ominous black shadow silhouetted by the sun. Osborn shielded his eyes before Henry walked back to his wagon. Ray stood outside the open door as Osborn rose and peered in. Lou sat on the bed, rocking back and forth with her hands on her ears.

"Let's head back a bit from the sound," said Ray.

"Yes, yes. Farther away from the chaos. Farther away." Osborn entered the wagon, bringing up the stairs behind him. The wagon turned as Osborn sat next to her on the bed. He pulled a pair of nose plugs from a drawer and offered them to her with an open hand. With closed eyes, she didn't respond to him, continuing to rock back and forth. He raised his hands to hers on her ears but hesitated and couldn't bring himself to touch them.

Sitting beside her, he studied her out of the side of his eye. Like her, he started swaying his body, gradually reaching cadence with her rocking. Her eyes opened slowly to his, locking on them like two children swinging on rope swings and holding hands. Her pleading eyes softened, and her rocking slowed.

Osborn followed her cadence as Lou brought her hands down from her ears. A weak smile came to her lips. Osborn turned to her hand with its piano-playing fingers. He reached out and took it in his grasp, stopping it like a father stopping his child's tantrum. He turned back to her face with tears streaming down it.

Palm up; he offered the nose plugs again. "An extra pair. I also use these in my ears for noise. Yes, the noise. Try them."

She took them and put them in. "There's something special about you. I've never met a man like you before."

"I've never met anyone like you either. No one like you."

Lou laughed and sniffed up the tears. "You surely haven't met a woman that wears men's clothes."

"Suppose that's the truth, yes."

Lou wiped the tears from her cheeks. "You wear strange duds too, Osborn."

"How's that? How's that?"

"Not like any man I ever met. The fanciest, most handsome duds any man could ever wear. You wear a coat of kindness, a tie of tolerance, and a hat of humanity." She smiled at him before leaning against the closet wall and closing her eyes. Her jaw relaxed, and she pulled her feet up on the bed, curling up into a fetal position.

"Lou, would you like a pillow?" Taking a pillow, he hesitated, then bumped her with it. Eyes closed; she took it. Osborn curiously stared at her as she fell into a deep sleep. Her feet crept toward him like a snake until they touched his leg like a bite. He jumped off the bed, and she spread out, taking the length of it.

"Ray! I need to sit upfront with you." The wagon stopped, and Osborn came around to the bench.

Ray glanced over to him as Hoady resumed their journey back. "Don't ya want to stay back there with your girl?"

"She's not my girl." "Your friend?"

"She fell asleep and took the whole bed."

"Kicked you out, eh?"

"She did not kick me out. I told you she fell asleep."

Far enough away from the sounds of war, they found the army hospital tents, pulled in, and climbed down. "General!" Ray yelled from the other side of the wagon. "Uncle!" Osborn came around the wagon.

"How much for a portrait?" asked General Sedgwick while carried by two bearers and followed by seven junior officers.

"General! Hope they didn't get you too bad," said Osborn as he walked with them toward the hospital tent.

"Got me in the shoulder, wrist, and leg. I would like to have a portrait before they cut my leg off." Blood stained his uniform, but the general appeared in good spirits, most likely from the bottle of whiskey he held in his left hand.

"Well, it depends on what type of portrait," replied Osborn. "That metal kind. The tin one."

"A tintype is only five cents."

"Boys take me over to the gentleman's tent on the way to the hospital."

Both bearers laughed. "Sorry, General. You're going straight to the hospital."

"I know they're gonna take my leg. I want a photo with it before they cut it off."

"Ain't gonna do it, General. We's got other boys still out there." "Suppose that's true, son," said the general, taking a swig of whiskey.

"My portraits of soldiers with peg legs seem always to reveal the soul, yes, reveal the soul of those who've conquered fear on the field of battle."

The general's head snapped to Osborn. "Again, so well played. Bravo! I believe you're right, sir! Come see me later with my new wooden leg!"

The dusky orange sky carried the diminishing echoes of battle from the east. "Sounds like the battle might be coming to an end," said Ray as they set up their tent behind the hospital, the quietest spot near the division. Ray and Osborn set up Lou's embalming tent next to theirs, leaving Lou in the quiet wagon as they did.

The evening brought most of the soldiers back to camp, many of them wounded. Ray and Osborn made supper with Lou's salt pork. They ate it in front of the wagon as the parade of wounded headed toward the hospital. Henry and Ben rode in with several soldiers on their wagon's roof.

"Have some supper for ya," said Ray. Henry and Ben jumped down and came over, leaving their horse hitched.

"Starving," said Ben.

"How was it?" asked Osborn.

"It was real warm fighting. I mean, good business, but a lot of boys killed today," said Henry.

"I ain't never seen nothing like it. Fields of dead," said Ben, turning to Lou. "You'll be busy tomorrow, girl."

"Is it over? Is the battle over?" asked Osborn.

"So, I hear. Lee's forces began withdrawing across the Potomac to Virginia."

"No pursuit?" asked Ray. "Not yet, at least," said Henry.

Osborn turned to Ray and said, "We gotta get out there first thing in the morning. First thing."

Ben shoveled in food but stopped and said, "Naw. Ain't no rush in my estimation. There's dead as far as the eye can see. Some say the bloodiest day of the war. It'll take days to collect them all."

An owl hooted the late hour from a nearby tree. Osborn tossed and turned, listening to it in bed. He rose and stepped over Ray, asleep on the floor. After putting on his clothes and boots, he entered the night air, greeted by the moans and cries from the hospital's wounded. He walked away toward the rows of tents housing snoring soldiers.

Osborn sniffed the air, smelling the sweet, smoky scent of wood-burning. He disliked the smoke but loved the smell of it. Walking off to find it in the dark, he allowed his mind to fixate on his methodical pace. Two soldiers' silhouettes lay ahead of him, warming their hands over a fire in a barrel. They remained silent and offered no greeting as he joined them and put his hands out, warming them as they did. With peripheral glances, he attempted to ascertain whether they accepted him. Osborn flinched at every snap and pop from the wood in the fire.

Another man with a dark overcoat and hood joined them with his hands over the fire, making a square. Osborn tried to see his face within the shadows of his hood but could not. The man stood, swaying back and forth, hands outstretched. As he took out a flask and put it to his mouth, his hood fell back—it was Ben. Tilting his head back for a swig, his eyes opened in recognition. "Oh, it's you," Ben slurred before swallowing and capping the flask, not offering to share.

He stuck out his palm, looking at it before wiping it on his pant leg and putting it out for Osborn's. Osborn ignored it. Ben looked at his snubbed hand and back to Osborn with confusion.

"Did I offend?"

Osborn's eyebrows squished together. "Offend who?"

Ben's creased brow deepened. "Offend you. You will not take my hand."

"I do not take anyone's hand. I don't like to be touched," said Osborn, like everyone felt this way.

Ben's eyes flashed. "You are a strange one."

"I have been called peculiar often. I prefer the word. The C is a sharp consonant."

Ben studied Osborn's face under half-mast eyelids. "Something about you, I can't put my finger on."

"Yes, please don't. I don't like to be touched."

Ben shook his head. "No, no, I mean…" Ben's facial gestures gave the impression of him talking to himself. "So, I heard you figured it out on day one."

"Figured it out?"

"You know." Ben leaned in close, breathing his moist and rank whiskey breath on him. Osborn blinked, coughed, and waved away the air. "Oh, sorry, yeah, I been drinking. Did I get any spittle on ya?" he said, wiping Osborn's jacket.

Osborn leaped back from it with an, "Ah! I do not like to be touched," he said, putting the nose plugs in his nose.

"Oh, yeah, sorry. Boy, you are a touchy one."

Osborn shook in exasperation, saying, "I told you, I told you I am not a touchy one. No, not a touchy one."

Ben reached back into his pocket for the flask. "Fine, fine. I got it." He flipped up the flask and took a swig. Capping it, his eyes walked up and down Osborn. "You knew right away she's a she."

"Hmm?"

"You knew right away about Lou. You know, she's a she. The clothes didn't fool ya. The short hair. You know, she's a female."

"Oh, yes. I knew right away. She is beautiful."

Ben shook his head again from the thought. "Never heard that before. I mean, I'm happy you think that. She's a great kid. She's my niece, yep. I don't know any woman around who works with the dead. I ain't saying… I mean, she's a damn good embalmer. Just most women wouldn't be doing this type of thing," he said while swaying back and forth. His eyelids slowly blinked as he took another swig. "You said she's beautiful. She ain't never courted no one before, so you'd be the first."

"I don't want to court her. I just want to be friends. Best friends."

"No courting, eh?" He leaned in. "You know she did the embalming on Willy Lincoln, right? She tell you that? Yup, her and her father. Her father is my brother," he slurred with spit flying into the fire and took another swig. "Yep. She tell you that? She's a damn great embalmer. A natural." Ben swayed, and his eyes rolled back. The soldier next to him grabbed his arm to steady him. "I think she likes ya. You might reconsider the whole courting thing."

"I'm sacking in," said one of the two soldiers. No one responded. Ben took out the flask again and took another swig before putting it away without offering.

"But, yeah, she's a great kid. I saw you two in the wagon. I believe she likes ya. And smart as a whip too." Another swig. Ben stepped back, catching a tent stake, and fell. Osborn instinctively reached out but pulled back his hands at the last second. Ben collapsed to the ground. The soldier went down to try to pick him up. "Naw, I'm fine. Leave me." The soldier rose to his feet and regarded Ben as he lay snoring. A big snort woke him up, and he said, "Ya might reconsider the courting thing. Yeah, reconsider..." Ben's head fell back, and his snoring grew louder.

"Your man's up the pole. Luckily, it's a decent warm night. He'll be fine with that wool coat," said the soldier. Osborn stared down at Ben with his words still in his head. He took a deep breath, turned, and walked away, the fire fading behind him. Drawing nearer to her tent, he thought about courting. Wouldn't it be wonderful if that could be? If she would want that from him? If she would want a man that didn't like to touch? Was that even possible? What about children?

The closer he came to her tent, the faster his heart and mind raced. Notion after notion crossed it until an excuse came to him. Reaching the last group of tents before hers, he stopped.

Three sergeants, up late, sat on barrels playing cards. "Looking for someone?" asked the heavily bearded sergeant.

"No, no. That's my wagon right there. Right there." The bearded sergeant turned back to his friends with a shrug. Osborn's feet defied him as they stepped away from his wagon and to the direction of her tent. Thankfully, they stopped inches from her tent flap.

The evening air cooled the sweat on his face before he pulled back the canvas flap. His feet walked in with a mind of their own into the center of the tent, her tent. Dark as a tomb and quiet as coffin air, Osborn froze and waited for his eyes to adjust. He stood with the dirt floor beneath him, enclosed by canvas and held up by poles. Here's where her breath mixed with the air filling the space.

A sound came from his left. Breathing, her breathing, calling him like a siren's song. He shuffled toward the sound, hands outstretched like a sleepwalker until his right shin found the bed. Quietly as he could, Osborn went to his knees and rolled to his back next to her cot. The hard dirt floor stuck to the sweat on the back of his neck as he viewed the tent ceiling with occasional glances to her wood-framed cot for movement.

She is sleeping right next to me! Right next to me! I am sleeping with her! His thumping heart and rapid breathing roared in his ears. He feared she would hear it. He removed her brown cloth from his pocket. Unfolding it, he brought it to his nose and mouth, covering it. The scent of her throughout, he sucked it in, breathing her soul into his lungs. His shoulders relaxed, and his breathing slowed.

This is what it would be like if she was more than a friend. If she was mine and I was hers. And if she accepted my proposal of marriage, we would be husband and wife. We would be sleeping near each other just like this. I would hear her breathing while she slept peacefully. I believe I would kiss her now. On the lips, and I can feel her lips press on mine because she loves me and...

Lou flipped over, facing him. Osborn froze and sucked in a deep breath to hold it. Nothing. He rose slightly to peer at her face. Phew! She's still asleep. Oh, my goodness, she is so beautiful when she sleeps. Without her spectacles, I can see her eyebrows. So sweet the way her cheek squashes up against the side of her nose.

Lou's hand flopped off the edge of the bed. Osborn quickly retreated, becoming a statue on the dirt floor.

Her hand is so dainty and fingers...

He raised his hand, index finger pointed toward hers, slowly moving to it until a millimeter away. I want to...

Snoring came from behind him. If he wasn't already lying down, Osborn would have fainted. He dropped his hand and tilted his head back in the dirt to the inverted view of her father asleep on a cot. Her father's snoring grew louder by the second. Returning his attention to her finger, he slid the ridges of his fingerprint across hers. *I'm touching her!* He yanked it away, holding his breath with excitement.

Oh, how I wish it! My greatest wish would be to hear you call to me, your arm raising the sheet, inviting me in. I take it from you and submerge myself under, joining you in the enclosed world of our own. We will be the only two humans within it—my hand slides across your skin, smooth as porcelain. You whisper words of adoration in my ear as candles shimmer around us. My hand would move across your body, exploring it like a homesteader finding a more beautiful valley over each hill rise. . .

CHAPTER 14

"Osborn... Osborn?" his eyes opened to Lou's confused face, peering over the edge of the cot—eyes that grew wide as teacup saucers. "What... what are you doing here?" Osborn glanced to his left. Henry stood over him with the same confused expression. Lou's finger motioned a circle around her nose and mouth, her eyes narrowing. Osborn grabbed the cloth off his face, pushing it into his pocket.

"I don't know," said Osborn. "Did you sleep here last night?"

Henry set his fists on his hips. "This is highly inappropriate, Mr. Roche."

"Highly, highly inappropriate, highly inappropriate," agreed Osborn.

"Are you sure you're all right, Osborn? Father, can you get him some tea?"

"Tea? No. Get up, Mr. Roche," said Henry, his head tilting from side to side, asking silent questions. "Did he touch you at all?" Henry asked Lou.

"No, Daddy. I woke up and found him here."

"I wanted to ask a question. I must have fallen asleep."

"What was the question?" asked Henry.

"I can't remember it now. Can't remember."

Osborn jumped up to a stand. "I believe you should go," insisted Henry.

"I'll try to recall the question. I don't remember. I'll try to recall it," Osborn said as he stumbled backward, retreating from the tent. The morning sun assaulted his eyes, blinding him momentarily. In his daze, he collided with something solid—Ben's broad chest. The sunlight framed Ben's head, creating a radiant halo that made him seem almost divine. Ben loomed over Osborn, his gaze intense and unyielding, as if a god had descended to pass judgment. *Sinner!*

Sinner! I read your thoughts last night, Sinner! Your evil thoughts. You shall be damned for all eternity!

"Didn't I see you last night?" asked Ben as Osborn moved past him. "Where ya going?"

Without responding, Osborn walked around to the front of the wagon.

"Where were you last night?" asked Ray as he made breakfast. Osborn made for the wagon and shut the door behind him, leaning against it. "Uncle?"

Solitude. His heart slowed as his fingers searched for the brown cloth in his pocket, bringing it out again and sucking her into his lungs.

"Excuse me," Henry said from outside the wagon. "Is your uncle here?" Osborn stiffened.

"He's inside the wagon," said Ray. Osborn's hand darted to the wagon door but slowed and silently pushed the slide lock across.

"Do you know where he was last night?"

"He slept with me in the wagon."

"Apparently, you sleep well because I found him in there, and this is nothing to smile about, young man."

"I'm sorry, Mr. Cattell. I don't... I mean, what would you like me to—"

Osborn brought his ear closer to the door. "They need to be kept away from each other. Do you understand the importance of this?"

Ray remained silent.

"Louise can never marry. I've told you if two people with this affliction were to procreate, it would be a calamity. They both need sterilization, and I don't believe their minds could handle intimacy. It would destroy them both!"

"I can see you're upset, Mr. Cattell. I will speak to him about this, I promise."

"There is no need. We will be moving our tent. I do not wish to see either of you again."

Silence. Osborn's head turned about the wagon's interior. *What is happening out there?*

"Mr. Roche, you hear me in there?!" said Henry as he pounded on the door. Osborn's eyes went wide. "You stay away—"

"Get the heck away from the wagon," said Ray. "I'll deal with it. Now that's enough. Get on outta here."

"Get your hands off me, young man," exclaimed Henry before his footsteps walked away.

His body frozen, but his eyes moving in every possible direction, Osborn jumped when the doorknob jiggled. "Open the door. He's gone," said Ray. Osborn slid the lock open, and Ray's head popped in. "Is that where you were last night?"

Osborn immediately began organizing, avoiding Ray's eyes. "Thank you. I'll be out in a second."

"What?" Ray waited for a response. "You know the collodion doesn't go there. It goes where you took it from."

"I don't like it there anymore."

"You slept in her tent?"

"Ah, silver nitrate goes here."

"Did you sleep… in her… bed?" asked Ray, salivating for the answer.

"Farmer's reducer? I was looking for you."

"Did you…touch her?"

Osborn wheeled to him. "Ray!"

"Listen, I don't care."

"I am your uncle, and this is not the conversation—"

"Listen to me. I think it's fine. I'm on your side, Uncle. If you like her, you like her. That sits dandy with me. But that old man's got his tail up. I don't know if he'll let you see her again."

Osborn stopped, deflating like a balloon, and dropped his head. "I like her, Ray."

"I know you do. Listen, I'll pack up out here, and we'll head out to the battlefield. Maybe you can search some pockets, make some new friends. That'll make you feel a bit better."

"Maybe another day. I think I need to rest, to rest, yes. Today I don't want a new friend. I don't want one." Osborn sat back on the bed and fell to his side with his head on a pillow. Taking out the brown cloth, he squeezed it in his fist and brought it to his chest like a shipwrecked sailor clinging to an oak board, with no land in sight.

"Maybe another day," Osborn muttered, his voice shaky. "I think I need to rest. Yes, to rest." His eyes darted around the room before settling on the bed. "Today, I don't want a new friend. I don't want one." He sat heavily on the bed, then collapsed sideways, his head sinking into the pillow. His hand fumbled in his pocket, retrieving the brown cloth. With a desperate grip, he clutched it to his chest like a shipwrecked sailor grasping a lifeline.

The wind whistled about the battlefield of Antietam as Hoady pulled them down a dirt road, clip-clopping at a Sunday's pace. Ray kept turning to his uncle's sullen expression as he drove. "You needed to get out, Uncle. I couldn't just let you stay all day in the back of the wagon. Look, I told you it's a beautiful day. We'll get some good photographs today. I just know it."

Both their jaws dropped as they viewed the battlefield. The dead lay scattered over hills of green grass like blue and grey sprinkles on peppermint ice cream. They rode their wagon down the dirt roads, stopping here and there to pull out the stereoview camera for a photo.

Osborn stood studying a dead private, his upper body lying over two hay bales and his feet on the ground. "Ray, I want to try something different. Lower the tripod to its lowest setting for this shot."

"That's gonna be strange."

"You know I hate that word."

"Well, it's not gonna look right."

"Just because no one has done it doesn't mean it shouldn't be done. I want to try different angles than people are used to. Different angles, yes."

Ray developed the first photo and exited the wagon. "It's interesting, Uncle, very interesting."

"I knew it would be. See that church over there? Let's put the camera behind that, that, that broken steeple and have the dead men on the other side of it be in focus," said Osborn. Ray shook his head, confused, but followed as Osborn set the camera and focused.

"But the steeple will block a portion of the shot, Uncle."

"Yes, I want it to."

"And it'll be out of focus. Why?"

"Yes, it will, and I want that. It is called depth of field. The dead soldiers will be in focus in the background. You must trust me. You must trust me."

Ray developed it and exited the wagon. "I like it, but I'm not sure if others will. The steeple is out of focus," said Ray, handing it to Osborn.

"But you see, Ray. The viewer can see this is a church steeple even with it out of focus and can see the dead in the background. It's a metaphor, Ray. It's a metaphor that these young men died as God looked down upon them. The photograph is now telling us a story as books do. It's a story with irony, Ray. The house of God in front of death. Don't you see, Ray?"

Ray looked at the photo again, confused. He turned around to his uncle and then back to the image. His mouth opened without words until he said, "You truly amaze me. That is brilliant. I see the story now."

"Yes, yes. You see it, you see it," Osborn said as he clapped.

"I see it, I see it."

"Let's do more. Let's do more!"

"Yes, let's do more! Let's make stories with photographs!" said Ray, bouncing excitedly.

Heading south down the Smoketown Road toward a cornfield, they came to a slight rise in the road and stopped. The way ahead was impassable, heaped with dead Rebel soldiers dying on top of each other as they tried to climb a wood fence.

"I don't believe I have ever seen so many dead. This must have been some battle. Some battle," said Osborn.

"Were they trying to attack or retreat?"

"For their sake, let's say they were trying to attack. Yes, yes, trying to attack."

Stretcher-bearers, as well as other photographers, collected the dead in the distance. "I believe I see one of Brady's guys over there. Stereoviews of this battle are gonna be in every store across the country," said Ray.

"Watch the bearers. Find a spot where they haven't yet discovered. But I believe there's not enough combined silver nitrate amongst all of us to capture everything that happened here yesterday."

"Let's see if we can find some gems," said Ray, pointing to a wooded area off to his right. "Let's go into the tree line over there and see if they fought thataways." They moved their wagon off the road and set up their rebuilt dark cart, similar to Brady's carts but smaller and with a dark canvas that could be tied at the photographer's waist, eliminating light seepage.

Ray pushed it across the field toward the woods, with Osborn carrying the tripod over his shoulder. They had to dodge a body every few feet until Osborn stopped. A young Union private lay on his back with eyes wide and hands raised with bloat and rigor mortis. He had a quarter-sized blackened-red hole in his forehead. In one hand, he held a fountain pen and, in the other, a notebook.

"He died while writing instead of dying while fighting, while fighting, see?"

Ray turned to him and watched him briefly before saying, "Go on. We got all day." Ray sat next to the dark cart and picked the grass. Osborn went to his knees, opening the notebook gently and reading. A confused expression came to his face, and his eyes turned to a Rebel body three feet away. Osborn crawled over to him.

"What? That first one not good enough to be your friend?" asked Ray with a smirk.

Osborn searched the Rebel's pockets, bringing out several items and returning them before turning to Ray. "Can I tell you a story?"

"No. Not unless it's a photographic story."

"It's a true story. True story about these two young men."

"So, you admit when it's a true story?" replied Ray lifting his lip in a half-smile.

"This Reb, his name was Davis. This private over here, his name was Robert. Robert found Davis here dying, came over and started writing his family a condolence letter, a condolence letter. In the middle of battle, I assume. He got shot through the head just before he finished it."

Ray rubbed his cheek, staring at Osborn. "Why are ya smiling about it?" asked Ray.

"Oh, no, not smiling… I mean, I'm not smiling about the young man's death, no. I was just thinking that it's so interesting."

"It's so sad."

"It's both sad and interesting. Listen, 'Mama, Fear not for me, for I had a good death. I know you will be delighted to have my final thoughts on paper. Thanks to this Yank boy for writing it. I am accepting of my fate and believe Jesus is ready to be at my side. I wish you could be with.'"

"It ends there?"

"Yes."

"Hmm," said Ray, picking some more grass. "You should search him more and find out where he lives and send that letter on for him. Maybe even return the favor for the Yank."

"I don't like to take anything, Ray."

"You'll just be taking the—" The sentence was shattered by the crack of a rifle and the whizzing of a bullet slicing through the air. Instinctively, they both ducked, Osborn's scream piercing the sudden chaos.

A hundred yards off, an old Union soldier ran toward them with his pistol. "Don't move! Don't move an inch, or I'll get ya!" he screamed as he ran toward them. They slowly raised their hands above their heads and rose.

"We're photographers! We're photographers!" yelled Ray, blood pumping.

"What the hell are you doing with that body?!" yelled the soldier.

"I told you that's our wagon over yonder. We're photographers!"

"Then what the hell are you doing with that body, I asked ya?!" he said, putting his hands on his knees, panting and out of breath.

"We thought he might be alive. Just making sure."

The soldier pointed to the body. "Alive? With a hole in the head?"

"The other one, and listen, my uncle over here is a Union captain. Commissioned by McClellan himself, so if I were you, I'd watch yourself."

The old soldier's hands still held his knees. He shook his head at Osborn, frozen, eyes shut, flapping his hands. Still panting, he said, "Captain? I don't see no uniform, and look at him, is he a feeble-minded boy or something?"

"He ain't. You just scared him, is all. My uncle is a respected photographer," seethed Ray.

"It's true. I am a captain, and I am not feeble-minded. Not feeble-minded. And I hate that word."

"I thought you was grave robbers!"

"Well, we aren't," said Ray, rising and dusting himself off. "Where would you like the camera set, Uncle?"

The soldier stood up straight and holstered his pistol. "You almost got killed for that photograph, boy."

Ignoring the soldier, Osborn turned to Ray. "Remember the story, Ray? Put the notebook back into Robert's hand. Put the camera behind that, and we'll photograph Davis. The story will be told by the photograph just as I told you."

Ray's eyes opened wide with his grin. "Yes, yes. Brilliant."

"Disgusting, if you ask me," the sergeant muttered, his eyes narrowing as he scrutinized them. "Well, all right then," he added reluctantly. "I'll leave ya to it." He turned and walked away, but every few steps, he would glance back over his shoulder, his gaze lingering on them as if expecting to catch them in some act of deceit.

"You handled that well back there, Uncle. Getting better at shocks like that."

"Thank you," Osborn said, carefully setting the camera into position. Nearby, Ray struggled with the notebook, trying to place it back into Robert's frozen, blackened hand. The stiff fingers refused to hold it, and the notebook kept slipping to the ground.

"Just hold it there like he is holding it. I won't see your fingers if they're off to the left, and it'll be out of focus."

"All right."

After developing the photograph, Ray closed up the dark cart, and they resumed their trek across the field, heading towards the woods on the far side. "That one will make for a remarkable story, Uncle. Another amazing photograph, one after another. I don't know what's gotten into you."

"Gotten into me? Nothing has gotten into me, Ray. We just didn't have breakfast."

They stepped from the field and entered the west woods. The land sloped steeply in front of them, covered with a dense layer of pine needles that had accumulated over the years. Granite outcroppings jutted out from the earth like islands in a sea of gold. Towering loblolly pines, eighty feet tall, permitted only filtered sunlight to reach the ground.

"Leave the cart," Osborn instructed.

Ahead up the slope, specs of blue spotted the pine needle floor. "I see some bodies up ahead," said Ray. With labored breathing, they climbed the slope, and the soldiers' lifeless forms came into view.

"It was hand to hand in here, no limbs missing. This boy here took a bayonet. This one too, and this one was shot up close. Dang! This boy dropped cash money right here!" exclaimed Ray.

"Let it be. They'll shoot you for that. Tread lightly." Osborn went up farther, climbing up a stone. "I'm gonna go this way," he yelled back to Ray. "This side. There's a bunch over here."

Ray ran over. "Dang, it looks like a checkerboard of blue. They're all scattered about so even like God placed 'em there."

With Osborn out of sight, Ray called, "Hey, wait up!" He caught up to Osborn in front of a smashed drum lying next to a boulder. Osborn cautiously circled the boulder with Ray in tow. "It's the boy. The drummer we..." said Ray, trailing off.

"Yeah," replied Osborn, standing above him on his self-made deathbed of pine needles. The boy had arranged his legs straight with his feet together and his hands crossed over his chest, mimicking the repose of a coffin. On either side of him, two-inch tintype photos encased in frames were carefully lined up, each frame facing him, forming a photographic halo around his ashen face.

Osborn's cheeks quivered as he fought back tears. "Are you... Does this upset you?" Ray asked, his voice trembling.

Osborn squinted, torn between the urge to see and the desire to close his eyes. "He, he, he was speaking to Lou and me."

"I remember," Ray murmured.

"He's just a boy, just a boy. Why would they kill a drummer boy? They're not supposed to kill drummer boys, no. Who would do that? Who would? Off-limits, off-limits."

"Yeah," said Ray pointing to the encircled tintypes. "How did this happen? Someone set him up this way?"

"No. He did it himself. See the leg wound? Probably, bled, bled out. It took him a while to die. He most likely got shot, got shot, yes, hiding around the other side where the drum is, and he crawled over here, dug it out, set out his kin to have smiling faces about him. He prayed, crossed his arms, and left to meet his maker, meet his maker," said Osborn, turning away from the boy. "Remember his name?"

"No. I don't think he mentioned," said Ray.

"I'm gonna search his pockets."

"I wouldn't with that old man about."

"Lou was with me when we met this young man. She would want me to."

Ray shrugged his shoulders, walked around to the boulder's backside, and picked up the drum before climbing up above Osborn and the fallen drummer.

Osborn dropped to his knees, carefully picking up each tintype and reading the inscriptions on the back. He found the one he had photographed—the boy hadn't had the chance to mail it yet. As Osborn adjusted the boy's position, his fingers searched the pockets for any treasures, anything that might provide a clue. Wait! His fingers recognized a small locket with Florentine finish engraving. Inside was a photo of the boy's parents. Osborn put it back gently.

His rear pant pocket contained three letters from his mother. William was his name, but they all called him Billy. He had three sisters and a father, also in the army. Osborn recalled that his father had passed. He read all three letters and pulled up Billy to replace them when the whiz of a bullet smacked the boulder, spraying shattered granite all over him.

Startled, Osborn ducked instinctively, his heart racing as he shielded Billy's letters with his body.

"I shoulda knowed! I shoulda knowed!" cried out the old sergeant, running up the slope.

Osborn threw his hands up as more granite splintered from a second shot. "Ouch!" Osborn's mouth and eyes opened wide as he raised his hands again.

"Shoulda knowed!" he said out of breath walking nearer, gun pointed. "Don't you surrender to me, you dog gone, grave robbin', child touchin'. Drop those hands and come at me!"

"I wasn't! I wasn't!" Osborn's face scrunched, trying to hide from the terror.

"Don't you go weepin' on me, grave robbers!"

Osborn's hand slowly descended into panicked flapping. "You drop them hands, and I'll show ya—"

With his eyes closed, Osborn heard a heavy thud, followed by a gasp, and then all fell quiet.

"Uncle! Uncle!" Osborn slowly opened his eyes to see Ray standing where the old sergeant had been. "We gotta get up on outta here," Ray urged.

"What happened?!" asked Osborn, his head jerking about.

"I dropped a stone on that old coot," Ray said, his head turning to the man on the ground. Osborn followed his gaze. Bleeding profusely from the head, the sergeant lay at the feet of Billy.

Osborn's eyes became as large as saucers. "Oh my! Is he dead?!" "Don't know, don't care. We gotta get on outta here," said Ray starting off, but turning back to Osborn, not moving. "If you don't come now, I'm gonna grab your arm and pull you," pleaded Ray. "You're not gonna like it."

"I'm going, I'm going." Osborn ran down the hill behind him until reaching the cart at the edge of the tree line.

Ray took a deep breath as he grabbed the cart and walked out as if nothing had happened. "Walk! Walk, Uncle. Let's not attract attention to ourselves." Attempting to feign calm, Osborn threw his hands behind his back and slowed to a walk, but instead of his typical gait, he adopted a peculiar dance step. Ray caught it out of the corner of his eye. "What in the devil are you doing?" Ray hissed through clenched teeth.

"Taking a stroll in the park, taking a stroll in the park, taking a stroll…"

"Well, stop taking a stroll. Walk normally! Like you always walk! You look like a bullbat."

Osborn halted abruptly, his face flushing with anger. "You know I hate that word!"

Ray jumped in front of Osborn. "We don't have time for this, Uncle. You're gonna get us shot." Instead, Osborn shut his eyes tightly and tensed his body. Ray's hands tensed to fists by his side. "Stop it. Stop it!" Osborn stood frozen, tense. "Oh, that's it!" Ray exclaimed, grabbing Osborn by the arm and dragging him across the field with one hand while pushing the cart with the other.

Osborn screamed, "Don't touch me! Stop! Ray! Stop! Ray! Stop!"

Stretcher-bearers, a hundred yards away, turned with bored curiosity. Ray shouted to them, "Just looking for our kin is all!" He reached the wagon and flung the back door open. "Get in."

Steaming mad, Osborn glared at Ray and said, "We will discuss how we shall handle, we shall handle this differently next time."

"Fine by me," replied Ray. Osborn climbed in, and Ray slammed the door shut. Ray climbed onto the bench and turned Hoady to the north.

"Ray!" Osborn called out to him from inside the wagon. "Ray, did I tell you about Billy?"

"Who?"

"The drummer boy we just saw back there."

Ray shook his head. "What do you mean tell me about him?"

"His twelve-year-old brother would tease us relentlessly!"

Ray tossed his head from side to side. "Oh, no, please, Uncle."

"We plotted revenge so many times. But it was that one time…"

Ray slapped the reins to move Hoady faster. "I'm not listening."

"I lived down the road from Billy when I was five. He was one of my good friends. His sister would follow us around, wanting to play with us, and when we wouldn't let her, she would spy on us. We both thought the preacher's daughter was the most beautiful girl we had ever seen. She had short brown hair and looked like a lot like Lou…"

CHAPTER 15

Dearest Lou,

We are in Mississippi now. Every day I wonder what you are doing, where you are. I wish I had taken a portrait of you so I could have it now. My portraits are another way for me to collect friends, similar to Miss Tabitha. I sure wish I had collected you...

Ray peered into the wagon where Osborn sat at the desk. "Writing another letter to Lou? You don't know where to send them."

"I'll save them until I know. Until I know," said Osborn, concentrating on his letter.

"How many is that? Do you write one every day?"

"No. Every other."

"You'll be fine, Uncle. There are more fish in the sea."

"I swim in a very small pond. Very small pond."

"You should finish up. We got a long line waiting." Osborn peered out the wagon's window. A long line of soldiers waited to take their portraits.

"Just about done," replied Osborn.

"Can you do this at night? They line up earlier now since they all read about us in the battle. They want to hear the story again."

"You should tell them. They like you better."

"You always say that, and it's not true. They want to hear from the brave photographer. Not the brave photographer's assistant."

Osborn folded the letter, and they both proceeded to the portrait tent. Twin brothers stood in front of his camera—one with sergeant stripes, the other with corporal stripes.

"Oh, I forgot the plate," said Ray, heading back to the wagon.

Osborn studied the twins and asked, "Can I ask you, boys, a question—"

"Captain Roche!" The voice interrupted from outside the portrait tent. Osborn jerked his body down at the surprise, closed his eyes, and froze. Major General William Rosecrans, the division's commanding officer, came bursting through with junior officers' entourage in tow. The twin brothers came to immediate attention. "I saw your photographs today. Marvelous! Simply astounding," said the general as his eight junior officers filled every open spot in the tent. He stared at Osborn, his excitement turning to confusion. "Mr. Roche? Are you feeling all right?"

Osborn calmed, opened his eyes and stood up straight. "My photographs, but where?"

"One of my junior officers told me they were selling out from every shop in Nashville," he said, whipping up three stereoview portrait cards in one hand and his viewer in the other.

"Memphis, too," added a junior officer.

"Exciting stuff! It was the photo of the cavalry about to charge that got me. And I have a telegram here for you that I took the opportunity to read. Looks like you're going to be famous, Mr. Roche."

"Why would I be famous?"

"Why your daguerreotypes of the Battle of Seven Pines, of course. Like I said, they are selling out," he said, sucking on his pipe. The smell annoyed Osborn. He tried to wave it away.

"We were still waiting on word from my publisher," said Osborn, taking one finger and pushing his spectacles up on his nose.

"I just so happen to have the very word you have been waiting for," said the general, pulling out and waving the telegram in the air. "A telegram from your publisher. If I might." The general brought it out an arm's length away and squinted. "Mr. Roche, congratulations are in order! Simply magnificent work. Forgive my late correspondence, but I have been selling out of your stereoview card photographs across the globe. Yes! Across the globe! Quite a considerable success. Also, we will launch this in a very large-sized photographic book. We are thinking fifteen inches tall, twelve wide. Make it big! Think of some titles for the book. We would appreciate your presence at its debut in Washington on May 12th. Please telegraph us post haste if you can attend. I will also set up meetings with the press for publicity. I know you do not like to do this, but it is simply essential and will send your career to new heights. We also have book signings scheduled for you in several other cities. You have become quite famous here in New York. All funds received so far have been transferred to your account. A complete accounting will be sent to you next week as per our agreement. Please keep me apprised of your whereabouts, and if it is possible, you can attend your book debut. Sincerely, Anders Anthony, The E. & H. T. Anthony & Company, Publishers & Distributors of Photographic Views." The general tossed the letter to Osborn. "Congratulations. You're famous. The next time I see you, I will expect an autographed copy."

"My pleasure, general. My pleasure."

"Safe travels," said the general before heading out the tent flap. The junior officers followed him out, all with a pleasing nod to Osborn as they exited.

"We're getting a portrait from a famous portrait man!" said the twin with the sergeant's stripes.

"How about that?" said Ray, raising his brows.

The face of the twin with the corporal stripes lit up. "You should paint 'The World-Famous' above your name on your wagon," he said, gesturing the sign in the air. "The World-Famous O. Roche Photography."

"I like that," said Ray.

"I like that too," said Osborn with a gleam in his eye. "And it would cover the bullet holes."

CHAPTER 16

"It's very busy here," said Osborn as Ray guided Hoady into the center of Nashville. The town bustled with activity: people walking and shopping, carriages traveling up and down, and a street musician playing My Days Have Been So Wondrous Free on the accordion. Osborn waved away the smells from street vendors selling fried fish, baked potatoes, and brandy balls before inserting his nose plugs.

"You getting worked up?"

"I'm feeling a bit anxious. The people and the smells."

"We could have camped outside of town with the division."

"I need my bath, Ray. I need my bath. Let's find us a place to stay quickly."

Ray passed by a meat pie vendor. "I gotta have one of those."

"What? What's that?"

"A meat pie. Want one? I'm gonna get me a meat pie."

"There is nowhere to stop, Ray. Find a place to stop first."

"Do you want one or not? Take the reins," said Ray.

"Please, thank you," replied Osborn as Ray jumped off the slow-moving wagon and headed to the meat pie vendor.

"Two, please." Ray handed him ten cents for the two pies and turned into two young women blocking his path. A blonde and brunette with powdered cheeks and dresses showing off their ankles. His eyes traveled from head to toe.

"Did you see this boy's eyes grope you, Hattie?" said the blonde.

"I did indeed. I could practically feel 'em," said Hattie as she sensually bit on her fingernail. "A man should buy a lady supper before she lets his eyes crawl over her curves like that. Don't ya think, Caroline? Those for me?" she said, her eyes on the meat pies.

"You're the portrait man," said Hattie as she wrapped one hand around the back of his neck.

"How did you know I'm the portrait man?"

"We saw you jump off that wagon," added Caroline.

"Come for a little poke?" said Hattie with a sly grin, forcing a laugh from Caroline. "How old are you?"

"Uh, I…" stammered Ray.

"We ain't good enough for ya? I can show you things you ain't never seen," said Caroline as they laughed again.

"Naw, it's just my uncle is just over…"

"Well, go on with ya, then. We've got work to do," said Hattie as she pushed Ray away. His heel caught a loose wood plank, tripping him into the entrance of an establishment and sending the two meat pies flying. Music and laughter filled the richly appointed room with red and gold wallpaper. Four men sat at the bar to the right, drinking and talking to a bartender. Scantily clad women walked about wearing bloomers and corset-covered blouses, while others sat on luxurious couches with men from all classes of life.

Ray went to his hands and knees, searching for the meat pies on the wood plank floors. Spotting the first, he crawled over to it. From there, he spotted the other. As he crawled to it, a yellow bell dress blocked his path. Her hand reached down, picking up his meat pie.

"Is this yours?" An attractive middle-aged woman towered over him with a blue equestrienne top hat cocked to the side. "Well, if you don't answer, I'll eat it."

Ray navigated the bustling boardwalk, weaving through the throng of people until he reached the wagon, where an irate Osborn awaited him. "Where did you disappear to?!" Osborn demanded, his voice edged with frustration.

Ray handed him a warm meat pie and gestured toward the saloon across the street. "I got us two rooms over yonder," he said calmly.

Osborn shifted on the wagon bench, his eyes scanning the busy sidewalk. The town buzzed with life around them. "What place?"

"The one over on that next street. See those young ladies at the boardwalk edge? There," said Ray, taking a bite and pulling up his pants at the back with one hand.

"Isn't that a saloon?"

"A hotel, too," he said with his mouth full.

Osborn did a double-take of the hotel ending on Ray. "I need a bath, Ray. I need a bath. I'm not staying there if there isn't a bath."

After stalling Hoady, Ray and Osborn hauled their bags inside. Osborn's eyes widened as he took in the room, filled with young ladies dressed in revealing clothing and wearing a bit too much makeup. "What kind of hotel did you get us, Ray?" he asked, his anxiety mounting. "I'd like to get to our rooms."

They began weaving through the crowded space, Osborn taking special care to avoid touching anyone. A parasol suddenly dropped before him as they passed a table, blocking his path. Osborn hesitated, the tension in his shoulders palpable as the lively chatter and laughter around them seemed to close in. "So, you're the portrait man," said the woman in the yellow dress.

"How did you know that? How did you know?"

"This boy here," she said, pointing to Ray.

"So, what is it? The boy says you're famous," said Hattie, sitting beside her.

"Yes, yes, they say I am."

Caroline stood, leaning against the wall. She circled a finger around her face and said, "Just like the boy, his eyes are looking everywhere but here." The ladies giggled.

Ray cleared his throat. "It's an artist thing."

"An artist thing, eh?" said Hattie, surveying Osborn. "Well, I'm a work of art. Would you like to photograph a work of art, mister?"

Osborn turned to Ray with a sick expression. The woman in the yellow dress raised her parasol and said, "All right, all right, ladies, it appears we have two gentlemen here. Treat them with respect. Please let me introduce myself. I am Miss Della, the owner of this establishment."

"A pleasure, Miss Della. And I am Osborn Roche, but I must be off…"

Again, her parasol dropped like a toll bridge pole, stopping him. "Indeed, it is a pleasure. A photographer, eh? Well, now, the ladies have suggested an interest in portraits from you. I would like to discuss a business proposition in connection with that."

"Well, certainly. We do both tintype and albumen paper prints…"

"Mr. Roche, why don't I buy you a drink?"

"I am sorry, Miss Della, but I do not partake in spirits."

"Oh, are you a godly man?"

"I am, but I admit I have been remiss in my attendance to the congregation."

Miss Della's index finger beckoned him to bend down. She leaned in, her lips brushing a little too close to his ear, and whispered, "Mr. Roche, I have more than spirits for you to choose from," she said, her words slow and deliberate, each syllable dripping with implication. "You do see a lot of fine, nice young ladies around me who would be delighted to meet a man of stature such as yourself and even, quite possibly, conduct a business exchange, such as, say, a portrait for a poke."

Osborn's eyes went to the ceiling. "I believe I need Ray."

"I'm sorry did I offend—"

"I'm right behind you. Please excuse us, Miss Della. I think Mr. Roche needs his rest."

Ray and Osborn headed up the stairs as Miss Della called to them, "You just think on it, Mr. Roche."

The sparse room featured a dresser in the corner and a window overlooking the alley, but its centerpiece was a big brass bed covered by a red quilt. Osborn sat on it, reading *Madame Bovary*, a gift from Lou. He had made it a habit to read up to the next folded page, where she had stopped. As he reached into his pocket for the familiar cloth, the bedsprings squeaked with every movement. A sudden knock at the door startled him. "Yes?" he called out.

Ray opened the door and leaned against the frame. "Good morning. Did you sleep well?"

"Yes. Quite."

Ray gawked at him, waiting. "Now you're supposed to ask how I slept."

"Oh, yes. Did you sleep well?"

"Yes, I did. Now come outside with me. Let's see Nashville. It's a beautiful day. We can take a look around. We can meet people."

"You know I don't enjoy meeting people, Ray."

"I can meet people then…like… girls. Traveling with an army doesn't provide many opportunities to meet girls, and we are in a city where there are girls."

"I don't want to meet girls."

"I know you don't. *I do.* You can just accompany me. You need to get out and see the sights."

"I want to read and take my bath today and get going tomorrow."

"Tomorrow? We just got here! I've never been to Nashville. You have to give it a week at least."

"A week? A week of not working?"

"At least five days. We've never taken a day off."

Osborn put his face back in his book. "Three days."

"If I can find work around here, will you stay longer? We can do them right in here. I'm sure Miss Della would let us. It'd bring in more potential customers for her."

Osborn looked him up and down. "All right, no more than four days, and we need at least six customers a day, and that's a summer holiday. That's a summer holiday." Osborn returned to reading as Ray shook his head.

"Fine by me. I'll round up some right quick," said Ray, accidentally bumping into Miss Della as she approached from behind. "Oh! Pardon me, Ma'am!"

"In a hurry, young man?" Her smile was a curious mix of a mother watching her son play baseball and a cat toying with a mouse.

"I'm sorry, Ma'am, just headed out."

"I'm here to see Mr. Roche on a... specific matter."

Ray grinned. "Of course, he needs to get out," he said, sidestepping around her. Miss Della entered and closed the door behind her. She sauntered across the room like an actress on stage, her parasol serving as a prop.

"Why, hello. I hope you are feeling better. Are you?" She released each word softly, her voice wrapped in a sweet Southern accent. "I am, thank you."

"I hope I was not the—"

"And are you feeling better today?" he interjected.

She paused, her mouth left open from his interruption. With a confused expression, she said, "Why... I... am just fine, thank you for—"

"You are welcome," he interrupted again, grinning at his perceived display of manners.

She cocked her head to the side and frowned. "Do you not like to look a lady in the eyes? Or have I offended?" Miss Della continued her saunter, her eyes narrowing slightly as she gauged his reaction.

"Please do not take offense. Do not take offense."

"I can understand that I do offend people in some circles. Not that I try to."

"No. Please, no. You have not offended me in any—"

"Are you shy?"

"Some would say that, but I'd say I just am of a peculiar nature as has been described to me."

"Peculiar, huh? That makes you considerably more interesting than most men," she said as her smile grew wider. "And I see a lot of men." She batted her eyes at half speed. "Mr. Roche, can you tell me your Christian name again?"

"Osborn."

"Would you mind if I called you by it?"

"Not at all, not at all."

"Is there a Mrs. Roche?" She tossed her hand back with a flair.

"No. Just myself and Ray, me and Ray."

"Your son?"

"My nephew."

She gestured to the book in his hand. "What's that you're reading?" Her demeanor quieted the room and made the moment stretch on. Osborn nervously smiled at the oddness of it.

He brought it up. "Madame Bovary by Flaubert." Osborn felt the weight of her gaze. The room seemed to hold its breath as he struggled to find his composure.

"Oh! I don't read much, but I've heard of that one. I've heard it is very scandalous. Just my kind of story."

"Is there anything I can help you with, Miss Della?"

"Ah, a man who gets down to business. A trait I find most appealing in a man. Why, yes, there is. Like I said last night, my girls would like to have portraits done."

"Yes, yes. Ray and I were thinking we might do portraits in here. In here, yes."

"Delightful. I can bring you several customers."

Osborn frowned. "Oh, but not a portrait for a poke, not a portrait for a poke, no."

"No?' she pouted.

"No, Ma'am. Not a portrait for a poke."

Miss Della stopped her sauntering and faced him. "Hmm, there is something about you, Osborn. Hmm," she said, tapping her finger on her pursed lips. "Indeed, you are peculiar, an interesting form of peculiar. But there is something else about you. Something I cannot put my finger on."

"No, you cannot. I do not like to be touched."

She stopped and leaned into him. "Touched? Really?" "

Really. I do not like the sensation."

"Like anywhere?"

"Correct, anywhere. I do not like to touch or be touched."

"Not even on the pecker?" she said with a deviously questioning tilt of her head.

His eyes opened. "Especially that."

"Hmm, interesting. Never met a boy who didn't like that."

"No, I cannot bear it, cannot bear it, no. There are only two people that have held my hand. My mother and a special friend."

"Ah. I see now. Who is this special friend?"

"Miss..."

"You don't have to tell me," she said quickly, continuing the saunter. "So, Mr. Roche, you are... forty?"

"Forty-one."

"You ever been married?"

"No."

"Got a special friend, never married. Hmmm. Is this special friend, a man?"

"No."

"I see, a woman. And she can touch you?" Miss Della winked at him.

"Not in the manner you are thinking. Not in that manner."

"Not in that manner? But you would like her to, hmm?"

"Miss Della!"

She sharply turned to him. "Miss, miss, miss Della!" She whipped up a smile quick as spit. "You've never been with a woman. I'll be." Her eyebrows jumped like they hit a bump in the road. "Probably never even seen a..." She coyly lifted her dress to her knees and quickly dropped it teasingly with a big laugh. She shook her head as Osborn's eyes opened wide. "Oh, stop! A woman's body ain't..."

"Your questioning is highly... vulgar. Nonetheless, I have seen a woman's body, but a friend told me it didn't count because she was dead. And the army commissary sells photographs... special photo- graphs. Twelve by fifteen-inch ones," he said, making 'L' shapes with his forefingers and thumbs. "They cost a dollar twenty for a dozen. Yes, a dollar twenty."

"Riveting. Do you have one with you? I'd love to see."

Osborn's mouth fell open, not understanding why a female would want to see one. "Why... no... I... have never purchased one myself. I've just seen them in the hands of others."

"You in love with this special friend?"

Osborn turned away from her. "The thing I truly desire is her friendship."

She grimaced. "Friendship? From a woman? That's a first."

"My past never held any friends for me, so I made up friends in my thoughts. Now that I'm famous I..."

"Famous? For what?"

"My battlefield photography has turned into two photographic books which, in turn, have made me very popular. Ray and I are heading to several, several book signings now."

"Well, I'll be. But anyway, get back to your special friend."

"Yes, well, so now that I'm famous, it seems I have many friends, which is something I always desired, but it's her friendship I want most. She is so much like me. Peculiar like me."

A smile as sweet grandmothers' rose on Miss Della's lips. "Peculiar? Yes, you seem to be, Osborn. Most peculiar indeed. But honey, if I can see anything, it's desire. And sweetheart, I can see you most indeedy-do desire her. I can feel it," she said, fingers jangling out to him like a witch casting a spell. "You want a whole lot more than a friendship with her."

Osborn shook his head and faked a laugh through puffs of air from his nose. "I would not make a good husband. As I said, I do not like to touch or be touched. I have held her hand, but I believe that would be all I could muster the courage to do."

"Hmm, interesting. Something I have never come across. But I believe I know how to solve this agonizing predicament; you see, it's like learning to swim, and the water is frigid cold. Your body will shiver from the icy temperature, but then you get used to it…" she said, bending down, her face inches from his. "And… you… swim…"

Osborn's blank expression wiped off her smile. She stood back up. "What I am trying to say, Osborn, is the cold water is a metaphor for a woman's touch on your body and, well, you see, learning to swim is a metaphor for… a… poke."

Osborn's jaw dropped, and his eyes blinked with shock. She continued ostentatiously moving about the small room with her parasol as her dance partner.

"You think I am flippant, but I assure you I am not. You must train yourself. Educate your body on the pleasures of a woman's touch. Your body will become used to it and learn to enjoy it."

"I do not like to be touched, Miss Della."

"So, you say." She sharply turned but continued her saunter. "But the secret is… You have to start by touching just the one, iddy, biddy, tiny… secret… spot. And trust me, I know men, and I mean all men, like that spot touched."

"I don't think—"

"It's simple body education, and I am a tenured professor in that science. If you desire this woman, you can have her, but she will want an educated man, I assure you. There is no other choice but to come downstairs with me on your arm…" She stopped and turned to him. "No! The touch thing, I remember. With me by *your side*, to make you comfortable, and we will select a girl that's to your liking. Sound good?"

Osborn sadly shook his head. Miss Della let out an exasperated breath. "Oh, boo! You disappoint me, Osborn. It's not often I am disappointed."

"I am sorry."

"Well, then, you will just have to take portraits of my girls then. You don't have to be touched. Just simple portraits."

"It'd be my pleasure. We can do them right in here, right here."

"Wonderful, wonderful," she said as she moved to the door, taking the knob in her hand. "Tomorrow night, then!" With a slam of the door, a pouting silence filled the air, as if the room itself were sulking with her absence.

CHAPTER 17

Drops of rain pinged against the tin roof of the room. The air was thick with the scent of developing fluid and the faint, musty odor of old wood.

"Please hold still and... Good. Thank you," said Osborn, adjusting his spectacles as he finished taking the photograph of a husband and wife. The couple, dressed in their Sunday best, looked slightly stiff but pleased. "Ray will develop the portrait next door and bring it to you downstairs in about fifteen minutes," Osborn informed them with a polite nod as they exited.

The couple left, and Ray swiftly followed, carrying the precious glass plate. As the door closed behind them, Miss Della entered, bringing with her a waft of perfume that momentarily masked the chemical tang of the room. She moved with the grace of someone accustomed to commanding attention, her presence instantly altering the room's atmosphere.

"That was your last customer. Can we start on my girls now?"

"Certainly, certainly."

"And you won't be shy, will ya?"

Osborn tilted his head to the side, confused. "Shy? No, I have been taking people's portraits for years."

Miss Della took the small oak chair and brought it next to Osborn, sitting in it. She leaned forward and lowered her voice. "Delightful because I want our portraits to be just like those army cards you spoke about."

Osborn's brow jumped. "Oh, dear. I don't do those kinds of portraits, Miss Della."

"Oh, boo! Osborn. You disappoint me again?" She pouted. "Can't you just avert your eyes?"

"I am the photographer."

"There must be a way," she said with the face of a child who dropped her ice cream cone. "Even if I did, it's Ray..."

"Your nephew?"

"Yes. He is only seventeen. It is not appropriate."

"Seventeen? Seventeen's old enough. Why, I knew what a doohickey was when I was knee high to a grasshopper."

Confused, he said, "Hmm?"

Miss Della leaned in and whispered, "Then do it without him."

"He is in the next room."

"Send him on an errand."

"I don't believe I need anything."

"Shhh!" She raised her thumb, gesturing towards Ray's room. "Make something up," she whispered, shaking her head and widening her eyes as if it were the most obvious thing in the world.

Ray walked in, holding the developed photo. "Uncle, I have the... Uh, what's going on here?"

Della and Osborn turned to face his suspicious gaze. "Uh, Ray, can you go out and find us some additional collodion?" Osborn asked.

"We have enough..."

"We'll need more. I'd appreciate it if you could do that now. Please, do it now."

Ray pointed to the ceiling. "And it's raining."

The pinging of raindrops suddenly ceased. Osborn pointed up. "I think it's stopping. Thank you, Ray."

Ray looked at the ceiling, then back at Osborn, wrinkling his nose as if he smelled a dead rat. Slowly nodding, he said, "All right, then. I'll need some money."

"Top drawer." Ray took the money and left.

As the door closed behind him, the room felt suspended in a moment of quiet tension. Osborn and Della exchanged glances, the corners of Osborn's mouth twitching into a nervous smile as he twisted his beard. Della arched an eyebrow and smirked, breaking the silence.

"Seems like you're quite the improviser, Osborn," she said, her voice dripping with irony. Osborn chuckled softly, the sound mingling with the last fading echoes of the rain.

Outside the staircase door stood Ray, peeking through the cracked door into the second-story hallway. The thin walls allowed the groans, laughing, squeals, and headboard banging through.

Miss Della exited a room first, her steps confident as she headed down the stairs. Osborn appeared next, crossing the hallway to Ray's room, emerging moments later with the portable development desk. Just a minute later, Miss Della returned, leading a beautiful young woman by the hand. The woman wore a green kimono robe adorned with yellow serpents, open at the top to reveal a corset-covered blouse that pushed her smallish breasts into an almost comically exaggerated position. Her feet were clad in stylish purple shoes and white socks with frilly collars.

Miss Della opened Osborn's door and ushered the girl inside.

Ray's eyes widened, and he couldn't contain himself. He jumped up and down, punching the air with his fists and covering his mouth to stifle his laughter or a scream. After about twenty seconds, he calmed down, shaking his head in disbelief as a massive smile crept across his face.

With his eyes wide, Ray could not stop himself from jumping up and down, punching the air with his fists, and covering his mouth to stop himself from laughing or screaming out. After twenty seconds, he calmed, shaking his head with disbelief as a massive smile crept upon his face. "Good on you, old man. Good on you!"

In the room, Osborn sat fidgeting with his camera, refusing to acknowledge them. Della released the girl's hand. "Wait in the hall a minute," Della told the girl, who walked back out.

Della shut the door behind her and approached Osborn with concern on her face. "You all right, Osborn? You look a little tense."

"I am feeling a little tense, a little tense."

"Don't put too much on it. I told my girls not to touch ya, and I ain't expecting you to do anything but take portraits. Only if ya change your mind or ya get to feeling a bit randy, my girls would oblige ya. Remember now, it might be a good thing for ya, Osborn. I believe you should think on it. It's educating your body, as I said, and ya might like it. I am certain it'd help you be more husband-like to that gal you're sweet on. Keep that in your thoughts. My girls could help with all that, I expect."

Osborn stared blankly at her. "Well, then, I am physically prepared for the first."

"I do hope you enjoy yourself, Mr. Roche." Della left, and the green kimono entered. She walked over to the dresser, crossed her arms, and scrutinized him before putting her hands on her hips. The bright colors of her clothes and painted face made Osborn anxious. He dove under the camera shroud.

"Where'd ya go?" she asked.

Osborn pulled out his hand and waved to her. "I am under here. Under here." His fingers wrapped around the brass lens cap and twisted it off. Her inverted image came into view.

"How should I be? Standing or sitting?" she asked as she sat in the chair and crossed her legs.

"However, you feel most comfortable. Most comfortable."

She stood up, walked around the chair, and threw her leg over. "Standing. I'm on my back all day. Shall I take off my clothes now?" Not waiting for his reply, she dropped her robe.

He tensed but calmed himself with a deep breath, and his thoughts went to his camera. The tension fell from him like the woman's robe from her body. The lens, the bellows, and the view glass stood between himself and her. His concentration went to his art, and her nakedness became a beautiful object to capture in a photograph.

She came into focus as he pulled apart the leather bellows. "I am Osborn Roche. What is your name?"

Her name popped out of her like a playful burp. "Peg."

"A pleasure, Peg. May I ask you a question?"

"Yep."

"Can you tell me of a pleasant Christmas morning in your childhood?"

Peg's eyes went to the ceiling before she shrugged her shoulders and jutted her chin out to him. "Why?"

Osborn came out from under the shroud. "Excuse me?"

"Why do you want to know that?"

Osborn slid the dark board in with the wet plate. "It helps me reveal you. To see more than the outer you."

"You reveal me?" She glanced down at her nakedness. "I'm the one revealing to you."

Osborn spoke with the soft kindness of a grandfather and said, "What I mean is, I'd like you to tell me of a pleasant Christmas morning because the audience of the photograph will see more than your skin. More than skin."

"They don't want to see that, Mister. Everyone just wants to see the tits and fanny. That's how it is." Both her voice and expression flashed resentment toward him. It confused him. He put his hand at the ready on the lens cap.

"But I believe the..."

"Take the fucking portrait, mister."

He sucked in a breath and flashed his eyes at her before saying, "Please hold still," and pulling off the lens cap. "Those are not the manners for a lady. Thank you." She covered her nakedness with the kimono.

"That it?" she asked, walking to the door.

"Yes, yes." Osborn removed the plate and walked over to his portable development desk.

"Send the next one in?"

"No, not yet, please." A quick and unusual encounter for him, but he knew he had the portrait he wanted before the image exposed itself to him through the red glass. Soaking it in the last bath, her soul floated up and hovered there. The pubic hair, breasts, hips, and waist of a woman stood with one stylish purple shoe defiantly up on the chair. But the photograph revealed something else beneath the surface. There she stood, a scared little girl hiding from painful memories that she would like forgotten.

He set it to dry and prepared the next wet plate. The joy of capturing what he needed fighting with the thought of her anguish. "I'd like to meet the next lady," he called out.

The next girl entered, similarly dressed but with no corset under the barely tied robe. She walked directly to Osborn sitting at the desk, both arms still inside the dark box. She stood centimeters from his shoulder.

"You can make yourself comfortable over on that far wall. I'll be right with you, right with you."

"Della says I ain't supposed to touch you," she uttered in a scratchy voice. "Unless ya want me too."

Osborn finished the wet plate but kept his arms in the box. A tall woman, she towered over his left shoulder, staring down at the top of his head. "Hey," she said playfully. "My name's Francine. I heard yours is Osborn." His hands pretended to work inside the development box. "Hey," she repeated as she dropped her robe to the floor.

"Please stand over there. Over there." He turned to the left and nodded to the wall behind her. His eyes flashed wide with her brown triangle of pubic hair twelve inches from his nose.

She grinned at his reaction. "Would you like to take a portrait of that?"

"Thank you, no. Thank you, no. Please pose over there."

"Fine by me." She strolled over to the background, leaned against the wall and brought her nails to her mouth. Huffing a moist breath first, she polished them on her breast and asked, "Sitting or standing?"

He studied her as he walked over to his camera. "Whatever you feel most comfortable. Most comfortable, yes." Osborn dropped under the shroud to focus when a thought came to him; It's perspective. I'll change the angle. "No, on second thought, can you sit?"

"Sure." She sat in the chair as he brought a box over and placed the tripod on top. He took a book and put it under the camera's backside, angling it down to her. "Whatcha doing?" she asked.

"Finding out who you are."

"Told ya already. Francine."

"Francine, may I ask you a question?"

"Sure, you can." She spread her legs apart. "Want my legs like this?"

He brought her into focus and came out from the shroud. "However, you feel most comfortable, most comfortable. May I ask you a question?"

"Already said ya could. You say everything twice? Are you gonna take my portrait?"

"You ever go to the fair in your youth?"

"Course I did. Didn't everybody?"

"Yes, yes. Now, tell me a story of when you were there and had the best day ever."

Francine's attention moved about the room as Osborn had his fingers on the lens cap. She shook her head as if a mosquito landed on her cheek. "You have another question? I ain't had no good days there."

"Uh, well, sure. Yes, yes. Can you tell me of a pleasant Christmas morning in your childhood?"

Osborn watched the wheels turn in her head with the tiny motions of her brows, lips, and cheeks. A slight, quick wince preceded her tear filled eyes coming to him. "Please hold still."

He replaced the lens cap as she shook away the feeling. "That's it?" she asked.

Osborn came down from the box with the plate. "Can you send the next lady in?" Francine raised her eyebrows and left.

The door opened, and the third girl entered. "I'll be right with you. Need to develop one and prepare yours. Prepare yours."

Her painted face strolled over to him with curious green eyes. He glanced up at her before turning back to his work. She also wore a silk robe, a purple one with red flowers. Instead of stylish shoes, she wore a pair of large, worn men's cowboy boots. Without saying a word, she meandered over to the wicker-backed chair in the corner, sat in it, crossed her legs, and leaned over, resting her arms on the top leg. With a tiny stick, she picked her teeth.

Osborn finished the plate and brought it to the camera. "Please, it'll be this chair over here. Over here," he said, pointing.

She rose and walked over, shuffling her boots across the floor like a bored child. She sat in the chair and pulled a whiskey flask from her pocket, taking a swig. Her attitude suggested a reduction in leg height on the tripod. He wanted her to be as dominant as her attitude in the portrait. She scraped tooth plaque with the stick before turning to him. "You want to fuck me after this? Della says you don't like to touch. You'd like to touch this." She dropped her robe to her waist. Osborn's eyes explored her skin, but what he searched for lay far beneath it. He went back under the shroud to focus.

Staring directly into the lens, she asked, "What? You like boys?"

Osborn came out from the shroud and put his hand on the lens cap. "Of course. I am a boy." He waited a long moment before asking, "Do you? Do you like boys?"

Quiet as a whisper, she replied, "No."

"Please hold still."

After the last girl left the room, Miss Della flung the door open with the portraits in her hand. Osborn caressed the smooth finish of the camera as he sat at the development desk. Miss Della ogled him, hoping he would turn to her; her lips turned to a frown.

"I'm sorry, Miss Della," he said as he fidgeted with his camera, unable to look at her.

Her eyes flashed with surprise. "About what? That ya didn't let none of my girls tutor you? You're a sweet one, Osborn. Too sweet for this world."

"No, the portraits."

She shook her head with confusion and brought them up in her hand. "What's wrong with them? They are exactly what I wanted. Seductive. I can see why you're famous."

Osborn jerked his head back. "Don't you see more?"

"More?"

"Yes. It's in their expressions, their eyes." He walked over to her and pointed to the portrait of the first girl, Peg. "You don't see that?"

She shook her head. "She looks beautiful, spicy, seductive. One of my best girls."

"Look at her eyes. Her soul is there. I revealed all their souls in those portraits. That is what you are seeing, what you are seeing. To create a beautiful portrait, I need to reveal more about them. Reveal their soul. All the master painters did it."

She scrutinized the photograph. "Soul? Hmm, well, that's nice, Osborn. But I see seduction and money in these."

"You call it seduction, but I see pain. The portraits reveal their pain. There seems a high level of anguish in each of them. Can you see it there?" His eyes moved to Peg in her hands. "They have had tragic pasts, or they are disgusted by what they are doing with all these strange men. They have never been loved or have lost it somewhere," he said as Miss Della's eyes filled with tears. "Look at each portrait, and you'll find…"

"Why would you tell me this, Osborn?"

He stopped. "Pardon?"

"Have I not been kind?"

Osborn stiffened. "Forgive me, Miss Della. I did not…"

Miss Della's sweet voice went hoarse. "Why would you be so cruel to me?"

Osborn blinked rapidly. "I don't understand."

Miss Della pulled out a handkerchief, wiped a tear from her eye, and said, "I believe this collaboration of ours has come to an end, Mr. Roche."

Osborn stood, soaking wet in the darkness of the night, the rain camouflaging the tears streaming down his cheeks. Hoady waited patiently, already hitched to the wagon behind him. Ray rounded the corner, about to ascend the back staircase of the saloon, when a faint whimpering in the darkness stopped him. He turned and squinted, trying to make out the figure in the gloom.

"Uncle?" Ray called out. He approached slowly, his shock growing with each step.

"She kicked us out, Ray. She kicked us out."

"What?"

"Miss Della kicked us out, Ray."

"What happened?"

"She kicked us out!"

"You said that? But why?"

"I saw her girls, Ray, naked!" Osborn slammed his foot down in the mud.

"It's all right, Uncle. So, Miss Della is angry at you for seeing them naked? But I thought…"

"No, she's angry at me for seeing much more than that! I saw their complete nakedness. I don't understand women!" He slammed his foot into the mud again.

"All right, we'll talk about it later. Let's get you into the wagon. I'll drive."

"I got out all our stuff. All our stuff."

"That's good. Let's light the stove in there and get you warm. We'll just find a spot away from here."

Ray helped Osborn into the wagon and loaded the stove with firewood. Osborn wrapped himself in a blanket, shivering. "I didn't get paid for the portraits neither, Ray. Not for the portraits."

"Can't win 'em all, Uncle." Ray lit the stove, the warmth slowly beginning to fill the space. He stepped back out into the rain, climbed up onto the wagon bench, and urged Hoady forward. The horse's hooves plunged into the mud as they set off through the cold, relentless downpour.

Osborn's voice rang out from the back, echoing through the night. "And I never got my bath!"

CHAPTER 18

It took nineteen, twelve-hour days of travel to reach Washington. The wagon carried them down Constitution Avenue toward the White House. Since the beginning of the war, it had been occupied by thousands of encamped troops, supply dumps, horse stables, mess halls, and latrines. The capital city stank like a cesspool.

The E. & H. T. Anthony & Company, Osborn's publisher, had made arrangements for them to stay at the finest hotel in the city, the Willard, on the northwest corner of 14th Street and Pennsylvania Avenue, a block from their offices. They arrived mid-day and found a stable to park the wagon and house Hoady.

The Willard was the grandest hotel they had ever seen, with a continuous brick facade curving smoothly around the corner. A doorman greeted them, opening the door for them like royalty. They entered one of the three giant halls with two broad oak staircases leading to the rooms. They walked up to the front desk clerk, a perfectly dressed gentleman thirty years of age.

"Mr. Roche, a delight. We have been expecting you for days," said the clerk. He leaned over the counter, putting his hand to the side of his mouth and whispering, "Your publisher showed me your latest book. Just brilliant."

Amazed by the grandeur of the room, Osborn didn't hear him. "Thank you. Very kind of you," replied Ray as he signed the guest ledger for them.

"You have the suite. Seventh floor."

A line of people stood outside the E. & H. T. Anthony & Company's bookseller shop, waiting for Osborn to sign their copy of his book, Portraits Of A Nation Divided: The Battle of Seven Pines. Osborn's anxiety grew with the size of the line.

"I will ask their name, and you will write it, then write something like, 'nice to meet you,' then sign your name," explained Ray. "You don't even have to look up. Maybe say thank you or something and hand them back the book, and we'll move on to the next person."

"Thank you, Ray. That should work."

His head down, Ray's plan worked until the eighth person. Through his lowered brow, Osborn spied two pairs of trousers. He stuck out his hand for a book and took it, but Ray said nothing.

"Ray? Ray? Name, please."

"I'm so proud of you, Osborn. You're now the most famous photographer in the world." Osborn's eyes snapped to Lou's flickering irises beaming at him. His painful longing slipped away, happily drowning in the pools of her eyes, floating down into their depths with the dying smile of Romeo on its lips.

"Hello," he said. "How would you like me to sign your book?"

She handed her copy to him and said, "To my best friend Lou."

She waited for him to finish and said, "…with love, Osborn."

His left hand reached out to hers, taking it in his grasp as he wrote the final words. Ray's mouth went slack at their touch. Osborn flipped her book shut and reunited with her gaze as he held her hand, not wanting to release it.

"Uncle, I know you… probably… well, there is a long line…" said Ray empathetically.

"Can you wait for me? Wait for me?" Osborn asked.

"I've been waiting my whole life for you, Osborn. Another couple hours won't matter much."

When the four last people stood in line for their books to be signed, Osborn continually turned to Lou as she waited with her uncle Ben against the far wall.

"Name?" asked Ray of the next person in line.

"John," said the man, staring at the top of Osborn's head, hoping for him to recognize him. "I loved your photographs, sir. I wish I was there with ya." Osborn signed without giving the man what he wanted most, his attention, because his attention stood twenty feet away.

"Thank you," said Ray as he took the next book and laid it down before Osborn. "Name?" Ray asked the third to last person in line before turning to their publisher's representative, Anders, standing next to him. Ray said, "The batch of photographs you hold in your hand were mostly taken at Antietam. I'm telling you, Anders, they are amazing. It should be another book. And Osborn wrote quotes and stories beneath each one. It's like he tells stories with every photograph. You will see."

"Wonderful. I will get these to my boss right away. So, the next three stops on the itinerary are Baltimore, Philadelphia, and New York. You will present a copy of the book to General Howard at his home in Baltimore. All of the newspapers will be there," said Anders.

"Name?" asked Ray to the second to last person, and turning back to Anders, asked, "Who is this?"

"General Howard? Osborn photographed him as he sat wounded. He lost his arm from that wound and received the Medal of Honor. He is recovering at his home in Baltimore. You will present a signed book to him in front of the papers."

"Name?" asked Ray and, bending down to his uncle, said, "This is your last book, Uncle."

Osborn finished and handed the book to the last woman as she grinned like a thrilled schoolgirl at Osborn. Ray told her. "Thank you," for him.

With his eyes stuck on Lou, Osborn rose and walked over to her, arms raised for an embrace. Her arms went up in expectation of it before he stopped inches away, dropped his arms, and took a step back. "How have you been?" he asked.

"I've been…"

"We should get on outta here," interrupted Ben. "I need to talk to y'all about something. When's your nephew coming?"

They stood grinning at each other like two naughty children as Osborn said, "Shortly. They are working out our itinerary for the tour."

"So, y'all be headed out of the city?" asked Ben.

"Day after tomorrow," Osborn said absently.

With a concerned expression, Ben said, "Hmm. Maybe you should make it tonight."

Osborn sat across from Lou at a small table for two in the vast expanse of the Willard Hotel's dining room. The room was so large that waiters prayed their food wouldn't get cold on the journey from the kitchen to the tables. Three years prior, it had hosted twelve hundred guests for a ball in honor of British minister Lord Napier, but now, at two in the afternoon, it was nearly empty. Osborn and Lou's meals sat before them, barely touched.

Lou's finger idly traced the rim of her wine glass. "It seems like forever since I saw you last," she said.

"But it wasn't forever. I believe it has been only seven months. Seven months, yes. Oh, and eight days."

Lou smiled at him. "You haven't eaten much."

"I, well, I am not very hungry. And you, as well. You are not hungry?"

"No. Me too. It's because I'm so happy to see you, Osborn. Are you happy to see me?"

Osborn twisted his beard. "Yes, yes, very."

They both fell silent, the clinking of cutlery from a distant table the only sound breaking the stillness. Lou held her hands on her knees under the table. Osborn grinned, leaned over, and lifted the tablecloth to her fingers moving about. He returned to her smiling face, and she brought her hands up to show him. "Yes, still doing it. Did you miss me, Osborn? I missed you."

"I did. Yes, indeed. You should read the box of letters I wrote to you but didn't know where to send."

Her face brightened. "Box of letters?! Oh, I have to read them." "I wrote I miss you at the end of each one. Sometimes I'd even write it at the beginning."

"How many letters?"

"Sixty-eight."

Lou gasped and said, "Sixty-eight? That is the sweetest thing."

"Yes, all on albumen photographic paper. Ray was quite upset at that. Quite upset."

Ray and Ben sat a few tables over, speaking in low voices. Ben waved his hand at them and called out, "Hey, if you're finished with your meals, come on over so we can talk."

Osborn and Lou reluctantly rose, walked over to their table, and sat with them. Ben took a pull from his whiskey glass, turned to Lou, and said, "Ya know how we spoke about you going with them? You still good with that?"

"Yes."

The question confused Osborn. "Going with us?"

"Yep. Like I was telling your nephew here, her father was going to do something awful to her." He leaned closer to Ray and Osborn, put his hand to the side of his mouth, and whispered, "He was gonna take her to a doctor and fix her so she can't have children. Now that's just meaner than a sheep-killing dog." Ben took his hand away and sat straight. "Yeah, but that doctor shit… That ain't gonna happen on my watch. I just packed up the second wagon, put her in it, and left him there. He's gotta be madder than a mama wasp. But he'll be looking for her, that's for sure."

Ray turned to Osborn. "I suppose we can take her on the book tour with us," said Ray.

"Certainly," said Osborn.

Ben shook his head. "No, ya can't. Soon as the advertisement about your book tour was in the paper, she found it and was looking at it every day. I mean every day. Henry finally took it away from her and ripped it up. She just found another one."

"And I bought some of your stereoviews. Although I don't have a viewer," said Lou.

"I knew these two took a liking to each other early on and told Henry as such. I know he's figuring I'll bring 'em together. But they should be. I believe it's God's will; it is. But the thing is, he knows your tour. Every stop."

"What do you suggest we do?" asked Ray.

"Don't do it. If they gonna be together, I'd suggest you end your book tour right here and now. I know him. He won't stop until he finds her."

"We will leave the book tour, Ray. For Lou's safety."

"Leave the tour? Are you sure about that, Uncle?"

"We must."

"Then I gotta tell Anders. He will not be happy," said Ray.

"I'm sure he will be happy after seeing my next batch. And we can also sign some books, sign some books, yes. I'll do them for him tonight, and he could sell those. They think highly of me. They will understand."

Ray tapped his fingers on the table and said, "I hope so. You have been with that publisher since the beginning."

"I'll be headed out in the morning. I'd suggest you all do the same," said Ben.

Ray sat back, taking a deep breath through his nose. "I suppose.

How much stuff she got? We don't have much room."

"One suitcase."

"That's good."

"Yeah, nothing much," said Ben before turning to her and placing his hand on her shoulder. "You want it this way, right, girl?"

Simultaneously, Osborn and Lou both said, "I do."

CHAPTER 19

"Do you remember when we worked together on Miss Tabitha?" asked Lou. She sat with Osborn and Ray in front of the campfire. Seven hours of awkward silence sat with them since they left Washington. Osborn, relieved she broke the silence, closed his eyes, and nodded slowly.

Lou tilted her head at him as if she'd seen a cuddly kitten and said, "Aww, was it that special for you?"

"Uh, oh, no. I was just thinking, uh, yes, I remember that night."

"Remember the sleepover? That was fun."

Ray shook his head and stood. "I do not want to know, and I believe I must see to my necessaries," he said before walking into the night.

Osborn stuck his index finger into the air, recalling. "The sleepover. Of course I do. I remember."

"Do you remember the story you made up about Miss Tabitha?"

"Yes, yes, I remember it. I have a good memory."

"Can you tell me the story? I remember you said she got married."

"Yes, Tabitha and I met when I lived in Philadelphia. She became my friend, and she wanted me to call her Tabby. She always wanted to talk to me. She didn't care about my peculiarities, my anxieties. She and I became real good friends. I mean, not very best friends like you and me are—"

"Are we again?" asked Lou. "Because you were awful quiet on the way here."

"Always, Lou." The night hid her blushed cheeks. "Anyway, we got married, the end."

Her head twisted to him. "Wait! You got married?! You told me you didn't want to ever get married."

Two distant gunshots cracked the sky from the Union camp a half-mile up the road. Drunk soldiers played fiddles and drums.

Ray pulled up his suspenders as he returned to them from the darkness. "We should have set up further back," Osborn called out to Ray. "Keep a bit away from the boys yonder, a bit away, yes."

"They'll sleep soon," replied Lou, picking up the plates from them. "I'll clean the dishes over in the creek."

"Uh, no. No, Lou. I will do that," said Osborn. "You two cooked supper. I'll clean up."

"Uh, well, I will escort you. These boys are young and a bit raucous. A bit raucous."

"I'd love the company just the same," she said. Osborn picked up the pot and brought it as Lou brought the tin plates and utensils. They walked in the moonlight toward the creek. "Is it strange having me with you and Ray? Is that why you were so quiet? I don't want to get in between you two."

"Ah! You said it. The 'strange' word. It's not strange—" He turned to her profile. Moonlight reflected off the creek water behind her.

She interjected, "It's peculiar."

"Yes. It is peculiar, but it's the best kind of peculiar, and I am pleased to have you with us." They reached the river and squatted to clean their dishes.

"The first day we met, you told me about your mother," said Lou.

"A rose in a sea of grass, she was. She had the posture and elegance of the finest stallion and held her head high as a proud queen. I loved my mother. The only person I could ever stand to touch me. My only friend. Until now."

"She had the same eye condition I do?"

"Yes, but God painted hers green."

"Was she ever teased?"

"I don't believe so, or she never told me. Very little made my mother smile and even less made her sad. I am a lot like her in that way. At only two events did I ever see my mother express emotion: Funerals and weddings. At funerals, she would dab her eyes with her handkerchief, and at weddings, I would see her small crease of a smile."

"Other children made fun of my eyes—called them names."

"Your eyes are beautiful. God painted them in the prettiest of colors."

"You are the sweetest man in all creation."

They stood and shook the water from their dinnerware as best they could before returning. Away from the creek, the open field revealed a star-filled sky above it. Ray sat by their campfire some fifty yards in the distance. She stopped, turned to Osborn, and said, "I won't get in the way, Osborn. I promise I won't get between you and Ray."

"That was never my concern, never my concern. I believe I feel anxious, anxious, yes. You asked if I missed you before. I don't believe I have ever missed someone before, and with you, yes, I missed you, and now here you are. Here you are, yes. I am happy. Happy anxious, happy anxious, yes."

The moonlight reflected off a tear in her eye. She shook it off with a giggle before turning and running back to the wagon like a schoolgirl playing hide and seek. She yelled back to him, "I've never had someone like you. I've never had a friend, let alone a best friend."

She ran to the wagon and helped Ray put away the stools for the night. Left alone on the field, Osborn said to himself, "Me either. Me either."

Osborn walked over and followed Ray into the wagon. Lou stood by the door, and Osborn turned back to her, attempting to read her face.

"Where… should I sleep?" she asked cautiously.

"Oh, yes. A lady. We must have protocols. New protocols," said Osborn as he searched the room nervously. "What will you require? I've never lived—"

"I know what she needs, Uncle," said Ray, appraising the room. "Lou, you can sleep here on Uncle's bed, and we'll have to move the gear off the bunk beds."

"No, no. We cannot do that, Ray. Must not. It will be disorganized. I cannot have it disorganized."

"Then just off one bed. Move that to the floor," said Ray. "No, no. Disorganized. I need it a certain way."

"Then you figure it out, Uncle. I just gave you two suggestions."

"Lou takes my bed. I take your bed on the floor, and you can hang the hammock above me. It'd be a quick clean-up in the morning."

Ray clapped his hands. "I love the hammock. Sounds like a great idea."

Lou grinned. "Wonderful," she said.

"And each evening, you may dress first for bed and in the morning—"

"I wear long johns like you all do. I don't have any lady unmentionables."

Silenced, a flush came across Osborn and Ray's cheeks.

"Oh, I hope that wasn't inappropriate to mention. What I mean is… Well, all right I'll dress and let you know when I'm in bed."

"Yes, and in the morning, Ray and I can dress outside."

"Or I could just face the wall if it's too cold," added Lou.

"Delightful, delightful," said Osborn.

Ray rolled his eyes. "Okay, then. We shall exit for you to dress, and I'll retrieve the hammock from the cabinet below."

The men climbed out, and she climbed in. "Have a wonderful time getting dressed," said Osborn.

"Thank you," replied Lou before she shut the door.

Ray came in close to Osborn. "Have a wonderful time getting dressed? Why would you say that?" Osborn's mouth opened, unsure. Ray continued in a low voice, "You're anxious. Think about what you say. I know you like her, but that was stup—" Osborn tapped his foot with a pinched expression. "I mean, well, just think about it more. Try to say things a fine gentleman would say."

"Thank you, Ray." Ray turned and opened the outside cabinet below the wagon bed, pulling out the hammock. Osborn walked back up to him and asked, "What would a fine gentleman say?"

"I don't know, just not that."

"But—"

"Well, maybe, like, 'May I close the door for you?' or 'We'll be right out here' or 'Let me know if you need anything.'"

Osborn tapped his forefinger on his lips. "Yes, yes. I see. Thank you again, Ray."

The following morning, Osborn woke up to Ray's back in the hammock above him. He turned to Lou, already awake, smiling down at him. "You must like the floor. You're in the same spot I found you in my tent that morning."

"I suppose, yes, I suppose I am."

"I've been watching you sleep," she said. "You're quiet, but Ray snores."

"I don't snore?" asked Osborn.

"Not that I heard. At least not this morning. Did you hear me snore last night?"

"Snoring can't be as bad as someone talking before others have woken up," interrupted Ray.

"I'm sorry—"

A knock on the door stopped them. They turned to it. "Hello. I heard y'all awake in there. Want to find out when y'all are gonna be setting up shop?"

Ray stepped out of his hammock and unhooked it. "We're gonna have some breakfast first," said Ray, balling up the hammock and opening the door to a Rebel soldier.

The soldier grinned up at Ray. "Oh, morning. Sorry to wake ya. There's a herd of us wanting a tintype. Our last daguerreotype man left us."

Osborn sat up from the floor, his eyes locking on the gray uniform. "Give us an hour. We'll be right with you."

"Thank you, sir," replied the Rebel.

Ray shut the door and turned to Osborn's wide eyes. "What happened to the Union?" Ray whispered.

"Must have moved out. Let's dress and get to work," said Osborn. All three put on their clothes as fast as they could. They froze at another knock.

"Give us a minute. We'll be right with you," said Ray.

"Naw, can't give ya a minute. Ya gotta open the door now, I 'spect," said a different southern voice. Ray opened the door to a Rebel colonel on horseback. He had his pistol in his hand, resting on his saddle pommel. Two other soldiers stood, pointing Fayetteville rifles at them. "Hello, Captain Roche," said the colonel. "Let me introduce myself. I am Colonel Thomas T.

Munford, commander of the Second Virginia Cavalry." The colonel spoke with a slow, calm confidence weaved into the drawl of a fine southern gentleman. "I saw that stereoview card of yours. General Howard? Quite a photograph. Heard he lost an arm. He's a crazy son bitch too. They were speakin' 'bout that photo in the papers. But they also mentioned the photographer is Captain Osborn Roche of the Union army. It was all in the papers."

"It's an honorary title, sir. He's a photographer," said Ray.

"Yessir, that's what I read. Alls I gotta do is make sure y'all ain't got no weapons in there. So, get on outta there and let my boys check."

They all climbed out with their hands held high. One soldier went in while one checked their clothes. After checking Lou, the private backed off, confused. "This one's a gal," said the private.

"How's that?" asked the colonel.

"I just touched her titty."

"Touched a titty? Well, lucky you, son," said the colonel, turning to Lou. "You a gal?"

"Yes, sir."

"That's fine," said the colonel indifferently. "Forgive my man's impropriety."

"No weapons," said the private, ransacking the wagon. "Delightful. So, now, my commanding officer is Major General Jeb Stuart of the Army of Northern Virginia and the 1st Virginian Cavalry, and it seems you have arrived on a prodigious day. The general has requested a full field review by General Lee. He has named it the 'La grande revue befitting his reputation of a beau sabreur.' It will include all of our nine thousand calvary and four batteries of horse artillery, and we will be charging in replicated battle," said the colonel before shaking his head. "All this right before a fight with the Yankees." He turned back to Osborn. "When we rode in early this morning, the general saw your wagon and requested your presence at the review for portraits, and after that, he'd like the honor of meeting Captain Osborn Roche and breaking bread thereto. Do you accept this invitation?"

"Of course I do. Most certainly. Most certainly," said Osborn.

"Delightful, then return to your wagon and follow along."

Osborn, Lou, and Ray sat on their wagon's bench, following the colonel and his two regular soldiers down the road and deeper into the camp filled with thousands of Confederate troops. Although they had set up sometime in the night, it looked like they had been there for ages. The road became thick with men headed in the same direction to watch General Stuart in his grand review. Other troops marched in the distance, some in roll call, others ate breakfast. Osborn, Lou, and Ray passed by soldiers shaving, writing letters home, and playing card games.

Ray turned to Osborn and said, "What in the Sam Hill did we get into?"

"I believe we will be fine, Ray."

Ray turned to Osborn in surprise. "Well, look who's the calm one."

Reaching the parade grounds, Osborn and Ray set up the camera and tripod. They saw the Rebel cavalry preparing in the distance. "May I do something to help?" Lou asked.

"I believe we have it," said Ray.

"I would like to help."

"There is nothing to do, Lou. Go ahead and wait on the wagon bench and enjoy the show."

Colonel Munford galloped over to them. "We shall start shortly, coming from the East. The general would like a photograph as we pass by."

Osborn shook his head. "But it will be blurry. I cannot have you moving."

"But your photograph of General Howard? Didn't—"

"He had fallen off his horse. He wasn't moving. He wasn't moving."

"I will inform the general," said Munford before galloping away.

The onlookers applauded the soldiers on parade. Osborn turned to Lou up on the bench behind him. Her sad expression called to him. "Stay by the camera just in case they stop. I wish to sit by Lou."

"But, well, alright," said Ray.

Osborn walked over and climbed up, sitting next to her. "Have you seen General Lee?"

"No." Lou's moving fingers twitched about faster than usual. "Are you all right?"

"I think I miss my father. This is the first time I've been apart from him."

"But, but he was going to…"

"Yes, he didn't want us to be together, and I'm a grown woman now. But I still miss him. I can't help it. To me, he was like how Ray is to you."

"I unders—" The sound of bugles turned both their heads. He handed her nose plugs, and they both set them in their ears. The audience applauded as cavalry officers charged out toward invisible enemies, swords drawn. Behind them, horse-pulled artillery crossed the field with divisions of marching troops following behind.

Newspaper reporters and civilians stood among the crowd of soldiers. Osborn searched the crowd and said, "I wonder if Lee is here. I would relish a portrait with him." A rush of warmth ran up his neck as he felt Lou's hand clasp his on the seat. He turned to it, then to her. From the side of her eye, she watched Osborn instead of the parade.

With a grin, he turned back to the parade and said, "This is quite a spectacle, isn't it?"

"A wonderful spectacle," she replied.

Colonel Munford came galloping from the head of the columns of men, accompanied by six other cavalrymen, including the dashing General Stuart himself. Stuart sat atop his horse, dressed in his finest uniform with a red-lined gray cape over his shoulders, a yellow sash around his waist, a hat cocked to the side with an ostrich plume, completed with a red flower in his lapel. Ray turned to Osborn with urgency, motioning with his hand to come over for the portrait.

"Sirs, please take our portrait now. We will hold steady," called out Colonel Munford.

Lou's hand felt warm and soft on his. He turned to Ray with a smile on his lips, saying, "You can take this one, Ray. You can take this one."

A master carpenter had crafted the dining table from the heart of a massive oak tree felled in the woods near General Stuart's home in Patrick County,

Virginia. The single slab of oak, twelve feet long and three and a half feet wide, boasted a lacquered finish that brought out the rich brown and yellow hues of the wood, polished to smooth perfection. Around this impressive table sat Ray, Lou, and Osborn, joined by Colonel Munford and five other cavalry officers: Brigadier Generals Wade Hampton, W.H.F. "Rooney" Lee, Beverly H. Robertson, William E. "Grumble" Jones, and Major Robert F. Beckham. They all awaited General Stuart's arrival.

"...the only weapon to fight it as they capture a moment of it, like capturing one soldier from time's endless army of soldiers," Osborn concluded his usual eloquent speech.

Colonel Munford laughed heartily, shaking a finger at Osborn. "I truly enjoy this man here. And yes! He does his part, contributing to the historical record of the war for southern independence."

They all sat behind fine china, sipping Kentucky bourbon from crystal tumblers as they exchanged pleasant conversation. After an hour of waiting, Osborn finally voiced the question on everyone's mind. "May I ask where the general is? I thought we were supposed to meet him this evening."

Colonel Munford leaned back in his chair, a wry smile on his face. "Ah, the general is a very mysterious man. There are times we do not see him for days," he replied.

"We'll end up in a skirmish and, voila, there he is, sword out, making a charge," said Rooney with a grin.

Grumble Jones leaned forward, his elbows on the table. "Most nights, he sleeps in the trees like a jungle cat. He's probably out there now with his medicine man."

"Medicine man?" Osborn asked, intrigued.

"That's right. He travels around with a Choctaw Indian called Seven Leg Spider. Always with him, never leaves his side," Jones explained.

"Taught him everything he knows," added General Robertson, his voice low and ominous, as if recounting a ghost story. "Sometimes making him quite... unpredictable, I'd say."

"Of course, that's why we are so successful in hit and run tactics," Rooney noted.

"The general's unconventional ways," Grumble added with a nod.

"A word of advice," Major Beckham interjected, "If you ever see him, I'm warning you, do not approach him."

"There are only a few of us who can and even fewer who can speak to him," General Hampton said, the table nodding in solemn agreement. "And he just lost his best friend at Chancellorsville."

Concerned, Osborn leaned in. "No, not his best friend?"

"Stonewall Jackson, yes," confirmed Robertson, and the officers bowed their heads in respect.

"I'm so sorry to hear that news," Osborn said softly, turning to Lou. "My best friend means so much to me."

"Yep. But when you eventually see General Stuart, there is no mistaking him. He is larger than life. And he always travels with his medicine man," Rooney reiterated.

General Beckham slapped the table, causing the empty plates to rattle. "Damn it to hell. We've waited long enough. Let's eat." He glanced towards the tent flap and barked, "Bring it in!"

The tent flap opened, and the aroma of a long-awaited meal filled the air. Four soldiers in white gloves brought in the plates of fried chicken and green beans, setting them on the table. The colonel turned to Ray and Lou. "And you both are Mr. Roche's assistants?"

"I am," said Ray.

The colonel turned to Lou. She shrugged and slumped down in her chair before turning to Osborn and Ray. "I… I don't know what I am?" A tear formed in her eye.

"Oh, Oh, Ma'am, I…did I say something?" stumbled the colonel. Grumble, Robertson, and Beckham turned to the colonel.

"Ma'am?" asked Grumble.

Lou ran out of the room, and Osborn went after her. A few feet outside, she stopped with her face in her hands. Osborn walked up to her. "Did the general offend you?"

"No, no, it's not that."

"What is it, Lou? I'll help you."

"Yes, that's just it. I, I'm, I'm very happy to be with you, Osborn. I guess I'm a little homesick. You do your photography, but embalming was who I am. The thing I'm good at. I see you with your camera, making your art."

"All right, I will teach you everything I know about photography. Would you like to help with it?"

"I asked you, and you and Ray don't need my help. And, well, I just wish I could continue my art. My embalming. That is who I am."

"I understand. I understand completely. We will purchase supplies for you the next chance we get."

Her eyes beamed. "Truly?"

"Of course, truly."

"You'd do that for me, Osborn?"

"Anyone would do that for their best friend. Anyone would, yes."

Osborn led Lou back to the table, gently patting her back as she wiped tears from her cheeks. "Forgive my behavior, gentlemen," she said, her voice trembling slightly. "I don't know what got a hold of me."

"No, no, my dear. The young man here explained the situation," said the colonel reassuringly.

"Please accept our apologies, Ma'am," Rooney added. "We were inattentive, shall I say. Being away from home and surrounded by men all the time can make you that way. So, I understand you are an embalmer?"

Lou brightened immediately. "Yes."

"A young lady doing the devil's work is quite unheard of. The sight of the dead does not disgust you?" asked Beckham.

"It does not. Women are natural caretakers. I am simply a caretaker of the deceased," Lou responded confidently.

Osborn interjected. "Lou here embalmed little Willy Lincoln. Willy Lincoln, God rest his soul."

"God rest his soul, indeed," said the colonel. He turned to his comrades and, under his breath, said, "Too bad it wasn't his father." The table burst into laughter.

"Well, my boys here all call me Rooney, but my complete name is Brigadier General William Henry Fitzhugh Lee—"

Grumble, Robertson, and Hampton burst into laughter again. "Oh, now, here he goes," said Grumble, shaking his head.

Rooney gave them a sidelong glance before continuing, "General Lee is my father, and I can tell you, we need embalmers. The topic has been brought up."

"This division needs an embalmer," added the colonel, creating a smile on Lou's face that lit up the room.

"We would love to send our boys home proper," said Hampton.

Lou shook her head and said, "But I don't have any of my equipment."

General Robertson leaned over the table with an evil grin and whispered, "Then we must acquire that for you at the next engagement," as if it was a secret plan.

Lou clapped her hands like a giddy child handed a birthday cake. "Now that we have that taken care of, I'd like to suggest that in addition to the new science of embalming the departed, we have a famous artist of the new art of photography in our presence, gentlemen," said Munford to the other five officers. They all nodded and smiled at Osborn. "But I must bring up that unfortunate discovery," added Munford, clearing his throat. "The discovery that you are an honorary Union captain, are you not?"

"Well, yes, but..."

Ray interrupted, "But, but he was just given..." Munford's hand went up, silencing him. "Don't fret yourselves. The general is a generous man and has already given you the approval to stay. He is very interested in you, Mr. Roche, very interested. But for my own satisfaction, are you Union, or are you Southern sympathizers?"

"I have no political proclivities, no. But that is also to say I do not hold allegiance to any army. General McClellan gave the moniker to me, to me, thinking I might be jealous of another photographer to whom he also gave that moniker. I was not jealous and am not jealous. I felt it rude not to accept it. Felt it rude, yes."

"My uncle is an artist. That's all he is," added Ray.

"Of course, of course," Colonel Munford said. "But now I must beg of you an indulgence of the general's. He specifically asked me to request this indulgence and would be simply delighted if you were to grant it."

Osborn's brow rose. Grumble Jones again leaned in and said, "Trust me, it's not just an indulgent request."

"Of course, of course," said Osborn.

"He asked if you would be so generous as to renounce your Union rank of captain and..." said Munford, turning to the others with a mischievous grin. "Allow him to bequeath upon you the Confederacy's rank... of major."

Osborn beamed as Lou and Ray sat dumbfounded. "I would be honored, yes honored," said Osborn, barely audible.

"Then it shall be done," said Munford raising his Kentucky bourbon into the air, those at the table joining. "Raise your glasses, gentlemen..." he said, turning to Lou. "And fine lady. Here's to *Major* Osborn Roche of the Army of Northern Virginia."

"Here, here!"

Munford stood, pushing back his chair and keeping his glass raised. "And now General McClellan," he said, his voice louder. "You can take your shitty, little, honorary rank of captain and stick it up Mr. Lincoln's ass!"

CHAPTER 20

Ray and Osborn spent the next three days capturing portraits of the men and documenting camp life through their photographs. Lou followed along, carrying the tripod, until the sudden roar of cannon fire froze her in her tracks. She ducked and sat down, eyes squeezed shut. With another volley, she rocked with fear as the few remaining soldiers in camp grabbed their guns and rushed toward the fight.

"We need to get her to the wagon, Ray," Osborn said urgently.

"I can see that. I'll get her," Ray replied, moving towards her. "Let me pick her up and bring her back to the wagon."

"No," Osborn interjected, gently slipping his hands under her arms and helping her to stand. "Lou, Lou. It'll be fine. It'll be fine." Ray sucked in a breath as Osborn added, "Let's get you back to the wagon."

"You're touching her, you're touching her," Ray sputtered in disbelief.

Lou opened her eyes to find Osborn holding her. Despite the tears streaming down her face, a smile broke through.

Ray put the tripod and camera on top of the dark cart and followed behind until they reached the wagon. Osborn brought her in, sat her on the bed, and covered her with blankets. "See, it's fine now. Are you feeling better? Feeling better? We'll move away from the noise."

They sat on a distant hill as the battle raged on, the sounds of war a haunting backdrop. Lou joined them on the wagon bench, a blanket wrapped around her shoulders for warmth. Below, the valley was shrouded in cannon smoke, flashes of yellow-orange lighting up the haze like distant lightning in a storm cloud. As the sun dipped toward the horizon, a bugle sounded the retreat.

"I believe Stuart's cavalry is headed north," Ray said, breaking the silence. "Do you still want to follow them? We could go back and follow the Union boys instead."

"I'd like to continue with them. I think we can get some interesting photographs."

"These boys have real good manners, too," said Lou. "That one boy who touched my lady part pulled his hand away faster than a snake bite."

Ray guided Hoady down the road, following the wagon tracks left by the two artillery pieces. After twenty miles, they spotted one of the pieces ahead, abandoned with a broken wheel. Both of them glanced at it as they passed by.

"At least we know we're going the right way," Ray remarked. "There they are ahead," he added, spotting Stuart's cavalry in the distance.

Colonel Munford rode over with his entourage and pulled alongside them. "Well, Major, I thought we might have lost you."

"Afternoon, Colonel," said Osborn. "Has the general been seen lately?"

"I haven't seen him. He might be ahead with the infantry," said Colonel Munford as he kicked his horse. "We will see you up ahead in the town."

The church bell in the town of Middleburg attempted to ring an alarm to the town's captured saviors. Rebel soldiers marched Union militia prisoners down the main street as Ray and Osborn parked their wagon near the courthouse steps, where other guarded prisoners sat.

Ray, Lou, and Osborn walked along the plank sidewalk, weaving around celebrating soldiers who darted in and out of shops, ransacking them for supplies and liquor. Two Rebels, struggling to carry a large barrel out of a doorway, knocked Ray ten feet into the street. The soldier in front dropped the barrel, spilling molasses everywhere on the sidewalk.

"Damn, son! Keep outta the way!" one of the soldiers barked.

Ray sat in the dirt road, legs sprawled wide, shaking his head in a daze. Osborn rushed to him, grabbed his shirt collar, and dragged him back to the sidewalk just in time to avoid an oncoming wagon.

"You all right?" asked Osborn.

Ray rose, dusted himself off, and said, "Yep, thanks for grab… Wait. You just touched me."

"Well, I believe—"

Ray turned to Lou. "You saw it? And he picked you up yesterday."

"He did," replied Lou.

Osborn shook his head. "Maybe so, maybe so, but I need a quiet place. I can feel myself…."

Noticing Osborn's face turning red, Ray said, "Okay, Okay. I see a place over there. It looks quiet. Let's get you in there and sit a spell, Uncle."

"Thank you, Ray."

The Buckner House Inn, already ransacked, sat at the corner of the main street. Osborn, Lou, and Ray stepped inside. To the right was an empty desk, and in front of them, a staircase led to the upper floors. The dimly lit dining hall lay to their left. They cautiously peered in.

"We don't have any spirits if that's what you're seeking," called a woman's voice from the bar. They walked in further, spotting the woman behind the bar, cleaning glasses. "Did you hear me? I said—"

"We heard ya," interrupted Ray. "We just want to sit a spell. My uncle here isn't feeling too good."

The woman's stern expression softened as she took in the sight of Osborn's weary face. "Alright then, have a seat. Ain't much left, but you're welcome to rest here."

They made their way to a table near the corner, away from the scattered remnants of the inn's ransacked interior. "Sit here, Uncle. Put your feet up on that chair," Ray said, gently guiding Osborn to rest. Knowing that darkness calmed his uncle, Ray walked across the room to close an open drape. As he reached for it, he turned and froze. A Native American stood against the far wall, arms crossed against his bare chest, staring intently at Ray. Next to him sat someone engrossed in a newspaper, the pages obscuring their face. Ray left the drape open and walked back to their table, his steps slow and measured. He sat down and leaned in. "Don't look now, but there's a strange Indian over to your left staring at me. And he doesn't look happy." Lou immediately turned her head. "I said, don't look."

She quickly turned back to Ray. "What's he doing?" she asked.

"Just looking at me." Ray dropped his gaze from the Native American and focused on his uncle. "Feeling any better?"

"Yes, thank you, Ray. We'll wait for the dust to settle out there, and then we'll get the camera and see what we can photograph," Osborn said, settling back into his chair.

The man with the newspaper dropped it to the table. Dashingly dressed in a uniform adorned with a yellow sash and an ostrich feather in his hat, he revealed himself to be General Stuart. "Photograph? Did you say photograph?" he asked, rising and walking over to their table. The cross-armed, stern-looking Native American followed closely behind.

"Yes, you are the photographer, aren't you? I saw you at my grande revue. I hoped it pleased you. I'm wonderfully delighted to make your acquaintance. Please forgive my manners for having not greeted you myself. My mother, God rest her soul, would be so displeased with my manners of late," he said as he stuck out his hand to Osborn. "Major General Stuart, most people call me Jeb, so very pleased."

"I'm sorry, general, but my uncle doesn't shake hands. Please forgive him. It's an artist thing, they say."

"It is an artist thing," added Osborn.

"I am quite an admirer of the art community," Stuart said with a smile that never faded. "May I sit?"

"Please," said all three.

From the side of his mouth, Ray whispered to Osborn, "And you reply...?"

Osborn sat up straight. "Pleased to meet you. I am Osborn Roche. This is Lou and my nephew, Ray." Osborn turned to Ray with a big grin, pleased with himself.

Ray motioned his head back to Stuart. "He took the photograph of General Howard after he was shot," added Ray.

"I am aware. Yes, yes! Delightful! General Howard was fighting under General Sedgwick for that one. So unfortunate when we lose a general on either side. My boys don't like targeting generals. They believe that enlisted men are more dangerous."

"Yes, and I would like to thank you, thank you, yes, for allowing us to follow along with your division."

"Oh, it's all my pleasure, dear sir," said Stuart as he turned to Lou. "And I understand you are an embalmer. Aren't you, my dear?"

Lou's face brightened. "I am."

"Well then, I have a surprise for you just out back." Stuart turned to the Choctaw. "It is out back, isn't it, Seven Leg Spider?"

"Mm," grunted Seven Leg Spider.

"Yes. It's right out back. All the equipment you need, I believe." "Oh my! Thank you, sir," said Lou.

"Thank me? No, thank you, dear miss. We are in need of your services. Now, you must excuse me," he said, rising. "I must attend to my duties."

Lou, Ray, and Osborn also rose. "Good day, sir, and thank you for everything," said Lou. After Stuart walked out the door, all three made a beeline for the back door. Sitting directly in front of them was Henry's wagon.

"Oh, my. Oh, my. I… That's my father's wagon. I hope nothing has happened to him?"

"Naw, the Reb cavalry is known for stealing these things all the time," said Ray as he walked over, opened the door, and peered in. "No damage, perfect condition. Looks like you inherited it." Lou went inside it while Ray walked back over to Osborn. "No horse. We'll have to move her stuff into our wagon." Osborn's eyes fell to the dirt. "Yes, it's a lot of stuff, and that means we will have to reorganize, and we will have to share space with her."

"Ooh, I will not like it. I will not like it."

With pursed lips, Ray took a deep breath through his nose. "Well, we—"

"But I will do it! We will share and, yes, I will share. That will be that!" said Osborn with a finger pointed in the air.

As Ray watched him walk off to help Lou sort through things, he said to himself, "I'll be. I guess that will be that."

The early morning fog descended onto the valley like a sky-roaming leviathan. Osborn and Lou walked into the town, which now resembled a ghost town with all the soldiers gone. The leviathan swept through the streets toward them, swallowing them like Captain Ahab in Moby Dick.

"It's so quiet now," Osborn remarked, wiping the monster's cool saliva from his cheeks.

"And even quieter with the fog," Lou replied, her voice hushed. "Are you excited to work side by side, Osborn? Are you as happy as I am about it?" She slipped her hand into his.

"I am." The wood plank sidewalks creaked beneath their feet until they found the end and turned down a residential street. The silence was almost eerie, broken only by the occasional distant crow of a rooster or the soft rustle of leaves in the breeze.

Lou swung his hand again as she did the first time they held hands. They walked by homes, admiring them. "These are beautiful homes. Wouldn't it be just wonderful to live in a home like one of these?"

"They are very nice. Very nice. We have a very nice home in Pittsburgh. Ray and I do. We will see it someday soon. Someday soon."

They continued up a hill, and the road narrowed as they walked up until it became a trail. "Shall we continue?" asked Osborn. "Let's see where it takes us," she said, taking the lead.

As they crested the hill, the fog turned into a drizzle. "Are you sure you'd like to go on? It's becoming damp. Damp."

She turned back to him. "I love the rain."

"I do not like it. My shoes are getting wet, wet, yes."

"Osborn, how much do you like me?" she asked without turning to him.

"I like you a lot. Yes, quite a lot. It is this damp weather I do not like, no."

The drizzle turned to rain as the narrow path crested the hill to a forest of massive rusty blackhaw trees, shielding them from some of the shower with its canopy of big waxy leaves and tiny white blossoms. "What is…?" said Lou before she squealed with glee, let go of Osborn's hand, and ran toward a mass of monarch butterflies among the azalea flowers. She slowed before reaching them, putting out her hands.

"Look at the butterflies. Beautiful," said Lou as several flew near, inspecting her until one finally landed on her arm. Fascination also bloomed on Osborn's face as he neared. One landed on his beard and another on his arm. Lou giggled as his eyes danced, and his lips grew into a smile.

"One of life's miracles, right," said Lou.

"Yes, oh, yes," he said, the damp weather forgotten.

Lou walked over to him with a monarch on her finger. "Look-it." She brought it up close to his face. It flew off, and they both laughed.

"Your eyes flutter just like their wings." The grin on her wet lips receded as she stood before him, and her eyes took hold of his, bridging a path between them.

"Do you want to kiss me, Osborn?" Rain glistened on her cheeks, and his eyes fell to the dirt road, turning to mud. "We can try it like how we tried holding hands. That worked."

Osborn's eyes snapped up to hers under his dripping brow. She held him there, not moving. He wiped the rain off his head, slicking down his hair. "My hair is wet."

Lou ignored him, slowly closing the distance between them. "If you don't like it, we'll stop." She raised herself to her tiptoes, her face inching closer. Osborn's brow furrowed as he instinctively tried to retreat. Lou wrapped her small hand behind his rain-soaked neck, stopping him and sending a shiver down his spine. His racing heart skipped a beat as she brought her wet lips to his in a warm, gentle kiss.

In a twitch of her flickering irises, he forgot about his wet hair, his muddy shoes, the rain dripping on his neck.

Strange, new, and exciting sensations washed over him, free from his usual concerns and worries. His mind swam in the small creek of emotions, with the current growing faster until it pushed him into the surging Mississippi of them. In the rush of the moment, this first kiss, he felt no fear or desire to stop. He dove into the torrent of these emotions, willingly sending himself over the edge in a barrel. As she began to pull away, he sucked in the moist air around her like a drowning man breaking the surface. He opened his eyes to meet hers, tasting the raindrops from her lips. They tasted like the sunniest summer sky.

CHAPTER 21

They followed General Stuart west to Upperville, where they set up two tents side by side. Minutes after the cannons thundered, Lou received her first "customers." Osborn assisted by removing their uniforms down to their long johns, but he couldn't bear to go further.

"That's fine, Osborn. I'm paying Daley, the negro man that works in the hospital, to help me get 'em up on the table, and he's making caskets for me. You go on and do your photography."

With the battle winding down, Osborn left Lou happily embalming bodies, more of which lined up outside her tent, and he and Ray ventured out to photograph the battlefield. The recent rain had turned the roads into a muddy mess. As they navigated the terrain, General Grumble Jones and General Hampton galloped toward them, their horses splashing through the mire.

"Think we won the day?" asked Ray.

"Only fools sell the skin before they've caught the bear," replied Hampton, perplexing Osborn at the metaphor.

Grumble said, "I believe we took the day. Stuart was over by the Shenandoah River. Follow this road, and when you see a group of trees to the west, head that way. He should still be there. I believe I would like a portrait when you return, Major Roche."

"Certainly, certainly. It shall be on the house, on the house for stealing that wagon. And for you as well, General Hampton. For you as well."

"We did not steal it. We acquired it, Major Roche," said Grumble.

"Oh, wonderful, wonderful. That's much better than stealing it."

Ray slapped the reins on Hoady. "Funny, they call you major."

"Why would that be funny? It is true."

"Yes, it is true. I mean funny… Well, I don't mean funny. I suppose I mean doggone good. Good things seem to come to you, Uncle. You were an honorary captain with the Union. Now, you're an honorary major with the Rebs. You are a world-famous photographer. You've photographed the vice president, McClellan…"

"I don't believe major is an honorary rank," said Osborn with a touch of arrogance.

Ray snickered. "Oh, well now! I believe you may be correct. They never did add that word in."

"Ray, speaking of portraits, I no longer wish to use the tent. It takes up too much room with Lou's things now. We should leave it here."

"We put all of our equipment in there."

"All of our equipment is in the dark cart, too," said Osborn. "I was thinking, in addition to the questions I ask, if I were to photograph the subject in their natural environment, natural environment, I could bring out their essence even more. Do you see?"

Ray nodded and said, "Yes. Yes, I do see. Interesting. Even brilliant, I'd say."

"Yes, yes. Like photographing a lion in the jungles of Africa instead of the zoo."

"I agree. Let's try that."

Following the general's directions, Ray halted the wagon and pointed to the gray uniforms clustered in the group of trees ahead. They parked the wagon and pulled out the dark cart, wheeling it toward Stuart's men gathered near the Shenandoah River. The soldiers were preparing to make their way across the water.

"Time to go, men," General Stuart loudly whispered, gesturing the go-ahead signal with his arm.

Osborn and Ray quickly set up the camera and readied two plates as seven hundred men and their horses crept out of the woods and into the river. At twenty feet out, small arms fire erupted from the embankment on the opposite side. The water flowed waist-deep, and the men squatted low, trying to make themselves the smallest targets possible as they returned fire.

Osborn's hands shook slightly as he adjusted the camera. "Steady, Ray. We need to capture this," he murmured.

Ray nodded, focusing intently as he framed the shot. "Got it. Just a bit more..."

As the soldiers pressed forward, bullets zipped through the air, splashing into the water around them. The scene was chaotic, yet Osborn and Ray remained resolute, determined to document the bravery and struggle unfolding before them. In the center of the river, General Stuart sat atop his steed with Seven Leg Spider next to him. Stuart raised his sword as he called for a retreat. Osborn removed the lens cap on him with Seven Leg Spider in the background.

"Mount up and head north! We'll find another place to cross! And someone get my flask of bourbon!" said Stuart as his horse found its footing on the river's bank. As he dismounted, a soldier tossed him his flask. He caught it with one hand and pulled his sword again with the other, pointing the way as he took a swig. Trees around them shattered from cannon fire. Osborn and Ray ducked with every tree splintering blast.

Stuart walked over to them with a pleased smile. "Major Roche! Good to see you!" he shouted above the chaos, unaffected by the danger. Osborn's face scrunched, and his eyes closed.

Ray ran around the wagon to him. "I'm sorry, sir. He's having a panic."

"Nonsense! Nonsense! Osborn, good man, it'll be fine! The sounds of battle reinvigorate the youth of your soul!" Ray and Osborn hit the dirt with a second tree splintering explosion. Stuart and Seven Leg Spider didn't move.

"Yes, it may be time to leave," said Stuart.

"Uncle, it's time to go. You have to open your eyes to follow me." Ray pushed the cart ahead of him, with Osborn following. Cannon fire followed them into the field.

Reaching their wagon, Stuart stopped, oblivious to any danger. "Why, this is a Romani vardo caravan, isn't it? Beautiful," he said, turning to Seven Leg Spider. "Seven Leg Spider, can you please take my horse? I'd love to see the inside."

"Please, my pleasure," said Osborn before they climbed inside. Ray dismantled the dark cart while Osborn gave the Romani vardo tour. Not waiting for his uncle to finish, Ray sent Hoady in a gallop down the road away from the cannon fire, stopping a short distance away.

"Ray? Why are you stopping?" Osborn asked, peering through the small window.

"The Indian told me to stop," Ray replied from the wagon bench.

Stuart and Osborn climbed out of the wagon and walked around to where Ray sat. They found themselves in a thicket of trees about two hundred yards from the road.

"He told you? He's never spoken a word to me," said Stuart. "Well, he motioned, I mean. He didn't say anything." Seven Leg Spider gestured with his hands to Stuart. Stuart's brow furrowed with interest.

"He said we should stay here for now. There are Yankees close by."

"While we wait it out, let us make a portrait of the general," said Osborn to Ray.

"Ah, yes, a splendid idea. Let me get my sash and sword."

After they set up the equipment, General Stuart posed in front of a tree. "How did you meet Seven Leg Spider?" asked Osborn as Seven Leg Spider and Ray stood nearby.

"One day, he just showed up, and now I have this Choctaw following me everywhere I go, sleeping beneath my bed. I can only hope he would at least protect me if someone advanced on me. One can only hope."

After a few more of Osborn's questions, Stuart revealed himself when he spoke of his wife Flora. "Please hold still."

"Would you like Seven Leg Spider in a portrait with you?" asked Ray.

"Why, that is a splendid idea." Stuart gestured to Seven Leg Spider. "Come on over here, you old fool." Seven Leg Spider approached him, faced the camera, and crossed his arms. "He doesn't know a lick of English."

After his portrait, Stuart sat on a fallen tree beside Ray and said, "Take one alone of Seven Leg Spider. I'd enjoy having that. Ask him those questions of yours, Osborn. Ha!" Seven Leg Spider walked over and posed.

Osborn turned back to Seven Leg Spider. "Seven Leg Spider, where is your home?"

"Mmm."

"Tell me of your bravest battle." No response. "Tell me of a time in your life that you were truly frightened, frightened, like maybe when you were a boy." Seven Leg Spider shifted his feet. "Your mother. I'm sure you love her. Does she approve of you fighting with General Stuart?"

Seven Leg Spider stood for a moment before saying, "My momma loves General Stuart—"

"Please hold still."

Stuart burst into a spontaneous laugh, turned and walked two steps, then turned back to them with his hand covering his mouth.

Seven Leg Spider continued, "...She's prouder than hell of me. I wrote her and said I was General Stuart's right hand—"

"Well, snap my garters!" exclaimed Stuart. "You speak!"

"Yessum. I do. I'm sorry, General."

"You been running me around the barn all this time?" Stuart pulled out his bourbon flask and took a swig.

"To get close to ya, General. I mean, I got so much respect for ya and my momma—"

Stuart raised his hand to stop. "So, give me the bacon without the sizzle, boy. Are ya even a Choctaw?"

"No, sir. I'm from Florida."

Stuart slapped his knee and said, "Damn, all this time? Florida? Shoulda knowed." Shaking his head, he turned to Ray, exhaled exhaustion from his nose, and said, "Another one from Florida. Sometimes I wish they'd be fightin' for the Yankees."

In the evening, Lou, Osborn, and Ray sat in the wagon eating supper as the rain pitter-pattered on the roof. The stove warmed the room and dried the portraits hanging above the desk.

Lou pointed to the one with General Stuart in front of his tent with several of his staff. They all studied a map on a table. "I like that one of the general," she said.

"My favorite too. The general has intensity. So how did you do today, Lou?" Osborn asked.

"I did well. I made two hundred and fifty dollars."

Ray choked on his food. "YOU MADE WHAT?!"

"Two Hundred and fifty dollars."

"Very good, Lou," said Osborn.

Ray wiped his mouth in shock. "Good?! That's incredible."

"Thank you, Ray."

"We are in the wrong business, Uncle."

"We are in the right business, Ray. I am a photographer."

"I know. I'm just saying..." Ray turned to her. "I will never complain about the tent again, and if you need help, I'd love to learn."

"I would like to learn as well, Lou. Learn as well. We both would."

"How exciting! I would love to show you. Working together! Oh, my. I'm so excited. We will start tomorrow."

The following day, Ray and Osborn sat before Lou in her tent as she waved her long aspirating wand around like a schoolteacher. "We get fifty dollars federal money for an officer and twenty-five for a regular soldier. Always ask for federal money unless they don't have it. If they don't, make it seventy for an officer and forty-five for a regular. I pay Daley, the negro man, four dollars for every casket. With my father, Ben made our caskets, and we sold them for six dollars. We will do the same for federal bills, eight dollars for Reb bills, and make a two-dollar profit."

She wheeled over a sheet-covered body and removed the sheet on a colonel. His knee raised up, and his fists clenched in the air with rigor mortis. "I take the arms and move them about like this. Stretching them and removing the stiffness. Set the hands on top of each other. I put them lower for men, across the chest for women, like you saw me do for Miss Tabitha. Do you remember that, Osborn?"

"I do. Yes, I do."

"Always put the ring finger hand over the other."

"The left hand is the ring finger hand?" asked Ray.

"Yes. It is. Then I clean the body with this Ayers Moth and Freckle Lotion, especially in the mouth, because that decomposes first. Then, I set the features beginning with the mouth. It has to be closed, so you'll need to use one of my suture needles to draw a thread through the upper gums and tie it to the lower gums, pulling it together and closing the lips. For the eyes, I lay two coins on them to keep them shut. If you can't get to the customer that day, it'd be best to put the coins on his eyes the night before. They'll be permanent by morning, and you get to keep the coins. If it's a rush job, the customer keeps the coins."

Ray shifted in his seat, uncomfortably. "You call them customers? The dead men?"

"Yes. Now, I'd love help pumping the fluid into the artery because that can get tiresome. It has to be pumped at a specific rate, or the body will bloat in some areas and not in others. I will adjust the chemicals as we go along based on what I see the body doing. That's an art and something that has taken me years to learn and perfect. I add dyes to get the perfect color I want on the face, and I know how much to use and when to use it during the process."

"I'm both impressed and a little sick to my stomach," said Ray.

"Thank you, Ray. After we finish the work on the body and set the features, we lay him nicely in the box, put all his papers and other personal effects..."

"I would like to do that part," said Osborn.

"I figured you would," she said.

"Yep, I figured you would, too," added Ray.

"Then we nail the lid tight, write down the full name of the deceased with the address of his parents. Daley will come to take him to the train that will send him home."

"There seems a lot to it," said Ray.

"You'll have to learn with small steps. Shall we stop for now and have lunch?"

Ray rubbed his stomach. "I don't think I could."

"Well, we do need to do the portraits of Generals Robertson and Rooney today," said Osborn.

"I would like a portrait of Osborn and me, Ray. Can you do one?" "Lovely idea, Lou. Yes, lovely idea. Ray, please indulge us."

Ray shrugged his shoulders and said, "Well, all right. It'll give me time to settle my stomach."

Ray and Osborn set about readying the equipment. "All right, Ray, can you stand in my place so I can focus," said Osborn, diving under the black camera shroud. He pulled apart the camera's leather bellows, focusing on Ray and Lou's inverted image before coming back out and replacing the lens cap. Ray walked over, slid in the boxed plate, and pulled out the dark board. "We are ready and…"

"Wait, aren't you going to ask us questions?" asked Lou. Ray cocked his head. "Oh, you mean like he does?"

"Yes, those questions to get the soul of the subject revealed in the portrait, right?"

Osborn turned to Lou and said, "I already told you, yours is revealed so easily. There it is in your smile—"

"…Like a child when they pet a dog for the first time," she finished.

Osborn grinned as Ray said, "And you just revealed it. Please hold still."

After the ten-second exposure time due to the cloudy sky, Ray slid out the first slide as Osborn attached the small wooden box to the lens. "Okay, wonderful. And now my ingenious uncle will demonstrate the magnificence of his self-portrait invention!" announced Ray with flair.

"Really?" asked Lou.

"Yes, we are going to take a portrait with all three of us," said Ray as he handed the long dowel to Osborn.

"Dark board out, Ray?"

"Yes," he said, rolling his eyes like a bored child.

"Please hold still." Osborn pulled the mini dark board up with the wood dowel, holding it up for ten seconds before dropping it like a guillotine.

"Can you show me how to do it? I want to learn photography while you learn to embalm," said Lou.

"Of course," said Osborn. "It'll be my pleasure."

Sunlight beamed in through the red window as the second of the two portraits revealed itself in the developer bath. The three of them stood with stoic expressions next to each other in front of the big red wagon. Osborn held the wood dowel with one slightly blurry hand, and with the other, he held her hand.

"Aww, I love it, Osborn." Osborn ran it through the other rinses and baths before heating it over the oil lamp and handing it to her.

"Now, let us find a frame for those," he said, opening a cabinet. "Ah, yes. Here is one I've been saving for the perfect person," he said as he pulled out a detailed filigree silver double frame. "See, it is hinged and opens to two portraits. We'll put both of those in here."

Osborn put them in, closed it, and handed it to her. Lou brought it to her chest. "I will always treasure this."

The midnight moon hung directly above, casting a silvery through the window in the wagon. Osborn lay alone on the wagon floor, restless from the uncomfortably warm night. Mosquitoes skulked about—he'd already killed two. Ray, risking the mosquitoes, slept outside for the breeze, while Lou had chosen her tent. The wagon felt lonely without them. In the last few days, he had become used to seeing her arm hanging out from the bed above him as he fell asleep.

He covered his nose and mouth with the cloth, pinching it between his lips and touching the tip of his tongue to it before folding it and laying it on his forehead. As he stared at the wagon ceiling, thoughts of her filled his mind. Pulling the cloth off, he spread it above him with both hands, feeling the stitching, the thread, the creases, and the edging before bringing it to his nose for a deep, longing sniff. Her familiar scent wasn't as strong as it used to be.

Sitting up, he swatted a mosquito on the back of his neck and wiped it away with his blanket. He crawled out of bed and walked into the night. The crickets sang, accompanied by an owl as he circled the wagon. Each time he passed her tent, he glanced at it. On the fifth pass, he stopped, staring at the open flap before kneeling and crawling inside.

He lay on the floor next to her bed, just as he had that infamous night before her father caught him. She lay sideways on her cot, her face on the pillow turned toward him, her arm hanging out like every night, resembling Michelangelo's God on the Sistine Chapel—hand relaxed, forefinger extended. He scooted closer, directly under it, and his fingers found the brown cloth in his pocket, bringing it to life.

The sweat on her forearm glistened silver in the moonlight streaming through the tent flap. Osborn slid back and sat up, marveling at the sight. He took the cloth and gently slid it from the crook of her elbow down to her wrist. Like a reflex, her hand grabbed both the cloth and his hand. Caught like a thief, he froze. Her eyes opened, asking silent questions he had no answers for. Her hand released him, and he lay back down, pinned by her gaze.

He placed the cloth over his eyes and nose, breathing deeply through it before her hand reached down, swiping it away. Her fingers kneaded the cloth momentarily before she brought it up to her neck, sliding it across her skin. He swallowed hard as she moved the cloth down the top of her longjohns and across the contour of her chest, wiping the sweat from her breast.

Osborn closed his eyes as she pulled the cloth out and laid it gently back on his face, covering his eyes, nose, and mouth. Breathing in her lovely scent, he fell asleep on the dirt floor, happier than he could ever remember.

CHAPTER 22

Confederate soldiers milled about their tents, some eating dinner, smoking pipes, or heading off to the latrines. The atmosphere was more reminiscent of a hunting trip than a war. Officers sat at crowded foldable tables, drinking coffee and discussing the day's orders.

Colonel Munford trotted up on his horse, a beautiful light blue dress draped across his saddle. Lou and Ray emerged from her tent, wiping their hands with towels. The colonel dismounted and walked over to Lou, handing her the dress. "Miss, General Stuart found this for you," he said with a smile.

Lou held it out in front of her, gawking at it. "It's the most beautiful dress I've ever seen."

"General Stuart would love the pleasure of seeing you all at the ball this evening."

"Ball?" asked Osborn, coming out of the wagon.

"Indeed, hosted by the ladies of Middleburg. They are giving it in General Stuart's honor."

"I don't believe I would like to go. I would not like it," said Osborn.

"Uncle!" said Ray with clenched teeth.

"General Stuart would be disappointed if you could not make it."

"Where is it to be held?" asked Lou.

"The Buckner House Inn. In Middleburg. The same hotel you met the general at."

"I've never been to a ball before. I never learned how to dance," said Lou.

"I never did either," added Osborn.

"My dear! I would be honored to show you right here and now. It is simple," said the colonel, walking up to her and taking the dress away. He handed it to Ray before taking her hand and leading her away. "It's all done in a box step." The colonel let go of her hand and stepped away to demonstrate. "You must watch me too, Mr. Roche. We start with the left foot. Forward, side, close, back, side, close, forward, side, close, backward, side close…"

Lou stood aside him and mimicked his moves. "You are a natural, madam." He took her hand and put his other on the small of her back. "Let the gentleman guide you. I will start forward, and you will go backward. Forward, side, close, back, side, close, forward, side, close, backward, side close…"

Lou's smile grew as she turned to Osborn for his reaction. "Osborn, Osborn, look. I'm doing it! I'm doing it!"

The colonel released her, holding up one hand triumphantly. "Indeed, you did. It will be a delight to see you there tonight at your first ball." Bringing her hand to his mouth, he kissed it. She brought it back in shock. Her hand had never been treated so gallantly. "Until this evening," said the colonel before riding off.

Lou burst into giggles as she gaped at the back of her hand. She walked back to Osborn. "Can't we go, Osborn? I'd love it if you took me. I'll wear the dress."

"I thought you didn't like dresses?"

"Yes, but girls are supposed to wear dresses, and this is a ball, and I've never been to a ball before."

"Lou, if he doesn't take you, I will," said Ray.

She turned to Ray, "Thank you, Ray," before turning back to Osborn. He held his head low. Her piano fingers rapidly moved about as she asked him, "I want you to take me. Will you take me?"

Osborn stood in silence, eyes to the ground. She ducked down into their line of sight. "Osborn? It would be very special."

"I cannot touch you, Lou. It disturbs me."

"We've held hands, Osborn."

Ray leaned against the wagon. "And he picked you up and pulled me out of the way."

She stood up straight and turned to Ray. "Yes, he let me hold his hand, and he liked it."

"I think you can do it, Uncle."

She leaned in close to Osborn and whispered, "We kissed, remember?" She turned back to Ray, releasing their secret, "And we kissed once!" she said before bursting into giggles.

"You what?! Well, if you did that, you can surely dance," said Ray, walking away for another box.

"I can't do it."

Lou's expression fell. "You won't do it for me, Osborn?"

"I can't do it."

Lou's face turned from sadness to anger. She pulled the dress off the wagon bench to the dirt before walking into her tent. "I'll sleep in here tonight."

Ray walked over to Osborn. "What are you thinking? I think that's a big mistake. I think you should try it. I know you can do it." Osborn closed his eyes and gritted his teeth. With lips pressed tight, Ray rubbed the back of his neck. Before walking away, he said, "Fine. Just a suggestion."

General Stuart's cavalry had moved out sometime in the evening after the ball in Middleburg. Osborn suffered a sleepless night. He made breakfast, his attempt at an apology. Lou came from her tent. "Good morning, men," she said pleasantly as if she had never been angry.

"Good morning, Lou. Did you sleep well?" asked Osborn.

"Perfectly. You?"

"Well, no. Didn't you hear the men moving out last night? They were quite loud, quite loud."

Ray came out from the wagon stretching and said, "I heard them. Woke me up, but I was too tired to get up."

"I'm lucky I finished with my customers. I—" She turned and peeked in her tent. "Oh, goodness. I was thinking they might have forgotten their caskets, but they must have taken them in the night, too."

"Guess that means we pack up and find them," said Ray.

"It does, it does," replied Osborn.

After packing, Ray climbed up to drive, and Osborn sat next to him in the middle. "Would you like to sit next to me, Lou?"

Osborn's forehead creased with frustration after Lou walked past them and replied, "No, thank you, I'll ride back here."

CHAPTER 23

The evening sun dropped into the horizon like a shiny copper coin into the tithing box. They had been searching for Stuart's men all day. Lou sat in the wagon reading while Ray sat on the bench beside Osborn, who was driving. Ray restlessly napped, his head continually falling forward and bobbing back again. The road entered a thick forest of poplar trees that stretched across it from above, forming a dark canopy.

Besides the wheels, a different creaking sound caught Osborn's ear ahead. He squinted into the distance, the dim light of early evening making it hard to see. As they came closer, a dark shape hanging from a tree a hundred yards ahead became clearer. Hoady clip-clopped up to reveal a Union soldier hanging from a rope around his neck.

Osborn brought the wagon to a halt and pulled out his nose plugs from his pocket, shoving them up each nostril. The dead corporal, likely in his mid-twenties, hung three feet off the ground, eye level with Osborn. Most of his skin had turned a ghastly blue to black, his fingernails dark as coffin wood.

Ray's eyes snapped open at the sight of the hanging man. "Oh!" he screamed, recoiling into the corner of the wagon bench. "What in the Sam Hill?!" Osborn steadied himself, pulling out his knife and sawing through the rope above the man's head. "You could 'a warned me! That ain't fair, and I know you're laughing inside right now. That... oh, my does that boy stink." Ray reached for his nose plugs.

The knife cut through, and the soldier collapsed to the ground with a thud. The body landed as he hung, with his arms and legs straight to his sides.

"Why are we stopping anyway? Someone may do the same thing to us. Let's get on outta here."

Lou dropped the stairs and came from around the back. "Oh, my," she said with her plugs already in.

Osborn jumped down and walked in a slow, wide circle around the soldier. Ray rubbed his face with both hands and asked, "Where are we? Any sign of them?"

"I've been hearing shots and cannons, shots and cannons, but haven't seen anything."

Lou stood above the soldier. "Someone do it to him, or did he do it to himself?" she asked.

Osborn said, "Either Rebels or highwaymen or—"

"That's why we should get on outta here. Could be highwaymen about," declared Ray.

"I don't think so. I don't think so."

"It doesn't matter anyway! I don't care about this dead boy. Just another dead boy. Let's get on outta here." Ray sat back on the bench, crossed his arms, eyes to the sky, defiant.

"It's getting late anyway, Ray. Maybe we should camp here for the night." Osborn sat down next to the dead soldier.

"Next to this stinking boy? Are you mad?" "Ray! You know I don't—"

"All right! All right! I'm sorry."

Lou walked over and sat next to Osborn. "Oh, you don't like that word either?" she asked.

"No," said Osborn, shaking his head.

Ray continued, "But this boy stinks. How…?"

"Use your nose plugs, your nose plugs. Like Lou and I are doing." "I have them in! He still stinks. Just less so. If you want to stop for the night, let's head away from here so we can sleep in peace."

Osborn's hand crept into the soldier's upper left pocket, where he pulled a rosary. He displayed it to Lou like a treasure. "It's nice," she said, admiring it before Osborn returned it.

"He was a Catholic."

"I see that," she replied.

Ray scooted over on the bench. They sat beneath him, grinning at each other. He rolled his eyes. "Oh, no! Not both of you! We don't have time for this! Please, can we just go?!"

"We do have time, Ray. We have time. We should just camp here." Osborn pulled out a whiskey flask, again displaying it to her in both hands. "Beautiful flask. Empty, though," said Osborn.

"Very nice."

Ray jumped off the wagon bench and walked off down the road. "This…! I…! I'm leaving!"

"Found a Bible!" called Osborn to Ray as he stomped off.

Lou turned to Ray growing smaller down the road. "We should get him, Osborn."

"A comb! Sewing kit!"

Ray spun on his heels and walked back to them. "Uncle, I don't care. Did you hear me say that? I don't care. Now we gotta find Stuart. Remember photography…"

"Ooh, letters!" Osborn grinned as he brought a stack of them out, holding them up like a pearl from an oyster.

"Oh, my, what luck," said Lou.

"And now, two of you. I'm walking!" Ray spun on his heels and headed off again. "This is just fine on the battlefield. I wholeheartedly accept it. But now? There's a time and a place for everything and…" Ray's voice trailed off as he walked farther down the road.

Lou turned to him, now a distant image. "We should get Ray, Osborn."

Osborn took the stack of letters, handing half to Lou. "He'll come back. We'll camp here tonight. I have to read these letters. I can't take them from the man."

"Okay. I'll read my half, you read yours, and then I'll tell you about my half as we go find Ray."

"Wonderful, wonderful."

Osborn opened his first letter. "His name is Peter." "Yes, I see that."

Finding a photo, Osborn showed it to Lou. "Look, his sister." A cute girl stood in the picture somewhere between ten and thirteen, with her hair up in a bun and tied with a bow.

Lou squinted in the dim evening light to see. "Pretty."

The bats darted across the night for their dinner. Lou put down her tenth letter, put them back into Peter's pocket, and rose. "I'm going to sleep, Osborn. Goodnight."

"Goodnight, Lou," Osborn murmured, finishing his letter and looking down the road for Ray. Seeing no sign of him, he rose and removed the harness from Hoady before hobbling the horse for the night. He took a blanket and laid it on top of a pile of pine needles under the hanging tree, providing a partial shelter. Digging through Peter's knapsack, he found salt pork, dried fruit, a candle, and a candle holder.

Osborn lit the candle and ate Peter's army rations, absorbing the details of the soldier's life from his letters. An hour passed, and his eyelids grew heavy. Blowing out the candle, he pulled out his brown cloth and covered his mouth and nose. The cool night air filtered through the fabric as his eyes wandered to the wagon, then closed for the night.

CHAPTER 24

"Hey, Mister, wake up!" Osborn opened his eyes to the mean end of a burnside carbine rifle. "You pull them arms from that blanket slow as a fat cloud passing the sun." The brown cloth fell off Osborn's face, and he did as the Union private said. "Got any guns on ya?"

"No, sir," said Osborn as he sat up.

An officer on horseback adjusted himself on the saddle. He looked away with disinterest when he said, "Private, search him."

"Get up," demanded the burnside private. Osborn rose slowly, the blanket falling from him. He stood in front of four Union soldiers: the officer on horseback, the private with the burnside, another wild-eyed private with a Sheridan rifle, and a skinny private no older than fourteen. Osborn raised his hands as the private with the burnside handed the rifle to the wild-eyed private before patting down Osborn.

"I don't like to be touched."

"Well, I don't like touching you," said the burnside as he squinted at Osborn's face. "Hey, he's got some things up his nose. What's those things up your nose, boy?"

Osborn pulled out the nose plugs and held them in his palm. "They stop the bad smells."

"Hey, look what I got!" yelled a large sergeant from thirty yards away. The sergeant had a bushy, grey horseshoe mustache and had Ray at gunpoint with his hands up.

"Where'd you find him?" asked the officer.

"Half a mile down the road, just off it. Sleeping under a blanket."

"No guns," called out the wild-eyed private after rummaging Osborn's things.

"What's your story, mister? You a photographer like it says on your wagon here?" asked the overcoated officer.

"Yes, I am."

Ray spoke up. "And he's a captain...."

"Shut up, boy!" The horseshoe mustache poked Ray in the back with his rifle barrel. "Speak when spoken to." The wild eye reached down and took a letter from Osborn's bedding. He snapped it open with one hand and squinted.

"Well, we'll see about that," said the officer to Ray before turning back to Osborn. "Do you know this dead man?"

The wild-eye turned to the officer, lifting the letters in his hand. "It's Golding."

"I believe I do, a bit. I've been reading his letters," said Osborn.

The officer slowly rubbed his forehead. "Reading his what?" he asked as if he didn't care about the answer.

"If you would allow me to explain," asked Ray.

"Shut up." The horseshoe jabbed Ray again. "You ever learn manners?"

"You believe you know him, so how do you know him?" asked the officer. He wore a clean overcoat over a filthy shirt—muddy and worn boots on his feet. His gunpowder smeared face wore the expression of a man who had traveled a difficult path.

"I read his letters. Letters his family sent him."

"Read his letters? He sent you letters? Are you a moron or something? I'll put it a different way. Why are you with him?"

"This boy is a wooden spoon!" said the burnside with a grimace and shaking his head.

More irritated than scared, Ray said, "He ain't no wooden—" The horseshoe hit Ray in the head with his rifle barrel. "Ouch!"

"I told you to shut up," said the horseshoe.

"Looky what I found," said the skinny private walking from the back of the wagon with Lou in front of his rifle. The officer glanced at Lou and went to Osborn.

"To clarify, I should say, I found Peter here under this tree swinging by his neck, by his neck. I cut him down and found his letters. I read most of them, and from those letters, I believe I know him a bit, yes, a bit."

"Know him? Why that's just peculiar." The officer shook his head. Osborn smiled at Lou. "The perfect word!"

"Yes, exactly."

The wild-eye walked to the burnside and slapped his arm with the back of his hand. "He is a wooden spoon, ain't he?"

Lou turned to the wild eye with flaring nostrils and said, "You shush, you."

"Were you any part of hanging him? Not that I care. He's a deserter," asked the officer.

"He hung himself. We found him hanging. Found him."

"If it's how you say it is, and you came upon him swinging, how do you know he hanged himself, Mr. Photographer?"

"We found his rifle and knapsack leaning against the tree. If someone killed him, those would be gone."

"That don't explain nothing. You coulda killed him and didn't move on yet," said the officer.

"His hands were untied," added Osborn.

"Ya coulda untied them."

Lou pointed to Peter's wrists. "They were never tied. They'd have rope marks. And see his neck? It's snapped. He jumped from that tree branch and snapped it. He didn't choke to death from having a horse run away from under him."

"Who are you?" asked the officer to Lou.

"The name is Lou Cattell. I'm an embalmer. I know these things."

"Hmm, one of those folks that make the dead look alive?"

"Yes," she replied.

"And she's quite good at it," added Osborn.

"She?" said the burnside before walking up to her.

"You a girl?" Lou didn't respond. "You got crazy eyes. Hey Joe, get a look at these crazy eyes. Crazier than yours," the burnside told the wild-eye.

"You don't talk to a lady like that," said Osborn, gritting his teeth.

"And looky what she do with her hands. Why you do that girl?" asked the burnside.

"I've always done it."

"Always done it? Hey, Lieutenant, I believe we have two halfwits here. They's both odd."

Osborn lifted his chin and said, "I believe those are—"

"Uncle, please just—" said Ray before the horseshoe hit him on the head. Ray slowly turned to him. "I was trying to tell him to keep quiet."

"That's my job," replied the horseshoe.

"So, you just cut him down?" continued the officer.

"Yes, sir. I just cut him down."

"We found him swinging," said Ray before receiving another smack on the head. "Ouch! Dang, it all! Son of a bitch!"

"Ray, language, please," said Osborn.

The burnside walked back to Osborn, facing him, and said, "You robbing him?"

"No. Just reading his letters, and your breath smells."

"Ah, yeah? You can smell it with those things up your nose?"

"I can still smell it, yes, and it's awful."

"You were gonna rob him, though. Do a little light fingering?" said the wild-eye.

"Were you gonna rob him?" asked the officer.

"No. We were just passing through and came upon him."

"Damn! This ole' boy stinks!" cried out the wild-eye coming close to Golding's body.

The officer spat out chewing tobacco and said, "But you said you knew him."

"Yes, but from his letters and things in his pockets. I read most of his letters from his family."

"So, you were gonna steal the things in his pockets?" asked the wild-eye.

"No. I always put what I find back."

The burnside laughed, shook his head, and said, "Now, who does that? You gonna take something out, steal it, and put something back. It don't make sense."

The officer's brow furrowed. "You could be a Reb spy? Ya might as well tell me true cause I'll find out," said the officer.

"I'm not a spy. I'm on my way to Philadelphia for a book signing." Ray's eyes darted to Osborn.

"What's a book signing?" asked the wild-eye.

"He's a spy," said the burnside.

"Oh yeah! He's a spy," added the wild eye—the skinny private nodded in agreement.

"He is not a spy. He's a Union captain. Your superior officer," said Ray before another smack. "Dang it all!! I'm telling ya true!"

"And you said you were headed where again?" asked the officer. "To a book signing in Philadelphia."

The burnside took his gun back from the wild-eye and laughed.

"Captain? You ain't no captain," said the burnside.

Osborn ignored the burnside and continued facing the officer. "I am. I'm a captain. General McClellan commissioned me."

"That's true!" said Ray before yet another smack. Ray rubbed the top of his head.

The officer spat again. "Captain? I don't see no uniform."

"Yes, I'm Captain Osborn Roche. Captain Roche. I am a part of the general's staff."

"This strange son bitch a captain?! Ah-ha!" the burnside cackled before the other two privates joined in. "Ain't possible. He's a moron or something."

"You shush up, you!" said Lou.

"You shush up, crazy eye," replied the burnside.

"It's true," said Osborn.

Ray quickly turned around, facing the horseshoe. "It's true!" Ray pierced the horseshoe with his stare. It was a standoff.

"It don't say captain on your wagon there," said the officer, spitting more chewing tobacco. "Well, you are not in uniform. You're with a dead deserter. I'd say nine outta ten, you're a spy."

"He's a spy," repeated the burnside. "Sure enough," added the wild-eye.

"I say we need to hang y'all right here and right now," said the officer.

Ray turned; jaw dropped. "Lieutenant, I..."

"Ah! Ha! Naw. I'm just fooling!" The officer raucously laughed, leaned over, and spat again. Confusion appeared on his men's faces, not getting the joke. The officer turned to the skinny private. "You find any weapons in there?"

"No, sir."

"All right then, we'll just see about all this. We're going that way anyways, so's you can just follow us. Hitch up that mule.

Ray turned back to the horseshoe, twice the size of him. "That shit hurt!" The horseshoe shrugged and walked away.

"It's noteworthy that we came to the same conclusion from different means. I mean about how he killed himself and all," said Osborn as he sat in between Ray and Lou on the wagon's bench.

"Oh, yes, I suppose. Very noteworthy," replied Lou.

Osborn turned to Ray, driving the wagon. "Does that, does that feel good, Ray? The cloth on your head?" Osborn reached into his pocket for his own, twisting it around his fingers.

"Better than it did, I'd guess."

The soldiers walked in front and beside them, with the officer riding ahead. On the floor in the wagon lay Golding's body—the death smell floating around them.

Osborn recalled Golding's family letters in his head, repeating his siblings' and parents' names before creating a story in his head. A smile came to his lips.

"You have a story?" she asked.

"Yes, I do," he replied.

"Don't encourage him," said Ray.

"When I was a child, I remember my family sending me to visit this boy, Peter Golding—"

Ray turned to Osborn, straight-faced. "No, you didn't."

"Yes, my family sent me to visit Peter in Maine. The Goldings were distant relatives."

Ray shook his head. "This is so tiring."

Lou clapped. "Tell me, Osborn. I want to know."

Osborn turned to Lou and quietly spoke, "I would go on the boat with Peter when he and David would fish with their father. Their father was kind to me and showed me everything about fishing. It's a shame I can no longer recall how. I remember when he called me his favorite friend. We took the small dinghy out with his sister Alissa and tipped it over. She was so angry at us, but she didn't tell on us to their parents. Gwen wasn't even born yet, I believe."

Lou laughed. "I like that one." He tapped his forefinger to his lips as he tried to think up more of the story. Out of the corner of his eye, he could see her piano fingers moving about above her lap. His hand reached for one without turning to her, taking it in his grasp.

She turned to him, her smile disappearing. "I'd rather you didn't hold my hand anymore," she said, using two hands to pull it away.

Both Ray and Osborn turned to her. Ray immediately spun back to the road, avoiding the conversation. "I thought friends could hold hands," said Osborn.

"I've changed my mind. Only sweethearts hold hands."

The Union Army camped outside Winchester, Virginia. They followed the overcoated officer through the rows of tents, horses, cannons, and wagons. He turned to them, said, "Wait here," and walked into a tent. The wild-eye private sat on a barrel eight feet away, with the burnside private standing next to him.

"Sir, coming back from the schoolhouse, we picked up a man who says he's a Union captain but has no uniform," said the officer from inside the tent.

"What division is he from?"

"I don't know. Didn't ask him," said the officer.

"He a deserter?"

"I believe he's a photographer." The tent flap flew open, and General Sedgwick came rushing out with his six junior officers in tow.

"Mr. Roche!" said Sedgwick, recovered from his injuries. The soldiers came to attention for the general. "I've been expecting you."

Ray turned to the burnside. "See, fool?"

"Expecting me?" asked Osborn.

"I have. Please follow me." The general limped off with everybody in tow, following him through the camp. He stopped at his tent and turned. "Uh, excuse me, men. I shall have a private conversation with Mr. Roche. Thank you."

The men saluted and left as the general entered his tent, with Osborn following. Lou and Ray stood outside. "You kept your leg, General."

The general sat behind his desk. "Yes, I did. It's much better. I am looking forward to my next battle. Please sit, Captain. So, is that Louise Cattell out there with your nephew?"

"Why, yes, it is. Would you like me to bring her in?"

"No, it's fine. But I'm glad I found you first. It seems you are a wanted man."

"Uh, how's that? How's that?"

"I recieved a telegram from the war office. It seems Miss Cattell's father has quite a bit of pull around here. The order says to detain you for kidnapping."

The general's eyes went to the side of the tent when they heard Lou yell, "I am not kidnapped!" from outside.

Sedgwick turned to Osborn. "I can see that, and of course, I will not abide by these foolhardy orders. But I have to suggest to you that maybe you should leave the field of battle. Where do you call home, Mr. Roche?"

"Pittsburgh."

"A fine town. I'd suggest you go back there. It's far enough from her father. Are you in love with the young lady?"

Osborn froze. "Uh, well, I—"

From outside the tent, Lou asked, "Tell me what he said?!"

The general rolled his eyes and continued, "Well, whatever the case, it would be best to go, although I do indeed enjoy my encounters with my good friend, the world-famous Captain Roche."

"Good friend? Oh, my, that is wonderful news, wonderful news."

"And now..." said the general, pulling out his copy of Osborn's book. "I will have the honor of a signature." The general laid out the book in front of Osborn, also handing him a pen.

"To my good friend, General..."

The general interrupted, "Please write, General John Sedgwick."

"Oh, yes, of course. To my good friend, General John Sedgwick..."

"Sign your name and put down, 'fighting time with photography.'" Pleased with himself, the general rocked back in his chair.

"Indeed, indeed. Fighting time with photography, you remember. Fighting time with photography, yes."

CHAPTER 25

"Hoady doesn't like trains, doesn't like trains," said Osborn before Hoady snorted air and shook his head. "See that, see that? He agrees." Osborn, Ray, and Lou traveled along the road next to the Susquehannock River.

"I think it's you who doesn't like them," said Ray.

"I find trains a marvel," said Lou.

"I agree with Hoady," said Osborn.

"The canals will get us across the mountains in five days. Hoady will take six weeks to get to Pittsburgh," said Ray. "Charles Dickens did it. You read the papers. He's one of your favorites."

"Ooh, yes, I love Dickens," agreed Lou.

"Yes, but even he mentioned it was precariously steep. He didn't seem to like it much, didn't like it much. And the Allegheny Portage Railroad ends at Johnstown, and Johnstown is where Lou is from."

"Oh, yeah, that's not good. I forgot all about that. Why didn't you—"

"My father will not be there. It will be the last place he wants to go and has been since my mother passed away."

"Let's hope so. Maybe we should bypass Johnstown," said Ray. "Oh, no. We must stop and see Mr. Parker. We must. And Lou needs more embalming fluids and a new pump. He will have it. He will have it."

"Fine, but let's get it and get on outta there, to be safe."

Banana-shaped Conestoga wagons, loaded with pioneers heading off to the distant lands of the plains, crowded the barge dock. Lou held Hoady's reins on the wagon's bench while Ray walked in front, guiding the horse by the bit across the precarious gangplank onto the barge. Too nervous to watch, Osborn sat inside the wagon, eyes closed.

"Leave your horses or mules hitched up and set your brakes," called out the bargemaster. Lou pulled up the brake and parked their wagon inches away from two other wagons. With the barge full, it left little room between the wagons, making the only way to the rear a crawl underneath.

Lou turned to the wall behind her, cupped her hands around her mouth, and said, "We're set, Osborn."

"Thank you, Lou," he replied.

Ray climbed back up and sat next to Lou, leaning back to enjoy the scenery of the bright green grass-covered banks. Eight dark brown mules pulled the barge along the canal—four on one side of the canal and four on the other.

"How are we going faster than Hoady? Hoady is just as fast as those mules," said Lou.

"But Hoady gets to rest," said Ray.

"That's true. So, you grew up in the home we're going to?"

"Yep. Pittsburgh is my hometown. Although, I'd say this wagon is more my home than the home in Pittsburgh. Uncle and I travel so much."

"Yes, Osborn mentioned he raised you. I'm very sorry to hear you lost your parents."

"Consumption. It was so long ago, it seems."

"After they passed, he came to live with you?"

"Yes. My mother passed first. Two months later, my father was dying. They wrote to my uncle, and he moved in a week later with a bag and three large trunks. My father passed on two weeks later. I'd never met my uncle before. When he first moved in, he was incredibly awkward. I mean, even more than he is now. I would watch him like a bearded lady at a freak show. Everything about him was peculiar. After I found out he hated to be touched, I would torture him."

Lou turned to the grassy banks. "He told me."

"He did? Yes, but, oh, how I regret it now. Every morning, I'd wake up to breakfast and clean clothes. Every morning was like the previous day didn't exist. He'd be the same man, the same good man, always trying to make an angry boy happy. Then I learned he hated certain smells and all loud noises and—"

"Oh, noises. I just can't," said Lou, shaking her head.

"Don't say can't, he did. Well, he's learned to tolerate them. But the worst was he would never venture out. I always thought it was because he wanted to keep an eye on me, but no. He never went out. Like anywhere outside the fences of our home…"

"I was like that too."

"Oh, yeah?"

"Mmm, hmm. I could do it if my father were with me, but I always preferred what I was used to. Being with you and Osborn is my first time away from my father."

"Seems you're doing well with it."

"Thank you."

"But with him, he'd even have everything delivered, or I'd run to the store."

"What changed him?"

"The daguerreotype. He bought it so we could do something together in the house. Become closer and get to know each other, he told me. I thought it was interesting, but you know how he is; he became fixated on it. He worked on it, played with it, day and night. And then he couldn't stop himself. After he photographed everything in the house, he knew he needed to get out and photograph more. And his photographs were what changed my mind. Through them, I could see how he saw the world through his eyes. He'd explain the importance of the image in the photograph, and it gave me an appreciation for him and his wealth of knowledge. He is so smart on every topic. People misjudge him so often." Ray turned to Lou. "They misjudge you as well, I see, just like him. I did, too. I have to admit."

"You did?"

"I'm sorry to say I did. But you proved me wrong. You're just like him. You know so much. You're so skilled at your trade."

"Thank you, Ray."

"So, I don't want to butt into your relationship with him—"

"Friendship."

"Yeah, friendship. I mean, I don't blame you for being angry and all. I was there. I'd be feeling the same as you. But I know he's…" Ray leaned closer to her, lowering his voice to a whisper, "…in love with you." Ray sat back up, his voice returning to its normal volume. "I can see it. I've known him for a long time, and I can see it."

"That may be, but he's got to show me that. I've never had a fella, and I've never had a friend. Your uncle has been my first best friend, someone that likes me, and someone that is like me. He and I have gotten close real quick because we both never had friends, but maybe I got too close. Brought in more feelings and expectations than I should have. I mean, he is a handsome man, after all. But I have to forget those feelings. I don't want to lose him as a friend."

"I understand, and his aversion to touch? That's a tough one. You can't have a real relationship without it, but he has gotten over things. You never know. He could get over that eventually."

CHAPTER 26

Ray kept a nervous eye out for anything unusual as they pulled into Johnstown. A week away from Gettysburg, Osborn denied his request to stop and cover 'The World-Famous O. Roche Photography' on the sides of the wagon.

The town sat on the western side of the Allegheny Mountains and about seventy miles east of Pittsburgh. The final stop on the Allegheny Portage Railroad, a part of the Pennsylvania canal system. They pulled up their wagon to a large warehouse on the eastern side of the town. The sign read Parker And Sons Undertakers.

Six or seven models of horse-drawn hearses were parked inside the voluminous room, all either black or white. Coffins ranged from simple pine boxes to ornately carved ones, lying upon heavy-duty shelves. The warehouse housed everything a funeral could require. As they walked in, a young man emerged from the shadows and stopped them, pointing to the words painted on the wagon. "Excuse me, are you the photographer?"

"I am. I am."

"Augustus True. I'm an undertaker," he said, sticking out his hand. "I'm sorry, sir. He doesn't shake hands," said Ray as he and Lou came around from the other side of the wagon.

"Yes, I'm sorry, I do not shake hands, shake hands. The name's Osborn Roche."

"My uncle here is world-famous. He's done portraits for Generals McClellan and Burnside and Vice President Hamlin."

"I'm impressed. Are you here to see Mr. Parker?" asked Augustus. "I am. We are old associates, associates."

"I was just speaking to him about needing a postmortem photographer. Would you be available?"

"Possibly, when is it?" asked Ray.

"It's the day after tomorrow. Saturday. Here in town." "We were planning on heading west," said Ray.

"That's true, and we'd have to find a place to stay. It wouldn't be worth the client's money, money," said Osborn.

"I can offer ya a place to stay up with me. We have empty cabins, and it's only four hours from here.

"Hmm."

"We'll feed ya well."

"Yes, Ray. Let's do the job, job."

"All right, Mr. True. Let us take care of some business with Mr. Parker, and we'll follow you up," said Ray.

Osborn, Ray, and Lou continued in. Ray turned to Osborn and said, "We shouldn't have taken that job. This town gives me the shivers now that I know she's from here."

"We'll be all right, Ray. My father won't be here. He's at Gettysburg," said Lou.

"Osborn Roche!" said a grey-haired gentleman approaching with a smile. "My goodness, it's good to see you! If you'd let me, I'd be embracing you like a bear," he said, laughing. "And Ray, my stars, have you grown! How old?"

"Seventeen, sir." Ray stuck out his hand to Mr. Parker.

"My oh my. But you, Osborn! Your work is nothing short of amazing. I've read about you in the papers and your book and book tour. The stories! My oh my! That battle in Seven Pines? The wife was just worried as a fly in a glue pot. But here you are."

"Yes, we are on our way back to Pittsburgh—"

"Get the news about Joseph?"

"News? No news, no," replied Osborn.

Mr. Parker dropped his head. "We lost him at Antietam." Osborn stood unmoved.

"Joseph? No," said Ray before elbowing Osborn.

"Uh! Oh, yes, I'm sorry to hear that too, yes, sorry to hear that."

"He was with the local boys of the Twenty-third Pennsylvanian. We lost a lot that day."

"Well, we're sorry to hear that. We were there too," said Ray. "The fighting got warm there."

"And who's this?" asked Mr. Parker, gesturing to Lou. "I'm Lou, sir. Nice to meet you."

"You his gal?" He motioned his thumb to Osborn. "No, sir. Just friends."

"Well, that's acceptable, I suppose. Where y'all stayin'? You have to stay with us."

"We already mentioned to this young man that we would follow him. Follow him," said Osborn.

"Augustus was his name," said Ray.

"Oh! Good lad. Starting in the business. Yes, he has his first funeral coming up, and he just asked me about a postmortem photographer, and here you show up! I'll be. Hey, make sure you help him out if you're working with him. He could use your expertise."

"Certainly, certainly," said Osborn.

"Mr. Parker, we are in need of some embalming fluids and a pump," said Ray.

"For what?"

"I am an embalmer," said Lou.

"No! I'll be. And a woman too. I'll be. Now, ain't that something."

"My father is Henry Cattell, maybe you've—"

"No! You don't say! I know your father. I might have even met you when you was a youngin'. So sorry to hear about your mother years back."

"Oh, thank you. Yes, my father is traveling with the army now."

"Heard he did Willy Lincoln, yes. I'll be. So, how'd ya meet this one?" Again, his thumb aimed at Osborn.

"After the battle of Seven Pines, it was. Yes, Seven Pines, they called it," said Osborn.

"Of course, he'd remember," said Mr. Parker. "Let's get to your needs, but you must come over while you're in town. The wife would love to see ya."

"It'd be our pleasure, Mr. Parker," said Ray.

"Yes, our pleasure. Our pleasure," repeated Osborn before asking, "Can I use your bath when we come?"

The Romani vardo rolled into a farm with ten cabins scattered around it. They climbed off the wagon's bench as five people emerged to greet them. A beautiful young woman in a black dress walked up to Augustus. The other four—a white woman in her mid-thirties, a black man in his forties with salt-and-pepper hair, and two black women, one a little older than the other—stood around the porch.

Augustus brought the young woman over to the wagon and said, "Missus, this here is Osborn Roche. He's a world-famous photographer—and I'm sorry, I didn't catch y'alls names."

Ray stood with his mouth ajar, staring at the beautiful woman in the black dress. "Ma'am. I'm Ray," he stammered. The woman had striking eyes—one iris ringed in dark green, growing lighter toward the center, and the other the color of a walnut, trimmed in gold.

They gathered in the central room of the farmhouse, where a kitchen counter spanned one wall and a dining table, big enough for six, occupied the center. The Missus and Easter, an older black woman, brought dishes to the table. Abigail, a younger black woman, turned to Lou and asked, "You's a girl, ain't ya?"

Before Lou could answer, Thane, a black man, interrupted, "That ain't a nice—"

"Yes. I am," Lou confirmed.

"I knew it," Easter said with a nod.

"Yes, I saw it too," added Janey, the other white woman, her light brown hair neatly pinned in a bun, and her yellow print dress catching the light.

"Why you cut your hair like that and alls?" Abigail pressed.

"I worked for the army. They wouldn't let me work if they knew I was a girl."

"Men, please, help yourself to a plate of food and take a seat. We ladies are chatting," said The Missus.

"You fought for the army? A woman?" asked Easter.

"No. I didn't fight. I'm an embalmer."

"What's that?" asked Abigail.

"I met one while in the army," said Augustus. "They make it so a cadaver can last for a very long time and be shipped home."

"What's a cadava?" asked Easter.

Augustus nodded solemnly. "A dead body."

Lou turned to him. "You remember the man's name? The embalmer?"

"No. But he had a pockmarked face and reddish-grey hair."

Lou slowly turned to Osborn, then back to Augustus. "That was my uncle, Ben."

"Yes. I believe Ben was his name," said Augustus.

"Where y'all from?" asked The Missus.

Osborn chimed in from against the wall, "Ray and I are from Pittsburgh. Lou's from Johnstown. Yes, from Johnstown close to here."

The Missus asked Lou, "What's your last name?"

"Cattell."

The Missus pursed her lips. "Hmm, don't know no Cattells. But then again, I don't know many folk from Johnstown. Us mountain folk don't travel down the hill much."

"They call you The Missus. Why?" interrupted Ray. "Is that the name you were born with?"

"No. I'm a weeper. All the women kin in my family are weepers." "What's a weeper?" asked Ray.

"They mourn. Mourn for your family. You hire them," answered Osborn.

"Yes. That's right. I was born with the name Melody Ann, but all my kin calls me by Little Miss," she said, every word from her floating to Ray.

"Little Miss. Mind if I call ya by it, Little Miss?" asked Ray with a gleam in his eye.

"You being too familiar, boy. Gotta show respect to the Weeper. She's called The Missus," said Thane.

Little Miss batted her lashes. "It's fine, Thane. He can call me that."

"So, The Missus don't mean you're married?" asked Ray.

"No, I ain't. Never have been."

Ray smiled. "Is it morning already, 'cause I think this room just got brighter."

Thane slapped his hand on his knee. "Boy, how old are you?"

"Ray, that's enough. Enough," said Osborn.

"I'm seventeen. Old enough to know a beautiful woman when I see one."

The dining table burst into laughs and gasps.

"All right, all right," said Little Miss.

"My apologies if my words are distasteful, Little Miss. I meant no harm by 'em," said Ray.

"I don't mind it none. And it's not often a weeper receives a compliment from a handsome young man. I'm flattered, Ray. Thank ya."

"Well, with that, we'll be saying goodnight to ya," said Osborn. "Let's go, Ray." Osborn and Ray walked out into the evening air. "I believe that was rude, Ray. They seemed upset. The black man did, yes, he did."

"She's so beautiful. That Little Miss."

"Yes, she is. But you still have to be respectful. Respectful, yes."

"I suppose. Just couldn't stop myself, I guess."

"Hmm. Maybe I should have accompanied you in Nashville so you could meet girls. I should have."

Osborn stood outside the home the following morning as Lou came out with the other four women and stood beside him. Ray set up the camera in front of the home.

"What's he gonna photograph?" asked Lou.

"He wants to do a portrait of Little Miss," said Osborn. "He asked me if he could do it alone."

"He's got it bad for her, I believe."

"I believe that too. Yes, I believe that."

"I told Little Miss about the fair we saw. They'd like to go."

"Then, we shall."

After Ray finished the portraits, including one additional of Little Miss he made for himself, he asked, "Don't they have a daguerreotype shop down in Johnstown?"

"Not yet," said Little Miss. "Got one in Altoona, though."

Ray nodded thoughtfully and glanced over to Osborn before he said, "That'd be a good place to set up a shop, I'd say."

CHAPTER 27

The fairgrounds buzzed with life, dominated by massive circus tents, outdoor stages, food booths, and rows of carnival games. Children darted from game to game, their laughter mingling with the shouts of stage callers wielding megaphones, summoning crowds to vaudevillian acts. Politicians pontificated from podiums, coins clinked in the glass cup game, and bells clanged from the slamming sledgehammer.

Osborn led the way, with Lou and Ray trailing behind. Ray fixed his gaze on Little Miss's back, a wistful smile playing on his lips.

"Ain't she pretty?" Ray murmured to Lou.

"Very. You like her? You should go on up with her."

"She's got a few years on me. Don't want her to think me a little puppy dog."

"I didn't think she did. I thought she'd taken a shine to you when she first met you at the house. It looked that way to me."

"I thought it was too much. Too much," said Osborn.

Ray's eyes darted to his uncle. "How would you know, Mr. Roche? Maybe you should be thinking of doing more in your case. Much more, if ya know what I mean," replied Ray. With a slight smile, Lou flashed her eyes at Ray before he ran up to Little Miss. He walked with her over to a ring toss game. "Would you like to play? Can I buy you some rings?"

"Aren't you a gentleman. I'd love to play." Easter smiled with a sideways glance to Little Miss, elbowing her in the side, and walked away. Ray bought the rings, handing all of them to her.

"You take half. I want a bigger chance to win one of them dolls."

Neither winning, they meandered off again. Food vendors of ham sandwiches, baked potatoes, spice-cakes, and muffins lined the path. "Can I buy you something to eat or drink?"

"That would be nice."

Ray bought them hot pea soup with a buttered potato, and they ate it while listening to a fiddler accompanied by his six-year-old daughter singing.

"You travel around a bit?" asked Little Miss.

"Yes, mostly with the army. We do a lot of portraits, but my uncle's famous for his battlefield photography."

"Augustus just came home from the war."

"I gathered that. Is he your beau?"

"No, he's Abigail's beau."

"The young negro gal?"

Little Miss cocked her head. "That don't sit right with you?"

"No problem with it at all. The heart loves what the heart loves. You read much?"

"Don't find much time for it, no," she replied.

"I loved her against all discouragement that could be. Great Expectations by Dickens."

"Sounds pretty."

"Would you mind if I asked ya something personal?"

"I suppose it matters what it is."

"Suppose that's true. Well, I was gonna ask, and you can stop me if it's rude, but you're so pretty. Why aren't ya married?"

A small laugh came from her nose. "It's because I'm a weeper, Ray. These folk up here, they know me as the weeper. I weep for their kin, and they treat me, well, all weepers as, I don't know, unsociables. The women of my family have been weeping for generations. Everyone up in these parts knows the Fenn family. They know what we do. There's also a lot of tales about us. Things that ain't true but make a good story. Things like we're all black widows and kill our men off. It don't bother me none. I like what I do. It's in my blood."

"But men don't see past it? I mean, you're so pretty."

She stopped and slapped him on the chest. "Oh, stop, you. Tellin' a girl she's pretty more than three times could be a proposal in some counties."

After the fair, Lou, Ray, and Osborn sat outside on the porch rockers in the warm evening air. "I'll see if there's something I can help with inside," said Lou.

Augustus walked from his cabin across the way and asked, "I ain't late for supper, am I?"

"No, not yet," said Ray. "Hey, Augustus, tomorrow do ya think it'd be all right if I asked Little Miss to go into town with me?"

Augustus sat down on the porch step. "I think it'd be fine. She don't need a chaperone."

"So tomorrow, I won't be helping my uncle out. Would ya mind watching him a bit—"

"I don't need a chaperone either, Ray," said Osborn.

"He doesn't need a chaperone, but sometimes he says things that people take the wrong way."

Osborn twisted his beard. "Apparently, I don't understand most humor."

"And he doesn't like to shake hands—"

"I don't like to be touched, no."

With a glance at Osborn, Ray leaned down and tapped Augustus on the shoulder. He turned to Ray, who mouthed the words, "Watch him."

"The Missus tells me it's your first funeral tomorrow," said Osborn.

"It is, and I'd be much obliged to ya if ya could chaperone me. If you won't take one, I will."

That evening after supper, Augustus sat at the table listening to Osborn speak about his experience in the funeral industry and as a postmortem photographer.

Little Miss stood cleaning dishes as Easter dried them. Ray rose and walked over. "I'll dry those for you, Easter," he said.

"Well, I'll be. A man doing the house chores," said Easter. "I surely don't want to stop that now, do I?"

"And I surely want to see it," said Little Miss.

Ray took the towel and stood next to her. His head kept turning to her like he wanted to say something until he finally did. "Would you... Would you mind if... I mean, I'll be going to Johnstown tomorrow. Would you like to accompany me? What I mean to say is, take a walk around the town. My uncle and Augustus are going. They can take us."

"That'd be nice."

In the morning, Osborn and Augustus dropped Ray and Little Miss on Main Street in Johnstown.

"We'll see you here this afternoon, about three. The sheriff's office is right over there if he tries anything on ya," said Augustus.

"Oh, get on outta here, you!" she replied before Osborn slapped the reins on Hoady.

"Mind if I ask you a question?" asked Ray as they started off down the sidewalk.

"You said that before. What if I do mind?"

"He isn't your beau, but do you like Augustus?"

"Course I like Augustus."

"I mean, like him, like him? Have you taken a shine to him?"

Little Miss turned to him with a raised brow and said, "Augustus is in love with Abigail."

Embarrassed, Ray turned away and said, "It's none of my concern, but I didn't ask who Augustus is in love with."

"Well, the answer is no. I am not, and I am here with you, not him." She took Ray's arm and wrapped hers in it. An ear-to-ear smile spread across Ray's face. "Where's your favorite place to go here in Johnstown?"

"The saloon. We could wake snakes," she said with a devilish grin.

"You don't mean that."

"No, I don't mean that. I'm a weeper. That's like a catholic nun going into one."

"I've seen ladies from the temperance league go into one."

"Really? That must have been a hoot."

Ray glanced over at her as they walked. She wore a pretty brown and blue patterned dress with a long-waisted bodice, tight to the waist, and a blue bonnet. "I meant to tell you earlier, but your dress surely is pretty."

"You're just a man of compliments, aren't you, Ray? But it's kindly appreciated."

"I don't believe I am. I just say what I see. Is that a drug store up there? Do they have ice cream?"

"I believe they do. Let's go."

Ray and Little Miss ate ice cream and toured the shops of Johnstown before returning to the farm in the afternoon. Thane had prepared a bonfire for their final night. He pulled out his fiddle and bow and began playing. Lou laughed and danced with Easter and Little Miss while Augustus sat on a nearby log with Abigail.

Ray stood by his uncle as Little Miss danced by the fire. "The brightness of her cheek would shame those stars," said Ray.

Osborn glanced over to him. "Did you have a good time with her today?"

"Her virtues have taken up my thoughts. I feel tomorrow will be a sorrowful day when we leave."

Osborn turned back to Lou, dancing, and giggling. "I believe I have the same sentiments, Ray. The same sentiments, yes. I believe it's time for bed."

"Wait, Uncle," said Ray as he reached out, grabbing his uncle's arm but immediately releasing it. Ray froze, expecting a reaction, but none came. "You see? I just took your arm."

"Yes, Ray, why did you do that? You know that upsets me. Upsets me."

"Are you upset now? You're not. You just looked at your arm."

"But it still upsets me, Ray."

"But does it, Uncle? It used to upset you, but now…? You have changed or something. You have become used to it or…? Don't you see?" Ray pointed to Lou dancing by the fire. "She helped you. She took your hand and showed you that you could do that."

"Ray, come dance with me!" called Little Miss as she walked with her hand out to him.

Osborn wanted to meet Ray's gaze but couldn't. His eyes flickered across Ray's face as he said, "Go on, Ray. Go on." Little Miss pulled Ray toward the bonfire, and he took her by the hand and waist, dancing to the tune of Thane's fiddle. Lou stood nearby, clapping along, her foot tapping in rhythm with the music.

As she watched them, the smile on her face slowly faded. She turned to Osborn, her expression distant and filled with unspoken questions. Her eyes searched his, seeking answers he couldn't provide. Unable to face her, he turned away and retired for the night.

"Oh, damn the day," said Thane as he stumbled out of his cabin, squinting in the morning sun and pulling up his suspenders. "Shouldn't 'a drunk all that whiskey." Ray and Osborn hitched up Hoady as Thane ran off to the outhouse.

Easter came out after him, shouting, "Shoulda thought of that last night!" before walking over to Ray and Osborn. "Can I make ya breakfast before y'all go?"

"That'd be fine. I could use some. Thank ya," replied Ray.

"I'll see if they's up," she said before heading up the steps to the main house door.

A few minutes later, Lou came out from the main house yawning and said, "We getting ready to go? They are making breakfast for us."

"Yes, we're planning on it," said Ray. "Little Miss in there?"

"Getting dressed," replied Lou.

"Can you ask her to come out if she could? So, I can speak to her."

Lou smiled. "I will."

Three minutes later, she came out with Little Miss. "You wanted to speak to me, Ray?"

"Can I get a moment of your time?"

Little Miss turned to Lou, who told her, "You go on. I'll help with breakfast."

She came down and stepped up to him. "Now, don't start by asking me if I mind you asking a question," she said with a laugh.

"Naw, I won't. I wanted to ask you… Well, I gotta get my uncle and Lou to Pittsburgh. We are going to set up a daguerreotype shop there and an embalming office for Lou. They need my help, but if I were to come back here, would you be agreeable to courting me?"

Her smile flattened, and she turned away. "Ray, I really like you. You're handsome and smart. Any woman would want to court ya. But I'm a weeper, Ray. You wouldn't want a weeper. I wouldn't want to do that to ya."

"How do you know what I want? The very instant that I saw you, my heart flew at your service."

"I'll always be a weeper, Ray. You can't be taking me away from here. I'll always live here. It's what we do. I'll always be a weeper even if you courted me and even if we marry. You'd have to live here with us. It's a hard life for a man in this family. You'd be playing second fiddle."

The door to Augustus's cabin opened, and Abigail came out dressed and carrying a bag of belongings. "I'm going to throw in with y'all. Can you take me to Pittsburgh?"

"What?" asked Little Miss as Thane returned from the outhouse.

"I'm leaving him, Missus. It just won't work. We just don't work," said Abigail.

"Where's Augustus?" asked Little Miss.

"Augustus ain't here. He left early for a job in Altoona," she replied.

Thane shook his head and said, "Girl, ya can't just do that without tellin' him. That ain't right."

Osborn walked over to listen when she said, "I can't tell him, Missus. I can't, and I'm leaving with y'all." Abigail stormed past Osborn over to their wagon. "No one is stopping me," she added as she climbed in and slammed the door behind her.

Lou came out of the house and yelled, "Breakfast!" All their heads turned to her with concern. Lou's brows jumped before she said, "What? I only helped cook it."

CHAPTER 28

The journey to Pittsburgh had taken two days, all downhill. Lou sat next to Abigail on the wagon bed, listening as she spun tales of her life as a slave. Abigail spoke of how she ran off the plantation with only a pair of scissors for protection, how she found Augustus in a field somewhere in Georgia, and how his kindness won her over, and how they fell in love during the journey. It wasn't until the evening that she concluded her story, saying, "...But I saw folk won't be 'cepting of us. Never will, no how. And that's the last thing I'll say on the matter. Now, I'll be making supper, and I don't want no help. It's my way of paying my keep, and that's the last thing I'll say on that matter as well."

After supper, the ladies went to sleep in the wagon. Osborn sat alone, warming his hands in front of the campfire. Its flames caressed the logs like water over creek stones. The scent of Jasmine floated in the late evening air. Osborn waved it away and blew it from his nose as he sat on a stool in front of the fire. "What, you don't like Jasmine? I thought that was one you liked," asked Ray as he walked back from collecting more logs.

"Too strong, too strong."

"The ladies go to bed?"

"Yes, yes, they did."

Ray tossed the logs next to the fire. "I saw you tonight. You seemed sad."

"I'm fine, Ray. I'm fine."

"I don't believe you are fine. I see it." Ray picked up a branch and broke it over his knee. "You remember what I told you last night?"

"I remember. Of course, I remember."

"Have you thought about that? About the touching? That it could be all in your head?"

"It is not in my head! Not in my head."

"Maybe not, but it is something you can learn to do. Learn to accept. You have overcome similar problems." Osborn shrugged his shoulders.

Ray tossed another log in. "Uncle… I'm going to Pittsburgh with you and helping you get settled."

"Well, yes, of course, you are."

"Yes, but after I'm done, I'm planning on taking the other wagon and coming back here. Moving back here to court Little Miss." Osborn's eyes stayed on the fire as Ray continued, "I believe I'll be sick till I see her again, she's taken my heart so, and I want a family eventually. You taught me a trade, and I'm so thankful to you and for you. But I gotta do this, you see? I gotta do this for myself." Rare tears filled Ray's eyes. "And I think it's time you did the same." Osborn glanced up at him. The yellow-orange flames shimmered on Ray's wet eyes. "Inside that wagon is what you been waiting for your whole life. You're letting it get away from you."

Osborn's gaze returned to the fire as Ray sniffed up the tears streaming down his face. "You can do it. You are nothing short of magical. When you put your mind to something, you focus on it like no one can." Ray walked over to Osborn and stood next to him. "I'm going back. I'm gonna be leaving you, Uncle. I'm going back for love, and you need to do the same. It's waiting for you in that wagon, and you deserve—" Osborn rose and unexpectedly threw his arms around Ray, pulling him in tight. Ray gasped in shock.

"I love you, Ray. I love you, Ray," he said, tears falling onto Ray's shoulder.

Ray sucked in a halting breath. "I… I… I love you too." Ray wrapped his arms around his uncle, enveloping him like a cocoon around a caterpillar. They held each other in the tightest embrace, an embrace that would release Osborn with new wings into the bluest sky.

Lou and Abigail came out from the wagon, stretching and yawning. Having awoken early, Osborn and Ray sat on stools by the fire. "Good morning," said Lou. Ray and Osborn grinned at each other like they had a secret plan. "What's with you boys today?" she said, giving them a suspicious glance. "Something's going on here. I don't know what it is, but something's going on."

After they ate breakfast, Abigail gathered the pan, plates, and silverware to take to the creek with Lou. "May I help, Abigail? May I help?" asked Osborn.

"No, you men just sit on down, even you, Lou. I'll do all this. Y'all are helping me. I want to do my part."

"But I want to do them with Lou. With Lou, yes."

"I ain't gonna let you. You can just sit there. Let me do this—"

Ray put up his hand to Abigail. "No, Abigail. Let them do this," said Ray slowly, spreading the words out.

Abigail turned to Ray, unsure. "It's all right. I want—"

Ray interrupted, "And I said, let…, him…, do…, it." Both women's brows arched as they studied Ray's determination.

"All right, all right, here ya go, Mr. Roche," said Abigail, handing Osborn the pan and dishes.

Osborn and Lou walked off to the creek. Lou scrutinized him with side-eye glances. They went to their knees at the creek, washing everything with gravel. Osborn's heart beat like the wings of a tethered falcon trying to take flight. His head swam in dizzy circles to the rhythm of her hands in the water, cleaning the pot—he spun away to rid the thought.

"Lou, would you forgive me? Forgive me for not taking you to the dance?"

She turned to him. "Of course, I already did."

"But you didn't. You won't hold my hand."

"Osborn, you're my first best friend. I don't want to lose you. We got close, and maybe I thought up stuff about us in my head. Wrong expectations about us. Holding hands brings those expectations back, and I don't want that because I know you don't want that."

Lou finished and stood, facing him. He rose, locking his eyes on her with an intensity she had only seen once before.

Osborn's veins filled with passion like the arsenic fluid that flowed into her customers, and with a slow, prolonged exhalation from his lungs, he said, "I want that." The pot and plates slipped from his hands as he ran to her, taking her into his arms. His eyes were inches from hers, staring deeply. She dropped her plates as he held her close, his lips meeting hers in a soft kiss. Pulling away, he watched her suck in a surprised breath. Still holding her arms, he said, "I want that, I want that too," and asked, "Will you marry me?"

She swallowed hard as the tears streamed from her eyes. "I will."

Osborn kissed her again. "Will you forgive me for not taking you to the ball?"

She cocked her head with a questioning expression and said, "Um, well, I just agreed to marry you, so yes."

"Will you dance with me now? Dance with me?"

"How fun. Yes, of course."

Osborn took her by the hand lead up the creek embankment to the pine needle-covered floor under the trees. He placed his left hand on the small of her back and took her hand with his right. "Wait," she asked. "How? How did you? What happened so you can hold me?"

"It was Ray. He cares so much about me. So much," he replied as he took his first step forward in a box step. They waltzed around the tall pines as Osborn hummed the melody of Strauss' Blue Danube.

The wagon traveled a dirt road lined on either side by a dense forest of red oaks, black oaks, white oaks, and shagbark hickory trees. Osborn sat on the wagon bench with Lou and Ray on either side. Abigail lay on the bed inside, singing to herself. All four dressed in their best clothes. Osborn lifted his face to the sky—the sun's rays warming his skin. Lou smiled, shut her eyes, and did the same. A leaf slipped across her cheek on its descent. She opened her eyes to it on her lap, picked it up, and spun its stem between her fingers.

"We're here," said Ray, pulling Hoady into the same church Osborn had brought Ray when he was young.

"I have good memories here," said Ray.

"Yes, you always wanted to come here and go to the hot springs over yonder."

"And the fair in the summertime."

"Yes," said Osborn.

Puffy white clouds floated slow and low in the blue sky above. One, peering around the church steeple like a mischievous angel. The foursome walked around the unoccupied church for a spell before the church's last pastor, Preacher Corbin, stepped up, walking with a stoop. At eighty-six years old, the pastor, long retired, was now the church's caretaker, living a solitary life down the road. He frequently greeted visitors, giving them a tour and telling the old church's history.

Dank, humid, and smelling of musty drapery, the old church had fallen into disrepair. Sunlight streamed in through three holes in the old roof made by a thunderstorm. The holes pigeons in, and the pigeons lured the cats in. A family of cats lived precarious lives on the first level of beams stretching across the church and all around the inner edges. The pigeons dangerously flew above them, clawing onto the rafters or on the high stained-glass windowsills.

Lou and Abigail walked down the side aisle to an office behind the pulpit. Abigail carried the light blue dress General Stuart gave Lou for the ball. The office had two wood chairs and a cross on the wall. As soon as they entered, Lou dropped her clothes and stood naked in front of Abigail, a big grin on her face.

Abigail snorted a laugh. "You ain't shy now, are ya?" said Abigail.

"No, I like being naked."

Abigail shook her head before studying Lou. "You're a different one, aren't ya?"

"Osborn says we're peculiar."

"On the sunny side of peculiar, I'd say. Now, don't ya have any drawers?"

Lou pointed to her long johns. "Just those."

"Hmm, yeah, those won't work with the dress. Well, suppose you won't wear none. Let's get the dress on." Abigail helped Lou put it on over her head and buttoned it up in the back. "How's that feeling?"

"Scratchy, but airy with no drawers. I like it."

Abigail laughed again and spun Lou around to face her. "Don't be telling nothing about not wearing drawers."

"Oh, I won't." Abigail fluffed up the ruffles around the wrists. "Abigail, why did you leave Augustus?"

"You must've read my mind. I don't know why. I miss him now. Maybe I shouldn't have left. He was a good man, and I ain't met many of them."

"How long were you with him again?"

"Just a short time, but…sometimes a short time can leave a long-time mark on ya."

"You love him?"

"I believe I did. He was a sweet one. Y'all getting married reminds of him."

"Why did you leave him then?"

Abigail took a deep breath and released it. "The day I met him, I found him lying alone in a big ole' field. His horse was off in the distance. I was thinking he might be dead, lying there. I could steal it. But he opened his eyes. I remember thinking they were kind eyes, but he was still a white man, and I'm a runaway slave. He didn't make no move for me, and I had my scissors in hand to be safe. But after a spell, I saw he was a good one, didn't try nothin'. Didn't ask if I was a slave, runaway, or not. He was different than most, at least most I was used to, black or white." Abigail's eyes filled with tears.

"That makes you sad?" asked Lou. Abigail nodded. "I'm sad my father isn't here. It makes me sad, too," she said, her eyes turning to the floor. "I wish he could walk me down the aisle and be proud of me and give me away to Osborn, the only other man I've loved."

Abigail wiped her eyes and smiled. "Yeah, looks like you gotta good one there."

"He is a good one."

"Wasn't Augustus a good one?"

"Augustus?" Abigail started before turning her gaze to the sky. "Ya know, I've always thought most people are like stones. There's rough stones. There's hard stones, soft stones, and smooth stones, big stones and small stones, skipper stones, and stones you can scrub your feet with. Augustus is like a skipper stone. The best kind of stone. The kind of stone that fits just right in your hand and is so smooth it feels right in your hand. The kind you could whip across a lake and skip… nine or ten times. And that's a beautiful thing, across a flat lake when it hits like that. Yessum, Augustus is a skipper stone too, but I'm guessing since someone like me, that's been through it like I have, and ya seen all this stuff ya don't want to see and ya been all this thing that that ya don't want to be… I don't know, I suppose when I needed a ten skipper stone, Augustus only skipped nine."

"Osborn is my skipper stone."

Abigail's smile rose. "That be truest of the true. I believe what you might have with Osborn is that eleven-skipper stone."

Ray stood as Osborn's best man, waiting with the preacher for Lou to arrive. A sudden cat yowl and scuffle broke the silence, followed by a puff of feathers floating gently down. Preacher Corbin dusted them off his coat. He smiled politely and said, "From the wings of angels," before clearing his throat and continuing, "We don't have Mrs. Shelly at the piano today, unfortunately," the preacher told Osborn, although Mrs. Shelly hadn't played piano there for over thirty years. The preacher shouted to the back of the church, "You may proceed down the aisle, please! We have no music to accompany you!"

Entering from the vestibule, Lou proceeded down the aisle, escorted by Abigail. Osborn sucked in a deep breath and flapped his hands. "You all right?" asked Ray. "Calm yourself. It'll be all right. It's just us and your beautiful bride." Abigail brought Lou to Osborn, and Lou put out her hand. Osborn took it with one and wiped the tears with the other.

"Oh no, Osborn, you're gonna make me cry."

"I'm fine, I'm fine."

They stood facing each other as the preacher read the vows. When it came time for the rings, Osborn reached into his pocket and pulled out two. Osborn said, "These, these, these, rings are made from wire, wire we had in the wagon.

Ray helped me make them. They are not what you deserve, but, but, but, and they are not perfect, they have flaws, they have flaws like we have flaws, Lou. Or, at least, that's what we've been told all our lives, told all our lives, right? Both of us have been told that. But you see," he continued, placing a ring on her finger and then his own, "these rings are unique because they were made with love and care. They remind us that even with our imperfections, we are perfect for each other."

Abigail made everyone pork sandwiches, including the preacher, who locked up the church and took his home. "Where are you planning on going when we get to Pittsburgh?" Ray asked Abigail.

"I don't know. Just going is alls. I'll find something."

"My uncle and I spoke about it, and they wouldn't mind it if you'd like to stay on with them."

"Yes, Abigail. There are several bedrooms, several bedrooms," said Osborn.

"Stay on with y'all?"

"Yes. I will be investing in a daguerreotype shop and an embalming shop for Lou, so I will not be able to pay much at first—"

"Pay?!" she exclaimed, bursting out in laughter.

"Well, you let us know," said Osborn, standing and taking Lou's hand. "Lou and I are going to walk over to the hot springs." Osborn walked off with a wave of his hand.

"Don't stay too long. I want to get there before nightfall," Ray called after them.

Abigail turned to Ray with a suspicious expression. "You gonna pay me?! What I gotta do?"

"Stay with them, cook, clean, take care of the place and—"

"I can stay with y'all, *and* you gonna pay me?"

"I'm not. They are. And room and board, of course."

"What' s room and board?"

"A bedroom and food, of course."

"But why? Y'all don't even know me."

"I'm headed off, doing something I gotta do. I won't be with my uncle anymore. They wouldn't mind it none, and I would just feel a bit better. Well, you see, you have to watch out for both of them. You know what I mean?"

"You mean because of how they get all in a huff about small things?"

"Yes, but it's not small to them. It disturbs them. They experience life and people, and everything around them differently than we do. They are both highly sensitive. So sensitive that things that don't bother us do bother them a lot. They don't exchange pleasantries. They just say what they think. Watch for that. Sometimes it's bad. Sometimes you might have to explain away something he says. It can be embarrassing. You just have to blame it on him being an artist. Folks fall for that."

"He's an artist. I can say that. Is that what artists do?"

"I know my uncle works hard to appear like we do. I've taught him to recognize emotions in others, but he has to always be on the lookout for those clues which come so easy to us. I'm sure it's taxing on him. They are very smart people who will pay for a nice life for you, but they are like beautiful flowers, you have to water and protect them if you want that. If Lou panics, you go over and comfort her, tell her it's gonna be all right, and get her away from the situation that caused it. If he's in a panic, don't touch him. Never touch him. You get in front of him and tell him, real nice, to follow your voice out of danger and tell him you'll bring him nice hot tea, and you'll both sit on the couch, or you'll make him a hot bath—all pleasing thoughts. I'm sure Lou's the same. Get them to a quiet place and calm them. An hour of quiet solitude works."

"Sakes alive. I didn't see any of that coming from them."

"Can you do all that?"

"I can do it. I used to work for an old white woman, and she was as tough as a nickel steak. Ain't nothin'. So, what about you? Where ya off to?"

"Don't you know?" he asked.

"The Missus?"

"Yeah."

"She is a good sort from what I can tell, but I hate to tell ya; I think she got it bad for Augustus."

"I'm hoping not. Anyway, I gotta try."

"I 'spect."

"So, I can count on you with them?"

"Yessum, and I'm a might thankful for the offer, I tells ya true. Real thankful. It's a blessing, it is."

"Yep, I'll tell you, your work will be rewarded far more than money can. You will learn far more than you can teach, and you will be rewarded with real treasure. An unconditional love so powerful it will rearrange your heart."

Abigail turned to Ray with cheeks that rose and fell before her eyes sought out her shoes. Tapping them together, she said, "I could use a little heart rearranging."

CHAPTER 29

"And it has a bath. I'm excited to take a bath," Osborn said as they drove the wagon up Crape Street in Pittsburgh. A residential dirt street lined with hazelnut trees had two-story brick homes on either side with a scattering of vacant lots.

"My oh my, this home is lovely," said Abigail as they pulled into the back lot behind their two-story home.

"It is, Osborn," Lou agreed. "It has a bathroom inside with gas-heated hot water, four bedrooms, and a maid's quarters. Ray's father built it," explained Osborn.

Ray jumped off the bench and ran off as he called back, "Uncle, just park the wagon and unhitch Hoady. I'll be back out to stall and feed him after I open the place up."

"Go, go on and see it," said Osborn. Lou smiled at Abigail, took her by the hand, and they ran in the back door. Osborn unhitched Hoady before heading inside, removing his boots first before entering. The place smelled musty. He slid a finger across the dusty, lacquered dining table as he passed it, leaving a clean line. Osborn walked upstairs and into his room. Abigail and Lou held hands as they jumped on the bed. When Osborn walked in, they stopped and turned to him.

"This home is charming, Osborn. Is this our room?" asked Lou.

"No, this is my room, my room, yes," he said with a grin. "Do you like it?"

Lou crossed her arms, staring down at him. "We are married now, Osborn."

Osborn's eyes flashed. "Oh! Yes, yes. This is our room. Our room, yes."

Abigail prepared a celebratory supper of ham, potatoes, gravy, and string beans. Osborn, Lou, and Ray waited at the table as she put the last plate on and backed away, nervously picking her teeth with a fingernail. "Well, go on now. Go on and eat," she said.

Lou wrinkled her nose and said, "Well, sit on down so we can."

"Me? Naw, y'all don't want me to—"

"Abigail, sit on down. It's not that way around here. At least not in this home," said Ray. Abigail beamed, ran over, and filled her plate.

"Dang. This ham is delicious," said Ray.

"You like it?"

"Delicious, yes, yes," said Osborn.

After dinner, Abigail rose to clear the dishes. The table froze with a knock on the door. A second knock drove Ray to answer it. Abigail rose from her seat and backed away from the table.

Ray opened the door to the back of a large man. "May I help you?" asked Ray. The man turned to them, spinning a bowler hat on his fist. Pinned on his lapel was a constable's badge.

"Mr. Roche?"

"Yes," replied Ray.

The constable lifted his chin and peered down his nose at Ray. "You look a might young to be Mr. Roche."

Osborn rose from the table. "He is Mr. Roche, and I am Mr. Roche too, his uncle, his uncle. I am."

"Uh, well, I'm Constable Fletcher. Your neighbors saw the old place lit up. Everyone 'round here thought you were out doing that daguerreotype work."

"Well, we were. We needed to come home," said Ray.

"Oh, all right then. Well, I'm pleased ya did because I have a crazy situation I'm—"

"Peculiar, please, peculiar," said Osborn.

"Excuse me?"

Ray glared at Osborn. "Uncle, please," he demanded before turning back to the constable.

The constable continued, "It seems someone from the war office telegraphed us, and they say you kidnapped a young woman—"

"Kidnapped!" exclaimed Ray. "That is the most preposterous…!" \

"Well, now, hold on there. So, you don't know a Louise Cattell?"

"I am right here," said Lou, standing and walking over. "I was not kidnapped."

"Oh, well, sorry, Ma'am, but your father says Mr. Roche took ya according to the war office."

"Took me?"

"Kidnapped ya, it says."

"Do I look kidnapped to you?"

"Suppose ya don't but—"

"Mr. Roche and I are husband and wife."

The constable jerked his head. "Oh! Well, that might change things a bit. But, so you know, he says you are, and forgive me for saying, some kind of moron or some such. Dangerous, according to Mr. Cattell."

Simultaneously, they all responded, "Dangerous?"

The constable continued spinning the bowler hat around on his fist. "I can see you look…" His eyes walked over her short haircut and the men's clothes she wore. "…somewhat normal to me. But would you mind stepping on over with me to our office down the road? My sheriff will need to hear the which of the why and so forth."

Ray closed the gap between himself and the constable and said, "Constable, they were married earlier today. It's their wedding night. You wouldn't want to make it a bad memory, would ya?"

He lifted his chin again, his bowler still spinning. "I suppose I wouldn't. But I'll be expecting him in the morn. Fine by you?"

"Fine by me," replied Ray. The constable peered around Ray and said, "They told me at the office you were quite well known."

"World famous," replied Osborn.

"Yep," he said before rocking on his heels and saying, "Have a good night now."

As Ray shut the door, Osborn closed his eyes and flapped his hands in panic.

"It's all right, Osborn," said Lou. "Just sit down and breathe."

Osborn did as she asked, taking deep breaths until he calmed.

"Don't panic, Uncle. We will prove it all tomorrow. Let's not ruin your wedding night."

Osborn opened his eyes. "My wedding night, yes, oh, yes," he said, looking around the room. "Where did Lou go?"

A subtle smile grew on Abigail's mouth when she said, "She went to bed." Osborn's eyes turned to the stairs. A bit of light shined down from above. He swallowed hard. Taking a lamp with him, he cautiously walked over to the stairs. At the top, Lou stood swaying her hips in her night robe. Lamplight reflected off her happy, flickering eyes.

"Are you coming to bed?" she asked, her fingers moving as fast as Beethoven's.

"Yes."

Her smile pulled him upstairs. She followed him into the bedroom, lit only by their oil lamps. With the shutting of the door, he spun around fast enough to blow his lamp out. She stood with her back leaning against the door, staring at him.

"Hey, Osborn?"

"Yeah?"

"I can see you're getting anxious."

"Yeah, yeah."

"I am too." Osborn wanted to say something to comfort her, but he couldn't move. He stood staring at her and the great shadow she cast over the ceiling by the lamplight. "You know that time I asked to hold your hand, and you did? And that time, I asked if you wanted to kiss me, and you did?" She turned to her lamp; the only thing left illuminating the room. Her lips blew it out, leaving them in darkness. "Well, since we're married now and all, we should try something else."

The morning sun came through the gauzy curtains into the room. Osborn and Lou lay in bed. Lou tucked herself in his arm, head on his chest. The brown cloth lay on the nightstand next to his spectacles.

"That cloth. Where'd you get it?"

"It is the only thing I've ever stolen in my life. I stole it from you." Surprised, she sat up in bed, the bedcovers falling from her chest, exposing her breasts. He jerked his head away. His hands flew to his face, covering it.

"Osborn! Are you embarrassed?" she giggled. "We are married. It's part of being husband and wife." She ran her fingers through his hair, wrapping locks around them as he would with the brown cloth. "They're just a part of my body, and I'm your wife now. You can look any time you want, but if you're too shy about it, I will be modest for you," she said, laying her head back onto his chest and cuddling in close. His hands slowly came down. "You surely weren't shy last night." Again, his hands flew to his face, covering it. "Oh, goodness gracious. It's just a body. You've seen many bodies with your postmortem photographs."

"Miss Tabitha was the first woman's breasts I ever saw, and I don't remember it well because I averted my attention so quickly. So quickly."

"Well, I am your wife. You don't have to avert your attention from me. You've told me I'm beautiful so many times. I love that. I get butterflies in my stomach when you do that," she said, lifting her head for his reaction. "You know that's a euphemism?"

"Yes, Ray told me. Means you're happy-nervous. Happy-nervous."

"Yes." Returning her head to his chest, she continued, "I hope you find my body attractive too."

"I certainly do. Indeed, I do."

"You certainly did last night." Embarrassed, his hands flew to his face again. "Stop, Osborn. You are so handsome to me, and your body is a part of that, too. You're just a handsome, cuddly bear." She squeezed him, and his hands came away again, revealing a smile. "With embalming, I've seen so many bodies, you just become used to seeing them, and I've seen many, many penises." His hands repeated the action. She lifted her head to him. "None as handsome as yours, honey. Can I call you honey now? I thought it was so sweet when couples called each other, honey."

"Yes, yes, you may," he said, thankful for a change in conversation.

"Back to your theft; when did you steal a rag from me?"

"The second time I saw you. You washed your hands and arms with it. I was jealous of it."

"Jealous?"

"It was flowing over your skin, caressing you. Something I only wished I could do then. Wished I could do, yes."

"You brushed my arm with it that one night."

"Yes. I love the way you smell. It had your scent in it. I would breathe in the smell of you with it. I wanted more of that scent."

She giggled. "I know. I thought that was so peculiar. But also, the most romantic thing ever," she said, putting her hand through his hair. "That's why I rubbed it on my breasts that night." His eyes slammed shut. "That's what won you over, wasn't it?"

"It was your aroma from that place, that special place, so intimate, such a part of you around your heart and…Well, those things that make you a woman."

"Breasts."

"Yes."

"Where do you keep it?"

"My pocket. Always in my pocket. And when I die, someone will find it there and make up a story about me and you. Me and you."

"No. You'll never die," she pouted, her head resting on his chest. "Will you, Osborn? Never die. You have to promise me, promise me. And you have to say it like that, with two promises."

"I promise you , promise you."

CHAPTER 30

"You hitch up Hoady?" Osborn asked Ray as he sat in the corner chair of the parlor room. Ray lowered the paper in his hands. Osborn had dressed for the sheriff in his grey suit with a bow tie.

"You look like a new man in that suit. All that for the sheriff?" asked Ray.

"Thank you, Ray. Yes, I want to make a good impression."

"I'm ready," said Lou coming down the stairs in a man's grey suit and tie. "What do you think?" she asked as she modeled her suit.

Ray dropped the paper to his lap. "Is that my old suit?"

"I found it in your closet. It was a little dusty, but..." she spun around. "It fits."

"I wore that when I was twelve."

"Thirteen, Ray. Thirteen. I bought it for your graduation from Primary school. Primary school."

"Yes," Ray said slowly, recalling the memory.

"I was very proud. A very proud uncle, yes. But it now fits Mrs. Roche perfectly, perfectly."

Lou squealed, sending Osborn ducking down to a squat and throwing his hands on his ears. Lou ran to him, concerned. "I'm sorry, Osborn," she said, taking his arms and raising him back up. "I couldn't help it. You called me Mrs. Roche. That's the most adorable, lovely name anyone has ever called me." She smiled a moment wistfully before saying, "And I think I'm going to cry."

Osborn drew concern. "No, Mrs. Roche, don't—"

"Ah!" she squealed again with a giddy smile. Osborn dropped out of her hands to the floor. "You said it again!" she exclaimed, reaching again for him. "I won't be loud again, I promise." Grinning ear to ear, she turned to Ray. "May I find more clothes, Ray? After we come back?"

"Don't see why not. They don't fit me anymore." Ray set aside his paper and rose.

Lou turned back to Osborn and said, "Mr. Roche," as she put out her arm for him to take. Osborn took it and opened the front door for her. "Mrs. Roche," he said, his hand outstretched, showing the way. Lou slapped her hand over her mouth as they walked out.

"I'm a little scared, Osborn," said Lou as Hoady pulled them down Liberty Avenue toward the sheriff's office. "What if they take me away?"

"We are married, Lou. And they will see you are not what your father says. They will see."

"Ah!" gasped Lou, hands to her mouth.

Osborn tried to follow her line of sight. "What?"

"The wagon right there!" she said, pointing. "My father is here!"

"There it is," said Ray, pointing to a wagon in front of the sheriff's office with "Cattell Embalming" written on it.

"No, no, we can't go in," pleaded Lou.

"We will tell them we are married, Lou. It'll be—"

"He will convince them. He knows doctors. Look at the clothes I wear. They'll claim I'm insane or—"

Ray turned the wagon down a side street. Osborn turned to him. "Where are—"

"She's right. Let's not chance it. Let's go back and get Abigail. You all head out of town. I'll go over myself and see about this. If things are good, I'll send you a telegram, just let me know where you are when you get there. Or we can fix this through the courts later."

"Yes, yes, I believe you are right, Ray. I do not want to lose my insane wife."

"You can stay if you wish. Take care of the house," Osborn told Abigail.

"Naw. They find a negro alone in that place. I'm good as dead. I'd rather go on with you folk if ya don't mind me."

"Why is dead good?" asked Osborn.

"I loaded all your things in the wagon," said Ray as he loaded up the last box. "And I locked up the house."

"Of course, you can come with us, Abigail," said Lou.

Abigail shook her head, confused. "I don't see how they can do this," said Abigail. "Y'all are married now."

"But my father is here. He is a well-known man of science and will convince them I am not of sound mind."

"Ben told us he would say such things," added Osborn.

"Yeah, Abigail. It's safer for them. I'll deal with the sheriff. You all should get on out of here just in case her father convinces them that she's insane or some such."

Abigail smirked. "I know lotsa folk that go insane just from just being married."

"I suppose it's that time," said Ray.

Ray moved in and hugged Lou. Her head against his chest, she asked him, "Why do you have to go off on your own? I'm going to miss you so."

"Goodbye and good luck, Ray. I'll do right by ya. Do what ya said," said Abigail.

"Thank you, Abigail. Safe travels."

Ray walked over to his uncle. "Well, Uncle, I suppose the time has come, and I'm gonna hold you—something I never wanted to do as a boy. I look back on it, and... Well, I probably could have used your fatherly embrace back then. You're gonna make it up to me now by letting me be the one to let go first." Osborn nodded, and Ray pulled him in tight, holding him for as long as he wanted.

Holding eye contact for longer than usual, Osborn said, "I believe it came time for you, didn't it? It was always going to happen. I knew that. I knew that. Always going to happen, yes. It's in your nature to be a man and strike out on your own. Out on your own, yes. I was a good momma bird when you were a boy—doing something I didn't want to do at first, yes? But now, I see the reward for that, yes? You are my nephew but also my best friend, best friend. You're not my best friend anymore, Lou is."

Ray laughed. "Oh, all right then."

"But you are my friend and nephew. Just not my best friend."

"That's just fine with me, Uncle. Lou is the best best friend."

"Yes, she is, but now, now, I'm a good papa bird by letting you fly the nest. Yes, yes, I am letting you fly the nest. It's time I let you fly the nest, isn't it? Isn't it, Ray?"

"It is. And you've always been the best momma and papa bird, Uncle. The very, very best."

CHAPTER 31

Eight feet high and thirty feet across, they had painted 'Alice Dean' in grand red letters on the side of the eight-hundred-and-eighty-ton capacity sidewheel steamboat. At only six months old, it was one of the finest paddlewheels on the Ohio River with three passenger decks, a cargo hold below, and a wheelhouse above. Two massive black stacks towered into the sky, belching black smoke.

The enormous steamship loomed in front of them with its loading gangplank calling them into its cargo hold like a drawbridge into Dr. Frankenstein's castle. Having finished Shelly's book last year, Osborn's anxiety grew with the thought, but also from the precariously slim two feet on either side of their wagon. Osborn and Lou guided Hoady in, acting as blinders to the water below. After unhitching and stalling him, Lou and Osborn went to the wagon to retrieve their bags for the seven-day journey to Paducah, Kentucky. "You don't mind sleeping in the wagon, Abigail?"

"Don't mind it none. It's nice in there."

"We'll bring you food shortly," said Lou.

Osborn and Lou passed through a large passenger lounge filled with music and laughter on the way to their room. The door to their inside stateroom sat on the open-air corridor down the center of the ship. "This is nice," said Lou as she jumped on the bed, leaning back against the wall. "Do we disembark at Paducah?"

Osborn sat on the edge of the bed at Lou's feet. "Unfortunately, yes. We have to move Hoady and the wagon to another ship there. Then we head up the Mississippi to St, Louis. It's all wagon from there."

"Still not sure where we'll end up?"

"Indian territory. Somewhere around Fort Gibson. Still fighting going on out there, and there's work for both of us. It's also far enough away to never be found."

Osborn's passenger ticket read, Alice Dean, July 1, 1863. "Tomorrow's my birthday."

Lou sat up. "What?! You never told me that."

"I did just now."

"I mean before now."

"You never told me yours, either. Yours, either."

"April twentieth."

"All right, then."

"All right then? No, it's not all right then. I have to get you something. I'm your wife. I'm terrible if I don't give you a gift."

Without turning to her, he said, "You are a gift to me, Lou. You are the gift."

Lou stared blankly at the wall until her head cocked to the side. "I've got an idea! You stay here, Osborn. I'm going to the wagon. It'll be the best birthday present any husband could ask for."

After two hours, Osborn went down to the cargo hold. Abigail stood outside the wagon, arms crossed. "I don't know what's going on in there, and I do not want to know. I heard it's your birthday tomorrow. Happy birthday."

"Thank you."

Abigail called to the wagon, "Lou, Osborn's out here."

"I'm coming. I'm coming." A minute later, Lou climbed out with a square object wrapped in photo paper. Her smile walked up to him. "Got your present. Here it is." She handed it to him with her tongue in her cheek and her hips swaying side to side.

Abigail shook her head in disbelief. "I ain't never seen nobody so in love," she said before climbing into the wagon and closing the door.

Osborn's fingers started to pull back the first fold, but Lou stopped him with her hand. "No, wait. Let's open it together in our stateroom."

Once they reached the stateroom, Lou shut the door behind her. She turned to him with a beaming smile, excitement radiating from her. He had never seen her more thrilled. "Thank you, Lou, this is—"

"You haven't even seen it yet. Thank me after."

He carefully pulled off each corner of the paper, revealing the silver filigree folding portrait frame he gave her with their photo together and the other with Ray.

"Thank you, Lou. This is wonderful. Wonderful."

Lou grinned at him, fingers frantically moving about in front of her like a mad scientist with a secret plan. "Open it," she burst out with a laugh. Her hands whipped up to her mouth, covering it with anticipation.

He opened it, revealing the portrait they had taken together on the left side and a new, different portrait on the right. She had replaced the other photo with a self-portrait of her own making. In her photo, Lou lay on her side on the wagon's bed, head propped up with her hand, wearing nothing but her boots and a smile. Osborn's hand flew to his mouth in a gasp as Lou squealed.

Osborn and Lou leaned over the upper deck railing of the Alice Dean, anxiously watching all the people crowded shoulder to shoulder two stories below. A line of private school girls in blue uniforms weaved through the bustling crowd like a blue snake in a river, following their teacher across the Louisville docks.

They both jumped at the ship's whistle—the first of four warnings that the ship would be headed to their last stop of Paducah.

"Let's go to the wagon with Abigail. We can wait with her until the crowd gets smaller. Then we could get some food onshore," said Lou.

As they both headed down the stairs, a Union officer and two soldiers stood at the purser's desk. Passing by them, the officer said, "I'm looking for an Osborn Roche. Your passenger logs said he is on this ship." Simultaneously, Osborn and Lou's heads spun to each other.

"Mr. Roche?" asked the purser.

"Yes. He's with a Louise Cattell," said the officer.

Distracted by dockworkers mishandling cargo, the purser grimaced. "Please, just a moment." Walking over to the rail, he yelled, "That goes to the back! Not there! To the back!"

Osborn and Lou quickly continued downstairs and ran to the cargo level, where Abigail leaned out the open-air window next to Hoady. "Abigail, we have to go now. They found us through the ship's passenger logs," said Lou.

"Yes, yes. We have to get the wagon off here. They'll just catch us, catch us at the next stop if we don't, if we don't," said Osborn.

"Who's they? Your father? Is he here on the boat?"

"No, soldiers are here. They were asking for us by name," said Lou.

Abigail turned to the wagon. Its yellow letters screamed at her. "By name? You mean by that name?" she said, pointing to the wagon. "We ain't gettin' far."

"I'm sorry, Osborn," said Lou, "Your beautiful wagon."

"Oh, oh, oh," whimpered Osborn, walking in circles. "Not my wagon."

"We have to. We can fix it later," said Abigail.

"All right, all right," Osborn relented before running into the wagon. He came out with gloves, a rag, and a bottle of nitric acid. A few strenuous rubs on both sides of the wagon and the paint disap- peared from the wood.

Osborn's eyes fell from the wagon to the deck. "Our beautiful wagon, Lou. Our beautiful wagon."

A fish leaped from the muddy waters of the Mississippi, splashing back down with a loud plop. Lou looked up at the sound, her eyes widening with sudden curiosity. "Did you hear that?" she asked, nudging Osborn.

Osborn grinned, "Probably a big one. Think we could catch it?"

Abigail chuckled, still stirring the pot of beans. "With what? We don't have any fishing gear."

Hungry, they all stared into a pot of brown beans above the fire. Its contents; the same color as the river. They had been traveling all day and were somewhere south of St. Louis. Both Lou and Osborn relished the sticky sound it made.

"Hello!" a faraway voice interrupted.

"There's some fella over yonder. He's walking on over," said Abigail.

Lou and Osborn popped their heads up, and both pushed the spectacles up on their noses. A Native American man ran to them, his hand up in a wave. He wore a Confederate jacket, the cuffs and edges adorned with red fabric, no shirt, and black trousers held up by a wide, red sash. "Hello," he hollered again to them from fifty yards away. "May I come over?"

Abigail stiffened and said, "I believe that's a Reb jacket he's got on. Where should I—"

"Just sit tight, Abi," assured Lou from the side of her mouth. "Yes," Lou said to the man. "Are you hungry?"

"I could eat, yes."

"You are welcome to come. Welcome to come," said Osborn.

"Thank you. I am Moses Wolf," he replied as he sat cross-legged on the ground before the fire.

Osborn turned to Lou. "That is the manner you sat the second time I met you."

Abigail spooned beans into a bowl and handed it to him as she studied him with a side-eye glance. Moses shaved his scalp all the way to the crown of his head, leaving a thick, long ponytail of straight black hair.

"I am Osborn Roche."

"I am Lou, and this is Abigail." Their eyes greeted each other. Abigail spooned beans into three more bowls.

"Fine wagon," said Moses, nodding to it.

Osborn turned to it. Seeing his name gone and the oval of stripped paint bothered him. "It used to say, The World-Famous O. Roche Photography, Portraits Of All Kinds on both sides."

"O for Osborn?" asked Moses.

"Oh, yes. Yes, it is, yes it is. O for Osborn."

"The other side the same?"

"Yes. Both sides."

"The wagon was scalped." Moses laughed. His spoon dove into his bowl for another bite. "I know these things. I had one of those made for me. These phot… photo…"

"A photograph, yes, yes."

"Hmm. A strong word your tongue must fight to speak."

"It was originally called a daguerreotype because Louis Daguerre discovered the process to—"

"Your nation makes strong words, so other nations will never speak them."

"Well, Louis Daguerre was a Frenchman. He was from France. France, yes."

"Then France does not want you to speak theirs."

Osborn tapped his finger on his lips. "Hmm."

"You should call them… dugs or… mots. Something the tongue doesn't have to fight for."

"I call them portraits."

"Portraits, yes. Easy on the tongue. I have heard the word."

"Are you out scouting for your division now?" asked Lou.

Moses spooned the beans into his mouth as his eyes flashed to her questioningly through his brows. "Hmm?" His eyes darted to his jacket. "Oh, no. I am going home. I only wear this jacket because I have nothing else and the nights are cold. I remove it during my travels in the sunlight."

"Did you remove it from a dead soldier? A dead soldier? I always put it back, yes."

Moses held an empty bowl. "Like some more?" asked Abigail.

Moses handed it to her. She spooned him more beans and gave it back.

"No, it is mine. I am Chickasaw."

"What's a Chickasaw," asked Abigail.

Osborn burst in and said proudly, "The Chickasaws are an Indian tribe within the Five Civilized Tribes, which are the Choctaw, Cherokee, Chickasaw, Creek, and Seminole. They fight for the Confederacy. The Confederacy."

Moses aimed a thumb at Osborn. "Yes. My people have pledged warriors to the grey coats. They have told the five tribes we would be given our own state if our nations would help them fight, but now we've lost our Seminole and Creek brothers and half the Cherokee. They switched sides to the Yankees like cowards. They brought shame to the tribes. We Chickasaw only have our Choctaw brothers and the other half of the Cherokee to fight alongside. It was good to kill the white man, but I do not wish to fight my brothers of the five nations. I am finished with this war between your people. I want to return to mine."

Moses turned back to the wagon. "I remember the portrait they made of me with this box," he said with a mouthful of beans. "The first time I saw it, it was like a mirror, except it stayed still as stone. I believe it took a moment of my time here in this world, but the man handed it back to me on a tin sheet. A moment I can keep, but not a moment I can feel."

Lou smiled at Osborn before turning back to Moses. "That's similar to what he says," she said, gesturing her hand to Osborn. "His photographs capture a moment of time from time's endless moments."

"No, no. I say my photographs fight against time by capturing a moment of it like capturing a soldier from time's endless army, endless army of soldiers. Like time's soldiers are the moments of our life. Do you see? Do you see?"

"Hmm. Yes, I see," said Moses, staring at Lou. "Are you a medicine woman?"

"What is a medicine woman?"

"A person of great medicine that can make magic or travel to places beyond this world and return to it."

"No. I cannot do that."

"You have magic eyes that move about like a rabbit's nose. They have great magic."

Osborn rocked with excitement and said, "I believe they are as well. Yes, yes, they are magic, yes?"

Moses threw a narrow-eyed glance at Osborn and said, "Yes, they are." Lou's fingers moved as if they had a mind of their own. "And your hands...? Are you making magic with them now?"

"Oh, no. I... This is just something—"

"It calms her. It calms her. It does."

"You hide your magic," he laughed. "You fool your white brothers as O for Osborn fools them with his strong words that fight the tongue. I do not want to be on the other side of your anger, medicine woman," Moses said with a chuckle. His hand gestured to Osborn. "Are you his woman?"

"Yes, we are married," replied Lou.

He turned to Osborn and said, "The sun always shines on you if it is a medicine woman you lie with at night."

"No, no, the sun doesn't always shine on me."

"I think he means goodness or beauty is around you when you are with Lou, Osborn," explained Abigail.

"Yes, that is what I meant," said Moses.

"Oh, oh, yes. That is true. That is true."

Moses put down his bowl. "I've seen you since Nashville. We seem to be on the same path. Are you headed west through Fort Smith?"

"Yes, we are. We are," said Osborn.

"Where will you end your journey?"

"We are not certain," replied Lou.

"Letting the sky show you the way? I can be a better guide and show you the beautiful lands of my people if you take me there with you. My people live in the land you call Oklahoma."

"We'll take you there," said Osborn.

Lou turned to him. "All the way to Oklahoma?"

"No one I know is photographing that. I'll be the first."

"Remember, I need to work too, Osborn. I want to embalm."

"Did you say, embalm?" asked Moses.

"I am an embalmer."

Moses let out a "Ha!" with a slap on his knee. "You *are* powerful medicine! You cannot fool me. You have great magic in you. I have seen this embalming while fighting with the grey coats. The light has flown from the eyes, but you do not let death take the body. Your medicine, it is like his pho... photo..."

"Photographs," said Osborn.

"Yes. He takes a moment of time from the living, and you give it to the dead." Moses' slight smile turned from her to him. "He is the sun, and you are the moon of powerful medicines."

Lou smiled at Osborn. "We are the sun and the moon, Osborn. That's such a beautiful thing to say."

"This embalming…My people will think this strange—"

"I say peculiar, peculiar. It's a better word, yes."

Moses nodded to Osborn and said, "Another one of your strong words?"

"Well, it does have a hard-consonant C."

Lou interrupted, "Well, with the war, our soldiers are dying far from home, and they don't want to be buried in a place that is not with their families. I embalm them to be sent home, and their families can say goodbye to them in a proper manner."

"Hmm. There is even magic in your wisdom. I also want to return to my people. I need to die fighting for them, not for the grey coats. There are many of your soldiers in Oklahoma. Many blue coats and grey coats. When we get there, I will send you some. You can do your magic and send them home to their people and away from mine."

CHAPTER 32

Osborn drove the wagon with Lou beside him, unsure of their location or whether they were in Union or Confederate territory. Abigail hid in the back with Moses, sitting beside him on the bed, only emerging when they stopped for the night. In case the wagon was ever searched, their secret hiding place was a cabinet under the bed.

Outside of Little Rock, Moses finally walked freely alongside the wagon as they entered the Rebel-held city. As a runaway slave, Abigail remained hidden inside.

For the next four days, the wagon traveled alongside the Arkansas River, heading towards Fort Smith, the last stop before the vast plains of Indian Territory and the beginning of the California road to gold country. Passing the fort marked Abigail's freedom to walk in the sun. Moses Wolf, calling this wide-open land his home, walked into his living room of green and golden grass carpet, with ceilings of great blue sky and walls made of the horizon that could never contain him.

The wagon rolled along the flat, golden terrain. Abigail climbed up to the wagon bench and sat next to Lou. Moses walked parallel to them about eighty yards away, singing to the clouds. He bent down, scooped up a handful of earth, and brought it to his nose, inhaling its scent.

"That man ain't like nothin' I ever seen before," said Abigail as Moses threw the dirt into the air and continued singing. "And boy, can he sleep. That man slept the whole time back in the wagon."

"After he got out, he blossomed like a thirsty flower just watered," said Lou. Moses stopped singing and started talking to himself before running off to the horizon. "There he goes again."

"Where does he go?" asked Abigail.

"He brought us rabbit last time, rabbit. It was very good. Very good, I thought," said Osborn.

"Oh, over there," said Lou pointing to a Conestoga wagon in the far distance. "A prairie schooner headed west."

"Prairie schooner?" asked Abigail.

"Doesn't its white canvas roof look like a sail? See? It looks like a sailing ship crossing a golden sea."

"Yes, it does. I like that; a prairie schooner," repeated Abigail.

"Ahoy, Mate! Thar she blows, a white whale!" said Osborn with his hand to the side of his mouth.

The second rabbit roasted on the campfire spit as they all sat around it, eating their potatoes and waiting for the meat to cook. Osborn looked up from his plate. "How do you catch the rabbit?" he asked.

"I find its home, find a stone and wait."

"Who taught you all these things you know?" asked Lou.

"My family, my people, and the land itself, I have learned from all. The land is also my mother. It still provides for me, gives me a place to live and things to eat. I know what I know because she taught me."

"The land is your mother?" asked Osborn, confused.

"It is." Osborn followed his gaze to the stars for the answer.

The firelight danced on Moses's painted forehead. Earlier that day, he had painted it bright red with two yellow lines traveling down his cheeks from under his eyes. Osborn admired him from the other side of the campfire. "Why did you paint your face like that?"

"By the setting of the sun two days from now, we should be at a place you call Honey Springs. The grey coats have soldiers there, and that is where my

Chickasaw brothers will be. I painted my face for them. It has been two summers since I have seen them. I wear the paint so they will know me."

"We cannot go all the way with you, Moses," said Lou. "Abigail is a runaway. We will leave you a reasonable distance from your brothers and continue to Fort Gibson."

"I would have enjoyed showing you my nation, but I understand it is dangerous for the buffalo soldier woman," he said, turning to Abigail. "Our nation has many buffalo soldier peoples in it. We greet them with open hearts as our common enemy is the white man. But you are different, Osborn Roche, and you medicine woman Lou. You are the first white people I have enjoyed sitting with, and I can see you have the sun's light guiding you."

"Do you have any paint left?" asked Osborn.

Moses reached behind him and brought out two large leaves with yellow and red paint smeared on them. "I believe I have used it all."

"Can you show me how you make it?"

Moses smiled and said, "Will you paint your face, Osborn Roche?"

Osborn turned to his name smeared from the side of the wagon. "No, but I can use it for the wagon. For the wagon, yes."

The golden grass swirled about their calves as Osborn stood in the cool morning air with Moses. Puffy white clouds floated above them as Osborn proudly regarded his paint job on the side of the wagon. The wagon moved. "I believe they are awake. Awake, yes." Moments later, Abigail and Lou came out from the wagon.

"You're up early, Osborn," said Lou.

"Moses made me the paint. It is not as good as before, but come look, come look." Abigail and Lou walked around to them. Osborn had filled it in with a different shade of red, and in yellow, he painted *The World-Famous O. Roche Photography, Portraits Of All Kinds*, and under it, he painted *& Embalming* with *Gone From The World, But Alive Again In Our Hearts* below that.

He grinned at Lou mischievously. She giggled. "The motto works for both of us, you see?"

She beamed at him. "I do. It joins both of our worlds."

"Yes, our worlds. Like Moses, like Moses said, I am the sun—"

"And I am the moon."

CHAPTER 33

They approached Honey Springs from the south. Held by Union forces, Fort Gibson sat twenty miles to the north. Hoady pulled them onto a grassy meadow next to a lake turned gold from the sun's last light. A forest of dogwood trees grew two-hundred yards off to their left. The beautiful lake turned from gold to black as the storm clouds moved in.

The rumble of thunder heralded the rain. Soldiers on horseback came out from the dogwoods toward them at a gallop—eight of them wearing Yankee blue. Moses dashed and rolled under the wagon wheels, pulling himself up onto the axles and out of sight.

"Hey there," said a lieutenant as rain pelted him. He wore a young man's face with an old man's beard; long and prematurely grey. "You a photographer? We don't get many of those. Where ya from?" Three riders rode around, surveying the wagon.

"Pittsburgh," said Lou. "My husband here is Osborn Roche, the famous photographer."

"I can see that. And an embalmer too. It says it right there on your wagon. We could use an embalmer around these parts. What are y'all doing out here?"

"We are looking for things to photograph, photograph," said Osborn.

The lieutenant looked away with a sly grin. "I got an idea. A good place to start might be photographing us fellas. I think we'd be looking real good in a photograph, especially when we put that Chickasaw that was with you in front of us with his hands tied." As the lieutenant pulled out his pistol, the sky opened up. The rain fell so hard they didn't hear when he cocked it.

Lou shifted uncomfortably in her seat. "Uh…"

"He in that wagon? Ya might as well give him up. We seen him through the spyglass when y'all was coming up, and you can believe we'll be searching that wagon." Moses dropped to the ground, splashing into the rain-soaked mud, and rolled out.

"Good thinking," said the lieutenant, turning to a soldier. "Search him and bind him. Boys, search the wagon for weapons." He holstered his pistol.

"We don't have any," shouted Lou above the roaring rain.

"Just like you didn't have that Chickasaw? We'll check it out just to make sure." They bound Moses at the wrists by a long rope attached to a soldier's horse.

"There's a negro gal in here," shouted the soldier coming from the wagon.

"I asked for weapons, not no negro gals." The lieutenant turned to Osborn and Lou. "You two just stay on that bench and follow us."

"Where are you taking us?" asked Lou.

"To the colonel, but you'll have to sit tight till after the battle. We're just about to be hitting the Rebs hard. Tell ya one thing, though. I surely do know he's not gonna like that you were hiding a Chickasaw."

The dogwoods muffled the sound of rain as they entered. Blue coats stood among the trees ahead—an entire Union brigade composed of a battalion of the 6th Kansas Cavalry with the 1st and 3rd Regiments of Indian Home Guards. The soldiers took Moses and tied him to a tree.

"We have to do something about Moses," Lou told Osborn. "I don't know what we can do. I don't know."

"Mr. Roche! Mr. Roche!" A colonel on horseback trotted up to them. Assuming either an arrest or a handshake, Osborn stayed on the wagon bench. Lou went to her husband's side. "Mr. Roche! I am your greatest admirer. We work in similar businesses," said the colonel in a Scottish accent. "Maybe you've heard of me. I am Colonel William Phillips from the New York Tribune?" Osborn's eyes went to the sky. "Well, I am a colonel now, but I am still a war correspondent for the Tribune, and I know your work so well. It is certainly a pleasure and…"

The lieutenant stepped up. "Colonel, this man was hiding that Chickasaw over there. Found him under the wagon," said the lieutenant with a finger pointed to Moses.

Phillips' smile again disappeared. "Lieutenant, do you know who this lad is?"

"I believe I do. He's a photographer and an embalmer, and he was hiding a Chickasaw."

"Well, I'm sure he has a reason for that," replied the colonel turning to Osborn for his explanation.

Osborn lifted his chin and said, "That man simply showed us the way here, Colonel. As you know, I am a noncombatant and, and only documenting the war, with my photographs, with my photographs being my contribution, my contribution. It's the way I fight a battle for us all. I fight time. Time is the enemy to all men, an ally to none. My portraits and photographs are the only weapons to fight it, to fight it, as they capture a moment of it like capturing one soldier from time's endless army of soldiers."

Smiles rose on both Lou's and Phillips's faces. "Yes, yes, I know what you mean. Of course," he said thoughtfully, then turned to the lieutenant. "Haven't you read the papers? This lad is an army captain, and he was in the thick of it at Seven Pines!" His head spun to Osborn. "Brilliant work, by the way, Captain Roche."

Osborn's attention focused on Moses. "Thank you, colonel. About that Chickasaw over there—"

Ignoring Osborn, the colonel turned to the lieutenant and said, "Now go about your duties, Lieutenant," before turning to Osborn and saying, "I suppose this will be a very fortuitous time for you to arrive, Captain. I assume you'd like to photograph the battle?"

"Battle?" asked Osborn.

"Certainly, we are just minutes away from attacking." "Oh, my, how close is the enemy, the enemy?"

"Just over the valley in the tree line. Well, I must be off. Maybe I'll see you in the thick of it down there!" shouted the colonel as he rode through the trees.

Osborn turned to Lou. "Better put your earplugs in and get into the wagon, into the wagon. I'll try to—" Union cannons rained fire across the valley. Both Osborn and Lou shuddered, eyes wide. Lou slammed her hands to her ears and threw herself back against the corner of the wagon's bench as the men of the 1st Kansas Colored Infantry, a volunteer regiment, surrounded the wagon.

Osborn shoved in his earplugs before the bugler called for their charge, and in a whoosh, they all ran out screaming and firing. Shaking with fear, Lou fell to the ground, cowering by the wagon wheel in the fetal position. Osborn jumped down to her, pulling her in tight.

Abigail came running around to him, cradling and rocking Lou. "Osborn?" she said, kneeling. "Osborn, I'm here. Open your eyes. Let's get her inside the wagon." Osborn rose with Lou and brought her into the wagon, laying her on the bed. He tried to pull her hand away to insert an earplug, but she held steady as marble, eyes closed.

"She needs earplugs!" She needs earplugs!" he yelled over the sounds of battle. Frustrated, Osborn flapped his hands.

With Abigail's help, they peeled back a hand from Lou's ear, plugging one and then the other, before Lou's hands slammed back on. Lou curled up into a ball again. "I'm getting us out of here, Osborn. Sit down!" Abigail put her hands on his shoulders, and he shrieked, setting Abigail back. "Fine!" she yelled, before running out and closing the back. She jumped on the bench and turned the wagon away from the battle.

As they reached the same valley where the Union men had found them, the wagon slowed, the rain-soaked mud gripping the wheels and refusing to let go. Abigail climbed off and into the wagon, drenched from the relentless downpour. Lou sat rocking with her eyes closed while Osborn slept on the floor.

Wrapping herself in a towel, Abigail sat on the floor with her back against the door, shivering. "What did I get myself into?" she murmured, her voice barely audible over the sound of the rain.

They awoke to the caws of ravens and the shrieks of turkey vultures flying and hopping about in the morning sun. Their clothes still soaked, they wrapped themselves in blankets and stepped out of the wagon into the crisp, cool air beneath a clear blue sky.

"The battle must be over," Osborn said, surveying the serene yet unsettling scene around them.

"What happened to Moses?" asked Lou.

"He was gone when I moved our wagon. Army must still have him."

Osborn pointed to the woods. "Let's head that way, that way."

Abigail cracked the reins on Hoady as Osborn used a thick branch to pry the wheel from the mud. It came unstuck with a lurch, and after changing their clothes, they headed in the direction of the battle. Reaching the top of a knoll, Osborn pulled the brake on the wagon. The dead lay scattered across the battlefield below. "Oh, I ain't seeing that!" exclaimed Abigail. She jumped down and hurried inside the wagon.

Lou and Osborn switched their earplugs to their noses to block the stench. The Union dead and wounded had already been removed, leaving only dead Rebels consisting of mostly Chickasaw and Choctaw Native Americans, with a few white soldiers from the Confederate Texan divisions.

"I'll take a look around," said Osborn walking about the dead, glancing at their faces. Lou pulled her blanket around herself tighter as Abigail popped her head out the small window.

"What's he looking for?" asked Abigail.

"I think I have an idea," she replied before calling to Osborn, "Are you thinking of how to photograph?"

"Possibly, possibly," he replied absently as his mind focused on the dead Native American soldiers.

"He gonna do that portrait thing?" asked Abigail. Osborn stopped and kneeled by a dead Choctaw soldier. His hands went through the dead man's clothes. Abigail cringed. "What's he doing?"

Lou smiled and said, "He's making an Indian friend."

CHAPTER 34

Enclosed with tall log walls and earthwork fortifications, Fort Gibson stood near the Arkansas River. Inside its walls stood ten officers' homes, a two-story barracks, a hospital, a bakehouse, a mess hall, stables, and warehouses. It housed a mix of five hundred Cherokee, Seminole, and Creek Native American soldiers of the Union Indian Brigade. The fort also housed the 1st Kansas Colored Volunteer Infantry Regiment, borrowed temporarily from nearby Fort Scott.

They entered the gates in their wagon and parked it near the center of the parade field. "There he is," said Lou. Moses Wolf sat, head lowered, on the headquarters' steps with a guard holding the rope. A proud man leashed like an animal. Colonel Phillips trotted his horse up to them.

"So, Captain Roche, your wagon says embalming. Is that in your repertoire of talents?"

"Mrs. Roche here is an embalmer."

"Nice to meet you, colonel," said Lou.

The colonel grimaced. "A young lass embalming the dead?"

"My father taught me the trade. He embalmed Willy Lincoln." The guard holding Moses tugged the rope attached to him, yanking him up. They walked toward the stockades.

"Very notable. Well, Ma'am, I'd be pleased if you could—"

"Oh, colonel? May I ask a great favor? That Chickasaw over there, the one that brought us. He came all the way from Memphis to show us the way and visit his family. I don't believe he is a threat, and I'm sure my husband here will agree."

"But he is a combatant," said the colonel.

"Mrs. Roche is correct. He would do no harm. No harm."

"Would you have it in your heart to release him?" asked Lou.

The colonel turned back to Lou. "I tell ya what. We have several casualties from the battle coming in now. If ya offer your services to us, I will release him."

Lou smiled. "It'd be my pleasure, colonel."

The colonel grimaced again. "Is pleasure the right word?"

Abigail's nose wrinkled. "Unh-unh, not the I way I be thinking," she said.

"Matter of fact, you are a captain. I'd be pleased enough to offer ya up one of the officer's cabins for ya and meals in the chow hall if you'd stay on."

"We would want that. Absolutely, absolutely we would, yes," said Osborn.

"Wonderful," he said, pulling the reins on his horse. "I'll have my men help ya get situated."

The colonel trotted his horse to the man guarding Moses. The lieutenant untied him, walked him to the gate, and gave him an undignified kick in the rear. Moses stumbled, then turned back to the guard, muttering something inaudible before whipping around to face the prairie. His long black ponytail flipped forward and back as he continued walking away. Osborn's thoughts begged him to turn around and wave goodbye, but he didn't. He ran out of the gates without looking back.

Phillips' men helped set up the tent behind an officer's cabin, far enough away from the soldiers to avoid any sight or smell of the dead. Lou and Osborn moved equipment and chemicals into it when Abigail came running up to Lou, breathless. "Did you see inside the house?" she asked urgently.

"What?" asked Lou.

"That's our place. Right there. The soldier man told me so. It's got fine furnishings, a living room where I can sleep on the couch in front of the fire, and your own private bedroom for y'all. Come see."

"I can't now. We have a lot of corpses lining up. You fix it on up for us, Abigail."

"Yessum."

Lou glanced over at the bodies stacking up in rows outside the tent. Her fingers began to move rapidly, worry etched on her face. She went to the corner of the tent, sat on the dirt floor, pulled her knees to her chest, and began rocking back and forth.

Osborn turned to her, concerned. "You all right? Are you feeling—"

"I'm feeling anxious, Osborn. I always had my father and my uncle... you know, to work with. This place is a mess. The soldiers are stacking up. I have to get to work on them. I can't do this alone."

Osborn sat down beside her, pulling his knees in like she did. He matched the cadence of her rocking, and, for a brief moment, a quick smile rose and fell on her face. "I will work with you. We will work together. Together as a team, yes."

"You will work with me?" she said, stopping her rocking. "I'll show you more. You'll become a world-famous embalmer."

"Yes, yes. And when we have time, you can help me. I don't have Ray anymore, either."

"Yes! I would love to. I love you, Osborn. You made me feel better." Osborn stood and took her hands, helping her up.

"I'll set up the equipment while you work, while you work on your first customer. Then, I'll organize the chemicals between preparing a body and setting the features for you. We will be a team. Be a team, yes?"

Lou kissed him. "Together, we are the sun and the moon."

CHAPTER 35

Three weeks had passed since arriving at the fort. Osborn and Lou sat in their living room as Osborn read a letter from Ray. "Ray is courting Little Miss and has rented his own daguerreotype shop in Johnstown. He lives above it. From his letter, he seems pleased. Would you like to read it—"

The door flew open. "Hey, the colonel's here to see ya," said Abigail as she walked into the house with Phillips following.

"Captain and Mrs. Roche, hope I'm not disturbing anything?"

"No, sir," they said.

"Well, tomorrow, I will be meeting with the chief of the Long Hair Clan of the Cherokee. Would ya be able to come along and photograph us for the Tribune?"

"Wonderful, wonderful. I would like that, yes."

"May I come?" asked Lou.

"Of course, you may, Mrs. Roche. We will be heading out after morning chow."

"Yes, yes. Oh, colonel, Mrs. Roche and I have been discussing that since the battle at Honey Creek, there have been no engagements with the enemy, leaving Lou with no customers—"

"Customers?"

"Uh, no, embalming work, I should say, except for those two dysentery casualties—"

"Yes, the Rebs were the worse for wear at Honey Creek. We believe they are regrouping somewhere. Smaller Reb regiments have been wreaking some havoc raiding supply depots and stealing livestock."

"Well, yes, and we would like to ask your permission to cross battle lines to look for customers with them as well," asked Lou.

"But they are the enemy, lass."

"Yes, but we do not help them in any way. We only tend to their dead and send their boys home."

The colonel stuck out his lower lip. "I suppose, but I believe it would be too dangerous. They might think ya are spies or—"

"Embalmers are always allowed to cross lines in the east."

"But this is a different land. There are Choctaw and Chickasaw warriors, too. They don't care about any supposed rules. They'll be smiling as they do unspeakable things to ya both."

It was only last year that the Rebels held Fort Gibson," said the colonel as he rode alongside their wagon on the way to the Cherokee village. "But seeing all my men approach, they abandoned it, and I took command. We were just too much for them. Oh, Mrs. Roche, regarding your, as you say, customers, I was thinking, I will send a messenger under a truce to the Rebs. I will suggest they bring their departed to the fort gates under a white flag with enough money to pay ya and the wagon master to take the body out of here. That might work."

Lou clapped her hands with excitement. "Thank you, colonel."

The colonel pointed to the distance. "There it is over there."

The Cherokee village sat in the distance, forty homes dotting the plains alongside the Arkansas River. On the opposite side of the river, four acres of hickory and oak trees stretched out, a lush green contrast to the wide-open sky. Smoke rose from holes in the center of their thatched grass roofs, curling into the clouds above.

This big sky country was a place Osborn and Lou had only read about, and Abigail had only imagined. A few years ago, Osborn had never wanted to leave his small flat in Philadelphia and, later, the Roche home in Pittsburgh. He surprised himself with how far he'd come.

"It's so beautiful here, so beautiful, yes?" he said, his voice filled with awe.

"Oh, yes. I've never seen such beauty. Never ever in my life," she replied.

"This tribe here is a smaller group of the Long Hair Clan of the Cherokee," said the colonel. "They are called the Strangers. They are a peaceful clan. The chief's name is Moytoy. It means rainmaker. With the Cherokee, there's a peace chief and a war chief. He's the peace chief and is chief of the clan in times of peace. There's a war now, so another chief from the Wolves clan is the War Chief now. Prisoners of war, runaway slaves, and orphans from other tribes get adopted into this clan, thus the name; the Strangers."

Abigail popped her head out the side window. "Runaways?"

"Yes, Ma'am. They got a few here."

Their wagon, the colonel, and eight of his men rode in and past a mix of log cabins, waddle, and daub huts made from weaving limbs, vine, or river cane across strong logs and packed with clay and mud.

Children ran about the fields and between the houses. "Where is everyone? I don't see any parents," asked Lou.

"They're waiting for us in this big cabin here," said Phillips, pulling up to a log cabin the size of five to six in the center of the camp. "It's their ceremonial house."

The colonel dismounted and walked up the three steps to the wood deck in front of the deer hide door. "I'll be a while. After I'm done, we'll come out and take some portraits. Have a look around if ya like."

"All right, we'll wait. We'll wait." A warrior from the tribe pulled back the deer hide door from inside, and the colonel disappeared behind it. Osborn and Lou walked off with Abigail to wander around the village. The sun had moved to the western sky, casting long shadows. Black crows flew overhead, diving, soaring, and holding their positions against the wind, their shiny black wings gleaming. Women washed clothes in the river, beating the wet clothes with a club, wringing them out, and tossing them into a woven basket. Osborn walked over to them with Lou and Abigail.

Lou stood next to her husband. "What do you see?"

"Those women. There is such beauty in that. In that, yes. Beauty." Lou winked at Abigail, and they both ran off to the wagon.

"Let's pull the cap on this," he said, turning to the empty spot where Lou had stood. Lou had entered the wagon to ready the plate while Abigail brought the camera and tripod. Osborn took the tripod from her and began setting it up. The women by the river glanced over, giggling.

One of them approached. She had the face, the hips, and the gait of a man, yet wore a woman's dress. "You make paint for us?" she asked.

Osborn tilted his head in question. Abigail stepped up and said, "I believe 'paint' means portrait." "I would like to, yes. But I call this type of painting a photograph."

He or she burst into laughter. The women downstream laughed as well.

"Photo?"

"Photograph."

"We can see photo after you...?"

"Yes, I will give you one, and I will keep one for myself."

Lou walked over with the plate as his or her eyes walked over Lou's clothes. A curious expression rose.

"Hello," said Lou.

"Hello. I am Ahyoka."

"Ah...yo...ka?"

"Yes. It means 'she brought happiness' in you speak."

"I am Lou."

"You two-spirit? I no see white two-spirit."

Lou shook her head with confusion. "What—?"

"Captain Roche! You are needed now!" yelled one of the colonel's men from the ceremonial house.

Osborn picked up his camera. "We will have to do this another time. I am sorry, I am sorry."

"You come next sunrise? Make photograph then?"

Rushing the equipment away, Osborn said, "Yes, we will. Thank you."

"I in home of Mary Dunn. You come find me?"

"Yes. Tomorrow, we will come find you, Ahyoka. Nice to meet you," said Lou.

Osborn pulled up the brake outside the main village. The early sun shimmered off the river on the far side as fish flung their bodies out like circus performers. Each home in the village had a river of smoke flowing into the sky. Osborn, Lou, and Abigail wore winter jackets as they walked about, searching for Ahyoka or Mary Dunn's home.

People sat in front of their homes and walked about, engaging in daily activities. Children played in the distance, their laughter echoing through the village. Women worked the fields, tending to beans, corn, and squash. Lou spotted a ten-year-old boy running, chasing a pack of other boys. She put her hands out to stop him. "Mary Dunn?" she asked, hoping for some direction.

He skidded to a stop. "That's my grandmother," he said with a smile.

"Can you show us?" asked Lou.

"Yes. This way." The pack of boys turned and followed their friend. "Ahyoka is my sister. She told us you'd be here today. She is looking forward to seeing you."

"Your sister? Ahyoka is a woman or...?" asked Osborn.

Walking next to Osborn, the boy glanced up at him as if he didn't know the sun set in the west. "She is just like him," said the boy, tapping Lou's arm. "My sister is a two-spirit like him."

"What is a two-spirit? Two-spirit?" asked Osborn.

The boy laughed. "What is a two-spirit?! You know."

"No, I don't know, I don't know," insisted Osborn.

The boy pointed again to Lou. "He is a two-spirit. My sister is a two-spirit."

Lou shook her head. "I am not a him. I am not a man," said Lou.

The boy studied Lou skeptically. "But you dress as a man and your hair...?"

"I like dressing this way. These clothes are better suited for me."

"White people don't have two-spirit people?"

"We might if you explain what they do?" asked Lou.

"They have the gift of sight through the eyes of both a man and a woman. Don't you have that?"

"I don't know. I don't think I do."

"You speak English well. What's your name, young man?" asked Osborn.

"Stillwell Dunn, and they teach us all English in school. I speak Iroquoian, too. I can translate for you. My grandparents don't speak English."

"Ahyoka does," said Osborn.

"Not as good as me," said Stillwell as they reached the thatched roof hut of the Dunn family. Stillwell pulled back the deer hide door of the one-room house. They walked in, squinting to make out who was there and where to walk. Osborn stepped on a dog's tail. The dog yipped, turned, and growled. "Sorry, sorry, sorry."

In the center of the space, a firepit burned a constant fire, heating the room and cooking the food. Smoke from it rose to the chimney hole above, clouding the view across the fifteen-foot expanse. Words like "Ulihelisdi" and "Osiyo" came from the obscured shapes sitting around the room.

"They said welcome to you," said Stillwell as he walked them to one side of the room.

"Oh, thank you for having us," said Osborn, remembering his manners, as he, Lou, and Abigail sat upon the wide wood bench against the wall. The bench continued around the room, acting as a couch during the day and the beds at night. Colorful handmade blankets covered it for comfort.

From across the room, Ahyoka's smile greeted Osborn as his eyes adjusted. She wore a red dress with blue embellishments, several necklaces of colorful beads, and earrings made from deer bone that dangled from her earlobes. Her fingers weaved a ribbon into her braided hair.

Abigail scooted over to a black girl of about seven years sitting near them. "Hello," she said.

"Hello," replied the little girl.

"You speak English?"

"Yes."

"That's my sister, Yellow Grass," Stillwell called from the other side of the room.

An old woman ladled cooked hominy into two bowls from a large clay pot on the fire. As the little black girl pulled Abigail's hand, leading her outside, the old woman handed the bowls to Osborn and Lou. They waited for the spoon that never came before using their fingers. The old woman smiled with three teeth.

"What your Christian name?" asked Ahyoka.

Osborn sucked his fingers and said, "Osborn. This is my wife, Lou."

Ahyoka turned to Lou, puzzled. "You married to him?" she asked.

"I am a woman. I only dress this way because I prefer it."

Her eyes asked a question that Stillwell answered in Iroquoian before turning to Osborn. "She didn't know what 'prefer' meant."

"You no see through eyes of man and woman?"

"I don't believe I do. What difference is it? There is no difference."

An elder woman with a mane of long grey hair spoke Iroquoian to Stillwell. Stillwell responded in a back-and-forth conversation until Stillwell turned to Lou. "My grandmother says the truest two-spirit is one who can see no difference in vision between man and woman."

Lou raised her brows. "Well, all right. Thank you, I suppose." Osborn and Lou spent the remainder of the day outside the Dunn home, creating portraits of Ahyoka, her family, and several other women of the tribe. They all wore a mix of traditional Cherokee clothing colorfully adorned with buffalo hair, elk's teeth, or feathers and combined that with the typical American shirts, jackets, trousers, and dresses for the women.

"The little girl took me to meet her momma," said Abigail as she sat with Osborn and Lou on the ride back to the fort. "Her name was Nancy Dunn, and she is a runaway like me. The Dunn family took her and her brother in, and they took their name. She's married to an Indian fella I can't pronounce, some Cherokee word. Her brother's name is Charlie. They ran away together."

"How old is Charlie?"

"Looks about my age."

Lou turned to Abigail. "Oh. That's nice. Isn't it?"

Abigail grinned back at Lou. "Yes, it is. Osborn, are ya gonna be going again? I'd like to come if ya don't mind."

"Yes, you may," replied Osborn, his mind on something else. "These people are just like you, Lou."

"How's that?"

"I don't need to ask them questions to pull out, pull out their true nature. Who they are is right there in front of my lens. Stillwell made a few translations, but I didn't need it. Their faces reveal, faces reveal everything about them. I will create a book of Indian portraits. I believe these people are the most beautiful people I have ever seen."

Lou dusted off her shirt and pants. "You don't mind the way I dress, do you, Osborn? You still think I'm pretty?"

"I have told you many times how beautiful you are."

"I think you's pretty," declared Abigail.

"Course you're going to say that, Abigail. You're my friend. But he's my husband." Lou turned back to Osborn. "Why do you think that, Osborn? No one ever thought I was pretty. You are the only one. You are so different from everyone else."

"I told you why. That first time I saw you. What a wonderful moment that was the first time I saw you. The first day I saw your eyes flicker and wave at me the way a little girl excitedly..."

"...waves to her returning father," she finished with a smile. "Yes, I remember. But you know I'd wear a dress if you thought I was prettier in it."

Osborn twisted his beard. "You are like Ahyoka, yes, because, because she dresses the way she wants, she wants to dress, just like you do, just like you. She chooses who she wants to be. Her people love her and accept her. Yes, accept her, like I do you, Lou, like I do you."

CHAPTER 36

Osborn, Lou, and Abigail made the trip to the Cherokee village about every other day. Ahyoka always greeted them as they pulled up with Hoady and would stay with Osborn as he photographed all day. She had shown them the workings of the village, family life, farming, and government.

Osborn sat on a giant flat boulder overhanging the river, feet dangling off the edge. An elder of the tribe sat close to him as he waited for Lou to return with the glass plate. The sounds of the river and children giggling at its edge played on the wind. The caw from a crow broke the serene moment and sent a shiver up Osborn's spine. He hated that sound.

Lou and Ahyoka walked toward him. "In our village, you are what you are. We Cherokee people accept that. Want be warrior, you be warrior. Want fish, you fish. Want farm, you farm. I woman inside, Cherokee people accept I woman. Cherokee people accept you be, what you think you be. You think you eagle; you be." They laughed.

"You are a two-spirit, but your people call you a woman. Why?" asked Lou.

"Woman part stronger than man for me. Cherokee healer Mathew Curtis?" she said, pointing to the cabin where they had previously met him. "He want be called man. Man part stronger for him. Many two-spirits are healers for Cherokee people. Two-spirits have gift of see and feel. You understand?"

"Yes."

"I no feel call to path of healer."

As they neared Osborn, they found him in a one-sided conversation with the elder, who quietly sat with him, one leg dangling over the edge and his arms holding the other up to his chest. The elder nodded at his words.

"Red Horse Rider not know English," said Ahyoka as she walked over to him, giggling.

Osborn turned to Red Horse Rider before rising and said, "He seemed he was listening and interested, yes, interested."

"Hey, you two, I want you to meet someone," said Abigail as she walked up to them, holding the arm of a black man with a grey beard and salt and pepper hair. "This is Charlie Bates."

"Oh, yes, hello. Abigail has told us so much about you," said Lou.

"Good to meet you too," said Charlie. "You must be Osborn."

"You must be Charlie. You are a widower, and you were a buffalo soldier with the 1st Kansas Colored Infantry Regiment, and you were adopted by and now live with the Strangers Clan of the Cherokee."

Charlie laughed. "I see she did tell ya about me then."

"She did. I have a good memory. A good memory."

Osborn rocked in the rocking chair as he read Jane Eyre under the light of an oil lamp. Lou read The Woman in White next to him. Abigail sat on the couch, darning a pair of pants. She set it on her lap. "I, I need to say something to y'all." They both dropped their books and pushed their specs up on their noses. Abigail exhaled before saying, "I promised Ray and all, but I want to ask ya... Ya know I care for y'all, right?"

"Of course, Abigail," said Lou.

"Well, we've been here a few months now, and I seen ya settled in good, and all and, well, ya know the Cherokee don't treat us black folk no differently than themselves, ya know. The women run their homes and own 'em. They's respected. Growing life from their bellies as they do from the soil. Ahyoka's mama told me so. Some of 'em even being warriors. Hard to believe."

Osborn and Lou stared at her with grins on their faces. She took another deep breath. "Well, ya know Charlie, well, he..."

A knock on the door startled them. Abigail rose to answer it, cracking the door enough to stick her head out and keep the warm air in. She closed the door and turned to them with arms crossed. "The colonel put three dead Rebels out back for ya. They's under white sheets."

She turned to Osborn, beaming. "Will you help me tomorrow?"

"We'll make a day out of it, yes, I will."

Abigail shook her head in disgust. "A day for that? Mmm, mm, I have never ever seen two folk so in love. But as I was saying," she said, walking back and sitting on the couch. "The village just sits right with me, and I with them, and well, Charlie wants to be courting me—"

"You like that fella, Abi?" asked Osborn.

"Sweetest man I ever met and, well, I'd like to move to the village. Y'all wouldn't mind it none, would ya?"

Osborn said, "We, we, we never needed a chaperone, Abigail. We always wanted a friend."

Cold air whistled through the crack in the door, and snowflakes blew in under it. Osborn and Lou wore their heavy coats and winter pants. They jumped at a knock on the cabin door. Osborn rose to answer it, cupping his hands to blow warm air into them. A freezing gust blew in as he opened it to reveal a snow-covered Private DeBlois. The private scooted in as fast as he could, slamming the door behind him. Lou jumped at the sound. "Sorry for barging in, Captain. It's just that last time..."

"Oh, yes, yes, private."

"I couldn't find any firewood, sir. We're plumb out, and it's hog-killing cold out there. Can't go out of the fort to cut some for ya."

Lou sat on the floor in front of the smoldering fireplace. "Thank you for looking, private," she said.

"Yes, Ma'am. If I find some, I'll bring it," he said, scooting back out.

Osborn barred the door behind him. "I want to go home to Pittsburgh. I want to go home to Pittsburgh. It's cold here, and I want a bath. Oh, how a hot bath would—"

"I want to go to Abigail's," said Lou. It had been two months since she moved out.

"No, no, not with this weather, Lou. Not with this weather, no."

"I need to go there, Osborn."

"It's too far, no, no."

"You need to take me there. I really need to go. I need to speak to her." Lou pulled her knees to her chest.

"Are you all right? What's wrong, Lou?"

"I need to see her. I need to speak to her."

Osborn sat before her, rubbing her leg. "Speak to her about what? About what?"

"Woman things. I need to speak to her, Osborn. I'm scared."

Osborn jumped to a stand and flapped his hands. "Why didn't you tell me sooner, Lou? What is it?"

"Woman things. I just didn't. I need to speak to a woman. I need to see Abigail."

"Then we need to go, we need to go," he said, taking her hand and standing her up. Osborn and Lou put on every piece of clothing they had, and he grabbed every blanket they owned. He hitched up Hoady and headed out with Lou inside the wagon. On the bench, Osborn rocked back and forth to calm himself, hitting his back against the wagon and flapping his hands the whole way to Abigail's. The thick snow on the plains added four hours to a two-hour drive.

Standing before Abigail's deer hide door to her waddle and daub hut, they called to her. She opened it in shock. "Get in here!" She pulled them in, shaking. "Get out of these clothes, at least the top layer, and get over by that fire." Abigail turned to Charlie, her husband of a month. "Charlie, can you grab a horse blanket and stable their mule?"

Charlie threw on his jacket, grabbed a blanket, and ran out. Abigail rubbed Lou's shaking body with a blanket and sat her by the fire. "Get on over here,

Osborn. You're gonna kill yourselves coming out here during a storm. Which one of y'all thought of this?"

"I need to see you, Abi. I need to talk to you about something."

"What in the tarnation? Couldn't it have waited? This is simply mad."

"Pec, pec, peculiar, Abi," Osborn managed to say through chattering teeth.

"Take that coat off, Osborn, and sit on down by that fire. I'd rub you down too, 'cept ya won't let me."

"No, no, no, thank you," he said.

From his previous marriage, Charlie's children, Issac, four, and Nora, three, sat next to Bethany, sixteen, an orphaned Cherokee they had adopted into their family. They all stared at Osborn from the benches along the sides of the hut. "Hello," said Osborn.

Charlie burst through the door and pulled off his snow-covered jacket. "Your mule is dead. I unhitched him and was about to throw the blanket on him when he just plumb fell over dead."

Osborn gawked at Charlie, the wheels in his head spinning. When none came, he closed his eyes, raised his elbows, and slapped the air before him as he cried. Lou turned to him and burst into tears herself. Issac and Nora joined in.

Abigail rose to comfort her children as Charlie put his hands on his hips and said, "Maybe I shouldn't have said nothing."

Osborn woke in the morning covered in buffalo hide. The mud-covered walls kept the room cozy and warm, with the fire in the middle. On the other side of the fire, Lou sat with Abigail, a buffalo skin blanket covering both. They whispered to each other with Lou's familiar giggle sporadically thrown in.

"He's awake," said Abigail, pointing to him. Lou grinned, pulled off the hide, and ran over to him like an excited child on Christmas morning, wanting to wake her parents.

She kneeled on the rug before him, bringing her face close to his. "Osborn, Osborn, I've been waiting for you to wake up," she said with her flickering irises beaming at him. His silly grin didn't respond. She pushed him with a giggle and said, "You're doing it again."

"What, what? I didn't—"

"You're staring into my eyes. Stop. I want to tell you something."

"Tell me, tell me."

She took a deep breath, her eyes searching his face. "We're gonna have a baby." Osborn's smile faltered, replaced by a look of shock. "Osborn, what do you think? We're going to have a baby." He stared back at her blankly, a half-grin on his face. Slowly, the weight of her words sank in, and his expression softened.

Hearing sniffling behind them, they turned to Abigail crying. "Oh, now, don't ya go looking at me, here, don't be seeing me." Abigail pulled the buffalo hide over her wet face.

Lou turned back to his blank stare and half-grin. "Aren't you gonna say anything? We're gonna have a baby."

It took a moment, but Osborn's eyes filled with tears. "You are such a gift to me, such a gift to me."

Her thumb wiped away a tear from his cheek. "And I'm giving you a gift in return," she said with a poke of her finger into his chest. "You're going to be a father."

"I'm going to be a father."

"Yes, you are."

"I'm going to be a father."

Lou giggled and shook her head, her short hair tossing from side to side. "Yes, you are, Osborn. Yes, you are."

CHAPTER 37

"Eat him? I was going to embalm him," said Lou as she stood with Ahyoka, Abigail, Charlie, and about fifty members of the tribe surrounding Hoady's frozen, snow-covered body.

"We believe it is the circle of life. Your mule gives his life for others to live, and the dogs and wolves will take what's left," said Ahyoka.

"I don't know. I don't know. Hoady was with me for so long," said Osborn. "What about his spirit? He would not like it, I believe, I believe."

Ahyoka translated to the elder, and the elder responded. "Grandfather says he believes the mule would want this. It is in his nature. If man were not here, he would have fallen on the prairie for the wolves to live on."

Osborn shook his head. "I need to think on this. He was my friend, my good friend," he said, turning and walking away with Lou, Abigail and Charlie following.

"You wouldn't be able to move him, Osborn. He's too heavy anyway," said Charlie.

The fifty tribal members silently faced them as they walked away. Charlie escorted them into their hut before Abigail turned back to the tribe with an approving nod. Knives and axes came out from everywhere as the group turned on the dead mule.

Abigail pulled open their deer hide door and walked in, exclaiming, "Let's have a baby shower!"

"Let's say goodbye to 1863 and hello to 1864 with the hope that the new year brings us victory over the Confederacy," toasted the colonel to all the fort's officers and their ladies in the mess hall. Osborn and Lou sat with them at a table celebrating New Year's Eve.

"Here! Here!" cheered the soldiers.

Colonel Phillips walked over and sat with them. "My, my, you look ravishing in that dress, Mrs. Roche, just divine."

"I was married in it, and it's the only dress I own. I wore it for the occasion, but I would've rather not. I feel peculiar in it, and it's scratchy."

"Yes, I don't believe I've ever seen a dress on you."

"General Stuart gave it to me."

The colonel's eyes opened. "The General Jeb Stuart?"

"Yes. You won't mind if I don't wear it again?"

"Of course, Mrs. Roche, especially if he gave it to you," he said, laughing. "But I do appreciate you wearing it just for the ball. Very thoughtful."

"Osborn has something he'd like to tell you, colonel."

"Lou and I are going to have a child."

The colonel slapped the table. "Osborn, you old codger. Bully for you. Bully for you."

"I am not an old codger. I do not know what you mean. I do not know."

"Figure of speech, it is," said the colonel.

"It's a playful way of saying 'good lad,'" said Lou.

"Yes, I suppose it is," agreed the colonel. "Well, I wish I had a present for the happy couple. Wait, what's this," he said with feigned surprise, pulling a telegram from his coat pocket. "It is a telegram for you, Osborn. One from your publisher."

Osborn read, "Bla, bla, bla, bla, bla, Mr. Fontaine is working on the layout of your new book on Indian portraits. I think this book will be a huge success. The photography is remarkable, and I love your title, 'Portraits of Strength, The People of the Cherokee Nation.' Just lovely." Osborn put down the telegram, a grin on his face.

"Congratulations, Mr. Roche. Another successful book for ya."

"I'm so proud of him," said Lou.

"Tell me, what are the Roche's planning on doing? The war here on the plains is practically over. There will be few, if any, men to embalm or battlefields to photograph. Back to Pittsburgh or…?"

"We have only been here for four months and fifteen days. I feel there is more to discover. I am fascinated by the Cherokee people," said Osborn.

"I, too, am an enthusiast for the indigenous," replied the colonel. "We would like to stay on here for a while. For a while, yes. Would that be possible?" asked Osborn.

"But you would be celebrated on the streets of New York, I'm sure. A famous photographer? Certainly, Osborn. Have you thought about that? And I'm certain you are quite comfortable financially. You could purchase a beautiful home instead of living in an officer's cabin in a God-forsaken country."

"You know my peculiar nature, colonel. My nephew, Ray, tells me I am not good with people. Not with people, no."

"You say that, but…" The colonel put his hands out, gesturing to the crowded room. "Are we not with people here, Osborn? I believe you'd be fine. Nonetheless, you are welcome to stay on. And I'm sure there will be the occasional need for both a photographer and an embalmer," he said, standing. "And now I shall dance with my wife. Good eve."

"Good eve, good evening, colonel," said Osborn. The colonel walked off, leaving Lou and Osborn at the table alone, staring at the crowded dance floor.

"Take me to the dance floor, Captain Roche."

Osborn glanced at her peripherally. "It's crowded out there. A bit crowded."

"Remember General Stuart's ball? A wise man won't make the same mistake twice."

"May I, may I ask my wife to dance?"

She smiled up at him and said, "I thought you'd never."

CHAPTER 38

Ray Roche
Pittsburgh, Pennsylvania

Dear Ray,

There are more fish in the sea! Remember? And Johnstown is a pond compared to the sea of Pittsburgh. Lou and I were very sorry to hear about you and Little Miss but were excited to hear you moved back to Pittsburgh and about your new studio. That means we can be partners again. We will join you there in about six months when the child is of traveling age.

Have you seen the Cherokee book at stores? Anders wrote and said it was out for sale and doing well in New York. I was wondering if it was in Pittsburgh yet? It should help business at the new studio.

I forgot to tell you we lost Hoady not long back. I miss him, but I bought a young mule off a Seminole man. Thank you for sending me The Deerslayer. I have read it twice.

Yours, Uncle Osborn

"Did you tell him Abigail got married to Charlie, and she won't be returning with us?" asked Lou. Her feet disappeared under her seventh-month belly as she pumped embalming fluid into a fifty-two-year-old sergeant, dead from a whiskey-bottle-a-night habit.

"In my last letter, yes."

She changed feet on the pump, kicking a box of collodion. "Ouch. Osborn, why did you buy so much collodion? There are four boxes."

"I use more than you, and you were using my bottles, using the bottles that I will need."

"I can't use that much, but never you mind about that. Can you move them, so I don't kick them?"

"Certainly, certainly. I'll move them to the wagon. Into the wagon, after I pour this out." Osborn picked up the full pail of the man's blood to dump in the hole dug out back. He returned with Abigail carrying a Cherokee cradleboard. Lou pulled out the tubes from the body. Abigail's smile disappeared. "Ah, naw, I'll wait in the house."

Inside their house, Abigail sat in the rocker, holding the cradleboard. Osborn and Lou stood staring at her hair. She had always pulled it back and tied it into a bun. But now, it had grown out and into a big, brown, round head of curly hair. "What? My hair?" asked Abigail. Lou and Osborn simultaneously turned to each other and back to her hair. "Ya, don't like it?"

"Oh, no. We love it. It's beautiful. Don't you think, Osborn?"

"If you mean love in the 'I enjoy it immensely' way, then, yes, I love it."

"May we put our fingers in it, Abi?" Lou asked.

"Oh," she said, remembering. "All right, but did ya wash your hands? I don't want none of that dead man stuff on me."

"We did," they said simultaneously.

"Well, all right, then."

Standing on either side of her, they dove their fingers into it, their satisfying smiles producing "ooohs" and "aaahs" with an "It's so soft" thrown in there.

"Don't get too much pleasure there. It's getting a little peculiar.

Now, I wanted to give you this; it's a cradleboard for the baby."

"I love it!"

Abigail demonstrated. "So, you lie the baby on his or her back, put their feet at the bottom, tuck the baby in here with this little blanket, and tie these straps to keep the baby safe. This top keeps the baby dry or out of the sun, and then you wear it on your back with these straps. See?"

Lou pulled her fingers out of Abigail's hair to take it. "Strapped to your back, so you can walk about and work with the baby, ingenious." She sat on the floor in awe of it.

Osborn still stood with his fingers in her hair. "That's enough, Osborn," said Abigail.

"Thank you for letting us do that, Abigail. It's so soft," he said.

"And thank you for this, Abi. It's my first and only baby gift."

"You're welcome, Lou. I'm happy ya like it. Now, I got some news of my own; I'm with child as well."

Lou jumped up, wrapping her arms around Abigail's neck. "I'm so happy for you, Abi. We can raise them as siblings!"

"Wonderful, wonderful news, Abigail. Such wonderful news, yes."

"I'm five months or so behind ya, but they'll be friends for sure. So, I was thinking on stayin' with y'all when the baby's time gets near, sos I can be here with ya and help."

Osborn bounced from his knees and said, "Please, Abigail, I was going to ask, going to ask you, yes. I would not know what to do. I would not."

"There is a doctor here at the fort, but I'd rather it be you, Abi," said Lou.

Abigail reached for her hand, taking it. "That settles it then, back to my old spot on the couch when the time comes. We gonna have ourselves a baby."

A month and a half later, Abigail slept on their couch with her sixteen-year-old adopted daughter, Bethany, on the floor beneath her. A minute before the rooster crowed, they woke up to Lou and Osborn staring down at them.

"I think it's time," said Lou.

"We think it's time, yes," said Osborn.

"Light some candles," said Abigail, throwing the blankets off.

"You must try one of these cigars, Osborn. It's tradition," said Colonel Phillips as he, Osborn, and Major Jacks, a visiting friend of the colonel's, sat outside the cabin in the spring air, waiting for the baby. It had been three hours, and Osborn couldn't sit still.

"I do not like those. I do not like to be around them." The two men laughed. "It's been some time, some time. Does it take this long?"

"My first child took fourteen hours. It was also around this time of the morning as well. And I have to admit; I was drunker than Cooter Brown." said Major Jacks.

"Cooter Brown? Who is he? A friend?" asked Osborn.

The major tossed a curious glance at Phillips. "Naw, Osborn is an artist type. He hasn't been around much," Phillips told Jacks before turning to Osborn. "No, see here, Osborn, Cooter Brown is a metaphor for a drunken son-of-a-bitch."

"Oh, I see. Well, I don't see, but he's a metaphor. All right. Yes, a drunken son-of-a-bitch," said Osborn, nervously looking here and there. He stood up and peered through the window. "Maybe I should go in and make—"

"Leave the women be, lad," said Phillips. "It's women's work it is."

"Osborn pull the cork on this one," said Jacks, handing him a flask.

Osborn winced. "No, thank you. I do not like it."

"It'll take the shakes out of ya. Calm ya down. It's medicine."

Osborn grabbed it and took a sip. "Ug! That's terrible, terrible."

Thirteen hours later, Osborn and Jacks' heads leaned against their seatbacks, asleep. Phillips paced about, still smoking a cigar. Bethany bust through the front door next to them, tears streaming down her cheeks. "We need the doctor! We need the doctor now!"

All three men jumped up. "I'll go," said Jacks, running off.

"What is it? What..." said Osborn.

"She's bleeding bad. We need a doctor now!" she said again.

"Osborn, maybe you should go in there..." said Phillips as his panic took hold of Osborn. Phillips's voice faded away as the world, and his life in it, spun around him. The dread strangled his mind into submission until it all turned black.

He awoke in the wagon with Abigail at his feet. Her wet face turned to him and said, "You're gonna have to be brave, boy."

"What happened? Lou? The baby, the baby?"

Abigail swallowed hard, her eyes filled with sorrow. "Lou's gone, Osborn," she said, bursting into tears. "I'm so sorry, Osborn."

"But she can't be gone," he said. Abigail confirmed with a nod. "No, Abigail, no. That's not true. That's not true. There was only a twenty percent chance that she would die during childbirth. We took great care. She should not be dead. Please check again."

"We'll go see her together," she said. "Can I take your hand, Osborn? This one time?"

He shook his head. "I don't want to touch. I don't want to."

She rose, and he followed. Bethany sat holding the baby in the rocking chair, staring down at it. They passed her and entered the bedroom. Lou lay on the bed, hands across her chest covered with a clean white sheet. A pile of bloody sheets lay in the corner.

Abigail wept as she stood next to him, but no tears came to his eyes. Lou was sleeping, he told himself, or this was all a bad dream. Those flickering eyes could never be still. Her dancing fingers must always dance.

After ten minutes of standing there, Abigail asked, "What would you like to do, Osborn?"

"Like to do? There's nothing I'd like to do. There's nothing I'd like to do."

Abigail sucked up her tears. "I mean with Lou. What should we do?"

"Bring her back to me is what we should do!" he said, stomping the floor with his face to the ceiling.

"I'm gonna give you some time alone with her," she said, leaving the room.

Osborn walked around the bed, clutching her cold toes as he went. He pushed on her shoulder with no response. Pulling the sheet back, he climbed into the bed with her. Lying on his side, he pulled her close. He breathed in the smell of her hair, a scent he loved. Always in her hair, it held its subtle and comforting aroma even if she washed it. Many nights he would lie close and smell it. The scent had the power of sending him to places in their past where he could relive in his dreams. He found no word to describe that smell, but if it could emanate a sound, it would simply say 'Lou.'

Two hours later, Abigail opened the door and peered in. "Leave me tonight. I will set her features in the morning and prepare her. Prepare her, yes. Ray's suit? Would you make sure it's clean? Would you?"

"I will. Goodnight, Osborn."

"Goodnight, Abigail."

Osborn gathered all the equipment and brought it into the room. Sitting next to her, he took her hand and rubbed his cheek with it. "I won't be as good as you, but I'll do it as you taught me."

He stared into her eyes, knowing it would be the last time he would see them—those marvelous flickering irises now remained still. His fingers closed the light from them for their final time and placed coins to stay them. "I'm sorry if this hurts, Lou," he said as he sent the needle through her gums, tying them together. "But you must look your best. I know you want me to make you pretty. You always asked me if I thought you were pretty, remember?" Taking a pinecone from outside, he wrapped it in a cloth and set it on her belly. He brought up her hands and placed them on it to eternally set them in the position of the sea anemone he dearly loved.

He completed the entire embalming procedure in the time it took him to tell her the whole plot of The Last of the Mohicans. He stood back, proud of his work. "Abigail, she is ready."

Abigail came in. "You made her right nice, ya did, Osborn. She taught ya well. She looks so pretty."

"Ray's suit looks quite nice on her, quite nice."

"It does, it does. So ya gonna make plans for the service?"

"I should bring her home, bring her home, yes. She needs to be at home like all the soldiers we send back."

"Osborn, that's too far, I—"

"We send soldiers back home. I will embalm her. She taught me. She taught me. I will embalm her and take her home."

"But you have a son now. Yes, it's a boy. You can't leave him. You gotta think on that. You have a son. Now, don't ya think we should place her in the casket?"

"No, not yet, not yet. I wish to sleep with her again tonight. Again tonight, yes."

"All right now, if ya feel ya must. But we should be putting her in the casket in the morning, I 'spect."

"Morning, morning, yes, yes. In the morning."

Abigail crossed the parade field with the colonel at a fast gait. "It's been three days, and now he's saying she's just fine where she is like he doesn't even plan on burying her. I'm beside myself."

"I'll talk to him," said the colonel.

They walked in on him reading to her in the bedroom. "Osborn, my lad. It seems to be time to lay Lou to eternal rest, don't ya think?"

"She seems to be in eternal rest now, Colonel."

"But I mean, lay her to eternal rest in the ground, lad."

"I was thinking she should be brought back home. Brought back home like the soldiers."

"All right. We can send her back to her kin on the next train."

"Not to her father, no. Not to her father. And I must accompany her."

Abigail shook her head and said, "You have a son now, Osborn. You can't leave him, and I'm with child. I ain't going with you."

"The fort cemetery is a fine place. I'd be resting just right there if the good Lord saw fit," said the colonel. They waited for a response from Osborn, but he sat silently. The colonel shook his head, turned to Abigail, and back to Osborn. "We need to take her, lad."

Osborn threw the book against the wall, shut his eyes, and clenched his teeth. Abigail's eyes widened. "Oh, no," she said. "Let's give him a moment."

"I will not! Osborn, get yourself together, lad! She's gone. We need to take her. She needs to be set into the ground." Osborn's face turned bright red as he went into his typical air slapping panic. "Fine then! But we'll take her in the morning, whether you like it or not. It's for your own good, lad!"

The colonel stormed out, leaving Abigail. "Osborn, I ain't gonna be here for that. I'm leaving, and I'm taking your son for now. He needs a milking mother, and we's got a few with the clan. You want to think of a name?" Eyes closed, Osborn shook his red face at her. "All right then, we'll leave that for now. I'll be back for the services tomorrow afternoon. Goodbye, Osborn."

The following morning the colonel entered the bedroom with four men. Osborn sat in the same chair, dressed in his best clothes. The casket lay in place of Lou on the bed.

"Good, lad," the colonel said softly. "Now, ya might help us carry her to the gravesite." Shoulders hunched, Osborn stood. They all took a side, picked the casket off the bed, turned, and stopped. They couldn't fit through the doorway.

"All right, set her back, and we'll go two in the front and two in the back," said the colonel.

Outside the cabin, they paused, repositioning to carry the casket three to a side. The procession moved slowly toward the gravesite beyond the fort walls, where the vast prairie stretched out like a solemn sea, with islands of stubborn snow still clinging to the earth, the last vestiges of winter. Wind whipped across it, carrying the sharp snapping of the fort's flag, a solitary sound in the wide silence.

As they lowered the casket into the grave, the preacher's sermon began with only the wind listening to it. Abigail's family stood with Osborn, the preacher, the colonel and his wife, and the four pallbearers. After the final prayer, Osborn reached for the freshly dug soil, bringing it to the edge of the grave. The earth felt cool and soft in his hand, a connection to the world that still held Lou. He hesitated, reluctant to release it, but eventually, the soil slipped through his fingers, falling onto the wooden casket below, mingling with his silent tears.

After the service, the group made their way to Osborn's cabin for the wake. Once a sanctuary, the cabin now felt suffocating with people and their murmured condolences. Overwhelmed, Osborn slipped away to his bedroom, laying down on their bed. He pressed his face into her pillow, inhaling Lou's lingering scent, and fell asleep.

By four the next morning, Osborn had packed everything, including the tent and all his equipment. He left the cabin clean and orderly, shut the door with a finality that echoed in the empty space, and climbed up to the wagon's bench. With a sharp slap of the reins on Hoady Junior, his new mule, he set off without a word of goodbye. The fort receded behind him, a place he would never return to.

He only left behind two cases of collodion bottles, the very cases Lou had once kicked and asked to move. Those he had wrapped in the bloody bedsheets and put into the casket instead of Lou's body. They weighed about the same.

CHAPTER 39

Osborn's breath left his mouth like steam from a train, drifting away on the chilly spring wind. Abigail, returning from taking her adopted son to pee in the early morning hour, stopped in the middle of the dirt path twenty feet from her hut and squinted toward the river. "Go on inside now," she told Isaac, giving him a gentle pat on the butt.

She shaded her eyes with her hand, focusing on the silhouette of Osborn sitting next to someone on a boulder perched over the river. Pulling the thick buffalo skin tighter around her, she began walking across the yellow plain toward them, her steps steady and deliberate. The early light painted the landscape in soft hues, but the cold air bit at her cheeks as she approached the figures by the water. "Osborn?" Still dressed in his best funeral clothes, Osborn turned with Ahyoka. "Did you sleep last night?"

"Yes. I mean, yes, thank you."

"He told me of loss of Lou. I did not know," said Ahyoka.

"Yes, Ahyoka has been away, staying with family," said Abigail.

"I told him I wish I could see her off to great spirit."

As they spoke, clouds of their breath hung like tiny diamonds in the air, obscuring their faces. Abigail moved for a better view. "What are you doing here so early? Would you like to come over?"

"I left the fort last night. For good. For good, yes."

"What are ya planning to do?"

"I ask him to live with me. My heart would be happy for it."

"No, I want to take the baby to Ray in Pittsburgh."

Abigail turned her head away and back to him. "Take the baby?"

"Yes, and go back to Ray."

Abigail shook her head. "But the child is too young, Osborn. It needs a milking mother and you gotta do a lot to keep a baby happy. A whole lot. It'd be too much to take a baby all that way, Osborn."

"Oh, oh. So, well, yes, of course. Of course, it will be too difficult. Too difficult."

"Maybe in six to nine months if I can teach ya some things. Teach ya to be a proper father." A hawk circled above them, catching Osborn's eye. Abigail pulled the buffalo skin higher around her neck. "Osborn, your boy? I was thinking. I could be takin' care of him for ya if ya like."

"Yes, I'd like that."

"Then, are you planning on stayin' with us here?"

"Yes, yes. I don't want to leave our son."

"That'll be good. A child needs his father. And my child will be born soon, and I'll be takin' over the feedin' of your boy when my milk comes in. Your boy can be raised with mine. Does that sit right with ya?" Osborn turned to her, confused. "I mean, do you approve of me doing that for you and your boy?"

"Yes, yes, I do."

"All right, we'll do that. Now, do you want to live with us? In our hut?"

"No, uh, thank you, both, yes, thank you, both for the invitation, but I am comfortable in my wagon. It is what I am used to, used to, yes."

"Are ya gonna… What am I saying? It's cold out here. Come on over. Would ya like to meet your son?"

Osborn laughed. "Meet my son? Will he shake my hand? Shake it?"

"I mean, see your son and hold him."

"I would like that, yes." Osborn, Ahyoka, and Abigail walked over to their hut. Steam rose from a pot on the fire. The children stretched and yawned as Charlie threw on his jacket.

"Morning Osborn, you doing alright?"

"Morning, Charlie. I left the fort. Left it for good, as they say, even though it wasn't good. Wasn't good at all."

Charlie pursed his lips. "No, I suppose it wasn't, was it?"

Abigail raised his baby to him. "Here's your son, Osborn. Do you want to hold him?"

He shook his head. "Please, no, I don't want to touch him. I don't like it. No, I don't like it."

Abigail and Ahyoka turned to him in disbelief. "But it's your child, Osborn," said Abigail.

"But you know I do not like to touch. You can hold him for me. Yes, please hold him for me."

"Baby comes from your seed and belly of Lou," said Ahyoka. "It is a part of you as your fingers are to your hand."

"Osborn, how you gonna learn how to be a good daddy if you don't hold him?" asked Abigail.

Their eyes branded his face with a scarlet letter. Osborn dropped his head, glancing at them through his brows as they waited for him to change his mind. Instead, he turned and walked out of the deer hide door.

The wagon sat a ten minute walk away—a lonely red box on the wide-open golden plain. Hoady Junior grazed on grasses nearby. He pulled down the steps and climbed in. Lou lay on the bed at peace, hands on her chest as she had taught him, but in the sea anemone shape, he loved. He sat next to her, pulled out Last of the Mohicans, and said, "All right, let's finish this."

Around midday, approaching footsteps woke Osborn from a nap. He stiffened with the knock. "Osborn?" It was Abigail's voice. She tried the locked doorknob. "You in there?"

Osborn unlocked it, barely cracked it open, and peered out. "Yes, Abigail?"

"You coulda put the wagon a might closer, don't ya think?"

"I like it here." A half-mile of prairie grass grew between his wagon and the village. "Yes, I like it here, yes."

"Hmm, well, can I come in, or you come out? I need to talk to ya about the child."

Osborn slid out the door, shutting it behind him. "Yes, yes?"

"Would you like something to eat? We can walk on over to my place."

"Certainly, thank you. Thank you."

They started across the field, and Abigail gestured toward Hoady Junior. "That your new mule? He's a fine looking mule."

"Hoady Junior, yes. I call him Junior."

"Have ya written Ray, or do you want me to? Tell him what happened and that you're not living at the fort no more?"

"I will write him. I will."

"All right, so we have to talk about naming the boy. Did you and Lou ever discuss possible names?"

"We wanted to see the baby first before deciding."

"The Cherokee here name their children before the child has reached seven days. It's just something they do here, and they do a baptism of sorts in the river yonder. It's a real special time, and I think Lou would've liked it. Do you want to do that?"

"I like that as well. Lou would too."

"Can you think on a name?"

"I will."

"So, if ya plan on stayin', maybe you should think on moving a bit closer, don't ya think? 'Cause I ain't coming all this way to call you to supper."

The full moon illuminated the wagon with its pale grey glow. He removed his clothes to his long johns as he peered out the side window to the prairie in the distance, a sea of silver. A twinkle of light from his desk caught his eye. Lou's double portrait gift lay there. He picked it up and ran his thumb over its silver filigree surface before opening it. In the portrait, she lay smiling on her side upon the same wagon's bed she slept on now. He turned to her, lying flat on her back, moonlight brightening her pale complexion. She needed a touch up of skin tone.

Osborn closed the double portrait and crawled into bed, laying his thin body next to her. "We need to give a name to our son, Lou. What do you think? No, I don't want to name him after me. He reached over to his trousers lying on the desk. His fingers pulled out the brown cloth from his pocket and laid it over his mouth and nose. He sucked in a big breath and whipped it off. "You think so? I like it. I like it a lot. Yes, yes. I agree that is a good name, good name. Goodnight, my love."

The sun rose over the hills in the east. Its warm rays blasted him and the side of his wagon and made a long, cold shadow on the other side of it. He pulled up his suspenders and rubbed his eyes. He went inside and pulled his postmortem posing stands and rods out from under the bed. "I'm going to get you out today, today, yes. It's a beautiful morning, and we shall create the loveliest postmortem portrait ever created."

He set up the stool, posing stands, and camera equipment out in the sunlight and returned for Lou. "Now, how shall we do this?" he said, staring down at her, forefinger tapping his lips. After a moment, he reached down, and in one swift move, he pulled her up and over his shoulder. "Now, that wasn't too difficult." He brought her out and set her up, attaching the stands to her. Walking back and forth between her and the camera, he adjusted the stands around her out of the shot. With the guillotine box attached, he ran his fingers down its length and stood next to her. He placed his hand on her shoulder. "Please hold still."

Removing the glass plate, he walked toward the wagon. "I'll be right back, sweetheart, right back." About to enter the wagon, Abigail walked toward him from the other side. "Oh, dear." He put the plate on the floor of the wagon and ran back for her. "I'm sorry, Lou, we have to get you back inside. Abigail is coming." He unattached all the clamps and rods and climbed in the wagon, locking the door behind him. As he tucked her in, Abigail knocked.

"You awake? I got breakfast. What's all this stuff? You doing a portrait today?"

Osborn climbed out, pulling up his suspenders again. "Yes, I will be, yes today. Ahyoka, yes."

"All right, then. You want some breakfast?"

"I would like that, yes. I am hungry."

They walked in the cold shadow cast by his wagon. "I have a name."

"Oh, yeah?"

"Yes. We have decided upon Ishmael. Ishmael Ray Roche."

After breakfast, Osborn sat in the large ceremonial lodge with Abigail, Charlie, their family, Moytoy, the chief, and several other clan members. Mathew Curtis, the clan medicine man, held baby Ishmael out with both palms as he spoke Iroquoian. He brought him to the fire in the center of the room and passed him over and through the smoke four times.

Osborn's anxiety grew with Ishmael's crying. He shut his eyes, wishing he could shut his ears. Ishmael's cries grew quieter, and Mathew Curtis stopped speaking. Osborn's eyes opened wide when he felt Ishmael's body placed in his hands. Mathew Curtis's dramatic face backed away from him as he turned to his son in his hands. His skin as soft as Lou's. "Ishmael? Ishmael Ray Roche." Ishmael examined him with blue eyes. "You don't have eyes like hers, do you?"

Abigail sat next to him, wiping tears with her sleeve. "You're holding him, Osborn."

"I am. Yes, I am. I'm holding my son. My son, Ishmael Ray Roche." As Osborn's tears hit Ishmael, he started to cry as well. Flustered, Osborn handed him to Abigail and wiped his face as they all went out to the river.

Mathew Curtis stood in the shallows of the river, again holding Ishmael. Osborn stood near; his pant legs rolled up. "Be ready now," warned Abigail. "He's gonna dip him in the water seven times while sayin' a few words, and Ishmael's not gonna like it. He's gonna be wailing, so prepare yourself."

"I can handle it if I'm prepared."

Mathew Curtis spoke in Iroquoian, and Ahyoka translated, "When you were born, you cried, and the world rejoiced. Live your life so that when you die, the world cries, and you rejoice." Ishmael wailed as Mathew dunked him. Osborn slammed his eyes shut and tensed, trying to calm himself. After the seventh time in the cold water, Abigail wrapped the baby in a warm blanket and took him away. By the time Osborn opened his eyes again, only he and Ahyoka remained standing in the river. She stood smiling at him with a funnel shaped basket in her hand, made with river reeds and hickory branches.

"Naming your son good, Osborn. Now I show you catch fish." He agreed with a nod. Ahyoka walked out further and pointed to two walls of stacked stone in the center of the river. They formed a V shape but opened at the bottom. "We call it 'uga'yatun'i.' It trap to catch fish. You take basket and stand at small end. I walk upriver and scare fish to you. They go wide part and will go in basket."

"I understand."

Ahyoka walked off upriver. Osborn did as she said, standing ready with the basket. She picked up two stones and came toward him, kicking the water, yelling, and throwing the stones to the sides of her. After she walked a few yards, two fish popped in the basket, and he pulled it up, fish flopping about. "Good, Osborn." He handed the basket to her, and they walked to the riverbank. She dumped them, flopping on the grass. Osborn sat away from them on a flat stone.

"Come. We need more. Two not enough."

"Ah, I don't like the cold water. I don't like it, no."

"If you stay, you become Cherokee. You must learn." Osborn pulled out a handful of grass.

"Come." Osborn shook his head, pulling more grass. She waited until she laughed. "You are two-spirit as I. You don't see through man's eyes. You still warm my heart."

After an afternoon of taking her portrait and self portraits of them both, Ahyoka cooked them the fish they caught in front of his wagon. They sat on a blanket, eating in the light of the setting sun. The village and the river across the field reminded him of the first time he came here with Lou and the impression it had made on them.

"You take new wife, Osborn? I be good wife for you. My mother's home is mine when she is gone from our world." She motioned her hand to the sky.

"Lou would not like that. A single wife is a part of our culture. It is a part of our culture, yes."

"Lou is gone from our world, Osborn."

"But she is alive in my heart, and I... Just... Can't." She patted her chest. "That saddens my heart."

"I would not make a good husband—"

"I know this. You not like catch fish. You need me." She laughed.

"I would not make a good husband because I do not like to touch or to be touched."

She squinted with confusion. "Touch? This touch," she said, stroking her hand across her knee.

"Yes. I do not like it, no."

"You touch Lou."

"Yes, her and Ray, my nephew."

"What is a nephew?"

"The son of my brother."

Her eyes went wide. "You touched the son of your brother as you touch Lou?"

Osborn read the surprise on her face. "No, no, not as a man touches his wife. Just by hugging him, squeezing him with my arms, you know? Squeezing him with my arms."

"I see." Her eyes wandered across him. "No touch on man part?" Her eyes glanced at his groin.

Osborn's brows jumped. "Especially that."

"Especially that, yes?"

"No, no, especially that, no." Ahyoka shrugged her shoulders and pursed her lips. Osborn took another bite of his fish.

"There are many that call me peculiar," he added.

"Pe-cu-li-ar? What mean?"

"Strange. Not normal. Not like others."

"That is what meant to be. Every man, woman pe-cu-li-ar because every man, woman not like other." She pointed to the river. "We all like pebbles in stream. Not one like other."

They sat and spoke till night came. Osborn thanked her for supper, said goodnight to her, and climbed into the wagon. He stood above Lou as he removed his shoes with his feet. "I'm sorry I've been out all day. The naming ceremony made me cry. I wished you could be there." He lit two lamps and sat on the bed next to her. "They dipped Ishmael in the river seven times, and

Ishmael cried out each time, each time. You would not have liked that part. Not that part, no."

The wagon door flung open, and Ahyoka stood staring at Lou on the bed. Osborn turned away, refusing to look at her. He reached for his brown cloth, covering his face with his hands over it. "No, Osborn. No good. This bad, this bad. Lou gone from world. She gone from world." Ahyoka shook her head and walked away.

Twenty minutes later, Charlie held the lantern high, squinting down the path as he, Abigail, and Ahyoka walked toward Osborn's wagon. The dark night stole their light at only ten feet. Ahyoka slowed to a stop. "It was here," she said.

"Yes, it was," Abigail confirmed. Charlie pointed to the ground, the light revealing the flattened grass where the wagon had sat. The wheel marks headed east, off into the dark of night.

CHAPTER 40

Osborn paced back and forth outside of the wagon as it sat in a valley of golden grass. He flapped his hands up and down with a painful expression. "I know, I know, I know," he said to himself before he stopped and stepped into the wagon. "We'll find a spot nearby and…a hidden spot, and…I'll have to leave you in the wagon. I can take Junior. Yes, yes, we'll…I'll bring Ishmael back. I'll get him back."

Osborn climbed out and brought up the hinged stairs. Two steps away, he stopped. Something caught his eye a half mile away on the ridge. He squinted and shaded the sun from his eyes—four Native Americans on horseback watching him. One turned his horse away, and the others followed.

Running around the wagon, he climbed up and slapped the reins on Hoady Junior. The mule pulled the wagon up the hill. At the top, Osborn stood on the bench. A mile away, a thicket of hickory and oak grew along a creek bed—a good spot to hide the wagon. With no sign of the four Native Americans, he sat down and headed in that direction. "I found a spot for us," he called back to Lou.

He parked the wagon as close as he could to the creek under the limbs of a large oak tree. After he hobbled Junior, he went into the wagon and came out with several postmortem posing stands and a stool. Bringing Lou out next, he set her up next to the wagon. By the time he had finished, the sun had set. He lit the campfire and sat close to Lou, examining her silent face with her closed eyes and lips. "I can hear your voice in my head, but, but, but I wish I could hear it again in my ears. In my ears, yes. I'd give anything for that."

The thicket grew somewhere between three and four miles away from the Cherokee village and his son. Osborn let Lou rest in the wagon while he planned how to mount Junior. He had no saddle and would have to ride him bareback. Osborn jumped up with his belly landing on Junior's back. About to throw a leg over, Junior kicked, throwing him off.

"Junior! I need to ride you!" He brought him over to the wagon. Junior's back and the wagon bench were the same height. Guiding Junior next to it, Osborn squatted and jumped on. Junior jumped around, kicking until Osborn could hold on no longer. On the second day of trying, Osborn finally rode the mule.

Osborn rode along the far side of the Arkansas River and within its tree line. He wanted to be as close to the village as possible without being seen. Finding a good spot, he sat down, pulled out his field glasses, and patiently waited. He spotted Abigail and Ahyoka, but no Ishmael. With the sun setting over the mountains, he rode back to the wagon.

Over the next four days, Osborn made the ride back to the village. An oak tree provided the best viewing spot. From there, he had seen his son three short moments but still had no idea how to take him back.

Back at the wagon, the dark of night surrounded his campfire as Osborn made dinner in the moonless evening. With Lou sitting next to him, he flinched from a shriek in the darkness. Junior's head popped up from the creek, ears up and back. Another shriek came from a different direction. War cries! He unclamped Lou, picked her up, and locked themselves in the wagon. The war cries persisted as he gently tucked Lou into bed, and they continued until morning. He cautiously peered out of the window—nothing unusual. Junior meandered in the field, still hobbled and calmly eating grass.

Osborn stepped out to the birds singing and the creek babbling. He walked over and stood at the edge of the thicket—nothing but a beautiful day. Climbing on Junior, he headed to the village for the day. A mile into the ride, ten Native Americans followed from a distance. Sweat formed on the back of his neck, and he turned Junior back toward the wagon. The Natives cried out, bows and rifles in hand, and galloped away. They wore different clothes than the Cherokee.

That evening he listened to the more war cries in the night. In an early morning hour, he jumped when someone slapped his hand against the wagon wall, cried out, and galloped away into the night. "I have to do something tomorrow, Lou. Tomorrow. I have to get our son. But I don't know how to feed him and make him happy. I need Abigail. I need Abigail."

In the morning, Osborn decided to ride in and demand that Abigail give Ishmael to him. After all, it was his son, and he would tell Abigail that he had put Lou to rest and buried her. He needed to find the right spot, which he did. He will now take his son back to Pittsburgh and raise him with Ray. He mounted up and headed out with the story in his thoughts.

Outside the thicket, he stopped. A dozen Native Americans mounted on their horses a quarter mile away. Junior's ears went back. Osborn didn't know if he should go back or continue, and they weren't moving either. One of them kicked his horse into a gallop toward him. Osborn held steady, his anxiety growing the closer he came. He slammed his eyes closed and tried to disappear within his thoughts as the hoofbeats slowed.

"O for Osborn." Osborn opened his eyes to Moses Wolf, smiling at him atop his horse. A sudden relief came to him, his whole body relaxing.

"Moses Wolf," replied Osborn. Moses studied Osborn with a pleasing smile on his lips. A smile he had never seen on Moses.

Moses turned back to his companions on the ridge. He raised his rifle in the air and let out a war cry. Osborn flinched from it with his eyes wide as saucers. His companions cried back. Moses turned around to him. "May I sit at your fire? We can talk."

Osborn turned Junior around toward the wagon. They dismounted, and Moses brought branches to the smoldering fire. He blew on it and caught them on fire. They both sat down, warming their hands. Moses sheepishly nodded toward the wagon. "The medicine woman? Is she in there?" Osborn remained silent, and Moses' strange smile rose again. "There is talk, big talk about O Roche and his medicine woman."

"What big talk? Who is saying?"

"Some people say some things, and some people say other things. But they all say there is strong medicine with you, strong medicine from the medicine woman. The white soldiers are looking for you." Moses used his hands to tell the story. "The white soldiers are asking all the nations if they see you and your medicine woman. But the nations will not tell. They will not tell because it will bring bad medicine to them."

"Would you like something to eat, to eat?"

Moses slowly shook his head. "Many of my brothers have been here?"

"At night mostly. But we haven't been hurt. No, no. But concerned, yes."

"Ha!" Moses laughed. "They try to prove they are brave."

"Brave? How are they brave?"

"Medicine woman. They fear her. Fear her medicine." He laughed again. "They think I have no fear to talk to you. They don't know we traveled together. They think me bravest of warriors. Ha! I will get good wife for my talk to you." His smile faded. "Is she in there?"

"Yes. Do you want to see her?"

"No."

"What are they saying? What are they saying?"

"My brothers heard the story of you taking the medicine woman from grave and brought her back using her own medicine. She lies in your wagon like a..." He moved his hand across his other arm like an inchworm. "And she will appear like a..." Moses put both hands together, flying them into the sky.

"A butterfly," said Osborn, choking up, tears filling his eyes.

"A butterfly," repeated Moses.

"I did. Yes, I am waiting for that. For that, yes." Osborn sucked back the tears.

Moses exhaled through his nose and looked away. "The soul would have no rainbow if the eye had no tears." He turned and stared into the fire. "You should go now and take medicine woman. Go from here. Warriors will always want to be braver than last."

"They will try to kill us?"

"I do not believe so. The sun will always shine on you, O Roche. It would be bad medicine." Moses turned to the wagon. "But many fear when medicine woman becomes butterfly."

"Butterfly. Why?"

"The father of medicine woman take son away from Cherokee." Osborn's mouth dropped open.

"What?"

"The father of medicine woman brought soldiers, and they took son away on the iron horse that makes smoke. When she awakes without her son, she will be an angry butterfly."

Osborn jumped to a stand, hands flapping. "I must go, Moses. I must go find my son."

Moses stood. "I would help you if I could, but the iron horse will take them a great distance from my home."

Osborn spun on his heels, walking over to Junior.

Moses jumped on his horse and, before he rode away, said, "The Chickasaw never say goodbye. We say chi pisa lachike. It means see you later, O Roche. Always remember, you are the sun, and she is the moon of your great medicines."

CHAPTER 41

"Well, look what the cat dragged in?" said Mr. Parker as Osborn walked into his warehouse.

"Where? What did it?"

"Well, you, my boy, you."

"Me? A cat? Is that a euphemism?"

"A what? Eupha… Well, anyway, what the heck you doing here, Osborn. Good to see you." Osborn stuck out his hand to shake. "What?! Shake your hand? I thought you never…?"

"I don't and don't want to, but you looked so pleased to see me. I thought I would offer it."

Mr. Parker laughed. "It's fine, it's fine, Osborn. So, what are you doing here in Johnstown?"

"I am looking for the residence of Henry Cattell."

"Oh, are ya? Is his daughter here with ya? Lou, right?"

"No, she's not here."

"Oh, I see. Going to see her?"

"Yep, yep."

"Well, ya got any time to sit a spell?"

"Maybe later, yes, maybe later."

"Oh, all right. Well, it's one of the biggest homes in the county. Up county route two. Can't miss it. A big sign says Cattell, turn right and head on down there a piece. I won't say it's far, but you'll have to grease the wagon twice before you're gonna see the roof shingles."

"Grease?"

"Naw, that's a joke. But it is a far piece down the road, that's for certain."

Osborn couldn't tell the time by the half moon in the North Eastern sky. The sun had set six hours back, and he wanted to arrive at Lou's home in the darkest part of the night. The home lay on a secluded forty acre parcel of wooded forest land of red spruce, mountain ash, and red maple. Osborn drove Junior past it and off the road into the thick forest land behind it, looking for a spot far enough from the home that they wouldn't be found but also close enough to walk to daily. After a mile and a half, a river blocked his path. He set up camp, hobbled Junior, and climbed into bed with Lou for the night. "Goodnight, my love."

Morning sunlight filtered through the red maple trees surrounding the wagon. Wanting to explore the area, Osborn walked into the crisp morning air and toward the sounds of the rushing river. Walking along its bank, Osborn stopped in his tracks a mile from the wagon. A small cabin hid in the trees, overgrown with ivy, moss, and ferns. The door had either been kicked in or collapsed from age.

He cautiously approached it, stepping on ground that hadn't been walked on in years. Peering in, both he and a raccoon jumped when they saw each other. The raccoon added a vicious hiss before leaping into the fireplace and climbing up and out. Osborn went over and peered up. Honeysuckle vine grew down and into the cabin. Behind him, he found a small cot covered by a moth-eaten green blanket. Next to it, a bookshelf with six books. A reader lived here. Above the door hung a Springfield Model 1795, a single-shot, flintlock-based musket. The owner didn't take it with him when he left, and it wasn't taken by anyone else. This place doesn't get any visitors.

He reached for a book on a shelf close to the bed and opened it. All the text was handwritten with dates—a diary. He grinned as big as a man who had won high-stakes poker. Osborn put the book back and said, "Looks like you left me a lot of reading to do, reading to do, yes."

Osborn came out and into the sun, squinting up at it. No one had been here for years; this would be a better place to bring the wagon if he could get it here. Osborn counted his steps as he headed east, checking the cabin's distance to Mr. Cattell's home. Forty minutes into his hike, he saw the roof shingles. The house sat on a clear-cut section of the forest with a long driveway to the road. The same driveway he drove the previous night.

Staying within the tree line, he walked about in search of a nice spot. A spot Lou would approve of. Osborn stopped at two red pine trees growing a foot apart. Goldenseal bushes and bloodroot flowers grew in front of them. More than enough room to put his telescope. Plus, Lou would love the white flowers of the bloodroot, and it would provide them complete cover. They could see without being seen. Behind it all lay a bed of pine needles he could sit on; it was perfect.

He traced his steps back to the cabin and from there to the wagon. "I found a great spot to see Ishmael," he told Lou. "I also found a cabin. It's a lot closer to the house than this and a lot more secluded."

Osborn lit the wagon's lamps and took a deep breath. "How am I gonna make it without you, Lou," he said softly. The lamplight played on her pale skin. Her fingers drooped. No longer the "piano playing" shape he loved.

Osborn pulled out some beef jerky and sat with his back facing her on the bed. "The place I found is perfect. You will like it. It has bloodroot flowers, the white ones with the yellow in the middle." Undressing to his long johns, he climbed into bed next to her. He blew out the lamps and reached for his nose plugs before turning to Lou. "Sorry," he said as he put them in.

The following morning, he set out in the wagon toward the cabin. The ground varied with soft dirt, hard dirt, rocks, and boulders. The wheels crashed down, rolling over rough terrain, jostling the wagon about. A large boulder made it impossible to go forward. He'd have to take the rocky terrain of the river's edge.

Junior reluctantly stepped in the six inches of water on the bank and tugged the wagon over each stone. Straining, Junior let out a loud "Hee-haw." Osborn climbed down, walked up to him, and patted his neck. "I'll walk with you, Junior. We can do this. We can do this." With Osborn next to him,

Junior moved forward, his hooves slipping over each stone. The water grew to Osborn's knees. "Closer to the bank, closer to the bank."

Guiding Junior to the bank, Osborn felt the water grow deeper instead of shallower, rising to his waist and just under Junior's belly. His anxiety rose with the water level. He couldn't back up or turn to the center of the river; the bank was only twenty feet away. It couldn't get much deeper than this, he reassured himself. Taking Junior's bit, he moved forward, straining against the tide and rocky riverbed.

When the rear left wheel cracked and splintered as it came down the other side of a boulder, the back of the wagon began sinking into the rushing water. The other back wheel collapsed, and Junior hee-hawed wildly as the wagon pulled him back into the deeper part of the river. Osborn frantically held Junior's bit as the river swept them both back, the current tugging the wagon along.

Junior's eyes flared with fear, his hee-haws echoing in panic. The wagon bobbed in the current, its tar-sealed joints barely keeping it afloat. The weight of the hitch began pulling Junior under, dragging him back and down toward the river's bottom. Osborn went with him, refusing to let go of his bit. Junior's head was inches from his, terror mirrored in both their eyes. Holding the bit with his right hand, Osborn began frantically unstrapping the harness buckles with his left, fighting against the powerful current and the mounting dread that they might not make it out.

Junior's hooves kicked frantically for the surface. With one strap loose, Osborn held it as he surfaced for air, taking a deep breath before diving down again. He pulled himself by the strap toward his struggling mule. One last buckle freed Junior. The mule kicked and rose, coughing and sputtering as he swam toward the bank, away from Osborn.

Free-floating in the current, Osborn turned his head to see the wagon floating faster than him. Kicking off his boots, he swam as fast as he could. His heart sank as the wagon slammed against a boulder, smashing it. "Lou! Lou! No!" he screamed, his voice lost in the roar of the river.

Desperation fueled his strokes as he swam toward the wagon, fighting not to be swept past it. The Romani vardo's roof rose only two feet above the surface as water flooded into the crumbling wagon. Buoyant items popped out, bobbing on the water's surface like ghosts of their former life.

Osborn slammed into the side of the sinking wagon and pulled himself onto the roof. Desperate to find a way in, he crawled to the back and dove in, pulling himself inside the rear doorway and up to an air pocket at the ceiling. Only half-filled collodion bottles floated around him. Diving back down into the dark water, he quickly scanned the interior before swimming out and up for another breath.

As he gasped for air, he spotted her, floating thirty yards away downriver. "Lou! Lou!" he wailed, his voice raw with anguish as he swam toward her. The rushing river had calmed to a gentle current. He threw arm after arm, digging into the water, refusing to stop. When he reached her, he took her hand and went to his back, floating as she was, his arms outstretched and his weary eyes fixed on the blue sky.

"Why, why, why," he whispered, the words barely audible over the lapping water, before he began kicking for shore.

Junior's hooves click-clacked on the rocky bank as he waited for Osborn to wake up; a loud hee-haw finally did. Lou lay in his lap, soaking wet in Ray's suit. Osborn used all his strength to pick up Lou and bring her to Junior. He hoisted her up and over Junior's back and walked them up onto the forest's dirt floor. "Come on, Junior." Without reins or a bit, Junior followed Osborn as he walked upriver. They passed the remnants of his Romani vardo still smashed up against the boulder in the river, pieces of it still floating away.

The sun had dropped below the hills by the time they reached the cabin. He unloaded Lou and laid her wet body onto the cot. With the chimney full of vines, he set the fire in a pit outside. Shaking from the cold, he removed his clothes, including the brown cloth, from his pocket. He set them all out to dry and covered himself with a bear pelt he found in the cabin. Laying close to the fire, he fell asleep for the night.

He woke in the morning with Junior clawing the dirt with his hoof. "You can go now, Junior. I'm not going to hobble you, not going to. You are free to go." Junior replied with a snort and shook his head. Osborn checked his clothes—they were dry. He dropped his bearskin and put them on as fast as he could before wrapping himself in the skin again. Throwing another log on the fire, he sat by it and thought about Ray. "I wish you were here."

Junior wandered over to a meadow and snacked on dandelion flowers. Osborn's stomach growled with hunger. Crawling over to the meadow, he began yanking dandelions from the ground, eating them—root, leaf, and flower. Junior eyed him curiously as they ate together. After six dandelions, Osborn couldn't stomach any more. He sighed, knowing he'd have to find something else to eat. Everything he had was now floating somewhere down the river, lost to the relentless current.

With a bit more energy, he cleaned out the cabin and searched for anything of use. Wanting to sleep inside with Lou, he cleared the vines from the chimney. The cabin still had everything he needed: shovels, lanterns, oil, candles, tools of all sorts. Under the bed, he found more pelts, filthy from the mice making their home there. He cleaned them by whacking them with a shovel outside. Not as comfortable as the Romani vardo, but by evening, he had fixed the door and sat in a rocking chair in front of the fireplace.

Osborn took out the cloth and rubbed it on his face before taking a deep breath through it. He turned to Lou, still in her wet suit. He hadn't had the time to dry it. Returning the cloth to his pocket, he covered himself with the bear pelt for the night.

He awoke to the sounds of mice feet scurrying here and there under the cot, angry at the new occupant. He spent the day walking back to the river, scavenging what he could from the wagon. Only a wall and a wheel remained, smashed up against the boulder and held there by the current. Further downriver, he found two bottles of collodion, the jar of the yellow paint Moses Wolf gave him, and the wagon's door and drop-down stairs. He brought it all back to the cabin.

Lou and the moldy scent from her wet clothes filled the room. He didn't have his nose plugs to help. He stood outside the door, hesitating. She lay on the bed, the clothes clinging to her as Miss Tabitha's dress did. He went in and removed them, setting them to dry in front of the fireplace. Dismantling the wagon's stairs, he took two treads and fashioned a cross. He painted on it with Moses' yellow paint.

The clothes had dried by morning, and he took care in dressing her. After, Osborn turned to Junior and asked, "Can you follow me again?" Junior shook his head, but Osborn took that as a yes and slung Lou over his back. Osborn took the shovel and cross and set out for the perfect spot. His dread grew with each step toward it. Reaching it, he set her down and pulled out his telescope—no activity at the house. "This is the spot, Lou."

He took the shovel and stabbed the earth. Osborn recalled the stories of them as he dug the grave and asked her if she remembered. His sweat-soaked clothes clung to his thin frame by the time he finished the grave. He climbed in and set her gently down. Climbing out, he pulled the brown cloth from his pocket. He closed his eyes and brought it up to his mouth, inhaling her in, drawing her into the deepest part of himself. His eyes opened to her wrapped body as he took the cloth, wiped the sweat from his neck with it, and tossed it in to keep her company.

Two seconds later, he went to his knees to retrieve it. "I'm sorry, I need it." He stabbed the spade into the fresh soil and shoveled it on top of her. A sound they both loved, as soothing to his ears as the cloth to his nose.

With the grave filled, he picked up the cross and hammered it into the mound of soil. He stood back and read what he painted. "L. Roche, Embalmer." Bringing his hands up and spreading them across the sky, he said, "Gone from the world, but alive again in our hearts." Tired, he sat on the pine needle floor with his love next to him and their son sleeping in the home before him. "A peculiar circumstance, yes, peculiar, but at least we are all together." He brought the telescope to his eye. "I'll tell you if something happens. I'll watch for both of us, Lou. I'll watch for both of us."

Thank you for reading
Collodion,
book two of the
Death Shall Have No Dominion,
three companion series books.
If you would like to
know more about the author,
Greg Morgan,
or the other two books in the
series, please visit
greg-morgan.com

Please show us a kindness and leave a
review of Collodion by Greg Morgan
on Amazon.com or Goodreads.com.

APPENDIX

Historical People

General John Sedgwick knew Osborn well at the Battle of Seven Pines. (September 13, 1813 – May 9, 1864) He was wounded three times at the Battle of Antietam. Highest-ranking Union soldier to be killed in the war. Known for his ironic last words, "They couldn't hit an elephant at this distance."

James Ewell Brown "Jeb" Stuart (February 6, 1833 – May 12, 1864) was a United States Army officer from Virginia who became a Confederate States Army general during the Civil War. He never had a Florida man pretending to be a Native American friend, but Wade Hampton, W.H.F. "Rooney" Lee, Beverly H. Robertson, William E. "Grumble" Jones, and Major Robert F. Beckham were historical Confederate Generals and friends of Stuart.

General George McClellan (December 3, 1826 – October 29, 1885) From (November 1861 to March 1862) he served as general-in-chief of the Union Army. 24th Governor of New Jersey. Most historians have judged that McClellan was a poor battlefield general.

In Collodion, Colonel William Phillips was a friend to Osborn and commander at Fort Gibson. (January 14, 1824 – November 30, 1893) A journalist, a commander of the Cherokee Indian Regiment and Fort Gibson, U.S. Representative from Kansas.

Thomas T. Munford, commander of the Second Virginia Cavalry Munford served under Thomas J. "Stonewall" Jackson as commander of a cavalry brigade of two regiments. Munford was the colonel that "captured" Obsorn, Ray, and Lou and had him photograph Jeb Stuart's 'La grande revue, befitting his reputation of a beau sabreur' parade.

Osborn photographed Union General Howard after he fell off his horse at the Battle of Seven Pines. Howard was wounded twice in his right arm, which was subsequently amputated. He received the Medal of Honor in 1893 for his heroism at Seven Pines.

Osborn's nemesis, Mathew Brady, Photographer (c. 1822 – January 15, 1896) He photographed Andrew Jackson, John Quincy Adams, and Abraham Lincoln, among other public figures.

Doctor Samuel Howe was a nineteenth-century American physician, abolitionist, and an advocate of education for the blind. He organized and was the first director of the Perkins Institution. Said to have pioneered studies on autism.

Henry P. Cattell, Lou's father in Collodion, truly was hired to embalm President Lincoln's son, Willy, and later would handle Lincoln's body after he was assassinated.

Hoady, Osborn's mule, was an American Mammoth Jackstock Mule. It is a breed of North American donkey, descended from large donkeys imported to the United States from about 1785. George Washington, with Henry Clay, bred for an ass that could be used to produce strong work mules. Washington was offering his jacks for stud service by 1788.

Historical Places

The ship the Alice Dean (March 1863 – July 9, 1863) In June 1863, the Alice Dean served as a Union troop transport. Confederate Brigadier General John Hunt Morgan captured the Alice Dean. After it, for their own purposes, Morgan's men burned the Alice Dean.

The Willard Hotel is a historic hotel in Washington, DC. On February 23, 1861, amid several assassination threats, Detective Allan Pinkerton smuggled Abraham Lincoln into the Willard. There, Lincoln lived until his inauguration on March 4, holding meetings in the lobby and carrying on business from his room.

Fort Gibson is a historic military site located next to the present-day city of Fort Gibson in Muskogee County, Oklahoma. It guarded the American frontier in Indian Territory from 1824 until 1888.

Osborn's publisher, The E. & H. T. Anthony & Company, was the largest supplier and distributor of photographic supplies in the United States during the 19th century.

Historical Battles mentioned in Collodion

Battle of Seven Pines May 31, 1862 – June 1, 1862

Battle of Antietam, Sep 18, 1862

Battle of Honey Springs, July 17, 1863

Battle of White Oak Swamp (June 1862)

Cedar Mountain

Battle of Manassas

www.ingramcontent.com/pod-product-compliance
Lightning Source LLC
Chambersburg PA
CBHW021233060726
47590CB00005B/1747